THE UNFORGETTABLE REUNION OF
FOUR EXTRAORDINARY WOMEN

DIANA—independent, ambitious...she married in the '50s, protested in the '60s, slept around in the '70s...and is determined never to love again.

ELAINE—radical feminist...she found her politics and ideals couldn't comfort her when her long-term marriage fell apart.

JOANNE—single, successful, gorgeous...she desperately wants a child but is disillusioned with sex, with relationships...with men.

SUKIE—the catalyst...her death brings her friends together, and her diary will reveal their secrets and their hearts.

"HOT STUFF! Regardless of your age or sex, this book will hit you like a medicine ball to the gut."
—Rita Mae Brown, author of
RUBYFRUIT JUNGLE,
SOUTHERN DISCOMFORT,
and HIGH HEARTS

"Will assuredly and deservedly take its place with such other contemporary classics as THE GROUP, CLASS REUNION, THE WOMEN'S ROOM, and SUPERIOR WOMEN. In many respects, it is far more universal and therefore, more enduring."
—*The Asbury Park Press*

"A LOVELY, LONG REPRISE OF A GENERATION AND AN ERA. OUR MOTHERS AND OUR DAUGHTERS MAY BE SHOCKED BY *HOT FLASHES*, BUT THIS IS THE WAY IT WAS."

>—Jane O'Reilly, author of the 'Click' article in the first issue of *Ms.* magazine and *THE GIRL I LEFT BEHIND*

"There are almost 11.5 million 'displaced homemakers' in the country. Barbara Raskin has set out to write a book that will speak to every one of them...Raskin is a smart writer with an ironic voice and a knowing wit."

>—*Newsday*

"The warmest current...stems from its understanding of friendship itself."

>—*Publishers Weekly*

"INTERESTING, INSIGHTFUL BOOK WORTH READING...THE VIVID AND HEART-RENDERING PASSAGES...WOMEN DISCOVER THEMSELVES IN *HOT FLASHES*."

>—*Macon Telegraph & News*

"Barbara Raskin must have been taking notes while still in the cradle."

>—*Chicago Tribune*

"HOT, FLASHY AND WONDERFUL! Transcends its subject to provide an immensely moving portrait of cultural changes from the 1940s to the 1980s....THERE ARE PLENTY OF FLASHES HERE—OF WIT, HUMOR, INSIGHT, ANGER. BUT *HOT FLASHES* HAS MUCH MORE TO OFFER: IT BUILDS TO A CONCLUSION THAT IS POWERFUL, MOVING AND HOPEFUL."

>—*The Cincinatti Post*

"RICHARD BENJAMIN HAS JUST BOUGHT THE RIGHTS TO FILM THE MOVIE VERSION, IN WHICH BARBARA STREISAND HAS EXPRESSED INTEREST."

>—*Twin Cities Reader*, MI

"FEW NOVELS ARE IMPORTANT FOR AN ENTIRE GENERATION OF WOMEN....*HOT FLASHES* IS ONE....ONE OF THE MOST IMPORTANT, MOST TOUCHING NOVELS ON THE SHELVES...IMPORTANT TO YOUNGER GENERATIONS OF WOMEN AS WELL....ONE OF THE BEST NOVELS DEALING WITH THE 'MODERN WOMAN.' READERS WILL NOD THEIR HEADS IN UNDERSTANDING, LAUGH AND SHED MORE THAN A FEW TEARS. AND, NO DOUBT, THEY WILL WISH TO THANK RASKIN FOR WRITING *HOT FLASHES*."
—Chicago Heights, IL, *South Holland Star*

By now, there are 800 copies of HOT FLASHES in the window of the B. Dalton bookstore on New York's Fifth Avenue. It's a Book-of-the-Month alternate and has already been bought for a major motion picture by Richard Benjamin. [Raskin] has done "The Today Show" and *People*, and is prepping for a bi-coastal tour...HER BREAKTHROUGH NOVEL." —*The Washington Post*

"[A] cross between FEAR OF FLYING and THE BIG CHILL....Its appeal...should extend to all women and perhaps even to men—if they can stand the heat. Raskin's HOT FLASHES are filled with laughter, tears, love, and hate—like life itself." —*Booklist*

"I gave my copy...to my wife...She finished it on an airplane flight—and, she told me, she cried all the way from Atlanta to New York....WILL BE THE MOST TALKED-ABOUT NOVEL OF THIS FALL, I GUARANTEE!" —San Jose *Mercury News*

"AN INSIDE LOOK AT A GENERATION OF WOMEN GRASPING AT AND GRAPPLING WITH LOVE. IT'S BOTH SAD AND FUNNY. I ENJOYED IT."
—Judy Feiffer, author of *FLAME* and *LOVECRAZY*

"THIS IS THE STORY OF A GENERATION...HITS VERY CLOSE TO HOME...READERS WILL...SEE THEMSELVES DIFFERENTLY."
—*Sunday Advocate Magazine, Baton Rouge, LA*

NOTE: If you purchased this book without a cover you should be aware that this book is stolen property. It was reported as 'unsold and destroyed' to the publisher, and neither the author nor the publisher has received any payment for this 'stripped book'.

BY BARBARA RASKIN

Loose Ends
The National Anthem
Out of Order

HOT FLASHES

Copyright © 1987 by Barbara Raskin.

All rights reserved. No part of this book may be used or reproduced in any manner whatsoever without written permission except in the case of brief quotations embodied in critical articles or reviews. For information address St. Martin's Press, 175 Fifth Avenue, New York, N.Y. 10010.

Library of Congress Catalog Card Number: 87-16141

ISBN: 0-312-92801-7

Printed in the United States of America

St. Martin's Press hardcover edition/August 1987
St. Martin's Paperbacks edition/August 1988

10   9

BARBARA RASKIN

Hot Flashes

SMP

ST. MARTIN'S PAPERBACKS

Dedication:

for the men in my life: noah, jamie, keith, zachary,
sam, dick, and jedd
and for the women: andrea, aviva, barbara, bethany,
bobbie, charlotte, dorothy, emily, erika, glenda,
helen, isabel, jackie, jane, janet, jean, maggie,
monique, myrna, pat, perdita, phyllis, rebecca,
ronni, rosalie, sally, sharon, svala and zina

Acknowledgments:

I owe much gratitude to my editors, Tom McCormack
and Toni Lopopolo, who made it happen, and
to the National Endowment for the Arts
for helping so many
when help was most needed

St. Martin's Paperbacks titles are available at quantity discounts
for sales promotions, premiums or fund raising. Special books
or book excerpts can also be created to fit specific needs.

For information write to special sales manager, St. Martin's
Press, 175 Fifth Avenue, New York, N.Y. 10010.

CHAPTER 1

Hot flashes in midair:
We always looked good at airports.
We liked to visit hot countries.
We slept with strangers whenever we felt like it.
We learned a lot from our lovers.
Some of us learned that the fastest way to get ahead was to give some.
Eventually most of our husbands were listed in Who's Who.
We wanted everything, got it all, and then discovered it wasn't enough.
We have read and written many of the books about women like us and the way we live now.
Politically alienated, we squandered much of our energy.
We are a generation of Type-A, A-List, Number 10–type women.
We were such good friends. Really. We still are.

I am Diana Sargeant. I am forty-eight, a tenured professor of anthropology at Columbia University, and an internationally respected authority on female rites of passage. Because I believe that people invent their own memories and that the past has an unruly life of its own, I am frequently called upon to act as the official historian for my group of friends.

A generation must tacitly agree to remember certain things in certain ways and refuse to be dissuaded from its chosen version of the past. Otherwise the past won't stay put. If we're not vigilant about preserving our own history, someone will always come along and try to correct our memories. And then how will we know who we were or who we are now?

Some of my closest friends complain that I am addicted to generalizations, that I am too bold in extrapolating from my own experiences. I understand their discomfort, but I discount their criticism. I know most people like to believe they are unique and different from their cohorts. But because of my anthropological training, I see the group in the individual, the common experiences of a generation in the idiosyncrasies of a particular person. The part embodies the whole.

On the Friday evening of Labor Day weekend, 1985, while aboard the seven o'clock shuttle circling Washington National Airport, I experience a number of hot flashes. Hot flashes are rolls of unreasonable, unseasonable heat that create a rush—a flush that floods the face from neck to hairline. A hot flash is itchy, prickly and provocative—like a sudden spike of fever that produces a mean and cranky irritability. Sometimes I have as many as fifty hot flashes a day.

Totally absorbed in some intellectual problem, I will suddenly feel like I've just opened an oven door to lift the lid off a turkey roaster, allowing a stream of steam to escape and slap my face. Although a hot flash only lasts a few seconds, it reminds me of how I feel when I have to retrieve a lost ball in some itchy, knee-high weeds after finishing two sets of tennis on a hot July day or when I first enter a chalet following a ski run and stand by a blazing fireplace before removing my parka. A hot flash causes my face to sizzle like the backs of my knees when I've lain too long on my stomach at the beach or like the crown of my scalp when I'm forced to fish in a flat-bottom rowboat on an inland lake at high noon in August.

Clinically speaking, hot flashes are symptoms of menopause. But menopause is the *cessation* of a process, which means hot flashes are a manifestation of *nothing*. I don't understand why *nothing* should have symptoms. Unlike menstrual periods, hot flashes serve no purpose such as the sloughing off of old tissue or new issue. Their heat cannot be ·harnessed as energy for other purposes; like life, they are unpredictable, uncontrollable, uncomfortable and unfair.

More and more frequently nowadays, my hot flashes have begun to feel like urgent communiqués from the interior of a vast, dark continent—fast-breaking news items from my heart of darkness. Sometimes hot flashes trigger sudden insights into previously obscure experiences. Other times, in reverse fashion, a rush of revelations will release the heat like thunder after a flash of lightning. Either way, I have come to trust the wired insights that hot flashes produce.

Because I believe in epiphanies, I record most of these illuminations in a notebook that I carry in my purse. Since hot flashes are often cryptic, I try to decipher them as soon as possible, but often while I'm trying to do so, I get another hot flash that steams up my reading glasses so I can't even see what I'm writing. Anyway, while the Eastern shuttle dawdles over Washington in its usual holding pattern, I flesh out some of my airborne hot flashes for possible inclusion in my continuing study of Female Adult Depression Babies.

We always looked good at airports. We had style and our luggage was suitably battered. Even after air travel became more economical—democratizing the class of passengers—we still wore killer heels, dangling earrings, tight jeans and silk shirts whenever we flew anywhere, even on long night flights or short commuter

hops. For us, airports—like cafés, chalets and caba-
rets—were stages on which we felt required to perform.
We used such places as launch pads to expand our ca-
reer opportunities, improve our social situations, or ini-
tiate romantic adventures.

We used to have a fear of flying, but that passed.
Relaxed, we trotted through airline terminals, trans-
mitting our messages via the coded clicking of our high
heels on resonant marble floors. The sophisticated sig-
nals we dispatched could only be decoded by "special
agents"—men with sufficient imagination to tune in to
the suggestive dramas we felt compelled to stage. Deci-
phering our code required a certain affluence and a
familiarity with most of America's serious films and
novels. (This is not to say wimps and nerds did not
attach themselves to us. They did. We were usually gra-
cious in our dismissal of them, unless, of course, we had
time to kill over a couple of drinks and saw no special
agents around.)

The tic-tac-tac of our heels signaled that we were in
imminent danger of missing an urgent flight. Wearing
Hollywood-referential expressions that suggested both
dramatic destinations and mysterious pasts, we walked
in a way that whipped our hair away from our faces
and puckered our clothing in strategic places. We al-
ways carried large shoulder-bag purses that held every
legal, medical, financial, hygienic and cosmetic neces-
sity a forced landing on some Caribbean island might
require. However, we traveled with only a single piece
of beat-up designer luggage so we could make our
moves quickly when we changed our minds.

Since we had a habit of using travel as an escape from
boredom or disaster, we logged a lot of air miles during
the late fifties and early sixties. Lots of us kept a suit-
case partially packed and a complete cosmetic kit ready
to go at all times. A few of us routinely stuffed tissue
paper in the shoulders of our blouses so they wouldn't
get crushed when we folded them for packing.

We picked our destinations on the basis of our politics, money, movies we'd seen, assignments, assignations, or the whereabouts of parents, friends, former lovers or fast-breaking news. Often we arrived at ticket counters without any idea of an itinerary and when we ran away no one knew where to start looking for us. Indeed, if our ships ever came in, we probably missed them because we were out at the airport trying to get a tetanus shot.

As a group, we became proficient at making scenes in terminal cocktail lounges and actually developed a highly sophisticated repertoire. Sukie, who wrote several modestly successful novels during the seventies, kept wonderful files of such scenes. She alphabetized them in manila folders marked "Breaking Up" or "Wild Parties" or "Fabulous Fights in Public Places." Over the years, we channeled her a lot of material.

We liked to visit hot countries and consort with men who wore white suits designed for the tropics. Although terrified of customs officers, no matter where we went we always acted like travelers, never tourists. We liked to believe that once we arrived somewhere, we were "just there." We loved photogenic islands replete with reptiles and exotic flowers. Despite rumors of dangers, we tanned as much of ourselves as feasible for as long a time as possible. We liked our lovers to work on his-and-her matching tans. We enjoyed doing those sexual acts best done in the tropics on location. We were always keen to discuss Eurodollars, Vietnam, the Beatles and revolutions in Central America.

Often we slept with strangers. Or, rather, we slept with strangers whenever we felt like it—or when we deemed it necessary because of insomnia, intoxication, an old grudge or an inability to say no. Highly prone to panic attacks—an ethnic disorder common to Type A's such as ourselves—we used sleeping with strangers as a quick homeopathic cure for our unfocused, floating anxieties. Strange hotel rooms offered us instant oppor-

tunities to anchor our incipient hysteria. Like California, we fought our high-intensity brush fires with larger countervailing flames.

Back in the fifties, because we couldn't think of anything else to do, we carefully selected our china, glassware and silver patterns, registered at the nearest department stores, and got married so that we could proceed with our lives. Enthusiastically we embraced that institution which allowed us to abuse ourselves, antagonize our husbands, indulge our lovers, ruin our careers and spoil our children.

While many of our husbands became famous, most of us didn't. Regardless of their professions, our husbands became men-of-a-million-letterheads who eventually turned up in Who's Who. *We were unlisted, since there's no section for Muses; we were only mentioned as in: "He is married to the former blah-blah and has three children." Few of us accomplished half of what we were capable of doing. We squandered our expensive educations, mishandled our careers, and toyed recklessly with our talents. We took our husbands' work seriously and our own lightly. This resulted in long-term resentments, since we never found it particularly interesting sleeping with someone just because he was in* Who's Who.

We have had numerous abortions. Back in the 1950s, those of us who lived in the East went to Dr. Freddy in Pottstown, Pennsylvania. Judith holds our record for abortions with eight; she had one in Cuba before the Revolution and one after. Karen paid $2,500 for an abortion, received a general anesthesia, but later discovered she had not been aborted after all. She named her baby after herself and then gave her away for adoption. Some of us died from sloppy procedures. Nowadays we take our daughters downtown to some "pre-term" clinic and then out for an expensive lunch afterwards.

("Aren't you even going to kiss me first?" Glenda

asked the gynecologist as he started doing a pelvic on her. A humorless man, he immediately buzzed for his nurse to join them in the examination room.) We took the births of our children quite casually. We had our babies before natural childbirth classes requiring husband participation became popular. For us, there were no trendy home deliveries with some twenty-year-old midwife playing folk songs on a homestrung guitar while we counted contractions amid colorful pillows on our conjugal bed. Unlike Roberta, we did not sit on our own toilet during the last stage of labor.

Instead we were wheeled into a labor room, shaved, given an enema, and allowed to expel our babies amid a mess of excretions. ("Take a tuck for the old man," Patsy said to her obstetrician when he began sewing up her episiotomy after a twenty-three-hour labor and the birth of a nine-pound son. The doctor smiled but probably didn't do it, because Neal left Patsy when Jonathan was only four months old.) Although Mandy elected to have both her children by cesarean section so the chairman of her poli-sci department would feel secure about her returning for fall semester, most of us delivered our babies in the old-fashioned, nonscheduled way requiring long hours, traditional labor pains and the selection of two names—one for a boy and one for a girl—since we had no advance warning system.

Few of us had many children. Three were usually plenty. When there were more than three, they were likely to be by different daddies. Shamefully, in the fifties, we prayed for sons rather than daughters. Carola wanted a boy so badly after two girls that when she looked up into the ceiling mirror following her third delivery and saw the long umbilical cord still attached to the baby, she thought it was a terrific penis. Wrong. Carola named the little girl Heidi—after Castro's compañera—and decided not to try again even though she'd always imagined herself the mother of six strapping sons.

When our kids were little, we went to beaches a lot and taught them how to sound out T-shirts. Later, we taught them how to read from bumper stickers on cars stalled ahead of us in traffic jams and utilized the same slogans to explain the class struggle. When it wasn't summer, we overused inadequate day-care centers, took random jobs, worked for unsuccessful political candidates, wrote sporadically, read prodigiously, smoked, drank and did drugs.

Although most of our children turned out amazingly well, our first marriages usually failed. For decades we struggled with our first husbands, to whom we remain biologically related by blood through our children. Never very clear about the subject of our quarrels, we nevertheless kept fighting. Compulsive grievance collectors, we marred our marriages with melodrama. While some of us became battered wives, the majority of us suffered only internal injuries. Our husbands usually decided that our trial separations had worked out just fine.

We had sex frequently because we liked to get intimate fast and sex offered us the quickest possible connection. We liked to watch X-rated movies and get drunk or stoned before going to bed with someone new so we'd have an excuse for any excessive passion or genuine tenderness we displayed. Sometimes, because of the incestuous circle in which we orbited, we would ask men we slept with about the sexual performances of our female friends. We also exchanged notes among ourselves about our lovers. Once, X turned on to Y simply because Z swore Y had been her peak sexual experience. Unlike the next generation, we had few lesbian encounters. As Marilyn explained in Esquire, when we hugged our girlfriends, all we could think about was that they had such thin shoulders.

We learned a great deal from our lovers. As Sukie once observed, lots of us learned that we had to put out to get ahead and that the best way to get ahead was to *give some. We also acquired a great deal of information about politics, business, the arts and spectator sports. We could speak authoritatively about the NFL, the NBA, the NHL, the PGA, the USLTA, and even the WBA and WBC. We also learned how to handicap horses. You name it; we could fake it.*

We played a lot of tennis in a variety of hot countries that were often not much larger than some Class A golf courses where we drove carts for aging or lazy lovers. We have gone waterskiing, mountain climbing, trekking in the Himalayas, jogging, body surfing, deep-sea fishing and hang gliding. We have crossed mountain ranges in single-engine planes as well as jumbo jets. We have burned our eyelids at the world's most beautiful beaches and driven along dangerous roads in strange countries with drunken drivers during stormy weather to isolated places for obscure or obscene reasons. We have attended bullfights in Mexico and come home through customs carrying bloodstained banderillas for souvenirs and amphetamines in the hollowed-out heels of our summer sandals.

We have tried all sorts of exotic foods and erotic games. We have allowed an unreasonable number of obscene things to be done to us and enjoyed most of them. We have picked up tabs for fancy young men and allowed older ones to buy us extravagant gifts in exchange for various flavors of favors. Although fervent feminists, we loved men in the same way we loved movies. Men and movies added drama and texture to our lives; dating was the only distraction that interrupted our dazzling self-absorption. We liked men for the same reasons we liked fall fashions late in August, cold beer after a set of tennis, and buttered popcorn at a double feature. Like Happy Hours, men meant More, which for us meant Better. We have, however, finally learned that passion is not an end, only a means.

We weren't a clique or a crowd. We were a generation—although we didn't think that way. We believed

*ourselves to be the best and the brightest women of our
time. Regardless of where we were born, we left home
and moved to New York, Boston, Chicago, San Francisco or Washington, D.C. We thought there were only
five Zip—and maybe seven area—codes worth memo-
rizing in the entire country.*

  *Born during the Great Depression and named Judith,
Sharon, Arleen or Beverly by our bankrupt fathers and
frightened mothers, we always suffered from (a) psychological moodiness and (b) financial insecurity.
DEBs (Depression Era Babies) customarily feel deprived, regardless of what we achieve or acquire. Although tutored to expect entitlements, we are never
quite certain what is rightfully ours. An obsolete but
indelible memory of the Depression dollar is eternally
engraved in our minds, so that $10,000 always sounds
like lire to us. Since many of us survive on credit cards
nowadays, our cash flow remains a sitcom. We can still
discuss oral sex more easily than our annual incomes.*

  *We are a generation of Type-A females—grown-up
DEBs who disregarded all risks and used birth-control
pills, cigarettes, Valium, Percodan and alcohol all at
the same time. We also liked Dexedrine. Ah, diet pills.
We were never slim enough. We wanted there to be a
space-to-see-through between our thighs when we stood
on sandy beaches. There seldom was and our weight
fluctuations haunted us from decade to decade. We lost
and gained the same ten pounds year after year and
only pretended to prefer wearing loose long shirts outside our jeans instead of tucked in with a narrow belt.*

  *We are not, like the flappers, a happy-go-lucky
crowd. Many of us can be identified by the permanent
silver bracelets we wear around our wrists, pale raised
scars of unsuccessful suicide attempts. Lots of us have
had our heads shrunk and some of us have already had
our hearts, minds, and faces lifted in a variety of ways.
In self-defense, we tried to stave off bitterness with*

black humor, and because we were funny we were up-graded to hostesses' "A" lists so that we could flash our wit at their drunken dinner parties.

We have read and written lots of books about women like us and the way we live now. Most of our favorite writers turn out to have been feminists. We loved Colette, but we also admired her husband, who kept her locked up each day until she wrote a certain number of pages. We were early fans of Virginia Woolf and also of her suicide—the way she walked into the river, just like that. Boom. We like novels such as My Old Sweetheart, Play It As It Lays, Speedboat *and* Sleepless Nights. *Our biggest turn-on books are* Fanny Hill, Forever Amber *and* Lolita.

"We don't need husbands," Joanne once said. "What we need are editors." We also could have used road managers, salad chefs, certified accountants, fashion consultants, pit-stop auto mechanics, research interns, stenographers, and various other support staff. It was Joanne who said that the only "staff" she ever had was the infectious kind. What we all needed was a wife; we just weren't liberated enough to realize it.

Since most of the books we enjoyed were about women like us, many of us began writing fiction. We found this career quite suitable, since writing didn't require attendance at an office and could be conducted off-season during off-hours in an offhand, off-the-record sort of way. At the very least, writing could be used as an answer when someone asked, "And what do you do?" ("About what?" Alice used to reply before becoming an author.)

Unfortunately, narratives are difficult for us because our escapades, though often extravagantly dramatic, are essentially episodic. Since art is supposed to re-create reality, and because our lives don't seem to have much structure, many of our books are a little skimpy in the plot department. Sukie's novels seldom had any neat progression of events that concluded in an appro-

*priate crisis followed by denouement. The only thing
Sukie built—besides suspense—was some psychological
scaffolding for her heroine to scale.*

Superior women such as ourselves want our novels to
be better than those contrived, superpower spy thrillers
that invariably become best-sellers. Actually, we just
want to know about each other's lives right now and
how everyone's doing at the moment. Since we seldom
write letters, many of us publish novels or magazine
articles about our current circumstances as a way of
keeping in touch.

Unfortunately, at the present time, most of our
spiritual lives are stagnant. Although some of us practice liberation theology, and Jennifer is a leader in the
Sanctuary movement, too often we use our religions
only as metaphors in our fiction rather than rituals in
our lives. Judaism has become a joke, Catholicism a
crutch, the Anglican church a conceit, and evangelical
sects a required component in any so-called Southern or
black novels we produce.

Politically, many of us were members of the New
Left, which means we are now the Old New Left. Each
of us can remember what she was doing on the day the
Rosenbergs were executed. Indeed, Sylvia began The
Bell Jar *with a sentence dating her summer in New York
from their execution. That was a starting point for a lot
of us. We believe in nationalist revolutions, in the
impeding of imperial powers, and in the integrity of
the individual. That's it. Period. End of political report.*

We were such good friends. Really. We still are.

We gathered for the funerals of our loved ones, as
well as for weddings, divorces, separations, births, mis-
carriages, graduations, breakdowns, hysterectomies
and publishing parties. We came early and stayed late
to help each other. We loved to stay up all night, drinking wine and smoking dope or cigarettes, while telling
each other the same old poor-little-rich-girl stories
about ourselves that we liked to share. We are instanta-

neous, unnamed and unindicted co-conspirators in each other's battles against husbands or ex-husbands, lovers or ex-lovers, in-laws or outlaws, and unreasonable offspring. Like perennial high school juniors, we continue to discuss what we're going to be.

Actually, what we're all going to be is at least fifty by the end of the eighties.

A lot of us have permanent Pap smear appointments scheduled each year on our birthdays so we won't forget. We discuss biopsies, bonding, and bifocals with growing frequency. Since half of us get hot flashes already, we discuss what to do about them. The JAPs among us simply turn off the heat in their homes when they are having heavy hot flash activity during the winter. Our California contingent takes drops of a potion composed of flower extracts—hornbeam, mimulus, agrimony and cherry plum—four times a day. Our Eastern division uses estrogen, but arranges for breakthrough bleeding to avoid cancer. We all laugh at the notion that menopause implies "Men: a Pause."

Most of us are ecstatic about dispensing with birth-control pills, sponges, coils, diaphragms and nonrecreational condoms. We are thrilled about not having to buy any more tampons, sanitary pads, belts, shields, quilted mattress covers, Clorox bleach, calendars or Midol. We are delighted that we can finally throw away all our once-white panties bearing pale but indelible borscht-pink stains and buy fresh new ones that will never get soiled or spoiled. Needless to say, we are relieved that never again will we accidentally pull a Tampax—instead of a pen—out of our purses while scrambling to write a check or suffer a flash-flood while sitting on someone else's white sofa.

Although our nests have been depopulated, they are not completely empty. Currently, because of economic shortfalls, many of the yuppies we spawned have returned home to live with us. Avidly interested in acquiring a second VCR so they can pirate old movies, *they do not hesitate to ask us for money to help them accomplish this high-minded goal. Although some of them are married, most of them remain in heat and are busy exchanging old SAT scores for LSATs or MCATs. Our daughters worry about their eggs getting stale while they become lawyers and astronauts. Our sons are busy acquiring MBAs, BMWs and IBM-PCs. They read spread sheets or flow charts, discuss condos or condums, quote Dow Jones averages, do coke instead of drink it, and like bright lights and big cities.*

We are not yet ready to die. First off, we still have the kids' old dogs growing incontinent on our worn-out carpeting and nowadays we have to spend a lot of time coaxing them to eat. Also, we still haven't finished the ironing. We could never finish the ironing and there will surely be four thrice-dampened cotton shirts still waiting in their yellow plastic laundry basket when we finally throw in the towel.

Since we are not the sort to go gently into that good night, when we do succumb we want to be at home on our own comfy sofas. Long accustomed to bequeathing old party dresses to our cleaning ladies, at the last moment we will probably donate a selection of our used organs to some nearby hospital. One thing is perfectly clear. We have all decided upon closed-coffin funerals. If for some reason the coffins must be open, we want to be buried with our sunglasses on.

When the shuttle finally gets its landing clearance, I tuck my "Hot Flashes" notebook back into my purse and begin preparing myself for all that is about to happen.

CHAPTER 2

Sukie Amram died on the Friday morning of Labor Day weekend. She had been attending a special Senate floor debate when she collapsed in her seat in the Press Gallery around ten-thirty. The Capitol police called their rescue squad, but the medics said Sukie was dead before they arrived. She had suffered a massive cerebral hemorrhage. Outside in the corridor, Mary Murphy, *Newsweek*'s Capitol Hill correspondent, took charge and arranged to have Sukie's body transferred to Brownell's Funeral Home. Then she stuffed Sukie's purse in her briefcase, slipped out of the Capitol Building, and took a taxi to Sukie's house in Cleveland Park. There she rang the bell several times before admitting herself with one of the keys she found in Sukie's purse.

Although she knew Sukie was divorced, Mary Murphy first telephoned Max Amram's office. Max's secretary answered and said that Mr. Amram was in Europe. When Mary explained about Sukie, the secretary became highly agitated and said that the two Amram children were also in Portugal with their father. She then volunteered to contact the American embassy in Lisbon for help in locating them.

Next, Mary began flipping through Sukie's annotated Rolodex. One of her first calls was to Joanne Ireland, in New York City, who then telephoned Elaine Cantor, across town on the East Side, who then called me out on Long Island where I was spending the last weeks of August with my daughters. Elaine and Joanne were going to take the three o'clock shuttle down to Washington, where Mary Murphy was waiting for them. I said I would meet them at Sukie's house as soon as I could.

Because I couldn't get a flight out of Islip, I had to drive all the way back to LaGuardia. On the Friday afternoon of Labor Day weekend, the traffic, though mostly eastbound, was harrowing and the heat oppressive. The trip seemed endless as my shock shifted into grief and then gradually into panic. By the time I reached the airport at five-thirty, I felt fairly unhinged.

That doesn't happen very often anymore. Now that Leonard and I have been divorced for three years, my life is fairly disciplined. Indeed, I have largely banished wasteful emotionalism from my existence so that I function in a rational rather than a reactive mode. With considerable concentration, I have finally developed a control system for tuning out disturbing distractions and turning off disruptive relationships. Gradually I've taught myself to experience solitude as freedom and aloneness as wholeness. Mine is a distinctly 1980s philosophy.

I have a number of collegial friendships, plus one romantic interest—a man whose presence and absence are equally pleasurable to me. My two daughters are both happily ensconced at Yale. Loren is a junior in the English department and Lisa is a sophomore. I teach two courses at Columbia and devote the remainder of my time to research and writing. A year ago, I published a piece on "Adult American Depression Babies" in *The New York Times Magazine,* which catapulted me into my fifteen minutes of national fame. I did the "Today" show, as well as some local TV appearances, and last month *Vogue* ran a flattering photo of me in a story about "sleek, chic" academic women "making waves." My daughters tease me that next I'll be doing American Express commercials.

The flight to National doesn't land until 8:50. Outside the terminal, Washington is in the grip of its annual heat wave. Summers in Washington rarely progress or peak, so they can never climax and dissipate themselves. Instead, the humidity holds the city hostage well into September. The atmosphere swells like a pregnant woman past term, and the temperature rises until the heat lies like an overweight body atop the city.

The taxi I find is not air-conditioned, so when I finally reach Sukie's house, at a quarter to ten, I am drenched in sweat.

Elaine Cantor opens the door and I immediately fall into her arms. We cling together, sobbing and swaying in rhythm with our grief.

Elaine is fifty, short, round, dimpled, and originally both blond and cheerful. Born on the Lower East Side, but bred for the Upper, Elaine integrated her aggressive liberal politics and University of Chicago training to become a substitute English teacher in the Manhattan public school system in 1960. Since she was the most fervent radical of us all, she served as our political conscience and coach. Two years ago, after the breakup of her twenty-four-year marriage, Elaine quit working, let herself go, and gained thirty pounds. She told Joanne that she had stopped brushing her teeth before going to bed and that flossing was far beyond her at the present time.

Elaine's husband, Nathaniel, a rich corporate lawyer, gave her one of two houses he owned in the Hamptons and their East Side apartment. He then married a young TV producer and fathered a baby daughter. Elaine's two married sons come for Friday-night dinner with their wives and children every week. Recently Elaine threw the small plastic Weight Watchers food scale she'd bought for $12.50 into the garbage pail and replaced it with her Cuisinart food processor which she had previously considered too unsightly to leave out on the counter full-time. Now all the lemons and limes in her refrigerator have raw spots on their rinds where she's grated them to meet some recipe requirement.

When I hear footsteps behind us on the hall staircase, my heart begins to pound, but when I turn around it is not Sukie rushing toward me, but Joanne Ireland—sobbing and stumbling forward. As if changing partners for a slow dance, I turn to embrace her while Sukie's poodle, Happy, runs around in circles, barking shrilly at our performance. When we finally regain some composure, the three of us go into the living room, where Sukie kept her strongest window air-conditioning unit.

Unlike Elaine, Joanne Ireland watches her weight as intensely as she watches "General Hospital"—her one and only daytime soap. Joanne is a flashy career woman of forty-three. From an unhappy, dingy-lace-curtain family in Boston, she pulled herself together and, using Gloria as her role model, graduated from BU and moved to New York to become a writer. Tall, slim, and seductive, Joanne keeps her mane of thick, wheat-colored hair streaked with creamy blond flashes. Never married, she maintains an attractive, designer-decorated, all-white apartment on Central Park West by writing fast, breezy articles for *Vogue, Esquire, Playboy* and *Vanity Fair.*

Far and away the most glamorous of our group, Joanne is perhaps the least contented. Bitter about not having children, she recently began contemplating celibacy (*"Everybody's* not doing it," she told me last winter) as a skewed act of revenge against her many male admirers. While considering chastity, however, she remains sexually active, aerobically trim, borderline trendy, and emotionally unfulfilled.

Elaine has set up a branch mini-bar on the fireplace mantel, where she mixes me a gin and tonic. Sukie's long, narrow living room is furnished with dark, cumbersome Victorian pieces, plus a few tired upholstered chairs. The centerpiece is a cozy floral sofa where Sukie always curled up to "schmooze." On the walls hang her favorite Impressionist prints, still wearing the same frames they acquired when Sukie was in college. We are all old enough now to appreciate Impressionism once again. This reversal occurred about the same time we rediscovered our affection for African violets.

Sitting in the living room without Sukie makes me feel like an intruder. This time she has not invited any of us to come stay at her house. This time there are no salted almonds in the tarnished silver nut dish she kept on the end table beside the sofa. This time there are no plans to meet friends for lunch or a visit to the East Wing of the National Gallery the next day. This time is like none of the many times before.

During the sixties and early seventies—our most politically heady and personally happy years—we always crashed at Sukie's house when we came to Washington for antiwar demonstrations or civil rights marches. First we stayed there with our young husbands and babies, and then, later on as the war intensified, with our growing-up families. Since our political experiences are inextricably entangled with our shared memories of being young together, during the *shiva* / wake we hold for Sukie, we grieve for the past as well as for her—as if the past, too, were a fallen friend.

Because Sukie and Max had been active in the antiwar movement, they always knew where the marchers were to congregate, how to avoid arrest and where to go after the demonstration. Most often it was to the Amrams'. Many of the peace movement leaders stayed at their house, which seemed infinitely inflatable when space was needed. The Amrams had bought—for a song—and renovated a Victorian mansion in 1961, just before the Kennedy people arrived to acquire every interesting piece of real estate inside the city limits.

Sukie's house was casual and cozy in the winter, easy and convenient in the summer. On demonstration weekends, her living room would be carpeted in wall-to-wall sleeping bags until she mobilized the children to reroll and stuff them in the corners, where they slumped like unmarked body bags. Following summer demonstrations, we would return to Sukie's house, sunburned and exhausted, to argue about our estimates of the crowd size as opposed to "official counts," and to discuss the quality of speeches delivered on the steps of the Lincoln Memorial. In the winter, sometimes with frostbitten feet or fingers, we made our way back to warm ourselves in front of her large living room fireplace. At night there was always lots of Acapulco Gold, donated by Max's West Coast friends, and we would stay awake—long after our husbands and kids had gone to sleep—smoking and exuberantly exchanging confidences in Sukie's kitchen.

I knew the Amrams because Max and I had been students at Harvard together in the mid-fifties. Although I declared my major in anthropology early on, Max took a more circuitous route before entering the University of Chicago's Committee on Social Thought, where he completed his doctorate in social psychology. Eventually he accepted a position at American University and became chairman of the sociology department there.

The friendship between Max and me had always wavered between keen intellectual respect and dangerous sexual attraction. Max was undeniably handsome, brilliant and charming, but at Radcliffe I had begun to attain some distinctions of my own—so neither one of us wanted to risk pursuing the other. It was a standoff. Truthfully, I always feared Max was too much for me because back in the mid-fifties, nice girls had to giftwrap affairs in a patina of potential permanence. Hardly the marrying kind, Max refused to pretend we might be serious, so I avoided sleeping with him.

Because Max and I never actually dated, I felt comfortable about calling him when I came alone to the

March on Washington in 1963. It felt perfectly natural to resume our innocent, academic friendship and I eagerly accepted an invitation to stay at his house, where I met and fell in love with his wife.

Sukie.

Who could help loving her?

She was beautiful. She had enormous chocolate eyes and layers of dark curly hair that rioted around her face, tangling and untangling according to the weather, behaving hideously at the first hint of humidity. Sukie's hair was a hostile, destabilizing force in her life because it eliminated any element of self-determination in her public presentation. We discussed that problem for decades, even after white threads began basting their way through her dark curls.

When we talked, I used to watch Sukie's face as if I were reading the lyrics to a hard-rock ballad on the back of an album cover. Everything she felt surfaced immediately. Ideas played across her features like strobe lights and her emotions mobilized an endless array of expressions. Her squarish jaw, her slightly snubbed nose, and her unusually wide mouth—which created awesome, luscious smiles—were always in constant motion.

Since Sukie had no idea how beautiful she was, her insecurities and uncertainties created a distracting, but endearing, tentativeness about her. Unaware of the charm of her mannerisms, Sukie manifested all kinds of hesitancies. These made anyone watching her wait to see if she would actually light the cigarette clenched between her lips, swallow the bite of apple she'd taken, put down the child she had lifted in her arms, finish a sentence she'd started, take the spoon out of the cup before tasting her coffee, or answer a telephone ringing right beside her.

Her bittersweet brown eyes demanded constant dues from her friends. She collected absurdities, ironies, rumors, and outrages to refuel her spirit. "Come on," she'd beg silently. "Tell me a riddle. Talk about love. What's been happening? Aren't things crazy? Wild? Sick? Insane?" Savoring scandals, crazy juxtapositions, irreconcilable contradictions, she'd squeal, "Are you kidding? I don't believe it. I *love* it," about every outrage offered. She was an English major, with a poli-sci minor, searching for scenic material and larger themes.

Sukie wore dangling hoop earrings, jeans with loose madras shirts or bulky sweaters, use-contoured leather sandals, Chloe perfume, kohl eyeliner, a thin gold chain around her neck, and her heart on her sleeve. Merriment was her battery; laughter splashed color across her olive skin. Her favorite frivolous topics were food, fat, and famous people. She'd be dressed and ready to go, anywhere, for any reason, within minutes. Frequent eruptions of throaty, self-perpetuating laughter punctuated her speech.

After I'd spent several weekends at the Amrams', Sukie and I became best friends. It might have happened even if Max and I had been casual undergraduate lovers, but it was better not to have to overcome anything like that. It made the friendship between Sukie and me simpler and sweeter. As the sixties advanced, our families spent more and more time together and our children became enormously important to each other.

Before I had my first baby, I never knew how strong a need I had for community. It was only at Sukie's house that the various women who visited could release stifled cravings for companionship and luxuriate in the empathy that flowered around us. In the mornings we always felt incredibly rich sitting in Sukie's kitchen around her old, beat-up wooden table covered with crumbs and half-full coffee cups, while our children crawled across the floor or, in later years, toddled in to refill their cereal bowls before returning to watch "Romper Room."

Sukie had designed a long narrow counter that traveled along three walls of her irregularly shaped but spacious kitchen. Various sections of the counter served different purposes and a tall wooden stool on wheels allowed her to glide from one area to another, depending on her needs. Some of the counter space was designated for food preparation or for storage of oversized cooking utensils, but the corner closest to the kitchen table had been turned into a mini-desk. This area held a Rolodex, Scotch tape dispenser, stapler, a lethal-looking spindle flagging various bills or receipts, and a thin ceramic vase holding pencils and the Paper Mate cartridge pens to which Sukie was addicted.

With the affluent early-morning sunlight settling a crust upon the cream in Sukie's chipped blue pitcher and softening the butter in its pudgy white dish, we would sit around the table gazing at Sukie's kitchen possessions and talking about our lives—struggling to express our feelings about our families and our own personal destinies. Inevitably someone would hesitantly announce that she didn't feel she was actually doing exactly what she had originally intended to do. Twirling the flowered sugar bowl that always wore a sparkling choker of fallen granules around its neck, the doubter would lower her head so her hair half-hid her face, while she wondered aloud why life seemed so imperfect, why plans failed, friends faded, and dreams dimmed.

Uneasily we would watch the sunlight dance across the room to paint patterns on our bare arms, crisscrossed upon the table, as a unanimous silence spread among us. But eventually someone would explode with an enthusiastic inventory of all our assets—our important political activities, our wonderful husbands, and our lovely children busily extracting pot covers from the floor-level drawer of Sukie's stove. And then, each in turn, we would remark upon the wonders of our lives, reassuring the doubter that we had all taken the right path and done the right thing. Gradually, we would get high on hope again—certain that time would allow us to reconcile all our incompatible concerns so that our dreams might yet come true.

There in Sukie's sunny kitchen, with its scarred linoleum flooring and old tin cabinets, we would again feel the promise of creativity stir within us, like the soft foot or elbow of a baby pressing inside our bellies, and feel confident that we would eventually write a perfect novel, paint a perfect picture, cure some deadly disease or at least return to graduate school. Heady with coffee and hope, we would passionately assert that our families would flourish and that our loves would last even after we began to express ourselves and fulfill our own ambitions.

But when we had to leave that sweet warm kitchen, with the taste of coffee and cream still kissing our lips and the intimate touch of friendship still caressing us, we would grow frightened again and not want to leave. We would want to stay right there—in Sukie's house— forever, so that we could do all our chores together and charm each other's children along with our own. Because each of us knew that by the time we returned home, tired from travel, to our small apartments filled with the stale smell of our own absence, the rich communal sense of omnipotence would evaporate and we would again feel isolated and beleaguered, racked by our conflicted and conflicting dreams.

By 1963 I had completed all the courses for my Ph.D., spent two and a half years doing fieldwork in Amazonian Brazil, and moved to New York. A year later I married Leonard Satz, a successful civil rights lawyer ten years my senior, and moved into a large West End Avenue apartment. During the next four years I gave birth to our two daughters, Loren and Lisa, and finished my dissertation working mostly at night.

In truth, the period from 1965 to 1970 was the most frantic of my life. Domestic duties devoured me, and my children consumed me from daybreak until dark when they vomited me forth, frazzled and frenzied, to work on my dissertation. Worst of all, I discovered that most of my raw data didn't necessarily substantiate the theory I began to develop about female rites of passage in the Brazilian Amazon Mundurucu tribe. Since the research I'd designed was not totally aligned with the concepts that began to emerge when I started writing, and since there wasn't the slightest possibility of my returning to Brazil to gather new information, I had to juggle the data to fit the concepts.

Forcing my findings to conform to my theories was clearly a cardinal sin—the exact opposite of what I had intended or was expected to do. But even though time and circumstances skewed my methodology, Harvard accepted my dissertation happily and even commended my original (for that time) feminist analysis of the life stages of the Brazilian Indian women I had studied. Sometimes, however, I still feel uncomfortable about my unorthodox procedures and wonder if the shortcuts I took permanently marred my intellectual integrity.

Still, the sixties felt good to us because the present was always pregnant with possibilities, because right and wrong seemed easily discernible, and because we were still young and happy and in love with our handsome husbands and our bright, lovely children who played and laughed together, exhilarated by the camping quality of our Washington visits. Perhaps some moralist might say that when our country was waging a wrongful war, nothing should have felt so good. But the power we derived from our protest politics was heady and we have never quite forgotten how good it felt.

After a while, Joanne and Elaine begin to fill me in on what had happened while I was in transit from Long Island. They say that Mary Murphy turned out to be a sixty-year-old reporter who had been "out there on her own" for the last forty years.

"She said she didn't know Sukie well, but had always liked her. When we thanked her for doing everything, she got a little shaky and said that since she had no family, someday a stranger would have to do the same thing for her."

Having finished that unsettling story, Elaine then asks me to telephone Sukie's father in Chicago. Both she and Joanne claim I know him better than they do and for a moment my heart rises up in rebellion.

"Oh God," I protest. "I only met him once, maybe twelve years ago."

From what I knew, Sukie's father was a gray-collar fight promoter and gambler who had suffered so strenuously during the Depression that he never regained his psychological equilibrium. Those of our fathers who survived both the Depression and "Double-yew Double-yew Two," as they called it, had been left with deep scars that often made them erratic and unpredictable. My father had remained so silent about the war that I didn't find out until after he died, at the age of seventy-eight, that he had been a bombardier over Dresden.

Finally I accept the piece of paper with Mr. Smilow's Chicago telephone number and place the call.

He answers immediately. Our conversation is long and painful. There are moments when I'm not totally convinced that Mr. Smilow actually understands what I am telling him. One moment he seems to understand, but in the next he loses it. At several points he becomes incoherent.

"Now who did you say you are?" he asks for the third time.

I explain again.

"And what's your problem?" he coaches me.

I tell him our problem.

"That is impossible," he argues. "Is this a prank call?"

"I wish it were, Mr. Smilow. But everything I told you is true."

"Where are you?" he asks me.

"I'm at Sukie's house."

"Then I'll call back to see if you answer."

"Oh, Mr. Smilow."

"Well, I've got to talk to my sister and find a flight," he says. "I'll call you back tomorrow when I know something for sure."

He hangs up.

"I can't believe this is happening," I mumble, finally replacing the receiver. "I can't believe I just told a man that his daughter died."

We fall silent.

We are all DPs—Displaced Persons—from the land of Big Daddies, who became rich after the Second World War and bought the first new Buicks to roll off the assembly lines. Back from battle, they had donned gray flannel suits and enthusiastically joined the lonely crowd. Ignoring the Victory Gardens we had so feverishly tended, our dads built brick barbecue pits in the backyard where they directed cookouts on soft summer evenings. In the winters, when we had school snowdays, they sometimes stayed home from work to take us sledding.

Indeed, they spoiled us rotten because we were their Depression Babies. They never wanted us to know about roofing and siding or second mortgages. Nancy's father wouldn't even let her bring along her own toothbrush when they went down to Miami Beach for Christmas vacation because he liked buying her brand-new ones from the fancy gift shop in the glitzy lobby of the Eden Roc. As the fifties advanced, our fathers became more and more materialistic. They called blondes "broads" and joined restricted country clubs where they did the two-step on Saturday nights while arranging to two-time our mothers with the wives of their friends. Our mothers pretended not to notice.

Gradually our Big Daddies began to acquire slim blond secretaries, large real-estate holdings, blue-chip stocks and long pastel Cadillacs. They played the mar-

ket, thirty-six holes of golf each weekend, and 78 RPM
Harry James records on our new phonographs. They
overindulged us with pre-Freudian abandon because
The Interpretation of Dreams was never condensed for
publication in either *Reader's Digest* or *The Saturday
Evening Post.* Their favorite artist was Norman Rock-
well.

Regardless of their intent, our Big Daddies succeeded
in turning us into love junkies. Because so many of us
were both gifted and spoiled, we grew accustomed to
the kind of unconditional love they lavished upon us
and that's what eventually got us into such big trouble.
Although few of us ever lived in a castle, most of us
expected a rose garden behind the house. We also expected the men we married to be exactly like our fathers.

We believed that our young, inexperienced, imma-
ture and insecure husbands would know how to make
moves, waves, time, money, love and hotel reservations
with sophisticated ease. We believed they would know
how to raise flowers, children, shrubs, spirits, expectations, *their* salaries and *our* standards of living. We
thought they would be able to kill centipedes, tip
maître d's, park cars in small spaces and make us live
happily ever after. We were wrong.

Suddenly Joanne leaps to her feet. "I can't believe
this is the first summer we didn't take our vacations
together. Why didn't we do it? What made us change
our minds? Why'd we break our promise? Maybe that's
why she died—because, by all rights, we should have
been together at the beach this weekend." Then she
begins to sob. "I needed her so much."

"We all needed her," Elaine says firmly, determined
to keep our grief evenly distributed. "Sukie was probably the most important friend each of us had. Actually,
if you stop to think about it, we all only know each other
because of her. She was our center."

It was true. Elaine had gone to the University of Chicago with Sukie in the mid-fifties. Joanne had been her editor at *Mademoiselle* during the sixties when Sukie wrote a series of articles about women in the Kennedy administration. And my family had shared the most important parts of our lives—our passionate involvement in the civil rights and antiwar movements—with the Amrams.

"She understood me better that anyone else except Nathaniel, and now they're both gone," Elaine says bitterly.

Joanne and I nod.

"But look, there's something else, Diana," Joanne adds apologetically.

"What?"

"Some writing Sukie left out on her desk. It's from a diary or journal she was keeping."

She reaches down to reclaim a batch of papers from the floor beside the sofa and hands them over to me. Since it's clear they both expect me to read them immediately, I dig through my purse for my glasses, put them on, and begin.

CHAPTER 3

APRIL 1981

He left me on a Wednesday. Or was it Thursday?

Right away I began to feel an overwhelming desire to buy a pair of cowboy boots. What that wish signified, I didn't know. I simply felt certain that I needed some cowboy boots. So on Saturday morning I went to Georgetown and bought a pair of light tan, calf-high, heavily stitched Fryes. Because I was terrified of losing the past, I thought the boots might possess some special significance, but I couldn't think of what it might be.

I also began painstakingly mending the satin lining of the fur jacket my father had given me. I did a little sewing on it each evening. The fabric had frayed so the hem hung down below the bottom of the coat. It made me look shabby and poor. I tried very hard to fix the satin so it would stay in place.

Within a few weeks after Max left, time lost all its perimeters. Terror invaded and occupied me. I had always feared any lessening of intensity. I had spent my life fighting off diminishments. Now I was overwhelmed by loss.

I walked through my house as if it were a hotel lobby. I thrashed about in boundless pain for endless days and nights without any reprieve or respite. Security suddenly seemed like some old song no longer played on the radio. I stopped reading the newspapers or watching television. I was unaware that news announcers counted the days that the hostages were held in Iran. I do remember the day they were seized. I guess I saw the Yellow Ribbon Parade when they returned home. I remember nothing of the world in the interim. I miss my mother.

MAY 1981

I spend each day like a dollar. I shell out the hours like coins from my purse.

Sometimes I can't remember what I've done during a day or where I've been. I search through my pockets looking for parking garage receipts or carbon copies of credit card charges.

I hear voices, two voices—one male and one female. They are having a long conversation. Sometimes they say things Max and I said in the past. Sometimes they say things we never got around to saying. I listen all the time, but I am most attentive when I am alone in the middle of the night. My nights are longer than my days and that's when the voices become very loud. I know I am concentrating; I can feel my eyes staring with intensity.

I used to dream about men. Now I dream about men with other women. I dream about people doing things that hurt my feelings.

Frequently I dream about twins, about theatrical performances or about helicopters. Often in my dreams a helicopter is following me, fluttering above my head as I run down some dark, mean street. Sometimes there is machine-gun fire from the helicopters; other times the pilot tries to use the landing glides, like knives, to decapitate me.

In the middle of the night, when I wake alone, I review the names of all the great people I know were insomniacs. I hold this sleepless army in great esteem because they remained alert to their isolation. This must have been clarifying for them because insomnia offers an opportunity to run through one's repertoire of regrets. It is a stage on which to relive egregious errors.

I miss my mother.

I think about Blanche DuBois. I remember the Chinese lampshade she carried around to cover any naked light bulbs she encountered. I recall her nervous rearrangements of her hair to make it fall forward and hide her face. In the past, people often thought me most attractive when I felt I looked my ugliest. Sometimes I felt too ugly to have sex. Other times I felt so ugly that sex was the only way I could express my self-contempt.

If I don't see myself in mirrors or windows, I forget about how I look. Once in bed I can read, write entries in my journal, listen to music, feel cozy and content. But when I walk into the bathroom and see myself in the mirror, I cringe before the unbearable shabbiness of my future. I study my reflection, stunned by the unfamiliar countenance of a middle-aged woman. I only remember my young face, the one I wore from fifteen to forty, so that now its changes seem incredible to me.

I lay on the sofa thinking I could hear snowflakes falling outside. I remembered a Conrad Aiken story in which a character thought he could hear snow falling and I wondered if I was finally going mad. Desperately I tried to remember the end of that story, but I couldn't and the fictional snowflakes kept falling inside my head.

I was afraid of losing my mind, my children, my wallet. Max said he would give me money for another six months. It took me three weeks to call a lawyer.

Sex with Max was both simple and complicated. I can't believe I'll never feel his hands on me again. If he were dead I could accept it. But he is three blocks away, touching another woman.

"Get out of my life," he said to me over the telephone a few nights ago.

Several weeks after Max left, I called Diana in New York. She said that even if I had three husbands everything would still be exactly the same. I would still be home alone all day and have to go to the grocery, the shoemaker, the liquor store or the post office. I would still have to look for free-lance assignments. I would still have to do what I do. But her analysis didn't quiet me. I continued to flail about.

I found a psychiatrist, Dr. F. Karel, who prescribed several major tranquilizers for me. I took them with vodka. The combination totally disinhibited me. Within six weeks I was hooked on heavy doses of Prolixin, Valium, Elavil and sleeping pills. I began drinking a quart of vodka each day. I had blackouts and memory lapses. I gained nine pounds. My skin broke out; my hair refused to curl. I got deep dark circles beneath my eyes and developed a racking chest cough.

I paced the house, poured vodka into my breakfast coffee, ate peanut butter on toast, and trembled when I walked up the stairs. Sometimes I couldn't sleep, read my mail, take a shower or get dressed. Sometimes I fasted for four or five days; other times I felt starved and ate ravenously right from the refrigerator, slapping slices of American cheese on Wasp white bread and coating everything with mayonnaise.

Gradually I stopped recording the checks I wrote. As my identity dissolved, my signature became unrecognizable. Within the first month after Max left, the bank returned fourteen of my checks. Finally I went to speak with one of the officers. Mr. Proctor seemed sympathetic and said he would clear my checks himself. Later I heard about a doctor who was so afflicted by anxiety that during an attack his signature became a straight flat line so that no pharmacist would fill his prescriptions.

One day Dr. Karel said, "Sukie, if you don't stop acting out, you are going to lose your children, your friends, your reputation, and whatever money there is.

Believe me—if you don't stop acting crazy, you're going to lose everything."

I didn't believe him until it happened.

People kept telling me to be nicer to myself. I didn't know what they meant. Finally I decided it had something to do with flowers. Whenever I thought about the past, I had an urge to tuck some flowers in with my memories. In my imagination, I gathered hyacinths and anemones to weave around my thoughts.

I'm forty-five, look thirty-seven, and feel twenty-nine. I don't know which is worse. Because I'm forty-five, there are some days when I no longer feel like holding in my tummy. Some mornings I think, What the hell? I've been holding in my stomach for as long as I can remember and now I shouldn't have to do it anymore. But by nightfall I always feel my old sense of sexual responsibility return. Of course I have to appear slim and young, interesting and interested, composed yet available. That is my duty. To whom, I do not know.

I discovered a pattern I hadn't known existed. In the mornings I wanted to live, but at night I wanted to die. Thoughts of suicide made me sleepy, while ideas of homicide woke me up. In the mornings, before Max left, I always wanted my freedom; at night I cherished my security. Once he was gone all I wanted was to feel safe again—even for a short while, even for a single day.

We. Elizabeth Hardwick called we a "teabag of a word." I like that image but I never liked tea. For me, tea was always too closely associated with sore throats and tummy aches. Its smell always made me feel queasy. After Max left, the word "we" made me ache because I felt so singular. The sight of a couple put me into a panic. I felt as if no one would ever hold me again.

My heart kept racing, lurching forward, day after day. I told myself that nothing warranted such panic. No one had died. No one was sick. I could still count my blessings. But the silence of the telephone was a trembling reality that shattered me. My husband, my friend, my children's father, didn't love me anymore. I found it impossible to believe.

I have stopped going outside. The notion of going outside seems like the equivalent of a jailbreak to me. My self has become my prison—my prism of self-pity— and I don't want to leave it. Actually, I am afraid that if I went outside I would perhaps see some city-scapes—littered alleys, woebegone children, bag ladies, derelicts or crazies on the bus. If by chance I look out my bedroom window and see a couple hunching close together as they walk along my street, I stare down at them in agony. I study their intertwined hands, their arms wound around each other's waists, until they dis-appear around the corner. Then I feel my loss again with a piercing pain that leaves me breathless.

I do not want to start over. I want things to be the way they used to be. I want the past back. I want my old life returned to me intact and totally unchanged. I want the children to stay small cute sizes and never grow up. I want them always to go to the same school so they can walk back home together forever. I want Happy to stay inside the house so she won't get run over.

I want life to be like it was when I was a child and could recognize any dog that walked past my house, knowing it belonged to the Olsens on Vincent or the Carlsons who lived six blocks away on Queen. Or, if that's too much to ask, I just want everything to be the way it was when our kids were babies. I'll even take back all the stress if I can have the rest. Just give it back to me, God, please.

The whistle on my teapot has stopped whistling. Last Sunday I forgot I had water boiling, so it evaporated and the bottom of the teapot melted all over the top of the stove. Now I use a scratched old saucepan to make my instant coffee.

It's like my phone calls. Lately, a lot of my phone calls consist of postponements, cancellations or wrong num-bers. Even the man who inspects the furnace each summer telephoned last week to change his visit from July to August.

I live in a house in the middle of a city, yet I have raccoons in my walls. Since there is a city ordinance forbidding the killing of raccoons, my exterminator won't do a thing about them and I can't find anyone else who will. All I can do is listen to the raccoons scratching inside my walls every night, all night long.

My coordinated quilt no longer matches the sheets. For some reason the quilt faded faster than the linens so they no longer look like a set.

My GE iron no longer presses the small wrinkles out of my clothes. Tucks around the collars of my blouses have become quite troublesome.

Someone lost the little keys to the locks on my front windows so I can't open them anymore. I constantly feel deprived of fresh air.

My favorite dress, a two-piece black velour, is wearing out. The backside is growing sheer. The jacket still looks good but it doesn't cover the rubbed-away section on the seat. Also, the bodice has grown tighter so the waistband rides up on me. Without this dress, I might just stay at home forever.

I received a carbon copy of a charge slip from an Exxon gasoline station in a town where I've never been. My shaky signature is on the carbon, but I don't remember ever visiting Hershey, Pennsylvania. Hershey, Pennsylvania? Why would I go to Hershey, and if I did, was I drunk or did someone take me there and not tell me where we were? Did I get a chocolate attack in the middle of the night or is all of this just a metaphor? If so, for what?

I put my ficus plant out on the back porch to get a little more sunlight and someone stole it. Now, if I go anyplace, I keep looking for it. I know I would recognize it anywhere, even if it was mixed in with a bunch of other ficus or replanted in a different pot. To make matters worse, the roots of both my jade plants have begun rotting. I think human cancer must look like those gnarled clumps of squishy flesh.

After hours of loneliness, I would sometimes dial his number. Often he left on his answering machine even if he was home; "Screw you," the machine would say to me.

My humanity has begun to shrink like a woolen scarf mistakenly thrown into the washing machine. Inside I am shriveled up and misshapen. Panic prevails. I am aware that other people still seem to be engaged. There are processes, businesses, negotiations, plans, deals, relationships and affairs.

I believe I married too young, but I also believe that now I am too old to be betrayed, abandoned and deserted.

For a while Max and I had circular telephone conversations every day. We would rehash our lives.

You did this, you didn't do that, he would say.

You did this, you didn't do that, I would answer.

Then he would say, I did do this, but you wouldn't do that.

Now he says he has finally stopped smoking, that he is exercising daily and eating only health food. He is happy, he says, very happy. He says, "There was no other way for you and me. What happened had to happen." Now his life is simple and straightforward. He goes to his office only three days a week. He is developing a new syllabus for his classes. And he is happy living with her. He says, "She is very, very dear."

At night he is with the one who is very, very dear.

Why had I never taken walks with him, reached out to hold his hand, leaned across a table to touch his face at a restaurant, sat beside him at a party? Why had there never been any of those impulses, any of those stirrings?

Hurt. People must fear love after a hurt like this.

Outside the orbit of a man, I lack gravity, the force that tames my soul and holds me in place.

In the past, I always tended the wounded. Now that

I am hurt, I can find no one to help me. I never knew there was a time limit on rage and grief. People will take only so much and then no more. People get sick and tired of other people being sick and tired. They are bored by my obsession now. A lot of people think I've become a midlife crazy. Some of my dearest friends, no, most of my dearest friends, don't want to hear about it anymore.

That week had been a chaotic one in my life. Max had said he wanted to go away for a while to work on his book before he left on a week-long trip to Europe. He said he would find a motel or cabin in West Virginia. I thought it was a good idea and on Monday morning he left early to pick up a rental car. When he stopped back home to say goodbye, he kept watching the clock. I remember wondering why he was concerned about the time. I was laughing when I kissed him goodbye.

I spent the next four days researching an article about the diplomatic change-overs at the Nicaraguan and Iranian embassies following their revolutions. On Sunday night there was to be a large wedding party for Brenda and Phil at my house. Max came back from West Virginia on Thursday but left early Friday morning for an international academic meeting in London.

Over a hundred people came to the party on Sunday night. One of Brenda's younger friends brought his roommate along and the young man came over to greet me. He was puppy-dog friendly and finally asked if he could have my daughter's telephone number. He said he'd met her and Max in West Virginia the week before and wanted to call her. I gave him Carol's number without thinking twice. It took me the rest of the night to understand the meaning of what he'd said.

Max returned home the following Friday. It was a rainy October night. Because David was home studying, we went out for a drink at an almost-empty restaurant called Garvin's Laugh-Inn, on Connecticut Avenue.

As soon as we sat down, Max started talking about the conference he'd attended in London. I drank half my Salty Dog and then asked him whom he had been with in West Virginia. He looked at me silently for a very long time and then said, "It doesn't matter."

He was speaking truthfully, he always did.

"It does to me," I said. "I can't believe you were there with a woman. A young kid who came to the party for Brenda and Phil said he had dinner with you and Carol in West Virginia. Except Carol wasn't there, was she, Max? I can't believe you'd try to pass off some whore as our daughter."

Silence.

"Who is she?"

He didn't respond.

"I can't believe that after all these years, after everything we've been through, you can still do something like this."

"I love her," he said quietly.

"You love her?"

Silence.

Clichés crowd to my lips. "How could you do this? Why?"

"I love her."

"Who is it?"

"That doesn't matter."

"It does. Who is it?"

We went over it again and again, like scratching an itch, cracking a knuckle, picking a scab. He was stubbornly silent. I ordered two more drinks and lost more ground. He stayed cool and sober while I got messier and sloppier as my rage mounted.

"Who the hell is she?"

Silence.

Louder. "I said, who the hell is she?"

"Her name doesn't matter."

"Well what does?"

"That I love her."

"Oh shit."

Silence.

I unbuttoned my blouse, reached inside and pulled out my left breast. Then I sat perfectly still and finished my third drink.

"Oh fuck," he said. "Cut it out."

I left myself exposed.

"This is what I can't stand," he said earnestly.

"I've never done it before."

"You do other things just like it. Now stop it. Someone will see you."

Our part of the restaurant was completely empty. When I saw the waitress coming through the kitchen door at the far end of the room, I twisted my breast back inside my blouse.

"What's her name?"

"It's Elizabeth."

"Elizabeth?" Terror seized me. "Elizabeth from across the street? You're lying."

"It's true."

"You fucker."

Everything I had ever liked about him turned ugly before my eyes.

"Give me two more Salty Dogs," I called out to the waitress in a rude voice. "Do you love her?" I asked.

"I told you. Yes."

"You fucker."

"Go away for a few months," he said judiciously. "Go to Europe."

I lifted the bottle of ketchup off the table and poured it down the front of my blouse.

"I can't stand your craziness," he said.

I gulped down the first of the two drinks the waitress set on the table. When I'd finished the second, I got up and ran out of the restaurant and into the street.

Cars screeched and scattered in different directions. I stumbled down the center of Connecticut Avenue, seeking headlights that veered away before I could catch them. I could hear Max calling me and once, turning around, I saw him dodge a car in the middle of the boulevard in an attempt to reach me.

Suddenly a tall thin black woman was standing beside me, holding me with strict authoritarian hands.

"What's the matter? What's he doing to you? Do you know him?"

"Yes, he's my husband."

"Come along." The woman maneuvered me between several moving cars and then between parked ones until we reached the sidewalk.

"Is that blood on you?"

"No, it's ketchup."

"I'm a plainclothes policewoman," she said gently.

I sank against the woman's slim strong body.

"I'll take you home," she said.

She put me in her car and drove the few blocks to my house very slowly. I wanted to ride in that car with her forever. She must have known. She parked and we sat together in silence outside my house for a while. Finally I got out. I said thank you. She said, "Be cool." I said goodbye.

He was home already, in bed in his pajamas.

I stood in the doorway staring at him until suddenly I lunged across the room to begin hitting him, pulling his hair and thrashing his chest with my furled fist. Rage was driving me forward. The alcohol running through my system was mixing with my rage. I no longer knew what I was doing.

It was strange. From the moment he confessed his infidelity, I knew we would never be together again. Perhaps if there had been a glimmer of concern, if I had felt any love emanating from him as we sat in that restaurant, things might have been different. Unfortunately, it was over before I knew we weren't a "we" anymore. Because our marriage ended so abruptly, I've never been able to remember what must have been our last good time together.

Twenty years before, when we first came to Washington, we had gone out to an Italian restaurant with a foppish young friend named Jerry. It had been a classic 1950s Italian restaurant: wooden booths, candles stuck in Chianti bottles frosted with multicolored melted wax, red checkered tablecloths and the thick smell of cheese and tomato sauce. Max and Jerry sat together across from me and I had leaned back against the chilled wood of the booth to rest my head.

Gradually, I became aware of the man sitting directly behind me. He was talking slowly but steadily to a woman. As I listened to him, I was overwhelmed by a desire to see what they looked like. Stretching upward and turning quickly, I peered over the back of the bench.

They were middle-aged. The man appeared to be a slightly depressed salesman. The woman was a nondescript housewife dressed in an awning-striped cotton smock.

The man was explaining to the woman why he was going to leave her and their children. He said he was tired of her whining and complaining. He said he was tired of the children's constant demands. Also, he said, as if it were an afterthought, he had fallen in love with a woman who worked in his office. He was going to move into her apartment that weekend. He was going to give his wife and children four hundred dollars a month and he didn't want any backtalk.

I saw the waitress deliver two plates of spaghetti to them before bringing menus to our table. Max and Jerry were deeply engrossed in a political discussion.

My heart was thundering.

I felt my breath growing shallow. The smell of pizza and meatballs was gagging. There were crumbs in front of me on our checkered cloth from the Italian bread

Max and Jerry had crumbled. I saw butter frosting a knife that lay on the table. When the waitress came to take our order, I asked only for a glass of Chianti.

I must have known that some twenty years later the same thing would happen to me.

CHAPTER 4

"*T*his is wild," I say, shaking my head so my glasses slide down the sweaty bridge of my nose.

I am violently upset by the anguish of Sukie's journal. Having avoided such emotionalism in recent years, I am now overwhelmed at being subjected to it under the present circumstances.

"What do you mean?" Elaine asks.

"Well, I just didn't know Sukie had such a bad time of it. Actually I thought she was rather relieved to be finished with Max and finally free to do her own thing."

"She told you *that*?" Elaine gasps, straightening up in her corner of the couch.

"Well, not exactly," I waver. "I mean, I knew Sukie was angry at Max, but I didn't think she was strung out like *this*." I wave Sukie's pages in the air.

"God, Diana. For a famous anthropologist, you certainly don't understand much," Elaine groans. "What about that scene in the restaurant with the ketchup? I know that actually happened. Sukie was devastated by her divorce."

"Look. You know Sukie put on scenes in restaurants and bars. I mean she was *upset*, but she wasn't as distraught as all that."

"What are you trying to say?"

"Just that it wasn't really as bad as this makes it sound."

"Look, Di, you didn't see all that much of Sukie lately," Elaine testifies earnestly. "I came down here a lot. Also, I think she confided in me more because I'd gone through the same sort of thing just a year before she did. It's no fun being dumped even if you are a free spirit like Sukie. It still hurts. And it's perfectly clear to me now, in retrospect, that Sukie actually had a breakdown after Max left her."

"I don't know if you should call it a *breakdown*," Joanne interposes, looking dubious about such technical language being applied to Sukie. "She did sort of lose it there for a while, but it wasn't *exactly* a breakdown." She looks directly at me and then shifts into a discreet but meaningful voice. "She was doing an awful lot of drugs, though. Prescription shit."

I nod, but Elaine is still looking at me indignantly.

"You know, Sukie might have told different stories to different friends," I suggest. "She was a writer and she had a real sense of her audience." I let my voice drift off so I won't slide into any comparisons.

"I don't think you know what it feels like to have your husband divorce you, Diana. You *wanted* your divorce. You'd *outgrown* Leonard. You were bored with him and wanted to be free to do your work. Besides, you're different. You're not as emotional as Sukie or me. You try to avoid feeling *anything* too intensely," Elaine concludes with a sour expression.

I run my fingertip around the rim of my glass, somewhat injured by Elaine's analysis. My self-distancing is both conscious and conditioned. I grew up in a family that abhorred emotion. In middle age, I simply reactivated my own original predisposition to avoid obsessive behavior.

"A twenty-year marriage is hardly a one-night stand," Elaine continues even more fiercely. "You know, to this day, every time I read a good book I get an almost irresistible impulse to throw it in a Jiffy Bag and send it to Nathaniel. I know what sections he'd like best and

what would make him laugh. I could even underline it
for him if I had to. I've got *his* point of view in *my* head.
And I know it must have been the same for Sukie. Don't
you realize what that kind of split does to a person? It's
crazy time for the resisters—the ones like Sukie and me
who don't want a divorce. When a marriage breaks up
after that long a time, it's like a death." She begins to
cry softly.

"I think that's a fair statement," Joanne concurs. She
is pushing her thick hair away from her face, nervously
hooking it behind her ears. "But still, I know I mostly
saw Sukie in New York when she came up to work with
me, but I never thought her marriage was all that central to her identity. I mean, when we were really working hard on some article together, we always had such
a great time—just banging around my apartment in our
jeans and sweatshirts and pounding the typewriter and
laughing and eating and drinking pots of coffee. Sukie
could get high off writing. We both could. Or maybe it
was just the coffee. But we had such great times. And
to me, it never even felt like she was married. I mean,
I do know she had a lot of . . . men friends in New York
and that she was . . . pretty independent."

Elaine turns to look at Joanne as if she's just dese-
crated the flag.

"Anyway, it's all sort of . . . moot now," I whisper with
my lips quivering. "It doesn't seem to make much difference now that she's dead."

"Oh, yes it does," Elaine argues. "Because it tells you
how her life ended and what it was like right before the
end. You're always trying to generalize everything,
Diana. You're always trying to apply your own point of
view to our whole generation."

"Oh Christ, let's not fight now, Elaine, okay?" I ask
impatiently. "Let's not do a *Rashomon*. What difference does it make? Just forget it."

I get up to fix myself a second, stronger drink and
thankfully think of freshening Joanne's and Elaine's.

They both seemed pleased by my gesture and accept it as some sort of apology. Clearly we all want to stay together until our anger dissipates so we can draw some comfort from each other.

But I do see things differently from the way Sukie's other friends see them. By training I've been disciplined to detect generational forces and societal patterns within individual behaviors. Academically I practice discerning the common causes and concerns of discrete, highly variegated groups. Anyway, in this instance I am part of Sukie's generation; I too am an adult Depression Baby so I am personally aware of the sources and forces that influenced us. Indeed, from the time of our birth into families that had neither enough food nor space for us, many of us wondered if we were really "wanted" or just "accidents." Why would our desperate and frightened parents voluntarily have added another dependent to their struggle for survival?

Although Sukie may have appeared super-confident, enormously talented and totally charming, essentially she could never feel secure because she was her mother's daughter. Psychologically and financially buffeted by complex historical circumstances, our mothers believed they needed male breadwinners to avoid ending up on breadlines. They were probably right. Our mothers' generation was quick to forfeit independence and personal fulfillment in order to assure some security for themselves and their children. Consequently their major bequest to us was an imprecise—but imperiling—sense of helpless dependency.

Professionally, I believe Sukie's sense of loss was culturally as well as personally dictated. Depression Babies often responded to deprivation as if it were a call to arms. Like many other Americans born during the thirties, Sukie could get high off her losses. Challenges mobilized her for battle. Adversity inspired her to greater efforts and any uphill fight created a sense of drama that heightened her already intense determination. Many times I saw Sukie wrap some setback around herself like a ragged security blanket to give her confidence in the face of disadvantage.

Suddenly I feel another hot flash begin to mount. The skin below my neck starts feeling prickly and a rush of warmth spreads upward like a rash toward my face. Arching my arms, I lift the heavy weight of my hair up to the top of my head so that a little cool air kisses the back of my neck.

I glance at Elaine and Joanne. In their floral print sun dresses, they look like crumpled bouquets flung down and forgotten upon the sofa.

"Listen," Joanne begins.

But then the telephone rings. Since I'm the nearest, I lift the receiver. At first all I can hear is the sound of distance—rushes of air or waves of water.

"Hello?" I say loudly several times. Finally I hear Max's distant, but still strong, baritone voice.

"Diana? Diana, is that you?"

"Hello, Max."

"What happened?"

"She had a cerebral hemorrhage. She died right away. She was in the press gallery at the Senate."

"Oh God. The doctors couldn't do anything?"

"It was too late. Do the kids know?"

"Yah. I just told them a little while ago."

"How are they?"

"Awful now. They were great before."

"How are you?"

"I'm not sure. How 'bout you?"

"Okay. Elaine and Joanne are here too."

"Thank them for me. I've got a flight to New York in about an hour, but there's only one seat, so the kids aren't coming back until tomorrow. I get into Kennedy around seven in the morning and I'll catch the first plane to D.C. When's the funeral?"

"Monday, I guess."

Max is silent as he absorbs the fact that nothing has been arranged.

"Is Sukie's dad there?"

"He'll be coming tomorrow or Sunday."

"Okay. I'll see you before noon."

"Have a safe trip."

I hang up and repeat the conversation to Elaine and Joanne. Then we all stare at each other. For a long while we remain silent. We finish our drinks. We suck our ice cubes. We stare off into space. Each of us is physically and psychologically exhausted. We are also facing some major blockages. We are not yet ready to believe that what is happening *is* really happening. When we finally decide to go to sleep, Elaine says she'll fix the couch and stay in the living room because it's so cool. Joanne decides to use the guest room, so I take Sukie's.

The second floor of the house is much hotter than the first and Sukie's room is stifling. It is also a mess—not dirty, just confused. She hadn't made her bed before she hurried off to die. I turn on the air conditioner in the window and look around. Somehow everything seems more complicated than it used to be. I get the feeling that Sukie had been attempting to integrate the disparate parts of her existence and that the various strands had been drawn together here in her bedroom.

The head of the big sleigh bed is set against the double bay windows, and the mauve-colored sheets, sprinkled with pale yellow flowers, are tangled with a cotton quilt of irregular plum patches. The combination creates immediate chaos. Sukie's bookend bedside tables hold matching lamps with mauve shades. In fact, mauve is everywhere, bleeding and blending into the faded Oriental rug that covers the bleached wood floor.

I try to think of Sukie in relation to that color and finally decide she must have adopted Elaine's affection for it. We have all been friends for so long that sometimes we internalize each other's preferences. Each of us has occasionally bought a dress that was clearly intended—by style, design, color or, even worse, size—for someone else. Eventually these "mistakes" get forwarded to the appropriate person and we all joke and tease about them: "Sukie thought she was Diana and bought a white angora turtleneck." "Brenda thought she was Joanne and bought powder-blue suede slacks." "Elaine forgot she didn't have pierced ears and bought those gorgeous gold hoops she gave Myrna for Christmas."

On one side of the room stand a dresser, a large Victorian wardrobe, and a stout wicker hamper missing its top so that the jumble of laundry inside is visible. On the other end of the room is a desk created by a long board propped atop two metal filing cabinets. On it sit Sukie's old Selectric, crowded ashtrays, and mugs filled with stagnant white coffee. Magazines, books, newspapers, and piles of papers conspire to create even greater commotion on either side of the typewriter.

I begin to look around for some fresh linens. The knowledge that Sukie slept in her bed this morning makes the sheets seem contaminated. When I pause to think about it, the only disease Sukie had was death itself, but I still want to change the bed. In the closet I find some folded linens on the top shelf before being waylaid by the sight of Sukie's wardrobe.

As always, it seems to me Sukie wore costumes rather than clothes. Everything in her closet seems selected for some hypothetical photo opportunity staged so Sukie could present different visions and versions of herself. There are severe tweed suits and blazers next to voluptuous velour jackets and skirts. There are blue denim coveralls, jeans, and Western cowboy boots, but also bronze dancing slippers and a limp lamé cocktail dress half falling off its hanger.

It is also apparent that the clothes in Sukie's closet are organized by sizes. There seem to be sections for eights when she was slimming, tens for normal times, and twelves for use in case of emergency. Most of her dresses are Loehmann's anonymous designer models with torn-out labels. We have always worn discounted designer clothes and know the location of every outlet store in the country.

I change the bed, grab my little suitcase, and go across the hall into the bathroom for a shower. On a hook behind the door hangs a rosebud print nightgown I recognize as the one Sukie wore the last time she stayed at my apartment. I press my face against the gown for a moment, to inhale the sweet smell of her body, and the cotton caresses my cheek in return. Under the shower, I cry while the tepid water sobs past my ears and weeps down my body.

Afterwards, wrapped in a big blanket of a towel, I stand before the medicine chest mirror and look at myself. Beneath my tan, I am tired and shaken. My face seems out of focus, like a poorly developed print of itself. What I call my khaki—they're really sand-colored—eyes and hair seem more faded than usual after weeks at the beach. I believe eventually I will simply bleach out and disappear, rather than die.

Then, to abort any closer self-inventory, I exile the mirror by opening the medicine chest. And there is Sukie's drug collection—all the little bottles of time-release crutches to which so many of us have been addicted at various times of our lives. Smiling, I remember the last time Sukie stayed with me in New York. At breakfast she'd asked for some Sweet 'n' Low and I'd passed her two white saccharine tablets. Then, in silent amazement, I'd watched as she unconsciously popped them into her mouth like pills and swallowed them with a slug of coffee rather than dropping them into her cup.

We had a good laugh over that one; Sukie was a great laugher.

Instinctively I reach for one of the prescription bottles and, rather redundantly, read its label before extracting and swallowing two of the five-milligram Valiums. Then I palm the bottle, knowing Sukie would want me to have it. Given our stressful lives, none of us was ever beyond stealing popular prescription pills from one another. It was the only thing—other than time—that we ever took wrongfully from each other.

Returning to Sukie's room, I lie down naked on her bed so I can feel whispers of cool air from the window air conditioner. More and more frequently now I sleep naked because of nocturnal hot flashes that sting me awake like an electric heating pad, set on High, and forgotten in the bed. It always takes a while before I remember that I no longer have menstrual cramps, that there is no heating pad, and that I am drenched in sweat from a midnight hot flash that makes me glow like an iridescent object in the dark.

Staring up at the ceiling, I smoke one last cigarette and think about the section of Sukie's journal I'd read. The existence of any journal terrifies me because I know that is where writers corral their wildest feelings and censor emotions too savage to publish even in disguised fictional form. Of course I do not want to know all the pain Sukie suffered. Yet, because her journal exists, I am compelled to read it and I hear what she says. Actually, what she is saying is not that different from what a lot of our other friends have also been saying lately.

We have lived through a lot. Born to depressed families, we grew up fearful during the Second World War, came of age in the fifties when our country had gone crazy from prosperity, and entered college, at the time of the Korean "conflict," as the Silent Generation whose teachers were afraid to teach because of McCarthyism. We flourished during the civil wars of the sixties and endured the interminable seventies, only to find that the eighties began as a harsh and inhospitable decade for us.

Now a lot of us ache for a past we couldn't wait to finish when it was still the present. One of the saddest things about our generation is that during much of our lives we were out of sync with our own life cycles. Because of this, many of us were destined to suffer divorce and solitude at an unconscionably early age and stage in our lives. This is just a fancy way of saying that lots of us have many regrets and don't like being middle-aged singles alone once again. We still yearn with surprising nostalgia for the times when we each had a young family that folded like a fist protectively around us—a secure, but mobile defense shelter that could also be wielded offensively if necessary.

Jane said, "Whenever I dream I'm driving someplace, it's always in a station wagon that has two baby car seats in the back. I forget that all of that's over when I'm dreaming." Kay continues to hook stray rubber bands around the knobs of her under-sink cabinets as if she still had a toddler at home in danger of swallowing a lethal dose of ammonia. Anne says she can't believe she'll never again chauffeur a bundle of soiled white shirts around town in the passenger seat of her car, and claims she can still sometimes smell the odor of her long-gone husband in the front seat when all the windows are closed. Sometimes she buys No-More-Tears shampoo or Lucky Charms at the supermarket just to offset the cans of Soup for One in her shopping cart.

The endless tunnel of work, obligations and dependencies that we experienced during our twenties and thirties turned out to be the best years of our lives. The light, for which we kept watching, finally appeared at the other end of the tunnel only to be identified as a fast-moving express train bearing down upon us and our loved ones. And now that we've finally realized the value of the past, we feel doubly gypped because we didn't discover its worth until long after it was lost.

For those of us who married in the late fifties or early sixties, marriage became the center stage of our lives. It was here we introduced and played various versions of ourselves. Indeed, we also designed and cleaned the sets, cast the characters, wrote the scripts, directed the actors, and selected intimate audiences to watch our impromptu productions. When our first marriages ended, we felt as if we'd been flung off Broadway in the midst of a long-running play.

In retrospect, there were so many years of such great happiness that often late at night now we wonder how what has happened to us could have happened.

We are the first generation to learn that the equitable distribution principle in no-fault divorce does not mean the equal division of property. For that lesson we paid dearly, even though we felt we'd already paid enough dues. As Nancy wrote in one of her self-published poems, we will never again agree to accept the charges on any collect calls until we know precisely what they are and whether or not we have the right to defend ourselves against them. Nevertheless, most of us kept our slave names after we were divorced.

Despite all the reality sandwiches we've eaten, we're still hung up on the idea of marriage. Way back in the fifties, we learned that we "needed" a husband just as we "needed" a little basic black dress that could take us anyplace. It never occurred to us that two distinct human races—one of which dressed right or left, the other of which dressed up or down—might turn out to be fundamentally incompatible. Yet despite all our disappointments over the defections and deficiencies of our men, we still prefer them to freedom. We still expect some man will come along to light up our lives like a little asterisk twinkling above the prose sentence of our days. For us, six months without a man feels like a house without books—a situation that inevitably leaves us clinically depressed.

Some of us have already remarried. Informed as we are, we know that sixty percent of all second marriages end in divorce. That doesn't deter us from repeating ourselves since we've developed a certain equanimity in the departures department. After all, we have been rehearsing separations for almost half a century now and, during our original stints as single parents, we learned the necessary technique for folding a flat king-sized bedsheet alone.

None of us really feels old yet. In many ways we are living contradictions unable to age, gracefully or otherwise. We would never dream of adding a blue rinse to our hair, getting a perm, choosing sensible shoes for a social occasion, or going to the supermarket without wearing either eye makeup or sunglasses. We still curl our lashes, rub Preparation H on our faces before a cocktail party to shrink enlarged pores, and encourage friends who haven't yet done so to have their ears pierced.

We continue to believe our futures are full of possibilities and that we still might go to law school. We do not want to end up in Miami Beach sharing Happy Hour drinks and Early Bird Special dinners with ladies who play bingo twice a week and steal lipsticks from the Collins Avenue Woolworth's on Saturday afternoons. Having clung to rocks that crumbled into sand in our hands, we are now attempting to take charge of ourselves and to go forward in a dignified and orderly fashion.

I weep for a while before I fall asleep, but I sleep deeply until nine o'clock the next morning. Since I can hear Joanne in the shower, I simply put on yesterday's clothes and go downstairs in search of coffee.

CHAPTER 5

And there—in Sukie's dear, sweet, familiar kitchen—sitting at the table beside Elaine is Max.

He looks exhausted—dangerously, explosively exhausted.

Heartbreak, jet lag, and time warp have spoiled the Hollywood handsomeness of his face. Messy emotions have erased his sophisticated smile and dimmed his dramatic denim-blue eyes. Pain has shorted out his previously wired personality. The buttons of his rumpled shirt march diagonally, rather than perpendicularly, down his chest toward an off-center belt buckle that ropes in tired jeans.

He is externally disheveled and internally damaged.

His suffering summons me and, when he stands up and opens his arms, I trot obediently toward him. Like an abused child who turns for comfort to the guilty parent, I reach out in my grief to the man who hurt my friend.

Then a flash of shame, with a hot flash chaser, roars through me.

Above my head, Max groans, "The only thing harder than losing someone you love is losing someone you've stopped loving."

He is crying, his mouth pressed against my hair so I can feel the heat of his breath on my scalp.

"Too much," he moans. "This is too much. . . ."

"Why? Why? Why?" I complain rhetorically, thudding against him like a crib-banger.

Without quite seeing it, I feel Elaine avert her eyes until Max releases me and steps away.

Then I feel delivered, expelled from a warm womb into worldly danger. Max solders his hands onto my shoulders so as to steady and study me. We have not seen each other for five years. Foolishly I feel ashamed of how I may appear to him and, suddenly self-conscious, I step back and sink into a chair.

Immediately Max moves a chair next to mine.

"My God," he breathes. "You look fabulous, Diana." I stare at him.

He seems somehow more soulful than ever before. His dark hair and light eyes, his grainy skin and dune-colored stubble, remain handsome, but he seems softer and more accessible now. Wounded, he is no longer as intimidating as when he was totally self-assured and sexually judgmental. Hurt, he is less commanding and less challenging.

Now he looks expectantly back and forth between Elaine and me. Although neither of us has seen Max since he left Sukie, we know he knows we know everything. That is why he has now become our supplicant. He wants us to grant him some dignified part in this tragedy despite the ignominious role into which he's been cast. Clearly, after the bitterness of divorce, there can be no pretense of love. The best role for Max is as a supporting character who helps his children bury their mother.

But Elaine is hanging tough. She is sitting sullenly on the other side of Max, totally immune to his neediness. She is not about to forgive him and her toughness is displayed by a total lack of self-consciousness about her appearance. Addicted to loose, shapeless housecoats that she believes flattering, but which actually make her appear larger than she is, Elaine is now swaddled in a huge Arab caftan. She hasn't combed her hair and

clearly couldn't care less. There is a certain integrity in
Elaine's contempt for Max that encourages me to resist
his subtle solicitation of sexual deference in exchange
for his social approval.

"It was great of you to come right away," he says.

Max always opens affirmatively, playing the highest
card in his partner's strongest suit.

"How are the kids doing?" I ask.

"Not good. Neither one of them. Carol's all busted up.
Terrible." Max shakes his head. "And David . . . he's
angry because Sukie died all alone with everyone gone.
It's not good." For a moment he covers his face with his
hands. "They'll get into New York tonight and my folks
will pick them up and take them home to their apartment. Then they'll drive down here with Carol's boyfriend; she wants him to come. My parents will fly in for
the funeral."

The kitchen door swings open and Joanne appears.
Shocked at seeing Max, she freezes in the doorway and
unconsciously begins resealing the flap of her beige silk
wrapper by nervously tightening the belt.

Max stands up and moves toward her.

Despite an initial effort to restrain herself, Joanne also
rushes to him, weeping helplessly.

"Oh God, Max," she moans, collapsing in his arms.
"What are we going to do?"

"I don't know," he says, stroking her hair. "I don't
know."

Eventually she extricates herself from his arms and
stands, slightly bewildered, in the center of the kitchen.
Embarrassed by her emotional capitulation, she begins
tightening and retightening her belt again. Then, seeing the cellophane-wrapped *Washington Post* on the
table, she hurries forward to unwrap and open it.

"Elena is still hovering off the Florida panhandle,"
she reports, staring at the front-page headline. "Elena."
She lights a cigarette, nervously whips her creamy hair
back from her face with the rake of her fingers, and

continues studying the paper. But again the long chains of hair spill forward over her shoulders, reaching down to touch the beginnings of her breasts in the easy V-neckline of her pale wrapper.

"I thought they were going to start naming half the hurricanes after men," she complains, repeating the name several more times to herself in a whisper. "Elena. Elena was hovering over the Florida panhandle the weekend Sukie died."

In a flash we all taste our future memories of the present.

Suddenly Joanne starts leafing through the pages. When she reaches the obituary section she spreads the paper open and we gather around her. There at the top of the first column is Sukie's obit and picture. The photograph is the same one Sukie used for the book jacket of *Disorderly Conduct.* It is a serious picture that somehow makes her look like a thin Liz Taylor; she would have loved the *Post* for choosing it.

Suzanna Amram, 50, Dies
in Senate Press Gallery.

Suzanna Amram, 50, died yesterday in the U.S. Senate Press Gallery of a cerebral hemorrhage. A longtime resident of the District, Ms. Amram, a free-lance journalist, was working on an article related to Friday's extraordinary Senate session.

Ms. Amram was also a novelist and the author of *Laugh Lines, Fine Print,* and *Disorderly Conduct.*

Born in Chicago in 1935 and a graduate of the University of Chicago, Ms. Amram held a doctorate in English literature from Catholic University. Active in the writers' rights movement, she was a member of Washington Independent Writers, PEN, the Author's Guild, and the National Writers Union. She was one of the original members of Mothers Against the War in Vietnam.

Formerly married to Max Amram, professor of

sociology at American University, she is survived
by her two children, David, 18, and Carol, 20, of
Washington, and her father, Martin Smilow, of Chicago, Illinois.

Funeral arrangements are to be announced.

"Oh God," Elaine moans, staring at the newspaper.
"Sukie never finished her doctorate. She only said that
on one of her resumés when she was trying to get a
teaching job at some girls' academy around here. That
school where Jean Harris worked."

"Goddammit," Max curses as exasperation chases
weariness across his face. "Why the hell did she *do*
things like that? Why did she have to lie and ruin her
own obituary?"

Silence.

"Oh, who's gonna know?" Joanne finally asks. "You
think Catholic University is going to check through all
their records and demand a retraction?"

"They just might," Max says grimly.

"In *this* town? Where half the resumés in circulation
qualify as fiction?" Joanne is hanging in with a heated,
irrational defense of Sukie. "Are you kidding?"

"Look, we could call the *Post* and let them know
there's an error," I say uneasily, feeling ambivalent
about the seriousness of this crime.

"Oh sure," Joanne agrees sarcastically. "Sure. They
had a one-hundred-percent accuracy rating before this,
huh? Did you ever see their daily correction column?
Look, it's not that great an obit anyway. Only four
graphs. She deserved more than that. If we do something about the Ph.D. mistake, we should at least try to
have some real input into a new version."

"But it wasn't a mistake," Max insists. "Sukie lied."

"Oh, Max," I protest, suddenly adopting the opposite
position. "Sukie did enough good work that someplace
should have given her a damned honorary doctorate."

Max looks at me as if I've lost my mind.

Actually I am quite upset about this error in Sukie's obituary since I have long feared a similar fate. One of my most frequent nightmares is that after I'm dead, someone will discover how my theoretical generalizations about the Mundurucu were based on insufficient ethnographic evidence and then publish a critique of my dissertation that will discredit all my efforts, including later work that I researched most scrupulously.

"Look, we've got a lot of funeral business to take care of," Elaine says briskly. "We've got to take charge of things before everything gets out of control."

"Everything is out of control already," Max editorializes.

"We should have written the obit ourselves," Joanne insists. "I thought of going over to the *Post* yesterday afternoon to see what they were planning to use, but I just couldn't mobilize myself."

We all sit silent for a few moments listening to the air conditioner churlishly recycling some modestly cooled air.

"Here's the deal," Elaine finally says firmly. "We're going to eat a decent breakfast, so we can think straight, and then we'll decide what has to be done. Joanne, why don't you make coffee while I fry us some eggs?"

Joanne gets up and starts fussing with Sukie's coffee-pot. Within a few minutes she is confronting a variety of parts, scattered across the counter, that she can't reassemble.

"This is making me crazy," she complains plaintively. "How could Sukie use such a fucked-up coffee pot?"

"She didn't actually brew it in there," Max says. "She boiled the water in a teapot and then poured it through a filter into that electric thing. I had to buy her a whistling teapot because she always forgot she had water boiling."

A silence explodes and resounds around the kitchen.

"The whistle on that teapot broke," Elaine reports,

"and the pot melted all over the stove. It could have started a fire."

Max looks at Elaine as if she's a witch.

Immediately I hear the chorus from our past start chanting:

Even though our husbands *pretended* not to know practical things such as where we kept the Band-Aids, the kids' rectal thermometer, or our stash of safety pins and postage stamps, they clearly knew more than they let on. Even though they evinced eternal surprise that children needed appropriate age-and-gender gifts to take along to birthday parties or that nursery schoolers needed an interesting item for show-and-tell on Fridays, our husbands were hardly idiots and must have noticed *some* things. Max's memory of Sukie's complicated coffeemaking procedure validates her longtime contention that Max simply *feigned* ignorance in line with some strategy whereby a man couldn't be asked to do what he didn't know how to do.

I light a cigarette and listen to Sukie whispering in my head: "It's like not learning the language of a country where you're living so you don't have to participate. It's like I've got to translate everything for him. His dumbness doubles my burden. And he doesn't even know I have a burden." She had paused to think for a while. "The nature of my burden is such that I can no longer define it. I cannot *think.* I hate him. I mean I love him, but I hate him."

I know I should help make breakfast, but I feel too weak to stand up. My breath is caught within my chest, snagged like a pair of pantyhose on some sharp object. I know if I move I will irreparably rip a lung or some other interior organ—most likely my heart.

All I can do is watch Joanne holding Sukie's antique brass teapot under the sink faucet until it's full enough to set atop a crooked burner on the old gas stove. Previously, Sukie's brass teapot was for show-and-tell, not for use. All of us have similar personality accents in our kitchens because each of us independently decided, way back in the fifties, exactly what kinds of kitchens we wanted. What we wanted was *anything* that didn't resemble our mothers' Formica fortresses of the postwar years. Our trademark of independence was usually an antique, such as Sukie's teapot, that signified we had rejected Revere Ware and revered authentic Americana. It was our way of showing how different we were from our mothers' generation.

Our mothers were primarily housewives who belonged to ladies' auxiliaries, mah-jongg groups, PTAs, and canasta, book review, or country clubs. In the prosperous 1950s, our fathers bought them split-level homes with huge picture windows, country station wagons trimmed with wood, and airplane tickets to Florida every winter. Happily our mothers made tuna fish casseroles with crumbled potato chip toppings, desserts out of graham crackers, fancy hand towels for the guest bathroom, pot holders for Christmas gifts, needlepoint seatcovers for little footstools, and contributions to the March of Dimes because Sister Kenny was one of their heroines. Nowadays our daughters joke about making us happy by calling home to say, "Hi, Mom. This morning I lost ten pounds, passed the New York State bar, cleaned my apartment, and got engaged." We could make our mothers happy simply by calling home.

Back in the 1940s, after they'd forgotten all the headlines about breadlines but before they were corrupted by postwar prosperity, our mothers were sweet, pretty young women. Though they thought smoking on the street, visiting bowling alleys or wearing an ankle bracelet made you look like a whore, they were quite practical. Somewhat shy, they never looked at the Varga Girl calendars hung on the walls of neighborhood gasoline stations. No. Our mothers were much more modest; they believed in good behavior. They would never wear brown flats with navy-blue skirts and were always careful that their shoes, belts and handbags matched. They never wore their white high heels *before* Memorial Day and packed them away again right after Labor Day Weekend. They were fanatic about blotting fresh lipstick on a square of toilet paper several times so they wouldn't look brassy. They always kept the seams of their nylons straight and their powder dry.

During the war years, they were very brave. On weekends they crouched down in the garage and patiently tied old newspapers into bundles. They flattened out empty tin cans and went door-to-door around our neighborhood selling Defense Stamps to support the war effort. Proudly we watched the way they saved used Crisco in empty coffee cans to reuse again and again so they could hoard our ration stamps for butter to bake us beautiful birthday cakes. We felt proud of them when they went out alone at night to air-raid warden meetings, leaving us home in the care of babysitters, who set their hair with bobby pins they snapped open on their front teeth while they wrote sheer pale blue overseas "V" letters and listened to Crosby crooning over our Philco console.

But after the war, when our mothers quit their factory or office jobs to become homeroom helpers, Brownie leaders, and chaperones on grade-school field trips, we felt they'd betrayed us. Though they sewed the badges we earned on the sleeves of our Girl Scout uniforms, whipped sour cream into the Jell-O molds they made for dinner, and produced identically shaped Toll House cookies for ecclesiastical bake sales, we felt they'd somehow diminished themselves. Occasionally at night when they were feeling real frisky or flirting with our fathers, they tried to teach us how to do the Charleston. But by then we were totally disapproving and unforgiving toward them because they had become so enthusiastically conventional and energetically middle class, while we had remained disaffected, dissatisfied and depressed.

Miriam, who grew up in Salt Lake City, had a terrific

mom whom she hated passionately. Miriam was severely unhappy because she had no public way to prove her mother's malevolence. One day the young Pia Lindstrom arrived in Salt Lake City with her physician father to matriculate at Miriam's high school. Instead of being supportive of Pia, Miriam felt enormous jealous toward her because Pia's mother had actually run off with an Italian movie producer—the perfect crime that every adolescent girl wanted her own mother to commit. Essentially, our mothers were so nice they inhibited our instinctive rebelliousness.

"What exactly has to be taken care of?" Max asks in a voice now as rigidly frigid as his earlier one had been warmly reassuring. "What do we have to decide?"

I return myself to the present and its particular pain.

"A lot of things," Elaine snaps. "Where the service should be held. At what time. What sort of a service it should be. Where Sukie should be buried. If she should be cremated." Her flat, bitter voice skids to a halt. "Everything, Max. Absolutely everything."

Max stands up. "Okay. I'll stop by my place, take a shower, and then go check things out. I'll go over to Brownell's and see what the options are. I'll find out the whole drill and then come back here to brief you."

Instinctively each of us looks away. Clearly Max is going home to see Elizabeth and we are not yet prepared to acknowledge her existence.

"Anything else I should know?" he asks querulously.

The three of us shake our heads, so Max moves abruptly out into the hall.

We remain in the kitchen. Elaine eventually serves up three plates of eggs and English muffins. We pick at our portions; even Elaine can't eat. Finally we spread out the classified section of the *Post* and dump our food on it for Happy. Then we sit in silence, drinking our coffee, smoking cigarettes, and watching Sukie's dog enjoy our breakfast.

"Well, Max seems to be holding up all right," Joanne finally says.

"No reason he shouldn't be," Elaine shrugs. "He hasn't lost anything he cared about. Anyway, he was always charming and always will be, so I don't think we have to worry about him at all. He never lost any sleep over any of us. He always treated us like the crazy ladies."

"Not always," I correct her out of fairness to Max. "Not originally."

But Elaine ignores my defense as if it were a relic of ancient high-school boy craziness.

"Men like Max always get what they want when they want it because they're takers," Elaine says grimly. "They're winners not losers. They're movers and shakers. They're wheelers and dealers. They know how to protect their own little creature comforts. I'm sure this situation is kind of difficult for Max right now, but by the time the funeral's over, he'll probably be back here with Elizabeth—settling into Sukie's bedroom."

Joanne and I look at each other warily.

"Why are you looking like that?" Elaine challenges us immediately. "Max is—and always was—a flashy four-flusher, a show-offy, superficial kind of guy. Now he's just going through male menopause, that's all. Anyway, forget him," she says, shifting into her organizing mode, "we've *got* to make a list of all the things we have to do. We *really have to.*"

Traditionally, the writing of a list is a comforting procedure that gives us the illusion of being take-charge people. Inveterate list-makers, we quarrel briefly about who actually gets to write on the yellow legal pad Elaine finds, but since she is also the first to produce a pen, she wins.

Go through all of Sukie's papers including insurance policies, mortgages, bank statements, etc. etc. etc.

"That should be a real trip." Joanne stiffens her bottom lip into a downward slant of disgust.

Strangely enough, few of us married for money. That was odd since our mothers always said it was just as easy to love a rich man as a poor one. When Sondra returned home with a half-carat, emerald-cut diamond engagement ring, her mother looked at it and said, "May none of your troubles be bigger." We know this is a true story because Helen was there. Since women like us prefer living hand-to-mouth rather than nine-to-five, we never earned much money. Lots of us drive ten-year-old cars, wear coats that are even older, receive "insufficient funds" notifications on a regular basis, and think only of Ireland when we hear the initials IRA.

Since half of us are divorced, many of us are in dire financial straits, but it is only very recently that we began to wonder if we are eligible for any of our former husbands' Social Security benefits. We still have not learned how to manage our personal finances and now admit that our lifelong wish to see a comma in the balance of our bank statements is highly unlikely. We continue rounding off the amounts of those checks we remember to record and although we know how to double a sales tax to arrive at a proper tip for a waiter we are not able to do so if fractions are involved.

Go through all Sukie's manuscripts. See what Carol and David shouldn't see. Check for any new assignments she'd acc't, why covering Senate debate? Royalty statements, copyrights on her books?

Only a small number of us became successful. The biggest surprise about success was its failure to provide much satisfaction other than money. Failure felt familiar to us—intense, evocative and engrossing. Success somehow seemed limited or superficial and, anyway, usually arrived so late that any unexpected proceeds went directly to some college bursar's office for our kids' tuition. Unfortunately, not many of us sold out since few of us were offered the opportunity. At worst, we have been known to lease ourselves for limited periods of time.

Check S's jewelry, old letters, clothes, makeup, ap-pointments, library books, magazine subscriptions, etc., etc., etc.

Telephone Sukie's out-of-town friends who won't see obit.

"Wait a minute," I say. "We've got to break this down and be more specific."

"I'll make another pot of coffee," Joanne offers.

This is the same Joanne who once placed dishes into the bottom rack of a dishwasher horizontally so they looked like some swami resting atop a bed of nails.

Take Sukie's clothes to Brownell's.

Silence. No one believes herself capable of doing this.

"Damn it. We should've made Max take the clothes," Elaine says fretfully. "He was going there anyway."

"Call the obit department at the Post *and find out the drill over there,"* Joanne dictates.

Elaine records her remark.

Emboldened, Joanne says, "Get tough with them."

Absently, Elaine adds that comment to the previous statement.

"Think about an appropriate kind of memorial ser-vice," Elaine says slowly, in rhythm with her own writ-ing.

"I think we should wait on that until her dad gets here," Joanne says. She is standing at the sink, refilling Sukie's teapot again. "Unless we find something to read from her journal. Hey, how about that? Why don't we just read a selection from her journal?"

A small silence follows her remark.

"I don't think that's very politic," I finally comment dryly.

"Oh God," Elaine suddenly whimpers. "I wonder where Sukie left her car."

Her question hits me like a body blow. Sukie's car. Sukie is dead, but she drove herself to Capitol Hill and parked her car somewhere before she died. This thought causes my lungs to tighten up, decreasing the flow of oxygen to my brain.

"That's a problem," Joanne observes, returning to the table. "She might have left it in a space with a parking meter. It just might be collecting tickets somewhere."

"Call police," Elaine recites as she records her own words.

And then, suddenly, Elaine is stricken with grief and breaks out into loud grating cries, spiked with murmurs of "Oh God, oh God, oh God."

No one moves.

It is now clear that each of us will break down at different times about different things, recover, and then break down again later. It is also clear that each of us has different trigger points and pain thresholds. There is no predicting when or why a breakdown will occur. We each have to grieve our separate griefs when they overtake us.

Without any policy decision, we have established a certain routine of simply waiting until the crying person finishes or regains control. No one tries to comfort the mourner, because that could cause the grief to become contagious and spread. Instead, Joanne and I wait in silence. Finally Happy rises arthritically from her station near the sink and walks, nails clicking like typewriter keys, toward Elaine. Once there, she plants her front paws on Elaine's knees and looks up, inquisitively and sympathetically, into her face.

"Remember when Mailer complained about sleeping with single mothers during the sixties because he could hear their poodles' toenails clicking past the bedroom all night," Joanne asks in an effort to divert everyone.

Elaine is struggling to control herself. Finally the sounds she makes sound only like echoes of her previous cries. After a while she forces herself to her feet.

"You better go outside, Happy," she says, opening the back door for the dog. "Go take a leak."

"I can't believe Sukie had a root canal last week,"

Joanne muses. "She called me up to say how much it hurt. She could have skipped it."

"I wonder if she has another . . . appointment. You usually have three sessions. I mean, Nat had three in a row."

We sit stricken at the thought of Sukie's future appointments.

"They'll call here," Joanne says coldly. "Don't worry about that. My mother missed a dental appointment the day my dad died, and the dentist's nurse called up all pissed off to say they were going to charge her for the visit because she hadn't given them twenty-four hours' notice. So my mother said she was sorry but her husband hadn't given her twenty-four hours' notice either before his heart attack that morning."

"What about Sukie's magazine subscriptions?" I ask.

"She never paid those," Joanne says. "She was a real deadbeat. But I wonder if we could run a different picture of Sukie if there's a second obit. I have a terrific picture of her up in New York."

"Let's make our telephone list," Elaine urges.

Joanne moves over to Sukie's little kitchen desk and begins to flip through the Rolodex.

"You know Sukie kept two different Rolodexes," she muses. "She had some system for dividing up people, although I can't quite figure it out yet." She begins rippling through the Rolodex, flicking her nail across the alphabetized divider tabs so the cards fall back like dominoes. "She kept the ones for dead people in the back."

"Really?" I ask in a shaky voice.

"Uhum. But they're turned around backwards."

"How do you know that?" Elaine asks irritably. She could become quite severe at the first hint of frivolity.

"Because I know who those people are and they happen to be dead," Joanne replies curtly. "Different people have different systems."

"I don't believe Sukie did that," Elaine challenges her.

"Please, Elaine. Don't get all uptight *now."*

"Look, let's try to be serious," I interrupt as the air of hostility heightens. "We've got to finish making our list."

CHAPTER 6

"*I* don't want to do this anymore now," Joanne says sharply. "I want to read more of Sukie's journal. I want to see what's on some of those disks she left on her desk."

Quickly, Elaine stands up and begins to clear the table. This is her way of saying she cannot bear reading any more of Sukie's pain. So only Joanne and I walk through the dining room into the narrow side porch that was glassed in years ago to make Sukie a private writing room.

The computer table is set against the long expanse of warehouse windows overlooking her garden. Floor-to-ceiling bookshelves climb the brick wall of the house. Silently we gaze at her library. Even from the doorway I can see all the familiar titles crawling down the spines of editions that I too had carried around until finally planting them in my West End Avenue apartment. Sukie had the same undergraduate texts—early Modern Library editions of the classics—plus all the novels and critical works required by undergraduate and graduate English departments during the 1950s.

Joanne walks slowly past the books, studying the eye-level shelves where Sukie kept her collection of contemporary novels.

"The only catalogue system she ever used was gossip," Joanne breathes with a soft laugh as she inspects the titles. "Pure unadulterated—or adulterated—gossip. See how she's got *The Mandarins* in between *Nausea* and *A Walk on the Wild Side?* And her *House of Fiction* next to Tate's collection of poetry? There's Paul and Jane Bowles together, and Mary McCarthy next to Edmund Wilson, and Robert Lowell in between Jean Stafford and Elizabeth Hardwick. Did you read *Sleepless Nights?* And look. She's got Joan Williams's *Morning, Noon and Night* next to all the Faulkner, and Jean Stein's *Edie* on the other side."

I'm smiling now, enjoying Joanne's review of the books arranged by authorial relationships.

"See? There's *Hot Property* by Judy Feiffer next to Jules's collected cartoons, and Clancy Sigal next to Doris Lessing's stuff. Oh God. She's got Barbara Probst Solomon on the other side of Clancy, and Erica Jong next to Howard Fast. He was her last former father-in-law. And there's Antonia Fraser with Harold Pinter. I love it. Sukie's such a romantic. Look. She's put *Rubyfruit Jungle* next to Martina's autobiography, and Sinclair Lewis with Dorothy Thompson and Lillian next to Dashiell and Joan Didion with John Gregory Dunne and his brother's book, *The Two Mrs. Grenvilles,* on the other side."

"Right," I say, picking up where Joanne left off. "And look. She's put all our friends together. There's Ellen and Marge and Marilyn and Laurie and Ann and Ann-with-an-E. Everybody. And I bet they're all autographed, too. But see? She kept the youngsters separate. And of course all her divorce novels are together. Oh, but look, Joanne. She's put the older women in a group. Oh, how nice of her to do that. There's Mary and that marvelous Harriet Doerr and Diana O'Hehir and Grace and Tilly and Tess and Jane and Elizabeth. You know, most of them suffered even more solitary sentences than any of us did. They *really* had some rough times. I mean, their isolation was a *cultural calamity.* And they're all so nice and helpful now. Elizabeth wrote Sukie two sweet letters when her last book came out. Did you read Tilly Olsen's book about silences?"

I feel a rush of bibliophilic love for Sukie that makes me shiver. We had shared our literary lives as well as our political ones, and we had gossiped about writers as often as about friends. We had both spent a good portion of our lives reading. We read during long car, subway, plane, bus and train trips. We read while we nursed or bottle-fed our babies. We read on beaches and in bistros and in beds around the world. We remembered the places where we first read favorite books, just as we remembered certain rooms where we had slept with favorite lovers.

Lots of times we discussed fictional women in the same way we discussed our friends. We always remembered Madeleine, the woman in *Herzog* who instructed a luncheonette counterman to tear, not slice, her English muffin one morning while she was eating breakfast out with Mr. Herzog. From her we learned that a forked muffin surface absorbs butter better than a slick sliced one, which was the kind of practical information we liked to find in novels.

Of course both of us fell in love with certain characters because some detail about them broke our hearts. We worried about Charlotte, who sat around airports in Didion's *A Book of Common Prayer*, because she fastened her torn skirt hem with a safety pin, listed her profession as MADRE, and carried a designer handbag with a broken clasp. And we roared when Sukie noticed that Joan Didion and her husband, John Gregory Dunne, had both used the same "sit on my face and see if I can guess your weight" joke in recent novels. Missing from Sukie's collection, I knew because she'd told me, was a certain male writer (whom she refused to identify for purely selfish reasons) who thought all erected penises had a bend or curve in them. Sukie believed this author ignorant of comparative anatomy and was going to play dumb—but go for him if they ever met—just as she planned to do with Harry Reems.

In *Guerrillas,* V. S. Naipaul wrote that the skin that showed within the V-neck of his heroine's blouse was darker and coarser than anywhere else on her body, since that area was more frequently exposed to the elements. We would flinch from the impact of such a detail and then retell it to each other to demonstrate that *some* men saw and perhaps understood *some* things. Sukie believed that it was the second refrigerator in Philip Roth's *Goodbye Columbus* and the medicine cabinet in his *Letting Go* that unleashed the "telling" detail in American fiction. Also, since Sukie had actually known the redhead in the beginning of *Letting Go*—who wore her Phi Beta key on a chain around her neck even when she was naked, and carried her own special shampoo around in her purse to be prepared for unexpected stays at different men's apartments—she credited Roth with the early recording of female characteristics that, whether or not he "understood" them, ensured their survival.

So both Bellow and Roth were grandfathered into her short list of contemporary male authors who she believed wrote well about both women and children. Sukie kept André Dubus, Frederick Barthelme, Robert Stone, Kem Nunn, Russell Banks, Elmore Leonard, John Updike and Raymond Carver on her highly valued eye-level shelves because she thought they got right down there where women really lived. She loved Barthelme's motel sex, which she saw as a metaphor for our times, and the Carver hero who was shamed by the stench he left in his own bathroom on a morning when a sleep-over female visitor still had to take a shower.

Gradually Joanne and I move toward Sukie's desk and begin to browse through the pile of disks beside the computer. All of the envelopes are cryptically labeled JRN I, II, III, and on to X. Eventually, Joanne turns on Sukie's Kaypro, the same model she herself owns, and inserts one of the JRN disks into the machine. Then we stand side by side as Sukie's personal notes begin to unroll before us in green letters on the black screen. Hypnotized by the scrolling text, we huddle together as we absorb her pain.

OCTOBER, 1981

I am ill.

I lie on the sofa suffering strenuously.

Waking this morning I felt fear spreading through me like a tide oozing across a beach, erasing the damp sand castle of my identity.

From my sofa, I look around the living room at the furniture I know so well. So. These will be my chairs and lamps for the rest of life. I know their shapes and colors, their wounds and stains. I will sit, or lie, and gaze upon this furniture forever. How it is that I acquired these particular pieces for eternity escapes me at the moment. Even less explainable is why they suddenly seem unfamiliar.

I get up to turn on the phonograph, but the needle is bent and Jackson Browne wails instead of sings. I had wanted to hear some of the sad songs from Running on Empty, *but like a lot of other things in my house, the phonograph isn't working.*

I return to my nest.

Often when I lie on the sofa like this, I feel as if I'm in a hospital. I half expect someone to walk unannounced through the doorway, like a doctor making rounds. This hospital feeling always makes me want to suck ice cubes. During summers in the sixties, when we were all pregnant a lot of the time, we loved to spend long, lazy afternoons at each other's houses, lying outside on drugstore chaises, trying to get backyard tans while chewing on ice cubes. That memory always pleases me even though some medical person later told me that ice-cube cravings indicate a calcium deficiency.

I have been humming "Time on My Hands" all morning. Before, I seldom had a minute to myself; now vast wastelands of emptiness sprawl ahead of me each day. I frequently find myself humming or whistling old songs from the fifties.

About a month after Max left, I became a refugee. I slept in my clothes, unwilling to separate the day from the night. I carried all my essentials in my purse while I roamed through the city, often sleeping at other people's houses. I wrapped my toothbrush in tinfoil and tucked it inside a pocket of my purse.

On nights when David went to visit Max, I would drop in to a friend's house as humble and beseeching as if I were going to church. I would arrive around dinnertime so they would invite me to eat with them. After dinner I would drink so much they would be afraid to let me drive home and suggest that I sleep over. I always accepted their invitations gratefully since that saved me from another night at home alone.

I want my friends to help me. Sometimes they do, but most of the time they don't because they can't. If someone puts up a fight—says a reconciliation with Max is impossible or wrong—I get angry and cry. If no one protests, I wallow in my pain. What I want is my husband back and none of them can deliver. When my friend Jane, of the clear face creased only by laughlines, asked me to come live with her for the summer, I almost fainted from gratitude.

I want to hear about Them. I am not ashamed to ask. She is not well liked, but occasionally a friend will say something that wounds me. They say she is organizing some event for him and handling the details he can't manage alone. This makes me crazy.

My odysseys become longer and longer. I drive around town dropping in on people I haven't seen in years. I tell each person something different. Old chums

are called upon to remember the past, to testify to lost
moments of happiness they'd witnessed, to confirm the
years of comradeship, the decades of sharing. I demand
that they protest Max's terrible betrayal. I insist on the
injustice of his action. People are required to sympa-
thize, whether or not they know the particulars.

I am shameless, unembarrassed by my excessive determination to publicly assess the damage Max has
wrought.

After a while, however, my friends become tired of
my unannounced visits. My plight is no longer new or
newsy.

I am, however, interested in nothing else.

When I have no parties to attend or appointments to
keep or people to meet, I begin to dissolve. My incipient hysteria is stirred up whenever a block of time
materializes without any human parameters.

Suppressed hysteria impairs my perceptions. While
drinking coffee this morning, out of the corner of my
eye I saw a crumpled napkin on the floor and thought
it was a mouse. All morning long, I saw stationary objects moving. Also, my aural sense is off. I have always
heard voices, but now I hear people calling me. A child
of mine who was once small calls "Mommy," and my
bodily processes pause. But the child has been grown
and gone for a long while now. She no longer cries out
for me and anyway now she calls me Mother.

When I come off my uppers or downers and stop
eating for a minute, I realize that I am burning all my
bridges. Whenever I'm drunk, I announce that I married Max only because he was the first man who asked
me. Even though I was only twenty-three when he
proposed, I hadn't had time yet to know many men.
Perhaps that's why later I felt so gypped.

Lying on the sofa, I open my pink flowered notebook
which I keep nearby. I have divided it into various
sections called things like Love Notes, Class Notes, Sour
Notes, Bank Notes, etc., etc. I also have parts called

Here Are Some Things That Have Happened to My Friends; Here Are Some Things That Have Happened to Me; Here Are Some Things That I've Heard Recently; and Here Are Some Things That I Did Back When I Was Still Me.

Like some character in a Russian novel, I have begun keeping a list of slights and grievances in my notebook. This section is quite full. A lot of it is devoted to Miranda and how she betrayed me. Betrayals always drive me wild; I can neither forget nor forgive them. I nurse my grievances, explicate their details, contrive imaginative confrontations and plot my revenge.

This morning, instead of writing anything, I close my notebook and think about Her. I saw Her going into their apartment yesterday. She slipped into the entrance hall very quickly. She knew her way. She moved with authority. She looked efficient about going to visit my husband. Why not? He is hers now.

Her existence is an incitement for me to trash my own life.

I thought of her pride in getting my husband away from me—her taste of triumph at my torment. I imagine them discussing me in great detail, probing my motives for behaving insanely. My feigning madness terrifies Max. Actually, it scares me too; when I act that way, I believe it. In truth, although internally I am in total disarray, with some effort of my ever-weakening will, I can contain my craziness. When I purposefully unleash it, in order to punish Max, the real iguanas that slither out of my mind to scream insanities through my mouth terrify me as much as anyone else.

Occasionally Max says mean things to me over the telephone and I go wild. I want to reach out and hurt him in some way, to break through the intolerable barrier of his indifference. I am pulsating with need, unable to contain my emotions, shriveled with frustrated rage. I hadn't done anything wrong to him in any immediate sense. How could he do this to me?

For years he loved the enchantment of me—the heat of my insecurities, the mystery of my neurosis. He was enthralled like a fairytale prince by all that was wild and wicked in me. Then a bad witch came along, broke the spell I had placed upon him, and stole him away.

He was not my husband; he was my identity. My fusion with him was total. It wasn't even a question of love; he was my life, the joys and successes, frustrations and banalities, irritations and insecurities that constituted my existence. I never tried to separate my private self or experience from him. Everything was irrevocably joined at the hips of our lives.

We live alone now, David and I. According to U.S. Census figures, we are not alone. Ha ha. There are many other mother-son units such as ours. I have become what is called, for tax purposes, a Head of Household. My heart aches for my son who has become a divorce statistic. He is the fourteen-year-old who lives alone with an unhappy mother and sees his father once a week. What does that feel like? What does he think about inside that silent cocoon in which he now lives? Is he in a panic? Is he painfully resigned to his fate, experiencing his emotions helplessly?

Once I invited a child psychiatrist for dinner and afterwards I left the kitchen and went upstairs. Later David and I changed places. I sat at the kitchen table with the doctor while David went upstairs to watch TV. I asked the doctor what had happened. "Nothing," he said. "After you left, David said, 'I know why she invited you here, and I don't want to talk about anything. Everything's okay.'"

Before, our house was full of life; now it vibrates with emptiness. Friends of mine who have already gone through this say that living alone is unnatural—an act against nature, like keeping wild animals in a zoo. People were not designed to live the way David and I are living.

Before Max left, we received the 1980 census questionnaire. It requested the names of everyone sleeping at our house the night that the form arrived. By chance, there were six visitors staying with us at the time. Five of them refused to provide the personal information that was required. Like many Puerto Ricans living in New York, my houseguests did not want to be counted in the census. Neurotic anarchistic intellectuals sleeping away from home were another "depressed" minority not included in the 1980 census. Walker Percy calls such people "malaiseans."

Old friends find me wanting. I have apparently lost whatever qualities originally drew them to me. My house, which used to attract people like a brimming glass of wine, is now deserted. Fresh garden flowers no longer dance foppishly in vases set randomly around the rooms. Friends no longer fade in and out of my days. Kate and Diana and Joanne and Marlene and Aileen are all busy with their own lives. Diana has called a few times, obviously sensing my deterioration, but she's teaching full-time now and can't come here to be with me.

My house no longer summons anyone. If anything, we had too many wonderful friends. People frequently felt lost in our social shuffle. We liked our friends, but sometimes I grew tired of never being alone. Our friends often became wedges between us, draining our energies with demands to talk, smoke, drink, interact, relate, perform and give. Then I would complain to Max, saying I was wasting my time entertaining, making coffee and drinking, that I was tired of talking and putting out.

Usually after a night full of people we forgot to make love.

Making love. It was fraught with leftover feelings from the day—grudges, resentments, grievances. Being married makes it difficult to forget the days. The nights echo earlier commotion, the noise of the children, the unpacking of grocery bags, the emergency roar of a vacuum before the arrival of unexpected guests. Was it the work, the writing, the rush of life that distracted me from making love so that Max became only a target for my rage—a convenient outlet for all my complaints?

Will I ever feel like buying flowers again? Will I ever stop at the flower cart on Connecticut Avenue and buy a bunch of daisies to jam inside a jar and set upon my kitchen table? Will I ever again place cloth napkins beside my pretty brown pottery dishes and use separate plates for salads despite the extra work they create?

How could he have left his wedding ring in the medicine chest as if it meant nothing, as if he hadn't worn it on his hand for twenty years?

Unconditional love feels unctuous until it is lost.

So many sweet-sour memories—his fine, firm voice telling me things, teaching me, explaining. Why did I come to hate it then and yearn for it now? The resonance of his voice and its emotional tones haunt me. Now he talks like that to someone else.

What had I wanted from Max? Intimacy. But he couldn't deliver anything but counterfeit concern. What else? Passion. But his was unilateral; he couldn't inspire it in me.

One night at dinner I had seven glasses of white wine. Wine is worse than whiskey because it seems innocent. But wine is no more innocent than I am.

Hate corrupts and corrodes everything. Today I hate everyone. Mostly I hate myself—my face, my body, my breath, my weight, my anxiety, my self-indulgence, my neuroses.

Perhaps if it were a physical ailment I had, I would have more patience about going to doctors and clinics. Then I would probably want to get well. But taking an obsession around town, driving it out to the suburbs, sitting with it in waiting rooms, describing its symptoms to each new doctor, filling out medical office data forms, filing insurance claims—all of that is demoralizing. I created my own illness and now have to maintain it with constant medical care. I created my own madness and now must live with all that stems from its preposterous power.

Still I cling to my obsession, fearing its loss, liking its perks—the drinks and the drugs, the doctors and the dreams.

Was there ever a story written about a female Job—a woman blessed with everything, who lost it all within a single year? To me it happened very quickly, between one Christmas and the next. In 1979 I made a lovely pre-Christmas party for over a hundred people. In 1980 I went to a Christmas party where I got drunk in front of all my friends, wept, carried on shamelessly, lost one high-heeled shoe, and cut open my chin when I fell down the stairs while leaving. Because I couldn't find my car, I hailed a taxi, threw up in the backseat, and, opening the door, ran away, with the driver chasing me almost all the way home.

Of course I was unable to sleep that night. Fear and anxiety tumbled through my system and I felt physically ill. My body trembled. Remorse and regret flooded me. I tried to tell myself that I hadn't killed or maimed anyone, that I was just feeling ashamed of my behavior, but the panic persisted.

Hate, hate, hate. It's boring. It's monolithic. I feel so wronged that no one can do right by me ever again.

I slapped my son for saying I drank too much.

I hung up on my daughter who called from college.

I cut short a long-distance call from my daughter's friend who was confined in a mental hospital after having a breakdown. She had found an unlocked WATS line in some office and chosen to call me. I told her I was busy. After she hung up, I began crying, hysterical with guilt.

I decided to let my father take a taxi in from the airport when he came to visit me. He has telephoned every night since Max left to check on David and me.

He knows I am going under and, like everyone else, can find no way to help me. There is no way. With drugs and alcohol I can alter my identity in thirty minutes, erase the pain, release the rage.

I want my mother.

Something I'd been expecting all my life finally happened last year. My mother went someplace where she couldn't take me. Of course she promised to come back soon, but she never did. I always knew someday she'd do that.

When I was little, she used to go downtown shopping on Saturday afternoons and leave me home with my grandmother. All during those dark and chilly winter afternoons, my conviction that she would never return argued with my certainty that she would. Even after she reappeared, I remained convinced that the next time she went away I'd never see her again.

So last year she went out (to Mount Sinai Hospital for a bypass operation) and she didn't come back as she'd promised me she would.

I always knew that would happen. I always knew that she would leave me.

I don't miss her; it's simply that the sun doesn't shine as bright as it used to and I have no one to whom I can tell certain things, such as the fact I have a sore throat when I do.

It seems to me that if you have no one to whom you can say your throat aches, your life is a sad and empty thing.

In the mornings I always used to serve juice in wineglasses when we had stay-over guests. Max liked that a lot. Now I drink two cups of black coffee and smoke three cigarettes for breakfast, which I take alone. At night, when I lie down in darkness, I take Madness as my lover and embrace him feverishly; in the morning, I drink my coffee alone on the terrace of my mind and wait until Memory comes to join me for a walk down to the shore.

I became so crazy—or maybe it was because of all the drugs I was taking—I lost the curl in my hair. I had never had to worry about straight hair before. I said to myself, other women have had trouble with their hair all their lives; my problem was so new I had no right to complain about it. But suddenly having straight hair confused me. It made me feel like I was someone else.

Afterwards I came to believe that he had left me in the springtime. Actually it was nearly winter. Sometimes I remember the coat I'd worn during those days and nights, mildly surprised that I'd needed a wrap since I believed it was happening in the spring.

Once that winter, I roused myself enough to take David and one of his friends skiing. Approaching a chalet attendant, I asked, "Where do you buy tickets for the scare lift? I mean the chair lift? Oh well, never mind." I went back to the hotel and stayed inside the entire weekend, watching the skiers through the large picture window in the cocktail lounge.

Often on Sunday afternoons I would lie on the sofa and watch pro football games. I would watch and wait to see a single strand of long curly hair peek out from beneath the helmet of some heavy lineman huddling before a play. The boyish lock of hair always seemed totally incongruous on such a large athlete and invariably it twisted my heart. Sometimes I felt that the dark shadows beneath my eyes were as visible as the black grease worn by players to deflect the sunlight. Many of my perceptions were abnormally exaggerated.

On Sunday nights I would watch the football round-ups at the tail end of the eleven o'clock news to see replays in which a shapely receiver caught a pass, scored a touchdown, and then got down and boogied— all slim hips and rounded rump—before spiking the ball into the ground with sexual exhilaration. When the Commissioner banned spiking, I was sure it was out of spite toward women.

By late Sunday night I would be aching to feel the weight of a man descending upon me once again. I yearned to feel my own immediate, melting response to the authority of a male body. I have never sought out slim men because they seemed to lack magnitude. I always wanted more, rather than less, in everything. Especially in men. I loved large men, even if their shirts took much longer to iron.

I am an alcoholic who hates sobriety, an addict who abhors restraint, a hysteric who looks up that word in the indexes of psychology textbooks at other people's houses.

I view the next generation with skepticism. Max felt compelled to teach the new generation what he knew so as to tutor their better instincts. I liked to see how the generations differed. He savored the similarities, finding faith and hope in continuity. Max liked sleeping with me every night just as he liked finding a parking space on our own street, discovering the newspaper on the front stairs every morning, and having the kitchen chairs stay where they belonged next to the table. I liked things to change.

As soon as I wake each morning, my mind begins to leap about seeking a specific source for my pain. If I drank the night before, I try to remember what drunken phone calls I made, what fights I started with my son, what trouble I created. I cast about for the quickest route to remorse and find it. I think about what relationships I might have spoiled, which of my few remaining friends I might have insulted, what further damage I did to make any marital reconciliation impossible.

I am without steady work, without resources, without a support system to help me survive. I no longer have a lover or even an admirer. My children are bitter and angry; my father is suffering from my visible deterioration. He is glad my mother is dead so she doesn't have to see all this.

A few months after Max moved out, a woman was shot through the head on our front steps. The bullet ripped through her brain and smashed through my second-story bedroom window. Happy's barking woke me up. When I looked outside and saw the crowd starting to gather, I thought it was me I saw sprawled out front, I was that drunk. The next day there was a story in the newspaper about the shooting, but Max never called to see if we were all right.

What is weird to me is that someone who for years could be anguished by a splinter in my finger or a cooking burn on my wrist didn't mind a few months later if bullets shattered my bedroom window.

One day he cares about every cut or bruise, the next day he doesn't care if I die.

I just can't adjust to that.

———————————

"That was too fucking-A-much," Joanne says tersely.

We have turned off Sukie's computer and retreated back to the kitchen table.

"How could it be that none of us knew Sukie was having a breakdown?" she asks incredulously. "This is exactly like *The Big Chill.*"

"Why is it that anytime anything *real* actually happens to us, somebody always has to say it's exactly like some movie?" Elaine hisses. Her blue eyes sweep across the table to challenge Joanne. "Sukie dies and someone's got to say, 'God, it's just like *The Big Chill.*' This is *not* like *The Big Chill.* That guy committed suicide. Sukie just . . . Sukie just died. And also, *we* are not like *those* . . . survivors," Elaine concludes definitively. "We're very different."

Chastened, Joanne looks off into space.

And then, suddenly, Elaine screams.

"Aaaaaaahhhhhhhhhhhhhhhhhhhh."

It seems as if she had waited her entire life to scream

like that. She begins to stand up, but only succeeds in knocking over her chair.

Joanne, staring toward the door, turns her mouth into a perfect circle, but issues no sound.

Finally I turn around.

A tall young man, wearing a black T-shirt and long, lean jeans over heavy cowboy boots, is standing in the kitchen doorway.

"Je-sus," he groans. "What the hell's the matter? Whadaya screaming like that for? Didn't Sukie tell you I was coming over?"

"Who are you?" Joanne demands.

"I'm a friend of hers. Where is she?"

He moves into the center of the kitchen. He is perhaps thirty-five, but he has the ageless eyes of American men who have trouble coming to terms with themselves.

"How did you get in here?"

"I happen to have a key, that's how," he answers. "And Sukie knows damn well I come over every Saturday around noon. Maybe even earlier; it depends on if I work Friday night. What'd she do, go away for the weekend? I wasn't home if she tried to reach me."

This young man is clearly one of Sukie's types. She always had an enormous weakness for studs and jocks, allowing them to get away with things she wouldn't tolerate from self-proclaimed liberated men.

"What's your name?" I ask the young man.

"Jeff."

"Jeff?"

"That's it. Jeff. What is this? A press conference or something?"

Joanne stands up and walks toward Jeff until she is only a few feet away from him.

"Something's happened to Sukie," she says quietly.

I can hear him inhale extra air as if to cushion the news he's about to receive. He has blue-gray, almost childishly bright, eyes and straight blond hair that rides across his forehead. He reminds me a little of William Hurt, whom I like a lot.

"What'd she do?" he manages to ask.

"She had a cerebral hemorrhage yesterday; she died right away," Joanne answers gently.

Immediately he whirls around so that his back is toward us. Then he stands alone and silent for a few minutes. Joanne moves forward as if to touch him, but slowly retreats after a second. When he finally turns around, it is evident he is in extreme pain.

"Where's David? Didn't he go to Europe with his father?"

Joanne nods. "They were in Portugal, but they're on their way home now."

"Shit." Then he walks deliberately toward the refrigerator. "Where's Sukie?"

The three of us look at each other in even greater dismay.

"At a church? A funeral home? Where?" he demands.

"She's at Brownell's."

"Brownell's? Oh, shit. What a boojie place." He opens the Frigidaire. "No beer?"

"There's a couple cans behind that jug of wine," Joanne answers.

"Well, I loved her," he states matter-of-factly as he reemerges from the refrigerator. "I loved her and . . . she let me love her. She was the biggest thing that ever happened to me in my life. After Vietnam."

With that he anchors Sukie's sliding stool against the wall, mounts it, and wheels across the floor to park at the table between Joanne and me. Then he opens the beer can and begins to suck it.

"But that wasn't all we had going for us," he says. "I was also helping her with her new book."

"What book?"

"Sukie was writing a book?"

"Was it done?" I ask, hurt that she had never told me.

"Not done enough," he whispers hoarsely. "Not done

enough. And God knows, there's no one else but Sukie who could finish it."

"Well, don't forget, friends and editors completed works by Fitzgerald and Hemingway."

"No way," Jeff says, shaking his head. "No way."

"Maybe *we* can take a look at it. I've published quite a bit, and Joanne is a writer," I insist.

"Are you kidding?" Jeff asks me in a voice that is both insulted and insulting. "Sukie's book is a genuine comic novel. Didn't she even tell you about it?"

"No."

"Well, it's about one of your basic JAPs who decides to murder her husband after he walks out on her and it's the final word on Jewish royalty. Even the title was great: *Death Sentences.* See, the female narrator fucks up the murder attempt, gets charged with attempted homicide, and then handles her own legal defense in court. It's sort of a takeoff on the Jean Harris case; it's really a brilliant tour de force."

"I can't believe she was working on a book called *Death Sentences,"* Elaine whispers, shaking her head superstitiously.

"I was helping her edit it," Jeff says, studying the Amstel Light script on his beer can. "See, Sukie needed someone to take her seriously as a writer. And I do. I mean, I did." He tosses his head so that another layer of slick blond hair slides across his forehead. "I still do. My BA was in Lit." He mashes his now-empty beer can in one of his suggestively large hands, kneading it with thick strong fingers. "Sukie was a talented writer, but a genius of a woman."

Despite the fact that we are all in mourning, each of us is now looking approvingly at Sukie's young man. He is clearly a hunk with a heart.

Jeff gets up and returns to the refrigerator. "This is the last can of beer," he announces, surveying all the shelves before kicking shut the door. "Anyway, I've got

a complete copy of her manuscript over at my place."
He shrugs helplessly. "What a fucking loss."

We all nod.

It is clear Jeff wants to make Sukie's death a literary
loss as well as a personal one. And we want that too.
From his description, *Death Sentences* sounds like
Sukie's other novels, all of which explored the domestic
distress of American women. Despite the dark humor
that characterized her work, pain peeked out from behind her hectic prose, and her stories cringed beneath
the heavy cargo of despair they carried.

"But when did she start to write it?" I ask, still aching
because I hadn't known.

"Right about the time we met, I think. I never figured
out if she started writing because she was feeling better
or if she started writing and then got her shit together.
Anyway, by the time I met her, she was doing okay. I
wish I could take some credit for it, but I think it was
her shrink who got her wrapped up tight again. The doc
put her back together with baling wire."

Jeff's voice has begun to fade. His face is beginning to
crumble.

"All I taught Sukie was that it's nice to live in a place
with no telephone. Hey. Look, I'm going to go out and
buy us a case of beer," Jeff says. "We're really gonna
need it. But I'll come right back, okay?"

"Sure."

So he hurries off and we sit listening to his heavy boots
clomping down the hallway, the clatter as he opens the
door and then the rush as he slams it shut behind him.

"Did you know Sukie was seeing someone special?"
Joanne asks in a conspiratorial whisper.

Elaine grimaces. "You think *he's* special?"

"I didn't mean that way," Joanne responds defensively. "It's been a long time since any of us met any guy
who's *really special.* I just meant did you know she was
seeing someone on a steady basis? You know, once a
week like he said."

"No," Elaine answers firmly. "In fact, Sukie always said she didn't know from once a week when it came to men. Once a week was for getting your kid's braces tightened or ballet lessons."

"Well, he did have a key. . . ." Joanne pauses definitively and then gets up to pour herself a glass of white wine. Without asking, she fills a second goblet and hands it to me.

"Isn't it a little early to begin drinking wine?" Elaine asks irritably.

"You know there isn't any more beer," Joanne shrugs. Her shrug loosens the flap of her wrapper again.

I smile as I take a sip of the cool white wine.

Half an hour later, when Jeff returns with a case of cold beer, he also produces two fat, squat joints, which he lights in rapid succession and passes over to us.

"Go on," he says. "It'll help. No reason you should feel this fucking bad."

By one o'clock we are all stoned out of our minds.

"She used to come like an angel," Jeff says, breaking a lengthy silence.

Although we have integrated Sukie's young lover into our circle, and find it gratifying to hear how sexually happy our dear friend had been right before her death, none of us knows how to respond to Jeff's comment.

"I'll never be with anyone who can come like that ever again," he continues mournfully, hunched over in an attitude of deep despair.

"You mustn't let yourself get too depressed," Joanne comforts him. "Sukie wouldn't want you to feel that way."

Elaine raises her eyebrows.

I am vaguely aware of wolfing down some honey-roasted cashews from a can I found in one of Sukie's cupboards, pausing only occasionally to lick the sweet salt off my fingers.

Joanne, whose silk wrapper is verging on disintegration, reaches across the table to take some cashews and flashes the deep smile of her cleavage at Jeff, somehow suggesting her own outstanding orgasmic capabilities.

"No one else can understand how much she loved it," Jeff moans inconsolably. "She loved it. I mean, she *really* loved it. She could come eight, ten times a night. I think she got that way after she went through her change. I told her that. I really wanted her to believe fifty was nifty, that it wasn't just because of anything I did or the way I was . . . built or anything like that."

"I'm not sure you should be telling us all of this," Elaine says dubiously. "I'm not sure we want to know all the details. Why don't you . . . tell us how you met Sukie instead?"

She speaks in her best substitute-teacher voice and effectively castles Jeff off centerstage into a more sequestered environment.

Although he is clearly both stoned and drunk, Jeff rubs his stockinged feet (having long ago asked permission to remove his "shitkickers") and sweetly acquiesces to Elaine's suggestion.

"Well," he drawls, "I was driving my cab last summer and I picked Sukie up on Wisconsin and M Street. That's sort of my home base. In Georgetown. So as soon as she got in, I could smell this wonderful smell on her. It reminded me of something, but I couldn't figure out what. So finally I just asked her and she said, 'Vanilla.' She said that she rubbed vanilla all over her body because she was taking Antabuse to quit drinking and someone in AA had told her that perfume has too high an alcohol content to use when you're on Antabuse. You know, Antabuse makes you vomit if you get too much alcohol in your system—you can even die from it. So, hey, that was real interesting and I said you can always learn something new hacking, and that she smelled like some cookies my mom used to bake. I told her she smelled good enough to eat and that made her sort of

. . . laugh and well, I don't know, we didn't go straight to her house. I mean, instead we went out for lunch first."

Silence.

Eventually Elaine smiles rather tentatively.

Then Joanne smiles rather ruefully.

I burst into laughter.

Yup. That was Sukie. Our gal Sukie.

I laughed and laughed.

Good old Sukie. Never one to miss an opportunity.

Hot flash . . .

A guy comes on to us, we've got to respond.

That's who we are.

We were always that way and we're not about to change, even now—in the 1980s—when a lot of the fun has gone out of sex. Previously, although sex was often dangerous, it wasn't necessarily unhealthy. But now that AIDS makes people weigh love and/or lust against sickness and/or death, we have become Reformed Romantics and are beginning to edit our sexual resumés, which are a bit too long for this new AIDS era into which we've entered.

Having already made the leap from Hot Pants to Hot Tubs to Hot Flashes, we are not sorry that casual sex has gone out of style about the same time we have. Since childhood, we always hated missing out on anything. In the sixties, we not only wore hot pants, we internalized them and by acting them out, turned hot pants into a lifestyle as well as a fashion. Because of this, however, by the end of the decade, sex started to feel like a hot ticket on a cheap charter flight to Europe—over-crowded, overheated and inevitably overwrought.

By the mid-seventies, sleeping with strangers had begun to metastasize our anxiety rather than relieve it. Awakening too early on a dim morning atop a messy bed in an unfamiliar room of a large hotel overlooking some foreign city alongside a married man with no last name felt upsetting rather than exciting. By the end of that decade, making love with a stranger was like watching our own takeoff over a closed-circuit TV in a wide-hipped 747 that blew a tire on the runway so the entire flight was spent worrying about our chances for a safe—or at least a soft—landing. By the time we finally began our descent, we felt dizzy and our ears rang from the shocking loss of altitude, echoing the infernal, internal drop of our hearts into the lobby of our souls.

After splashing around in the seventies, we realized that a hot tub was not a form of self-expression and that even the largest didn't lend itself to swimming laps. By 1980, a certain self-consciousness had crept up upon us so that casual sex began to suffer from the same sort of minimalism currently afflicting contemporary American fiction. Like a Beattie short story, casual sex left us hungry again just a few hours later. Like detailed descriptions about miles of malls, casual sex finally made us nauseous from too much variety and too little meaning. We became interested in love once again.

When we first started fraternizing with the enemy, back in the early fifties, we were very different from the way we were when we actually started sleeping with them at the end of that decade. Back in junior high we were boy-crazy virgins, terrified of being carded. Teenage sex was something that only happened in the dark in uncomfortable backseats at drive-in movies. The few times we had the opportunity to "park" in a passion-pit, our buttons got played with more than our boobs, and we realized that the greatest danger in petting was the possible dislocation of the nylon stockings we kept stuffed inside our *ironed* training bras.

Because our mothers were whiplashed by the cyclical social reaction to the Roaring Twenties, they crashed when the market did and became quite prudish. They came down on us when we started to date, making more of making out than it warranted. Pressing mad money into our purses, they left the pole lamp lit in the picture window of our living rooms, as well as any outdoor porch light, so we couldn't even kiss a guy good night. Teenaged Depression Babies so confused sex with danger that, forever after, legitimate love felt noncarbonated and enormously disappointing.

"Hey. Pay attention, Diana," Elaine says impatiently. "We've still got to decide which dress to take to Brownell's tomorrow. That lady said shoes and . . . underwear . . . and everything."

"Underwear? You think she means a bra? No way there's a bra in this house," Joanne predicts. "But you know something? I bet Sukie'd like to be buried in that paisley print suit of hers. She really loved that suit and you certainly don't need a bra with it."

Silence.

"Why does anyone need a bra if she's lying down?" Jeff asks.

We look at him with stoned concentration.

"Doctors say big-breasted women should wear bras even when they're sleeping," Elaine eventually volunteers. As a teacher she feels compelled to provide some explanation for everything.

"That was hardly Sukie's problem," Jeff observes.

"Actually, Sukie once told me she was glad she was flat-chested," Joanne offers, somewhat defensively. "She thought she would have gotten into a lot more trouble if she'd been much bigger."

"That's probably true," Jeff agrees.

"Oh, really. This is getting sick." Elaine slaps her hand down on the table in disgust. "Why are we talking like this?"

"Because we're stoned," Joanne reassures her, sipping beer from a can.

"You know, things might have been better back in the old days," I say in my anthropological professorial voice. "If people still laid out bodies at home in their front parlors, we could dress Sukie ourselves. Right here."

Silently we share an image of Sukie laid out on the cabbage-rose, chintz-covered sofa in her living room where she'd always held court.

"Are you kidding?" Elaine squeals. "Do you really think Sukie would want all of us trying to dress her at the same time?"

"She maybe wouldn't mind if we did it with the lights off," Jeff volunteers. "You know that scene in *Terms of Endearment* when Shirley MacLaine tells Jack Nicholson if he really wants the lights on so bad he should damn well go home and—"

"Yah, we know that scene," I say swiftly to cut him off.

Except perhaps for Joanne, none of us likes making love with the lights on anymore and we are even careful to avoid motel rooms where passing headlights might penetrate ill-fitted drapes and illuminate our bodies in some torrid, contorted position no longer tenable if visible. Nowadays we protect our flanks from view with sturdy vigilance.

"Listen." Elaine begins to rev herself up again. "We've also got to decide who should be the pallbearers."

Each death word catches us up short so that we must pause to internalize it before responding.

"How many do we need, six, eight?" Joanne prompts us.

"How about me?" Jeff asks.

"Well, I was really just thinking about friends of hers," Elaine explains.

"Hey. Hold it." Jeff starts to stand up, but then slides back in his chair for lack of balance. "I *was* her friend."

"I didn't mean that," Elaine apologizes. "Anyway, even if we could find six guys who really were just friends of hers, everyone would still think they were her lovers if they carried her casket."

"Who cares?" Joanne asks.

"Max might," I suggest.

"Who cares if Max cares?" Elaine asks me. "The problem is, it just wouldn't look right."

"I can't believe you're still talking about things looking right, Elaine," Joanne moans. "I mean I really can't believe it." Then she turns her head to exclude Elaine from her next remark. "Listen, why can't *we* do it? Us and some of Sukie's Washington girlfriends?"

"I've never heard of women carrying a casket before," Elaine snaps.

"I don't think they're allowed to," I concur. "Jewish law doesn't even allow them to carry a Torah."

"Diana, there isn't any 'them'; 'them' is *us*," Joanne instructs me rather shrilly.

"Sorry," I concede immediately. "You're right. You're absolutely right."

I have already finished one can of beer and am solidly into a second. Also, it seems I become more stoned each time I speak.

"I think traditionally coffins are very heavy because the more they weigh, the thicker they are and the better they protect the body from . . . decay and everything," Elaine explains.

"Are you kidding?" I chide her. "They only make them heavy so they can charge more. They're heavy so they can be expensive. Didn't you read Jessica's book?"

"Well, it's not like we don't lift heavy weights all the time," Joanne observes. "Heavy weights belong in the shitwork department. That's how you can tell carrying a coffin is an honor. Otherwise they'd have had us doing it right from the beginning."

"Really," Jeff adds confirmationally, in a voice that sounds like it's coming in over a Sprint line.

"Anyway. Who ever said we can't lift or carry heavy weights? Remember when we had to get Sherry's car over the snowdrift in her driveway so we could take Ricky to the hospital? And remember the time Pat and Annie moved Sandy's grand piano when the floor in her apartment started to cave in?" Joanne is clearly getting carried away with the idea of carrying Sukie's coffin. "I definitely think we should do it. I think Sukie would really like it a lot. I can call up and ask about a light-weight model, like one of those aluminum rowboats or canoes they make. Those things hardly weigh anything; Sue and Meagan can portage their canoe for *miles.*"

"Coffins aren't made to order," Elaine protests with a touch of hysteria. "This isn't the Renaissance, remember?"

"Listen," I interrupt. "Let's do it. We'll ask as many of Sukie's friends as we have to, but let's do it."

And then, very slowly and shyly, Elaine and Joanne and I look at each other and smile. Because at that moment we suddenly realize that we are going to carry Sukie's coffin and we feel glad as well as sad for the first time since she died.

"It's sort of a . . . feminist statement," Elaine ventures.

"Oh, *please,*" Joanne moans. "Save your analysis or I won't be able to hack it."

Injured, Elaine switches tracks: "Maybe we should go out to a restaurant and get some . . . lunch. Otherwise we're going to get drunk sitting here like this."

"Drunk isn't the problem, stoned is," Joanne responds.

But Elaine persists and, finally, after a tedious discussion, Jeff telephones to order some pizzas. As always, our talk about food is fraught with suppressed hysteria. Each of us knows that to eat a pizza in a time of bereavement is to flirt with nihilism. I have several theories about American Female Eating Habits that I plan to publish someday.

"Did you know Joanne uses her neighborhood Chinese carry-out so often that she even orders her eggs from them?" Elaine tattles critically. "She just asks them if they have an extra dozen on hand they could spare and to deliver them along with her dinner. I guess they must use them for egg-drop soup or something."

Jeff smiles approvingly at Joanne for her ingenuity, and she then favors him with one of the long smiles that lights up her entire face. Jeff is not totally unresponsive to Joanne's beauty.

"Do you know why there are so many carry-outs in poor neighborhoods?" he asks.

A respectful quiet descends upon the table.

"Because poor neighborhoods have lots of rooming houses where the tenants don't have any kitchens, so if they want some hot food once in a while and can't afford a restaurant, they can buy it from a carry-out and take it home."

We discuss the political dimensions of Jeff's remark, which have many Sukie-like overtones, until the pizzas arrive. Jeff answers the doorbell, pays the delivery man and deposits the two large fragrant boxes on the kitchen table. Sitting down, he casually begins to eat his way through one pizza. We, on the other hand, go into a kind of schizophrenic spin. Each of us eats one slice of pizza and then picks at a second, knowing we will always remember this meal amid our memories of Sukie's death. As soon as we've finished eating, Joanne begins to feel ill. This is not unusual. Guilt-inspired nausea is quite common among our crowd.

The cardboard containers, stained by grease smears that look like North and South America, remain on Sukie's counter hiding our leftovers for the next few days, during which time we pick at and play with the remnants, first skimming off stray pepperoni, then onions and finally cheese. Although none of us would ever eat the crust, fingernail troughs can be seen where the upper strata of topping has been scraped away.

"Look, I've got a confession to make and a question to ask," Jeff says, establishing a serious tone as soon as he's finished eating. "Now that I think about it, I'm afraid I might have hurt Sukie's feelings, talking about wanting kids all the time. She never said anything about it, but now that she's . . . gone, I'm thinking it might have hurt her." He is chewing at his bottom lip, pondering the problematic past. "Did she ever say anything to any of you about anything like that?"

We all look at each other. Not only had Sukie never mentioned Jeff wanting a child, she had never even mentioned Jeff. In fact, she had continued complaining about the lack of decent men to date throughout the past year.

So none of us responds to Jeff's question.

"Okay," he continues, "on to part two. I know that you're all pretty foxy women and that you know the score and that you're smart enough to write pretty impressive articles, or even books, once in a while. Right?"

He waits until we all reluctantly nod our consent. We know, of course, what Jeff is going to ask. We know, from legions of other men before him, that he is now going to ask *how*, with so much going for us, we can be so goddamn insecure and unhappy. Of course, from past experience, we also know how difficult it is to explain the ideology of our unhappiness.

As Tolstoy would doubtless agree, all adolescent girls are unhappy, but each adolescent girl believes herself to be unhappy in her own unique and singular way. In truth, however, the high school unhappiness of *sensitive* American female Depression Babies was monumental because, during the forties and fifties, popularity was the only standard of success. Although we believed all the fifties fairytales we'd been told, we were born Outsiders. We were the girls whose bras the boys never snapped even though we wore tight Lana Turner sweaters. We were never loose enough to Lindy well and many mornings we went to school only because our lockers were there and that's where we kept certain contraband items like cigarettes, tampons and racy novels. Academically we always had difficulty because we didn't follow directions well.

It was always the other girls, the Prettygirls (sometimes even our very own sisters) who got to be student council reps, cheerleaders, homecoming attendants and prom queens. Even though we tried to imitate them, we couldn't. It was not that the Prettygirls were actually prettier than we were, but rather that they always looked like Nicegirls Who Didn't (But Who Really Did.) Primatively, we believed they possessed supernatural powers because their cashmere sweaters and Bermuda shorts kept their creases while the pennies they inserted in their loafers stayed put and, like the shoes, kept their shines. Everything about the Prettygirls stayed in place, especially their Nicegirl reputations which made our teachers think they were quiet, conservative, conventional conformists. This charade demonstrated that Prettygirls had magical powers more potent than reality and, of course, inimitable.

Prettygirls taught themselves private-school cursive script and used fat round donuts rather than dots over their i's and j's. With daring bravery, they crossed their t's with jaunty uphill slanty, rather than straight, lines. They all knew how to make dips: avocado dips for their Prettygirl pajama parties; deep dips to the floor when they jitterbugged at mixers; and—most wondrous of all—curvy dips in their bangs, which they set with magical bobby pins so that their hair *always did what they wanted it to do.* Later on, in the Kennedy sixties, they were even able to fall asleep with huge fat rollers affixed to their heads, creating big, beautiful Jackie! bouffants all night long—another thing we couldn't do and a major reason why we didn't all jump on the Kennedy bandwagon.

Like sorcerers, the Prettygirls, whose first names invariably ended in an "i", broke a limited number of enchantments in order to release a few Prince Charmings for themselves and left us only with a battalion of frogs who wore glasses. Eventually we came to suspect that their magical powers had something to do with hickeys because, unlike us, the Prettygirls started going *out* in tenth grade, *steady* in eleventh, and *all the way* in twelfth—activities that usually involved hickeys.

Gracefully, the Prettygirls made all the required costume changes from Bermuda shorts through pedal pushers, capri pants, gibson girl blouses, poodle skirts, crinolines, wired bras, strapless bathing suits and taffeta prom gowns complete with wrist corsages. They were elected Best Everything including Best Dressed even though they always wore their boyfriends' XL club jackets over everything except when they took their graduation pictures wearing Peter Pan–collared blouses, Revlon Pink Lightning smiles, White Shoulders perfume, a fraternity pin and their hair flipped up on both sides. Prettygirls had no acne, tummies, uncertainties, problem parents or academic concerns. Shortly after high school graduation, they all married the captain of the football team and sadistically asked us to stand up for them (as if they needed assistance) at their weddings—thus forcing us to buy many different-colored taffeta bridesmaids' gowns and to keep dyeing our linen pumps from lilac to fuchsia to chartreuse and then back again.

We couldn't—wouldn't?—do anything the way they did it. In truth, we couldn't even answer the questions posed by Kotex "Are You In The Know?" quizzes that ran in *Seventeen* and *Mademoiselle*. We didn't score well because we simply couldn't believe it was wrong to swim before the fourth or fifth day of a menstrual period. We weren't even prepared to acknowledge that periods *lasted* that long. Intellectually and artistically famished, we remained socially alienated wallflowers at the orgy, tortured by our own nonconformist instincts plus dreaded eruptions of acne. One of the few thrills of those years was our discovery of homemade brick-and-board bookcases—a design (imported into our sterile environment by some older sibling come home from college) which we immediately duplicated in our bedrooms.

Ignorant of the long tradition of dissent within our society, we were shocked and bitter—only a decade later—to watch rebels revered as heroes. Those of us who had suffered from "being different" during the fifties, and who would have killed to be "popular" back then, felt cheated as well as confirmed during the revolutionary sixties.

"The thing that killed me most about Sukie was how sad she was when I met her." Jeff grimaces from the memory. "It was awesome how sad she was. And even though I tried to loosen her up, and we did have some fun, she just couldn't take me seriously because I was fifteen years younger than her and because she had such a hangup about her age. And her weight. And her wrinkles. Shee . . . it! She had the whole schmeer."

Jeff picks up one of his boots and gently rubs the leather with a cocky thumb. He has now become a member of that vast army of male observers who see all our absurdities without understanding them.

"You know what I think? I think Sukie got hooked on that American propaganda about people being happy all the time. I think that's what caused a lot of her troubles."

He was, perhaps, right. Chinese parents never mention happiness when asked what they wish for their children. Grown-up DEB*s* can think of nothing else. We believe the Declaration of Independence guaranteed us happiness, not just the right to pursue it. What's troubling Jeff is the fact that we all look like winners but feel like losers.

The telephone rings and Jeff answers. He holds the receiver away from his ear so that a hysterical female voice at the other end of the line can be overheard.

"Yah," he finally says. "It's true. She's dead."

Now there is even more commotion from the incoming call and Jeff moves the receiver farther away from his face.

"Yah. Some of her girlfriends from New York are

staying here," he finally says. "Everyone's just sitting around the kitchen. They'll be here. Sure. S'long."

He replaces the receiver.

"That was Miranda Kriss," he says. "She lives across the street, but she's over near Annapolis and she just heard about Sukie, so she's driving back to D.C. She says she'll be here in an hour or so unless the Bay Bridge is fucked. Any of you know Miranda?"

We all shake our heads.

"But you know who she is?"

"Of course," Elaine answers impatiently. "She brought Max's girlfriend into the picture while pretending she was Sukie's friend."

"What makes her think she's welcome here, anyway?" Joanne frowns.

Slowly Jeff unfurls his lanky body and stands up.

"Yah. Well, she's a real bimbo, and I sure as hell don't want anything to do with her, so I'm going to split."

"But you'll come back, won't you? Tomorrow? Or Monday?" Joanne asks.

Jeff circles around the table, touching each of us gently on the backs of our necks or shoulders.

"Actually, no," he says. "I'm just gonna do a fade now and take a pass on the funeral. As long as Max and the kids are coming back tomorrow . . ."

We all stand up, protesting and arguing with him, but in the next instant he is gone, leaving only an enormous vacuum in his wake.

Each of us feels stunned by his departure.

"He's . . . he's a nice person," Elaine finally says, looking down the empty hallway toward the front door.

Joanne and I consent with our silence.

CHAPTER 7

I am tired.

The Hot Flash Flashcards from the past that keep appearing before my mind's eye are exhausting me. I am beginning to feel like an accident victim whose life runs fast-forward from beginning-to-end before the ultimate darkness descends.

"Look. I've got to take a shower," I say, rising slowly out of the chair. "I never got one this morning."

In truth, I want to be alone.

Upstairs, I draw myself a bath, but while waiting for the tub to fill I return to Sukie's bedroom and begin to canvass her desk. There are stacks and stacks of typed pages spread along its length. I survey the cover pages and eventually begin reading a segment dated April 1983. Immediately I get hooked and return to the bathroom to turn off the water so I can lie on Sukie's bed and read another section of her journal.

APRIL 1983

Late one Saturday afternoon I walk down Connecticut Avenue to Childe Harold's, an imitation pub I've always liked. Although there's plenty of action there at night, it's not really a singles bar and in the afternoon it's actually quite docile. Nevertheless, I still try to make a dramatic entrance because I long ago accepted the implicit challenge of any drinking establishment and automatically create a mental image of some fictitious female in extremis. *Then, when I enter, I am able to project an air of urgency for an anonymous and often oblivious audience to magnify the meaning of my arrival.*

I probably acquired my I'm-being-driven-into-this-bar-by-circumstances-beyond-my-control compulsion from seeing too many cocktail-lounge intrigue movies back in the late forties. I can never just sit down at a bar, buy a drink, smoke a cigarette, pay the check and walk away. Instead I must compose a furtive face and frightened attitude suggestive of some illicit mission—lacing leisure time with B-movie melodrama to make a boozy afternoon seem more dramatic.

Mounting a stool as if swinging into a saddle, I order my first Salty Dog and study the squadrons of shiny glasses and columns of whiskey bottles marching in duplicate across the mirrored wall. A sign above the bar reads: WASHINGTON AREA DARTING ASSOCIATION. *Over the stereo, Stevie Wonder is singing Happy Birthday to Martin Luther King. My heart is rinsed by a solution of pain.*

Elaine once told me that whenever I arrive someplace, I always look as though I've just returned from some mysterious adventure. Maybe once that was true, but not now.

Walter once said to me, "I bet you never walked into a bar alone and stayed that way for more than five minutes." He was right then, but not now.

Now I can sit alone for hours and no one even bothers to speak to me.

It's vibes, I think—self-contempt rather than self-confidence. Even losers love winners. Even a cat can look at a queen, Mama used to say when I was little.

But now I am bankrupt. I feel as if I were once incred-

ibly rich and then suddenly lost all my money. The idea of lost wealth never moved me before because it was too remote from my experience. But now I can understand the metaphor of money lost—the decreased potential, eroded power, missed opportunities and numbed expectations.

I believe that from this time forward everything for me will be division and diminishment, necessary losses rather than any embellishments.

Loss has become the theme of my life. Gone now are all the casual engagements, the accidental but inevitable encounters, the spontaneous spiderweb of associations and activities I always took for granted. Gone now is the invisible network of friends that served as my springboard, my lovely launching pad into life. All that was natural, easy and casual has evaporated. My center and my perimeters are blurred. Space, congestion, drift and definition have disappeared. Former affluence is all but forgotten. Men are only memories now.

From above the bar, Janis Joplin has begun singing her heart out about Bobbie McGee and an enormous emptiness blooms and blossoms within me.

Last week I called Elaine in the middle of the night, sobbing hysterically. She waited patiently until I got a grip on myself. Then I unleashed my longings for love.

"Look," she finally said. "We've had our flings and we've had our love affairs."

My heart paused in its pounding.

"What do you mean?" I demanded, immediately resentful, immediately determined to establish the differences between her and me.

"Those days are over," she said. "There are other things for us to do now."

"Like what?" I ask, helplessly frightened. Perhaps Elaine could survive alone, but there was no possible way I could.

"Like work. Like doing some support stuff for Nicaragua. Like going out to help Brenda with her new baby."

"Are you kidding?" I groan, feeling panic flutter and flower inside me. "That's it? That's all there is?"

"That's right. What were you expecting?"

"Well, I don't know. Something else, something more."

"Well, there isn't any more anymore."

"There has to be."

Elaine expelled an ugly laugh. "Look, you can fix up your house, spruce up your wardrobe, take a vacation. There's still things to do. It's just different now that we're alone."

I began to cry. "I want more," I sob. "A lot more."

"Then find it," she said.

She was finished. She had no more patience.

Elaine has always been militant about everything. Since she was my first friend at Chicago, I learned a lot of politics from her. But even back then she taught me things in a commandeering way. She always believed she was in possession of the truth so there was no room for any disagreement and since she was right ninety percent of the time, I let it be. But now that she's gotten older and more bitter, she sometimes scares me with her totalitarianism. Since she's no longer anchored, she's somewhat like a loose cannon aboard a ship on a stormy sea.

Her rage toward Nathaniel is no greater than mine toward Max, but her anger is much more comprehensive and indiscriminately anti-male than mine. Even at my worst, I don't feel or speak that way. Yet most everything Elaine says is true. I just don't like saying all the things she says. And I don't like to hear them said either.

Once when my life was very busy, I installed a call-waiting system on my telephone. The first day I had it, I heard the click indicating that a call was waiting so I switched lines.

It was a breather.

A heavy breather.

I couldn't believe it.

Telephone repairmen always used to ask me if I was Italian. For some reason I would say yes and then button my blouse up higher.

Now there aren't even any more telephone repairmen to come out to my home.

Once we went to a party that was held at the Golden Parrot Restaurant. It turned out that our waiter was an ex-student of mine. He told me I could have all the free drinks I wanted so I drank twelve piña coladas. Drunk out of my mind, I became frantically flirtatious and embarrassingly loud—laughing and joking and teasing everyone. I was very happy. When the dinner ended I invited everyone back to our house and led a giggling daisy-chain walk down Connecticut Avenue. As soon as we reached home, Monique and I curled up on opposite ends of the couch and fell asleep.

How drunk we were.

The dozen or so people who had accepted my invitation sat across the room from us and continued their conversation, trying to ignore our occasional happy snores. When the telephone rang I awoke, reached for the receiver, and said hello. I was silent for a moment and then, as people turned to look at me with concern, I said, "I'm sorry. I'm drunk and I can't wait for you."

Then I hung up.

"Who was that?" Max asked.

"My breather," I said and fell promptly back to sleep.

Apparently the telephone kept ringing after that until Max finally took the receiver off the hook.

When I used to go out for lunch I would always order two Salty Dogs from the bar and a chef's salad. Then I would ask for blue cheese dressing on the side—not because I feared finding my lettuce swimming in a pool of pink calories, but because I'd discovered you usually got more dressing if it came separately in a paper cup or creamer on the side. It was my way of beating the house and paying them back for using cheddar instead of Swiss cheese in the salad or cutting their tomatoes in slices rather than chunky quarters.

Depending upon my mood I smoke Merits to feel virtuous or defiantly tear off the filters for a hit like the kick of a Camel.

Now time mocks me. The past haunts me. The present provokes me and the future taunts me. My husband's betrayal has become my constant companion, always arguing for my attention. Only the hope of hurting him back can distract me from my obsession.

But there are no paybacks. That's the first thing. You don't get reimbursed for nice things you once did and you don't get revenge for the bad things others did to you. Nobody ever said that life was fair, but certainly no one ever mentioned just exactly how inequitable things could get. Even justice leaves a lot to be desired.

I used to have everything. I don't want to sound like an aging Hollywood actress, and indeed "everything" is relative—but still, in retrospect, it does seem as if I had a lot. We had unique, unusual children—handsome, intense, and yet very well adjusted. They were like beautiful jewels set into the bracelet of our marriage.

Now I feel as if I have nothing.

I spend each day like a dollar.

First I drive David to school.

Next I go to see Dr. Karel.

Then I drive to "my group."

Then I meet a friend for lunch.

Then I have a few more drinks.

I shell out the hours like coins from my purse.

Once I got an obscene call from a woman. It hurt my feelings more than any male crank call I ever had. I listened for a while before hanging up and then fretted for a week about who it could have been, afraid it was some woman I knew. I kept feeling that if I could remember the voice I would recognize it. I thought that the way she said the words and phrases sounded much different from the way a man says them. Somehow from a woman those words seemed more obscene.

Freedom, Janis sings, means nothing left to lose.

Not so long ago, novelists frequently borrowed that line to spin out their own complaints. They used it as a starter, the same way they used Tolstoy's line about happy and unhappy families.

I have come to understand that it is only my compulsion to transcribe my pain that smothers any suicidal impulses. The creative process is not all that mysterious. Put yourself at the drugstore and as soon as you think of toothpaste you will also remember mouthwash. Same for writing and music and painting. If you hang around long enough, you'll remember everything and begin to compose.

Before, when I was drunk, I used to feel beautiful. Now when I'm drunk I feel sad. And hungry. The vision of a toasted tuna fish sandwich floats into my head like a balloon in some comic strip. I know I am hungry. I haven't eaten for a long, long time.

I hear the staccato sound of rain outside Childe Harold's. A crowd of people enter the restaurant, noisy and drunk. They invade the place, clothed in collusion, emitting, like a heady perfume, the aroma of some earlier party they'd attended. Sitting down at a nearby table, they break into loud laughter and I feel an almost irresistible urge to run over and join them.

Why do I always feel that there has been some wonderful party somewhere to which I wasn't invited?

Friends who used to congregate around my table at Childe Harold—silently quarreling for space and inclusion—are gone now. I sit alone at the bar.

Maybe it was the abortions.

There were three of them.

I hadn't wanted any.

Of all the possible grievances I might have wielded, those were the only ones I never used. Somehow I couldn't use them—even as ammunition—because I could not bear to bring them up.

Perhaps he felt their psychological energy simply because I left them unmined.

Sometimes years went past and I never thought about them.

Once he brought up the subject and I looked at him angrily and said that maybe the right-to-lifers had a point. He walked out of the kitchen.

I take my address book out of my purse and read it to review which friends I have lost. I go in alphabetical order. It's funny. At this point in my life, the A's are most important to me. I suddenly realize I am carrying my past around like an old address book in my purse.

There are dormer windows in the front of Childe Harold's. They are level with the street so you can see feet going past, shoes shimmering in the light from outside. Colored flasks set upon the window ledge refract the light. A blond girl is silhouetted against one window, waiting for someone. Beyond the paned glass, rush-hour cars have begun jamming up on Connecticut Avenue, bottlenecking in the late afternoon.

I shiver. I have had four Salty Dogs. I am becoming drunk, anesthetized. The vodka creates a moat between my pain and my perception of it, making me a numb place to rest a bit while awaiting my amnesia. I have begun to welcome the blackouts that come more and more frequently now. Although they are frightening, I embrace them with gratitude.

A few weeks ago the names of dead people started surfacing in my Rolodex every time I used it. They began coming up like bodies on deserted beaches during the summertime. After a while I decided to discard the cards of my dead and wounded. I pulled out the ones for Paul and Ruthie, Orlando and Ronni, Jackie and Larry, and three of my father's brothers. I had no card for my mother because I knew her number by heart. Ha ha! I couldn't even do that one last tidying-up chore for her. Anyway, at the last moment I just couldn't bear to throw away the written names of my loved ones, so I turned them around backwards and hid them at the end of my Rolodex.

But once I'd started, I felt compelled to keep plucking out antiquated cards like yellowed leaves off a plant. Next I did the wounded-divorced families. That took even longer because I had to write out a couple of single cards for every single couple. Ha ha! Ha ha! In some ways, this chore hurt even more than discarding my deceased. Many old familiar friends are simply gone now. Marriages broke up and partners moved away or went to live with someone I didn't know. Previously stable children, whose car-pool schedules I knew by heart, ha ha, had suddenly gone into orbit and, like spies, never slept more than two nights in the same place.

Such rearrangements in my friends' lives forced me to make enormous reality adjustments. The universe I had once known was gone, but it remained clearly etched in my mind—remembered as irresistibly rich and deliciously secure. I no longer even know the addresses of friends who once shared my life with me. We no longer "no" each other. Ha, ha. Ha, ha.

I saw the card for my daughter tucked in under the A's between my plumber and her dentist. Is that what it's all about? Does a child you carried within you, and loved with a passion beyond any other, eventually become just another entry in your Rolodex?

Last night I sat down at my typewriter determined to relieve some of my pain by shifting a few of my thoughts onto paper. Some people lift weights without elevating their souls. I write page after page without ever saying what I mean. I cannot recreate the pain. I can only provide environmental evidence about the physical landscape in which the pain occurred.

One night last week the doorknob on my bedroom door came off in my hand and I couldn't get out. I *pounded for a long time and finally David heard me. He used a butter knife to wedge the door open.*

I had felt entombed—locked inside my own mind. Panic had pummeled me; the next day I had bruises on my body although I don't know how I got them.

Right after Max moved into his apartment, he began turning off the bell on his telephone so I could ring him incessantly and he wouldn't hear. I remained accessible although he no longer wanted access. He remained unavailable. The injustice and inequity of this situation choked me. Rage rose up like bile in my soul.

Perhaps he had always been unavailable.

I suppose clinically they would call me manic-depressive. Actually I'm so used to it now I just experience it as feeling emotionally busy most of the time. Of course it also depends on which pills I do. Ten milligrams of Valium first thing in the morning lets me get going. Depending on what needs doing that day, I take half to three-quarters of a Tenuate Dospan along with several cups of black coffee before noon. If there's not much going on, I take another half Valium and look around for someone who likes to drink at lunchtime.

In the future, if we need money, I suppose I can send David to ask Max. That doesn't mean we'll get it. How is it that I became dependent upon a man who hates my guts? How is it that he makes me feel old and ugly?

No matter what happened during our marriage, I was totally predictable and reliable. I always did the same things; I was always home to greet the children after school. Things stayed pretty much the same all the time. Now everything changes and fluctuates. Even my weight. I have to keep buying different pairs of blue jeans. I have Levi's in sizes twenty-seven, twenty-eight, twenty-nine and thirty. It drives me crazy guessing which pair I'll have to wear the next day, depending upon how much I've eaten.

I became a seller in a buyer's market in 1970.

Back then I was doing a lot of travel articles and I had

to go down to the Bahamas on an assignment. That's
where I tilted at the age of thirty-five. My editor wanted
a story about living cheaply in expensive resort areas so
I had to stay in a tacky, second-class commercial hotel
in downtown Nassau that looked like the stage set from
Separate Tables remaindered and exported to the islands. The place was crawling with obviously third-rate
British traveling salesmen.

When I went downstairs the first night for dinner, the
maître d' asked me to wait at the bar until my table was
ready so I walked through the lobby toward the make-
shift counter he indicated. A young man, already seated
there, watched me approach and then slid over one
stool to sit beside me.

"Do you have to wait for a table too?" he asked.

I nodded.

He was sleazy and unattractive. His teeth were absolutely British and terrible. His skin was murky and he
proceeded to ask all the obvious questions—why was I
there, was I alone, what did I do with my time?

I answered lethargically.

He asked what I drank. I said gin and tonic. He ordered me one and began to act as though he were my
escort. I sipped my drink while he studied my backside
surreptitiously. He started to ask more intimate questions. Finally the maître d' walked over to say my table
was ready. I stood up and smiled at the young man.

The bartender slid a single check across the counter
and the young man pushed it toward me. He already
had two drinks of his own on the tab.

"I'm yours for the taking," he said.

"No, thanks," I answered casually, although I was
stunned by that body blow.

It was while I was paying for my drink that I realized
I had changed from a buyer into a seller—that in bars
on islands around the world from this time forward, I
would appear ready to pay for companionship. I had

unknowingly crossed some invisible frontier between youth and middle age.

I couldn't believe it. I also couldn't eat. I went back to my room instead of into the dining area.

On Caribbean islands I am always suffused by a sense of adventure. Within days I darken and slim myself so strenuously that I am able to pass for a movie star checking out locations for future film projects.

I like it down in the islands.

I can even live with lizards. Although I'm phobic about rodents, and not totally happy when lizards have to travel across the ceiling above my bed, I can handle them when they stay on the walls. Once I heard that if one lizard bites off another lizard's tail it will grow back. The man who told me this said, "You can always get a piece of tail in the tropics." Then he winked at me over the top of his brandy snifter in a dark neighborhood bar in Old San Juan next to a small appliance repair shop.

Iguanas, however, are another story.

Resort towns always made me feel romantic.

When I was in my twenties, I knew how to emerge as a standout in East Coast resort towns that were well stocked with super-beautiful women. I mixed what looks I had with a carefully cultivated nonchalance that bordered on affectation. With dazzling instinct, I established an air of indifference—casually matched clothes, designer sunglasses, unbrushed hair and neglected feet—that somehow translated into a kind of careless glamour. It was sort of like going to Saks dressed like a slob and acting too rich to care.

Summers always licked me like a cat. I would envision hot highways waiting to be devoured, small towns wanting to be tasted, cool nights kissing sunburnt days, shadowy twilights infringing upon sandy afternoons, love scenes longing to be played out on dusky beaches. Once summer summoned me, I wanted to hold it in my hand like an orange and suck it dry, filling my mouth with its bright yellow color and letting its sticky sweetness drip down my chin.

But I am not near the sea now and it is not summer.

In 1965, Diana and Leonard, Elaine and Nat, Joanne and Karl, and Max and I took an oath to spend one month together every summer—to rent some huge beach house in a different place along the Eastern Seaboard each year. And we did it. We kept that promise. Now those holidays are like bright patches of light for me in the dark quilt of my past.

By 1980 I realized that I had not taken enough photographs. Of anyone. Now it is too late. A group of middle-aged strangers has replaced my beautiful young friends.

Still, there are snapshots other people took of us during our summer holidays.

In the sixties, when Max and Leonard and Nathaniel and Karl (Joanne's live-in lover for most of that decade) were with us—everything was different. Along with the smells of the sea and shellfish and sand and mildewed towels and dirty diapers and sweaty sneakers, there was always a sweet scent of sex in the air. On mornings when we only threw on cotton robes so we could hurry into the kitchen to feed our morning-hungry babies before we even showered, I was always aware of that odor. It was part of our then-sweet marriages and our summers at the shore.

Once when Leonard arrived a few days later than the rest of us, he slammed into the big wraparound porch, overlooking the sea, where we were all sitting in semi-darkness and said, "I swear I can smell sperm." And we had all laughed because we agreed and knew everyone made more love near the ocean than any other place in the world.

Back then, there was a male presence to draw a hard-edged frame around us.

Mikey and Allen, Elaine's sons, were six and seven when we first initiated our summer holidays together, so they were old enough to supervise our toddlers down near the water, and we could actually have tiny patches of time in which to talk. Also, at the beach, the men participated in surveillance since they were just sitting around talking anyway and could see the children without any extra effort. The only troublesome question was if they didn't see the children, would they realize they'd disappeared? Actually, the men were great about arranging amusements when the kids got older—fishing expeditions or bike rides or shopping excursions or trips to the boardwalk.

We spent the days in our bathing suits, slim again even if ghostly white stretch marks laced our tans and mysterious brown lines traveled down our midriffs, pointing like arrows toward our birthing areas. Those lines arrived with each new baby—just like our mothers—and then faded away after a year or two.

Now that there are only us women and our grownup children—who drift in and out for weekends with their friends and lovers—it's not all that much fun anymore. Now there are no excuses for laughing excursions to fast-food restaurants or late-night cruises along sloppy boardwalks that slosh with excitement, spilt soda, fallen popcorn and easy fixes.

My friends and I always sit in each other's kitchens when we visit so we'll be near the coffeepot, the liquor bottles, the food and the telephone. When we really settle down to talk we always go into the kitchen. It's in there that we excavate our old memories and explicate their meanings. It's there that we examine ancient confidences, as if they were poems, and reassemble memorable incidents from our pasts. Sometimes we talk substantively about our work, but most often we play with gentle visions of ourselves, testing different images just as we do when we try on each others' new clothes. More and more often now we can anticipate each other's conclusions about most subjects. That's nice.

My friends and I understand each other. Sadly, my dearest friends live in New York so that I feel distant from them and when I most want to inhale their beings, I can only hear their voices through a telephone. Perhaps I should move to New York to be nearer them when David goes to college, but then I would only discover that they have their own busy lives and I would feel hurt because they didn't have more time for me.

It would be especially that way with Diana. Diana has really gotten herself together. Although I don't know precisely in what ways she and I are different, it is that difference which keeps me searching and her settled. It is that difference which allows her to control her environment while mine buffets me around. Whatever it is—I want some of what she's got. I don't expect life to be easy; I only want a touch of ease before I die.

Would I have felt worse if Max had run off with Diana?

Both Loren and Lisa were very angry when Diana divorced Leonard. They refused to understand her rationale. She said there wasn't much she could do about that. She couldn't make them understand. She says it simply boils down to the fact that daughters and divorce don't mix. Her daughters blame her for their father's absence—for his no longer being home and always available to them.

Diana finished her doctorate, got tenure at Columbia, and now publishes all the time. She seems to take her success almost for granted. But, of course, Diana doesn't realize how intoxicating she is. She has no idea how handsome she looks—lean and loose and liquid, with her long hair turning beige instead of gray. She's not the one men go for first. Rather they watch her for a while because Diana is a knight who moves indirectly but with challenging results. When a serious, intelligent man becomes aware of her powers, he gets a contact high off Diana. Of course men love that—a free buzz is the best hook of all.

Max was always fascinated by Diana, even somewhat in awe of her. She is awesome. She's terribly smart, even if a bit erratic, and Max always respected her for that. I often thought Max might make a move on Diana sometime, but he didn't. At least I don't think he did. Diana would have jumped off a bridge rather than take up with Max—even though she had some feelings for him too.

That probably has to happen over years of closeness. We hung together because we mattered to each other. There aren't that many people in the world who really interest us, so there has to be a little covert lust. Who cares? Diana was like a little dinghy tied to the boat of our marriage. She bobbed along behind us in case of emergency.

———————————

I set the manuscript down on the bed.

So Sukie had wondered about me and Max; what's nice is that she didn't *worry* about us.

That sweetest of all triangles—two female friends and one's husband—is also the most dangerous. It is not like a boat and its dinghy. A married couple and a friend is more like a fast ten-speed bike encumbered by a set of training wheels that affords balance but slows it down. Actually our experience was what it was—three friends splashing around in a summer together, unself-conscious friendship lulling everyone into a false security. Ultimately, upset by so much excited and exciting closeness, someone makes a move—usually the husband who feels closed out or threatened by female friendships. Few women will break the taboo that disallows so expensive an indulgence.

Anyway, I always felt that the mild threat of my presence made Sukie a bit more demonstrative toward Max—a bit more affectionate than she usually was. I knew he missed that and somehow she couldn't or wouldn't provide it. When we were all together, she was more forthcoming and that made Max happier.

I Remember Mama.
Mama took me to see that play when it came to Chicago. I was ten and I felt something terribly important was happening to me as I sat beside her in that gentle Saturday afternoon darkness. I think I felt something important was happening because Mama had gone out on her very own, without even telling Daddy, to buy us two tickets to a play. But why had she chosen I Remember Mama? *Was it so I could enter that title in my journal now as I remember her?*

When I was eleven I broke my leg sledding on a big hill near our flat. After some time in a hospital I was brought home to continue my recuperation. Although I read and played with my dolls while listening to the soaps over my little radio, I became more and more demanding of my mother's time and attention. I needed to feel her nearness. One morning I begged and nagged her to sew my favorite doll—Patchie—a new dress. She told me she had some cooking and laundry to do, but if I played by myself all morning, by afternoon she would have finished a new doll dress and would surprise me with it. I agreed.

Over the next few hours I heard her working around the apartment. But when she brought in my lunch tray, there was a perfectly hand-stitched dress for Patchie. The only problem was that I hated the fabric. It was a garish red cotton with white polka dots.

"Ugly," I cried. "That's the ugliest material I ever saw. I hate it." And picking up the dress, I flung it across the room.

Never before had Mama ever become so angry at me. Now she stood beside my bed, her arms akimbo, her face white with rage.

"You spoiled little snot," she said. "When you were one year old I had only one dollar to spend for your birthday, but I walked downtown to buy you a sunsuit at Kresge's. And even though Papa started to make lots of money, I always saved that little sunsuit to remember how poor we were. And now you're so spoiled that you don't even think it's good enough for a doll dress. You're spoiled rotten, Sukie. Your daddy's spoiled you rotten. What am I going to do?"

Oh, Mama. I'm so sorry I did that. Maybe I was spoiled then, but I stopped being that way. I know how much you wanted for me, Mama, I know that you wanted the best for me. I know that you wanted me to be happy. But somehow I lost my way, Mama. Or maybe I never deserved to be as happy as you wanted me to be. Maybe I didn't deserve all the things you dreamed I'd be and do and have. Maybe I was spoiled and that's why I didn't get them. Oh, Mama. Why did you make me think I should have the best of everything and that I would be happy all the time?

There is one party from the sixties that I can remember with total recall. It happened during the October 1967 weekend Norman Mailer described in his *Armies of the Night*. An old friend of mine gave the dinner party with which Mailer opens his book. I made the apple cobbler that Linda served as dessert to her sixty guests.

In 1967, I was thirty-two. I know that as a fact, but I can't remember myself in my thirties. Those years blur, probably because I had no true consciousness back then.

I remember the photograph on the book jacket of *Armies of the Night. Thousands of people are forging across Memorial Bridge on their March to the Pentagon. Their faces are resolute and defiant. They are committed to stopping the war in Vietnam and challenging Lyndon Johnson for control of the country. They are determined.

That Friday afternoon I had returned home—after conducting three insipid interviews with three celebrated nonentities—to clean the house because two distinguished writers were to be our houseguests. After years of changing sheets for anonymous beatniks, hippies, civil rights workers and antiwar dissenters, I had finally been rewarded with two real celebrities—a Famous American Poet and a Great Literary Critic. Indeed, I made a special attempt at hospitality by replacing burned-out light bulbs in the guest room and setting out an assortment of matching towels, washcloths, and fresh bars of hotel-sample soaps before they arrived.

But even better—Diana and Leonard and the kids were there when I got home, and Diana, of course, helped me get things ready. We finally got the kids fed and bedded and then we giggled and acted silly while putting on makeup for the dinner party at Linda's. (I had already dropped off the Brown Betty.) After the dinner, we went to a political rally at the old Ambassador Theatre where Mailer lumbered drunkenly around the stage, rambling through an incoherent speech that concluded with his inviting everyone to a party at a familiar-sounding address that turned out to be our house.

Somewhere between four hundred and five hundred people trooped through our front door that Friday night. Whatever beer and liquor we had in the house was consumed. Cigarettes were ground into rugs, and people smoking grass burned holes in chairs, sofas and tabletops. Everything in the kitchen was devoured, and empty bedrooms were used for quick sexual encounters. Debris and empty beer cans were scattered everywhere.

At about 3:00 A.M. I approached the Famous Poet, who had a beautiful long-haired T-shirted girl draped around him, and explained the location of the guest room. Then I went upstairs to my own room and fell into an exhausted sleep.

At six the next morning, David, who was four months old, awoke. Although I still nursed him at that hour, I also fed him cereal afterwards in hopes that he'd be full enough to go back to sleep. Max was rolled up in an unconscious lump on the bed, so I carried the baby down to the kitchen to nurse him. Diana was already there with Loren. To see her in my kitchen gave me faith that somehow my house would get cleaned and restored.

At seven o'clock the telephone rang.

"Hello." A crisp cultivated woman's voice lilted through the receiver. "Is [the Famous Poet] there?"

"Oh sure," I said. "Wait a minute and I'll run up to get him."

But he wasn't there.

Slowly I returned to the kitchen.

"I'm afraid they've left for the plenary session already," I said breathlessly into the telephone.

"So early?"

"Well, it is a plenary session," I repeated.

"Well, please ask him to telephone his wife when he gets back."

"Oh yes," I said politely. "I will."

Years later, I am still fascinated by my natural impulse to protect the Famous Poet—to safeguard the male prerogative of "having fun" while in another city. I lied—not to protect his wife's feelings, but to hide her husband's infidelity for his sake—which, I now see, was the right thing to do for absolutely the wrong reasons.

As always happened on large demonstration days, people from New York who traveled to Washington with infants or small children telephoned upon their arrival to ask if they could leave some offspring at my house. Usually I got stuck babysitting, but today, since I was determined not to miss another march, I had engaged Mrs. Parrot.

All the adults except me left before nine. By eleven, when Mrs. Parrot arrived, Diana's two toddlers, my two, and two quarrelsome five-year-old boys from New York were installed in my house. Mrs. Parrot walked in on a mass of confused, unhappy children and the filthy, after-orgy mess. I finally disengaged myself and walked alone across town to the Washington Monument.

After listening to lengthy speeches at the Lincoln Memorial, the protesters started walking toward Virginia. They moved slowly, tens of thousands swarming toward Memorial Bridge. Still alone, I joined the crowd—and felt myself pressed forward by pushing, pulsating waves of people.

Halfway across the bridge I found myself caught up in an ocean of political hysteria. Fervor and fury ignited everyone. I was carried along by a tidal wave of antiwar passion. After years of disarray, the Movement was on the move. I felt simultaneously subsumed and enlarged.

Eventually I remembered that Mrs. Parrot had to leave by three o'clock. I had no idea of the time, but the sun was beginning to look suspiciously weak and westerly. I asked someone and found out it was almost two. Turning, I tried to wade through the crowd. As if fighting the current of a river, I pressed backwards against time and history, wondrous at the raw resolution of the people coming toward me. It took me half an hour to wind my way off Memorial Bridge.

Once back on the banks of the city, I could find no public or private transportation. The entire area had been sealed off, so I began to run along the river. I was engorged from having missed David's noon feeding and milk began to seep through my bra and blouse. I was afraid that Mrs. Parrot would actually leave at three and the thought of all those children alone in the house made me panic. I looked back at the crowd going in the opposite direction and knew I was missing history once again because of babysitting obligations.

I was panting, still out of shape from my recent child-birth. I started to cry. Mrs. Parrot was already in her coat when I reached my front door. I paid her and apologized profusely for being late. After she left, I nursed David and dealt with the other children.

That weekend has come to symbolize the sixties for me.

———————————————

I put down Sukie's journal and rush back to the bath-room and my now lukewarm bath. It is getting late. Miranda will show up soon and if I'm not downstairs Elaine will read me the riot act for leaving them alone with the villainess of this tragedy. I decide to just wash up at the sink and while scrubbing myself with a wash-cloth I think about the varying responses the others might have toward this last segment of Sukie's journal. Never having known Sukie's view of that weekend, I remember it totally differently, but that doesn't dis-credit Sukie's vision of it. While drying and dressing myself, I try to evaluate Sukie's judgment about events.

Certainly she had never been able to make up her mind about Miranda.

CHAPTER 8

What Sukie could never accept was that it all happened right in front of her—right across the street to be exact. Miranda Kriss and Elizabeth Morley rented the English basement opposite the Amrams' house during what I remember as the delicious designer spring of 1979. Later, Sukie told me that Max had come in from the yard one Saturday morning to say that a former student of his and another young woman were moving into the Nelsons' basement and he was going across to help carry some of their boxes.

Sukie met Miranda and Elizabeth later that day and liked them both, although Miranda struck her as the more interesting of the two. Both girls were graduate students at AU and the Amrams began to see them quite often, although it was mostly Miranda who was around during the daytime since she was writing her masters' thesis. That was the year Carol began applying to colleges and she spent a lot of time across the street with them discussing schools and careers. Because Miranda gave David his first driving lessons in her Karmann-Ghia, he also became her steadfast fan.

Sukie, too, discovered Miranda's unusual talent for initiating instant intimacies. Miranda had perfected the art of imitating the passionate exclusivity that colors close friendships. She had a reservoir of ingratiating tactics. At first she only did simple things such as taping

Carol's and David's favorite musical groups when they came over her eternally blaring FM, but she also clipped sports articles for David from out-of-town newspapers and sent Carol a dozen red roses upon her acceptance to Kenyon College.

Because Miranda was home all day, almost every day, she frequently accepted UPS deliveries for the Amram family, helped Sukie carry in groceries when she saw her unloading the car, and always telephoned before going to the supermarket to ask if there was anything Sukie needed. After a month of casual contacts, Miranda began dropping by the Amrams' late in the day when Sukie was puttering around the kitchen.

Then she would pour herself a glass of white wine and make herself extremely helpful during the dinner preparations. Miranda's obvious admiration of Sukie and her eagerness to help frequently forced Sukie to invite her to stay on for dinner. Max and the kids usually enjoyed that because Miranda had grown up in Washington and knew many of the politically powerful families about whom she told scandalous stories.

Indeed, Miranda was an endless source of gossip which she relayed with much gaiety—as if illicit love affairs were only amusing anecdotes and mischief itself never really malevolent. So-and-So's father, a former Secretary of Defense, was sleeping with So-and-So's mother—a former famous beauty—so that So-and-So Junior had the Georgetown house all to himself for the weekend, which was where Miranda had attended a cocaine party Friday night at which So-and-So appeared with his date What's-Her-Name.

Apparently Miranda had offered intimate details about famous people as if they were expensive baubles she specifically selected for the Amrams' enjoyment. She was also a superior gift giver. Her stream of thoughtful little presents never stopped. There were endless new novels from Kramerbooks and Afterwords, brash geraniums from Johnson's Flower Center on the first day of spring, baskets of herbs from the annual St. Albans School Fair, and elegant silk scarves with the label of a French boutique at the Watergate Hotel where Miranda worked out. Every few weeks she would appear with tinfoil containers of carry-out lasagna from some Georgetown pasta shop so that Sukie wouldn't have to cook, or some too-rich chocolate torte from Avignon Frères for dessert. Other times there would be a set of hard-to-get tickets for some sold-out rock concert at the Capitol Center for David and one of his friends.

On her birthday that spring, Sukie found a bouquet of helium balloons tied to her front doorknob first thing in the morning. Twice Miranda left bottles of wine she'd bought during an import sale at Woodley's Discount Liquor Store, saying she wanted Max to try them. Another time she gave Sukie a vial of Dexedrine, which had become popular and available on campus, and, on several occasions, some beautifully rolled joints of sinsemilla. Often there would be a large lamb or ham bone for Happy, neatly wrapped in heavy-duty tinfoil, left on the front doorstep next to the morning *Post.*

Miranda also began gifting Sukie with expensive castoff clothing she no longer wore. She had pressed an unpressed silk blouse upon Sukie as if it were a cotton T-shirt, saying it was too tight since she'd washed it. The shirt looked marvelous on Sukie, who could never have afforded to buy it, and she wore it endlessly.

Miranda never tired of driving Max to his office at AU when she was going to campus or dropping the kids off at their schools if she was up early enough in the morning. Since her parents lived on the Chesapeake Bay, she would often return from a weekend at the beach with baskets of chubby red country tomatoes, brown-paper bags full of zucchini—a vegetable that threatened to overrun the state of Maryland—homemade fruit jams or freshly baked breads.

As soon as summer arrived, there were insistent invitations for Sukie to use Miranda's Chesapeake Bay home since her parents had gone to Europe and Miranda was stuck in the city attending summer school. Miranda talked constantly about a lovely little Sailfish tied to a skinny but sunny dock under which millions of mussels hugged the rocks waiting to be harvested and devoured. In webby calligraphy on a pale blue card, she recopied her favorite recipe for the perfect Remoulade sauce to serve with mussels.

"Please go," she'd beg Sukie. "Just go yourself. You'll be able to finish your book twice as fast out there. And then Max and the kids can come out for the weekend. I'll even go with you the first time, to show you everything about the place."

So, early in June, Sukie and Miranda drove out to the Eastern Shore in the black Karmann-Ghia. Once at the house, Miranda explained how to use all the kitchen appliances and all the boating equipment. In great detail she explained how to find the mussels, where to buy bait, which markets in town had the freshest fish, and which nearby bar-restaurants offered the most action.

Eventually Sukie accepted Miranda's invitation and began going out to the Kriss's beach place mid-week and waiting for Max and/or the kids to join her on weekends. Later, Sukie told me about the wonderful times they'd all enjoyed out on the Bay before "the fall," when Sukie discovered Max had been having a heated affair with Elizabeth all summer. By spending so much time at the Bay, Sukie had offered Max unlimited opportunities to be with Elizabeth.

The few times Sukie came to New York after she and Max separated, and I had some free time to spend with her, she talked a lot about Miranda Kriss. She could never decide whether Miranda had been complicit in Max's affair and, if so, whether it was in a careless way. When I asked if she'd ever confronted Miranda, Sukie shook her head and said she had simply stopped speaking to her. Even after Elizabeth moved out of the English basement to take an apartment with Max, Sukie refused to respond to any of Miranda's attempts to reestablish contact.

Since I had never met or seen either Miranda or Elizabeth, I didn't have much feel for that situation. But by then Sukie was so distraught that her stories about Miranda were usually cut short by some spasm of grief or rage against Max. And, at that point, it would take all my resources just to calm her down, to curtail the amount of liquor she was drinking, and to try getting some food and/or coffee down her—none of which was easy.

When the front doorbell rings it is both too loud and too long.

"Hi, I'm Miranda Kriss," she says as soon as I open the door.

She smiles uncertainly, disclosing curiously long, although very white, teeth through the window between her lips.

Somehow Miranda Kriss is standing much too close to me, trespassing the invisible line where a visitor waits until invited inside. She is attractive in the quintessential American way—one of the golden girls who takes her grace for granted. She is wearing cutoffs and a white T-shirt beneath which slouch a pair of huge breasts. The T-shirt is loose, but her breasts are still obtrusive. They are like two rambunctious children from a previous marriage that a single mother tries to subdue in the presence of a man she's dating.

"You must be one of Sukie's friends from New York." Miranda's voice is calm, although her brown eyes are full of emotion.

"Yes, I'm Diana Sargeant," I say, assessing her in closer detail. She is indeed what Sukie always called a super-shiksa. She has a complexion more like a Brit than an American and her hair, which is the color of beer, spills close to her face. She is twenty-seven at the most.

"I live across the street," she says. "I got to know Sukie because Mr. Amram was my professor at AU. I know he's in Europe now. With David and Carol."

Then she begins to cry. She makes no effort to impede her tears or muffle her sobs. She stands perfectly still and cries matter-of-factly. Now I can see that she has cried before because the areas around her eyes are reddening in places where they were already chapped. Miranda Kriss is clearly in pain.

"Come on in," I say.

"I can't believe Sukie's dead," she whimpers. "What happened?"

"She had a cerebral hemorrhage."

Miranda sucks in her breath as she passes through the doorway. Once inside, she moves automatically toward the kitchen, and I can tell from her languid, leggy walk that she is totally comfortable with her large-framed, big-boned body and with herself. Her legs are long and have the kind of tan that looks inadvertent, a color acquired gardening or sailing rather than simply sunning. Sukie would have called it a goyische tan.

Miranda opens the kitchen door and then pauses before stepping inside. She is obviously surprised by the smoky air and the scent of marijuana.

"Hello, Miranda," Joanne says politely. "This is a pretty sad way for us to meet, but this is Elaine Cantor and I'm Joanne Ireland. I guess you met Diana already. Sit down. Wanna beer?"

Miranda sits down. I remain standing in the doorway because I see Elaine signaling me to wait there. When she gets up, I simply back out of the kitchen and wait for her to join me. She shuts the door behind us; then we walk into the dining room, which is still hugging the heat from the day. I flick on the window air conditioner.

"So what's her story?" Elaine asks impatiently. "What's she doing here? I mean, the question is, would

Sukie really want her to be here with us? Just because she's looking for some kind of absolution doesn't mean we have to come across just like that." She snaps her fingers rather close to my face.

"I don't know." I shrug. "Actually she's quite upset."

"That's not *our* problem," Elaine hisses. "And she *should* feel bad. She hurt Sukie a lot. Her. And Max. And her girlfriend Elizabeth. They all probably helped kill Sukie and now she just walks in here like she owns the place."

"It's her country," I say sourly, certain Elaine will understand. "It's always been her country; she can do whatever she wants here."

"God," Elaine curses. "It's not fair."

"The world's her convenience store. She doesn't have to watch out for anyone else."

Elaine shakes her head disbelievingly, but then silently acquiesces to my view and follows me back into the kitchen.

Joanne has unearthed several fresh bottles of liquor, a variety of mixes, and a large plastic ice bucket which she has set precariously close to Sukie's purse on the table. Without asking, she mixes me a vodka and tonic.

Then I sit down. Because of Miranda's arrival, everyone has changed places. Now I find myself in the chair Joanne usually occupies, which affords a view of Sukie's wall calendar hanging above the telephone. The sight of Sukie's handwriting makes my heart start chopping like an ax and at first I am unable to look directly at the squares in which she had penciled in appointments that now read like the dead imperatives of a crumpled old grocery list forgotten at the bottom of an everyday purse. It takes me a while to notice that Sukie had crossed out the first and last pairs of letters from Saturday, leaving TURD for the day following her death.

I shift around on the caned seat of the bentwood chair so as not to face the calendar.

"Well," Miranda says hesitantly, "I know what you all think about me." Her eyes make a complete circle around the table. Her hands are wrapped around her beer mug and though she appears nervous, she also seems determined to speak. "I mean, I know what Sukie must have told you, because I know what she believed. But she was wrong. I didn't set her up. I was heartbroken about everything that happened. When I found out what was going on between Max and Elizabeth— and that was hardly at the beginning—I didn't know what to do. I mean—well, maybe you all would have told her, but I couldn't. I mean I didn't, because I didn't know how to."

The three of us sit in silence. With our fingertips we trace the brown bracelets copied from the bottoms of a thousand hot coffee cups set down upon Sukie's table. We touch the fingerprints of cigarettes carelessly left to etch their shadows into the wood along the edges. Occasionally, Elaine uses a fingernail to chip at the mold of crumbs stuck inside the center seam of the table where the two leaves meet.

Finally, Joanne stands up to pluck some Kleenex from a box on the kitchen radiator and blows her nose with a few ferocious snorts.

"Someone should walk Happy," she says.

We all look over at the poodle lying in front of the sink. No one moves. No one wants to leave the table, the kitchen, the shelter of Sukie's home where her spirit is still in residence.

"Did you know Sukie was keeping a journal, Miranda?" I ask.

Her face tightens as she shakes her head.

"It's a real trip," Joanne comments grimly.

"Is it about . . . the split up?" Miranda asks.

"Yes." Joanne nods. "And it's the rawest piece of pain I've ever read."

"Does she talk about . . . me?" Miranda whispers.

"We haven't read all of it yet; there are parts all over the house," I say, not liking Miranda very much, but not necessarily eager to inflict any additional pain upon her. "They're in her bedroom and her study. On the typewriter and on the computer. They're everywhere. But so far I haven't seen your name."

"You probably will," Miranda says, gulping down some beer.

There is a very long silence now.

"But I'd like to ask you something," Miranda says, almost defiantly. "Why did Sukie take it the way she did? Why did she fall apart?"

It is Joanne who responds first. "You didn't meet Sukie until a few years ago, Miranda. You don't know what she and Max were like when they first started out together. You don't know how tight they were."

"After a long marriage," Elaine continues drily, "it's rather hurtful to have your mate leave you for a younger woman."

Everyone is tired now. Our eye makeup is smeared, our lips are licked clean of gloss or color. Elaine, who habitually runs her tongue around her mouth, has now done it so often that a narrow red rash outlines her lips. The dope we had smoked earlier has worn off and we are all feeling weary, although it is barely five o'clock.

Dusk has begun draining the light from the kitchen. Suddenly, sitting together like this around Sukie's table feels preordained. It is almost as if Sukie herself scripted this last scene, gathering an all-star cast of her oldest friends on this familiar stage to confront the young woman who first befriended and then—perhaps—betrayed her. The dramatic conflict seems to be whether or not our generation is still viable in the 1980s. The question seems to be whether or not we are outdated, outdistanced and outdone in this the new era of yuppies.

Hot flash . . .

Few of us have changed all that much with the passage of time. We're still rather old-fashioned and quite fifties-ish. We still follow certain trials, such as the Jean Harris, De Lorean and prize Pulitzer one, with great ardor. We are still enormously proud of Betty for kicking her habits, Joan her alcoholism, Jane her bulimia, and Liz for going on the wagon and losing all that weight. We are still mad at Mia for acing out her best friend, Dory, with André, at Joan Canwetalk for performing at the Republican Convention, at Shirley for becoming a space cadet, and at Natalie for drowning.

We still hate Scrabble, charades, crossword puzzles and prefer dogs to cats. At the piano we can play only chopsticks and remain frightfully insecure about classical music. Inevitably, we return rental cars ten minutes after the end of any bargain weekend, use our fingers to count the hours we've slept, and find it hard to resist American men who display foreign drugstore sundries on their bathroom shelves. Although we now wear glasses to read, cook, or make phone calls, and rely heavily on flannel nightgowns to stay warm—regardless of who's in our beds—we are still suckers for the *varoom* of a fast sports car, the grunt of a lover trying to hold back, and high-grade sinsemilla from Humboldt County.

Unlike our daughters, we do not consider Madonna a tramp. We love Anouk, Claire, Tuesday, Gena, Jill, Candice, Catherine, Diane, Lee, Sissy, Jane, Sophia, Carrie, Goldie, Mary and Elizabeth. We prefer Lily to Joan, silver to gold, bars to tables, Spanish to French, and south to north. We are still lazy about conjugating irregular verbs in foreign languages, figuring out the actual time when it's 17:30, trying to remember "spring forward and fall back," or determining the real cost of souvenirs when there are 1.7 escudos to the dollar. Even though we don't drink anywhere as much as we used to, because both Sheila and Jill met their current husbands at AA meetings, a number of us have joined

Alcoholics Anonymous—not to go on the wagon but, hopefully, to meet some nice guy who has.

Technologically, we are agnostics living in a computer age. We do not actually believe our tape recorders are working even if their red light is on. We cannot remember the kind of car we drove prior to our present one and we still frequently use contact paper for re-covering various containers—or for other spruce-up jobs around the house. Unfortunately, we believe that if we win the lottery, one of our children will get run over by a Greyhound bus, and that when we die—we will still have to change planes in Atlanta.

Although we have gradually become more interested in real-estate tax exemptions, aerobics, Keogh plans and adult extension courses, we remain vigilant against liver spots. While we may modify our traditional summer tans and forget to take our emotional blood pressure every morning, we have absolutely no interest in acquiring senior citizen discount passes. Although we do peer into the faces of bag ladies and bums to see if we went to high school with them, and read, rather than skip, newspaper articles about osteoporosis, we snobbishly feel that if we can't afford to see a flick without a discount, forget it. We still think of ourselves as sort of . . . fortyish, certainly not middle-aged.

While some of our youngest cohorts have suddenly begun delivering their first babies, most of us discuss root canals more often than birth ones. Although we probably have more biopsies than manicures nowadays, we still consider Tina Turner our main role model. When Gwensandra, one of the sexiest women we ever knew, was heard to say she wasn't "thrilled" with her new laxative, Sharon told her to knock it off—loud and clear. While using Tums, not for our tummies but as the cheapest source of supplemental calcium, and continuing our efforts to wear out the Star Wars sheets that our sons refused to take to college with them, we also persist in doing research on collagen treatments that fill out wrinkles and laugh lines, thereby postponing facelifts which we fear almost as much as old age.

Although we still need to take off for an occasional "mental health day," we are physically in good condition and are still mad at Marilyn, Natalie, Janis, Sue, Grace, Sylvia, Edie, Jayne, Sharon and Jean—as well as Sukie—for leaving us too soon. We wanted all the Dionne quintuplets to survive and grow old along with us.

Crazily enough, in a sexual sense the Change has been a change for the better for many of us. It actually catapulted a number of our slow starters into sexual athletes. Some of our newly aroused members, who actually still use the words *hot* and *dirty* as sexual adjectives, believe that multiple orgasms several times a week provide sufficient exercise if they also watch their diets. We still cannot swallow aspirin or cum. Although the majority of us do not frequent singles bars—since there is no way for an extra to star in a crowd scene—we will, upon occasion, place a well-written, elegantly edited personal in some presentable and plausible publication such as *The New York Review of Books*.

It remains clear that if some future right-wing government required us to sign notarized statements restricting our right to sleep with strangers in order to qualify for Social Security, we would never collect any of our allotments. Anyway, few of us believe that the Social Security Administration will still exist in the year 2000, when most of us turn sixty-five, so why would we give up a sure thing for a chancy one? After all, we weren't born yesterday.

Luckily, there are some advantages to getting old. Audrey, who has always suffered some chin whiskers, says she doesn't have to be quite as militant as before since they're coming in white now and don't show as much. Customs inspectors seldom even ask any of us to open our luggage anymore and though we move fewer drugs than we used to, we do, at every opportunity, smuggle black tulip bulbs out of Holland. Also, happily enough, we no longer feel compelled to finish every book we start, accept every social invitation we receive, or vote for the least bad candidate in either local or national elections.

Over the years we have belonged to local chapters of the National Society of the Survivors of Suicides, the Sierra Club, Amnesty, AA, AAA, ABA, ADA, ACLU, AMA, AAUP, NAACP, SDS, WIW, L.A.D.I.E.S. (Life After Divorce Is Eventually Sane), Snick, Weight Watchers, Displaced Homemakers, the National Writers Union, the Lawyers Guild, Physicians for Social Responsibility, Smokenders and NOW. Those of us who were eligible to do so dropped our memberships in the DAR or B'nai B'rith, and when we attend international conferences it's always as NGOs. Eventually we'll join OWL—the Older Women's League—as well as the Gray Panthers.

We are definitely going to have to brainwash ourselves into believing we qualify as senior citizens.

We are now, as the French say, women of a certain age. Although we can still flash gorgeous smiles, a lot of our teeth are loose because we have been grinding them and/or clenching our jaws, while presumably asleep, for almost half a century. Because top and bottom jaws clenched together exert two thousand pounds of pressure, nowadays our gums bleed more often than our hearts do. Those of us who suffer from temporomandibular joint syndrome know that ice packs in the morning help relieve sore cheeks as well as decrease unnecessary swelling around the eyes.

We have had a number of wonderful lovers. Although we were never the type to run out of a shower naked, we have flexed our love muscles so often that we could probably lift heavy weights vaginally. We always preferred isometrics to aerobics and have learned to live with what Charlotte calls our Jewish thighs. We are relieved to have stopped sending innocent rabbits to their early graves with our sunny urine, but we will never forget favorite lovers and the cosmic shudders they suffered in our arms. Currently our favorite anecdote is about the young girl who asked her eighty-year-old grandmother at what point sexual desire died and was told, "You'll have to ask someone older than me."

"I kept thinking that such a silly little affair would just blow over," Miranda offers in a dreamy voice. "I mean, I couldn't even think of Elizabeth and Sukie at the same time. Sukie was so superior. And I thought, why hurt Sukie by telling her about their tacky little affair when I was sure it was going to end soon."

"Well, if you really felt that way, why did you keep pushing Sukie to use your beach house?" Joanne asks. "That just gave Max and Elizabeth all the time in the world to get really involved."

"But that wasn't the way it was," Miranda protests weakly. "See, they were screwing their heads off in my apartment, and I kept thinking that one day, sure as hell, Sukie was going to drop by to have a beer or something and they'd be sitting around the living room half-naked. I wasn't their beard; I was trying to protect Sukie. Maybe you're the kind of friends who would have told her, but I couldn't. I just couldn't."

I watch fresh tears well up in Miranda's eyes.

Oh, how many times have we discussed whether or not to tell a friend about her husband's philandering? How often did a friend look shocked beyond words when she realized we'd known and never told her, never saved her from the humiliation that intensified her pain? Our discussions about infidelity always ended like our menstrual blood-spot debates. Should we tell a woman we see at a museum or department store that she has spotted the back of her skirt? Would she rather know the painful truth, and go home to change, or not know and simply deceive herself into believing it happened just as she was unlocking the front door, brainwashing herself into thinking no one else saw that scarlet letter of vulnerability, that discouraging red badge of helplessness, which—like the blood on Lady Macbeth's hands—appears despite all precautions.

"You were sort of playing God there for a little while, weren't you?" Elaine asks in a voice more inquisitive than accusative.

Miranda shrugs helplessly, and her large breasts twitch in sync with her shoulders. "Look. Sukie could have weathered the whole thing even after she found out about it. The problem was she just couldn't stop herself from tearing everything apart. *Really.* I heard about it from Elizabeth who got it straight from Max. So I knew right along about all the self-destructive things Sukie was doing."

"And what would you have done?" Elaine asks her.

"Well . . ." Miranda looks thoughtful. Her smooth face, shiny hair, and innocently flushed cheeks make her seem incapable of any artifice. "I guess I would've pretended I hadn't found out about it at all . . . that I didn't know anything was going on."

We all look at her with astonishment.

"From such restraint we don't know," Elaine says with a strong ethnic intonation. "And I for one could never learn it."

Regret appears briefly on the screen of her eyes but is then quickly deleted.

Now we begin to study Miranda in depth. It isn't just that we are old and she is young, it's that we are old and she is new. New women are much more premeditative than we are and can weigh the advantages or disadvantages of various alternative actions. Because they analyze all their options, they are more likely to be the conscious authors of their actions rather than the spellbound spectators we historically feel ourselves to be.

Although Elaine is racked with jealousy over Nathaniel's new baby, she is hardly the only one of our generation to complain about the inequities of contemporary marriage and divorce. Too many of us remain gray divorcées while our biological husbands marry younger women and father new babies. Although not new men, many of our former husbands are now new fathers, apparently having learned how to breathe through their mouths while bending over to change a dirty diaper—one of the many physical feats they were previously unable to master.

Nowadays our first husbands can occasionally be sighted walking the streets with their bad backs and new babies (who look vaguely familiar peering out of their Snuglis), apparently sharing child-care responsibilities with an enthusiasm that threatens to unhinge us. Having experienced little distress or drudgery during the raising of their first families, our biological husbands still have sufficient energy to start a new life and a new family, raising babies who are often younger than their own nieces and nephews, whose worn-out, yellow-stained hand-me-downs they must wear because many of their half-brothers and sisters are still in expensive graduate schools around the country. The new women, who married our old husbands, are apparently teaching them new tricks about co-parenting while we, who thought it was all over, continue coping with our erstwhile adult children who have come home to roost once again.

Of course some of these new women, who are now the new wives of our old husbands, do not necessarily understand everything our men expect or want from them. Everyone knows that George called up Colleen to request that she give his new wife acting lessons so she'd perform better in the films in which he wanted to direct and star her. And lots of people heard that Valerie had to rush over to help her old husband and his new wife when they brought home their new twins from the hospital. Fortunately, so far, none of us has either volunteered or consented to babysit with these infant half-siblings of our grown-up children so that the new parents can get away alone for a weekend. But that, too, may come to pass.

Marilyn did have the supreme pleasure of hearing, via the grapevine, that when her biological husband and his third wife, Sherri, moved to Chicago, the young bride began looking for an editorial job. Many of the editors she approached had known Marilyn professionally for many years and, noticing the young woman's unusual last name, asked if she was related to Marilyn. Desperate for work, Sherri finally said she was Marilyn's first cousin and, on the basis of that, eventually landed a job at the *Encyclopaedia Britannica* where Marilyn had started her career thirty years earlier.

So it is not as if our generation were either ignorant or naïve about younger women.

"You mean it wouldn't bother you if your husband of twenty years fell in love with a young student?" I ask, genuinely interested in Miranda's point of view.

"Yes, I'd care. But not enough to break up my marriage over it."

We all hear the reasonableness in her voice, but we are not privy to such self-control or in possession of the kind of self-determination that would permit such an enlightened reaction. To be perfectly honest, we have a real *thing* about original wives being replaced by younger new ones. We have heard far too many horror stories about longtime husbands running off with outrageously younger women.

When our friend Maxine's husband, a Miami rabbi, ran off with the young woman who was president of Hadassah at his synagogue and Maxine called Fritzie to tell her what had happened, she referred to her husband's paramour as "the shiksa." We all understood this was a generic rather than a genetic description, and we now use the term "young shiksa" indiscriminately when referring to *any* Other Woman—even if she happens to be older than the original wife and an Orthodox Jew to boot.

Judy (who didn't marry until she was thirty-seven when she fell head over heels in love with Michael O'Leary, the writer-in-residence at BU where she taught) had been married only two years when Mike ran off with his previous wife's youngest daughter—a girl named Ginger—who came to stay with Judy and Mike while visiting colleges in the Boston area. Since Mike had only done the right "extended formerly-blended family" thing by accommodating his previous wife and allowing Ginger—who had been his step-daughter for three years, five years earlier—to stay in his new home with his new wife, no one knew whom to blame. At least Ginger's mother had the decency to call Judy to apologize profusely and even suggested that if they worked together, they might successfully uncouple that unnatural couple—a suggestion that Judy politely declined despite the distraught mother's hysteria about her daughter not going to college.

"See, I saw Sukie differently than she saw herself," Miranda continues. "And I think that's what caused some of our problems." Her eyes are becoming a bit frantic now, darting from one to the other of us. "I guess I saw her as some kind of wonder woman who could do anything and handle everything. But instead, when she found out Max was screwing around, she freaked out. I've thought about it a lot since then. It was awful to watch a real nice family like that break up. But it didn't have to end that way. I mean, Sukie really went off the deep end with all her drinking and pills. She blew it.

"See, I've known Elizabeth Morley for years, so I knew how she operated. Her ambition was awesome and she wanted to get her doctorate more than anything else in the world. Oh, she really liked Max. In the beginning she was crazy for him and she knew he could help her a lot. But, when she finally got her degree this June and didn't need him anymore, she accepted a teaching job out at Berkeley. Max thought she took the job because it was so prestigious. But I know Elizabeth prefers operating alone in the academic world because there she gets a lot of mileage from being both good-looking and single. So when she didn't need Max anymore, she just split."

I am stunned.

Max is no longer with Elizabeth. The lovers are no longer together. I am still enough of a romantic to feel a slight twinge of disappointment. I suppose I want—at least—to believe in the permanence of those outrageously illicit liaisons that cause such catastrophic consequences. I suppose I want—at least—to believe in the authenticity and immutability of those perversely powerful passions that destabilize so many lives. If those don't last, what can or will?

Elaine and Joanne are also distressed by the news, although in different ways.

"Well, why couldn't Max see through Elizabeth?" Elaine asks.

Miranda looks at her with poorly concealed impatience. "Because he didn't want to, obviously."

That took care of that.

"You know, not every conniving woman gets her way," Joanne adds with convincing sophistication. "Lots of women want lots of things from lots of men that they don't get."

"I'm not saying Elizabeth didn't love Max. She did in the beginning. But she was just starting her career and I don't think she wanted to be bothered with a husband. She certainly wasn't going to stay here in Washington and I'm not sure Max could have moved to California and gotten himself a job comparable to his one here. Anyway, that's not important. I'm just saying that Sukie acted dumb. Well, maybe not dumb, but she sure didn't play her cards smart. She was holding a lot more power than she showed. She just didn't respond in as smart a way as she could have."

But then none of us was ever very smart in that way. We seldom mixed business with pleasure because we took both of them too seriously. We never tried to translate people into advantages. We were not "users" or "takers"; upon rare occasions we "chipped" just a little. That's why so few of us have decent incomes nowadays. We didn't make use of our connections when we had them. Since so many of us mismanaged our careers, the majority of our generation now remains mired in midlife money crises—doing a little free-lancing and invariably getting refunds when we file our Schedule Cs.

Although some of us persisted and pushed our way through to stable situations, most of us remain paralegals or associates (not partners) in respectable law firms, teachers without tenure (underpaid university adjuncts with unfinished doctoral dissertations), standup comediennes (without cafés or late-night talk shows), freelancers (without staff perks such as medical plans, stamp machines, stationery, WATS lines, or unemployment protection), mid-list authors (whose royalties never earn back their modest advances), and part-time professionals (without any hope of advancement.)

"I always used to watch Sukie and her girlfriends, you know—her Washington girlfriends like Kate Constant and Marlene Bennett—standing around in her front yard looking at her azalea bushes. And to me, from where I was across the street, they all looked so foxy and smart, I was jealous. And they all liked each other so much; that always got to me. And sometimes they had some of their daughters with them and you could hardly tell them apart because they were as pretty and young-looking and happy as their daughters were. At least that's the way it looked *from across the street,* if you know what I mean. Sukie was really different from my mother or my friends' mothers. Anyway, whether that was a plus or a minus for Carol, I don't know, but that's what I used to see.

"So the thing I couldn't understand was why Sukie got so scared when Max moved out," Miranda continues thoughtfully. "Carol told me Sukie was terrified of being alone and that she freaked out when no one was home with her. But I just couldn't believe that; Sukie was the strongest woman I'd ever met."

A glassy lake of silence forms, ruffled only by unspoken words.

Hot flash . . .

Depression Era Babies have always been fearful. Since our earliest days, we suffered from a wide range of symptoms. Some of us get wild anxiety attacks or night frights (Dierdre calls hers nightterrors). A lot of us get migraines and some of us can't swallow or stand up too quickly. We hyperventilate, harbor vague fevers and have constant bladder or yeast infections. Sukie had a phobia about high-speed highways, plus insomnia. Shirley suffers from eczema, Julie from asthma, Renée from psoriasis, Nora from heartburn and Carla from a bouquet of allergies. Charleen is plagued by middle-age acne and Brenda finally caught her roommate Mindy's vaginitis by sleeping with Mindy's steady after they broke up. Many of us have what doctors diagnose as psychosomatic neck, leg, lower back and heart aches.

We also have a panoply of phobias. Sharon can't drive across bridges. Once when she was down in the Keys near Marathon, Florida, where Radio Marti originates, she was listening to an American propaganda program, of which she could only catch the word *Communismo* growled in Spanish through the nasal passage of some Cuban fanatic, when she suddenly saw an unused railroad bridge, parallel to the causeway, that had actually been severed in the center to prevent its use by dragracers. At the sight of this, Sharon promptly fainted in the front seat. Luckily, Chuck was driving. All her life, Sharon has dreamed of bridges with their centers missing and when she finally saw one, it proved to be too much for her.

Judith also hates high-speed highways and accidentally knocked over and smashed her TV while rushing to turn off coverage of a stock-car race. Arleen is not crazy about escalators. She once had to flatten out on her stomach when we took the Dupont Circle Metro station "down" escalator, which is one of the steepest in the world. Most of the time now, Arleen rides the elevator reserved for handicapped people where she has struck up several serious friendships. Eleanor fears that the brakes in any car she drives will fail and that she will also. Helen is afraid of fractions, decimals, sets, stats and mathematical word problems.

Margaret is terrified of mushrooms. She cannot walk near the vegetable section of a supermarket. When she enters someone's home, she sits around worrying that she might accidentally see a mushroom and is often so anxious she actually has to ask her hostess if there are any mushrooms in the crisper of her refrigerator. She will not take a walk in the country or go to a museum where there might be a still-life painting of vegetables. Louise once pointed out to Margaret what, besides A-bomb explosions, most resemble mushrooms. But Margaret is not interested in discussing circumcised penises. For her, a mushroom is a mushroom.

Our California contingent remains terrified of earthquakes and continues to devise various methods of detecting tremors. Amy, who is one of our better younger writers, unconsciously uses earthquake metaphors in her short stories and habitually kept a glass of water beside her San Francisco bed to watch for surface ripples produced by early tremors. Ellen, of course, added insult to injury by having some of her characters atop

the Golden Gate Bridge *during* an earthquake. Even
Sukie thought that was going too far.

While we no longer have any fear of flying, a number
of us now harbor a horror of high-speed highways. Sukie
had begun monitoring fatal truck accidents on the Belt-
way that pinches the waist of Washington, D.C. Also
known as I-495, this six-lane highway features huge
semis that barrel along at eighty miles an hour, shaking
Sukie's little VW with vibrations as she scurried out to
Bloomies in the White Flint Mall.

Sukie also oversaw I-66, a speedy highway that
whizzes out of Washington into Virginia with special
HOV (high-occupancy vehicle) lanes established in an
effort to increase car-pooling. Since cars with fewer
than four occupants are required to use the inside
lane, some commuters bought store-window man-
nequins that they dressed appropriately and propped
up in their backseats to fool police into thinking they
qualified as HOVs. Sukie was deeply involved with the
ethics, practicality, and safety records of various HOV
systems.

I have thought about all this. It strikes me that we
used to have a fear of flying because we didn't like
relinquishing control over our destinies to jaunty,
craggy-faced pilots and slim-hipped, swaggering flight
engineers. Now that we're older and no longer resent
take-charge people, what we really fear is being in control. Responsible. A car hurtling along a high-speed
highway is the perfect objective correlative for this current concern of ours.

Sukie was afraid of the fast lane. She was also afraid
of highway exits, truck vibrations, rainstorms, mini-
mum speed limits, overly friendly teamsters staying
abreast with lady drivers in order to see one, mud spray
from passing cars, broken windshield wipers, blow-outs,
the different tempos at which different drivers pulled
onto the highway and ambiguous road signs.

Invariably every summer when we were at the beach, Sukie would ask me what she was supposed to do if she saw a sign saying Falling Rocks. Proceed? Abandon the car? Cover her head? Or if she saw a sign that said Bridges Freeze Before Roads? What did that mean? What was required? At this point in our lives, we have very little tolerance for ambiguities. Ambiguity is a one-lane one-way road leading to high anxiety.

Our fears have multiplied with our years. Many of us now dread charcoal lighter fluid, dead batteries, gas stoves, emergency landings, lead paint, soccer games, air pockets, contact sports, O-rings, falling air conditioners, unsafe sex, soft shoulders, pilot lights, white water, stampedes, off-season shellfish, liver spots and other up-to-date horrors. We see danger everywhere we look. We know what it is to feel constantly imperiled in a mortally dangerous universe.

The sound of the doorbell rattles me back into reality.

"Jesus," I groan, shaking my head as I get up.

This time it is Max standing outside, still damp from a shower, and wearing Levi's with a Polo T-shirt.

"Here's . . . the mail," he says, passing me a handful of letters.

I nod and turn to put them in an oblong basket Sukie kept on the tall thin radiator in her foyer. The basket is already stuffed. Apparently someone brought in yesterday's mail because I can see a number of unopened envelopes and a Fall Forecast flier from Woodies. The cover shows a suit that Sukie might actually have liked quite a bit. We know each other's tastes in clothing just as we know each other's shoe sizes, favorite candies and other weaknesses. We also know that we are all subject to flare-ups of fall fashion fever because, since childhood, we have measured time by academic, rather than calendar, years.

The crowd of mail in Sukie's basket makes me feel as if she is only out of town for the weekend and will return to deal with her unfinished business after the holiday. I can see bills through the sporty little windows of their envelopes and also one letter addressed to Mr. Max Amram. Not so long ago, Sukie had complained to me about how much time she wasted forwarding mail.

Nowadays we all spend more time looking up and writing down forwarding addresses on incoming mail than ever before in our lives. We still receive letters for ex-husbands, bills for former lovers and postcards for kids who have flown the coop or left the nest—depending upon the nature of their exit. Those of us who increased our incomes by renting out bedrooms in our empty nests during tight times still provide daily mail services for former boarders. Once in a while we'll even get a letter from some long-lost lover who suddenly wants to get together for a weekend in Atlantic City "ASAP." Sukie told me she once received such an invitation along with a SASE apparently addressed to some safe-house or business address.

I straighten out today's mail, along with the other letters, and then, feeling slightly dizzy, lead Max back into the kitchen. Since he is behind me, I feel rather than view his shock at seeing Miranda. Miranda is visibly upset by Max's arrival, but she regains enough composure to say hello as he hurries to the counter to fix himself a drink.

"So?" Elaine prods Max. "What's been decided?"

Max leans back against Sukie's little desk and takes several long swallows of his Scotch.

"The service is going to be Monday at three o'clock in Brownell's nondenominational chapel. I looked at it and . . . it seemed okay."

"Do you think Sukie's dad or the kids will mind it not being in a synagogue?" I ask.

"I don't think so. Sukie's dad is sort of a cultural, rather than a religious, Jew. And I think David and Carol will like this chapel a lot. Some staff person over there, an arranger or something, suggested we have an open-forum kind of service where any friends who want to speak just come forward. I thought that sounded pretty right for Sukie. What do you think?"

We nod. So relieved are we not to be responsible for the arrangements that almost anything Max planned, short of a circus, would sound fine.

"Then I bought one of the last three burial plots in the Rock Creek Cemetery. I haven't gone over there yet to look, but I saw a . . . picture, believe it or not." His eyes are glassy and he doesn't seem to be totally in touch with what he is saying. "It was expensive, but I'm sure Sukie's dad will take care of that. Oh. The lady at Brownell's said she told one of you about bringing . . . some clothes over there?"

We nod tensely.

"Did you find out about a . . . coffin?" Joanne asks.

"I took the one they suggested. The one they said was 'appropriate.' "

And with that, Max psychologically tunes out on funeral arrangements and turns toward Miranda.

"So," he says in a baiting voice. "I thought you were out at the Bay. In fact, I sort of thought Elizabeth might have gone out there to visit you before she went to California."

We all look at him. A shudder passes between us like a basketball during a pregame warmup.

Miranda loses the color in her face, and her longish front teeth suddenly begin ploughing into her bottom lip as she responds.

"I assure you she didn't visit *me.*"

Max shrugs, clearly stung by Miranda's show of solidarity with us.

"Well," Miranda says with false matter-of-factness, "I guess I'd better get going." Gripping her purse with white-knuckled hands, she nods goodbye to each of us, casting only a quick glance at Max. "I would like to

come back tomorrow if that's all right," she asks, looking toward me for approval.

I smile faintly and nod.

"I'll let myself out," she says quietly.

And then she too is gone.

CHAPTER 9

"So, what've you been doing here all day?" Max asks uneasily in the silence that coalesces after Miranda's departure.

"Not much," Elaine says. "Trying to get ourselves ready to start looking through some of Sukie's things, her papers and stuff."

"Have you come across her manuscript yet?" Max has his back to us as he pours himself a second drink. "David said she had a big hunk finished."

Joanne flashes me a cautionary glance, but during the second in which our eyes link and lock, Elaine invades our silence.

"A friend of hers who's editing it has it over at his place."

Knowing Max, I flinch in anticipation of his reaction to what he will erroneously consider an infringement of his rights as well as an abridgement of his authority.

"Oh Christ," he swears, shoving the scotch bottle back against the splash tiles. "What friend? Who?"

"It's just . . . a young friend of hers," Elaine answers nervously. "I don't remember . . . the last name."

"God damn it!" Max returns to the table and slams down his glass. "You let her last piece of fiction walk out of this house the day after she dies? I don't fucking believe it. You crazy or what?"

"Hey, Max," I say gently. "He *had* it. *We* didn't give

it to him, Sukie did. And if he hadn't told us about it, nobody would have known where it was."

"Well, who is he? Is it that lover of hers? That wacko Vietnam vet?"

Now we form a stony wall of silence. We are not ready to accept indignation from Max on any score.

"What the hell's his name anyway?"

"Hey, cool it, Max," I counsel, standing up to enhance my authority.

So he sits down again and tries to regain his self-control. Lighting a cigarette, he samples his drink. But he is clearly seething with anger.

"Look," he says more calmly. "It's not right. A million different things can happen to a manuscript under these circumstances. Just for openers, it can maybe get lost. Also, it can maybe get mangled by some phony editor or get published under someone else's name. Right? So I think we should go pick it up from what's-his-face." He turns inward for a moment, delving for a sound. "Jeff," he exults. "Jeff Conroy. Do you know where I can find his number?"

Silence.

But Max has been waiting for us to give him a hard time, so he's ready. "Well, let's just take a look in Sukie's little black address book."

And without a pause, he reaches out for the khaki shoulderbag that has sat in the center of the kitchen table since Mary Murphy deposited it there Friday morning.

Both Elaine and Joanne cringe.

It is a matter of protocol. The question is whether or not it is right to ransack a dead woman's purse. The question is whether or not The Enemy should be allowed behind allied lines. Although Max obviously knows Sukie's purse from a previous life, when it was in some sense community property, the question is whether or not he abnegated his access to Sukie's belongings when he aborted their marriage.

Instinctively, Elaine had made a move to stop Max at the very first moment, but then had stopped herself instead. So we all end up watching Max open Sukie's purse. He removes a see-through makeup kit, a crowded wallet, and then the soft, supple, black address book that Sukie had carried around the world. The little leather book is clearly tired; the corners are curled, the covers bent, and most of the black alphabet tabs missing.

"What do you want, Max?" I suddenly explode.

It is perfectly clear Max is worried that Sukie's new novel might be about him. *Heartburn* has frightened half the husbands in Washington. *Talk about endangered manuscripts.*

"What's *your* problem, Diana?" Max replies while his fingers continue rippling the pages of the address book. "I want to find this guy Jeff and get the manuscript back because it belongs to my kids. It's as simple as that. Okay? Anyway, here it is," he announces, somewhat appeased. "Jeff Conroy. Oh shit. There's no phone number, just an address. Well, I'm going over there—3203 M Street. Who the hell can live on M Street? It's all discos and bars." He begins to slip the address book into the breast pocket of his shirt.

"Uh-uh," I say. "Put it back in her purse, Max."

He does.

"And I want to come with you. Give me five minutes to get dressed."

At first he looks as if he's going to say no, but then he sits back down at the table again, so I hurry upstairs.

In the second-floor bathroom, I strip and slip into the shower. Under the hot spikes of water I think about Jeff. I think about Miranda. I wonder what happened between Elizabeth and Max and I worry about getting Sukie's clothes to the funeral home. I think about women and men and wonder how Sukie would want us to treat Max. I wonder about Max.

Lowering my head, I let the water rush through my hair.

Hot water, like hot flashes, sometimes reminds me of hot emotions I once endured but no longer harbor. The long habit of passion—originally produced by an adolescent obsession with popularity—has finally atrophied and freed me. Emotional promiscuity—the end result of my teenage compulsion to be liked—has evaporated at last. Male desire and approval are less important to me now. Ditto for the approval of family, friends and academic colleagues. How I feel in the presence of a particular person has finally become more important than how that person feels about me.

Wrapped in a bath towel, I return to Sukie's bedroom and open her closet. The sundress I've worn for two days is no longer presentable. I leaf through her dresses until I see a crinkled cotton skirt and blouse that remind me of Southwestern American Indians. Sukie liked to wear that outfit with some of the turquoise silver jewelry she collected and I always thought she looked beautiful in it. Slipping it on, I kick back into my sandals, grab my makeup kit, and return to the bathroom.

There, facing myself in the medicine cabinet mirror, I am suddenly besieged by a parade of faces—faces from a thousand public bathrooms around the world where I saw women, emerging from toilet stalls behind me, suddenly see themselves in an unfamiliar mirror and recoil with regret at their appearance. Instantly rejecting their own faces, they would begin to approach and reproach their reflections, furiously taking up arms against themselves with cosmetics they sightlessly clawed from the depths of their purses as they advanced, half homicidally, upon their images in the mirror.

Saddened by my thoughts of all the wounded women I'd witnessed reject themselves, I begin my own reconstruction—applying base, blush-on, eyeliner, under-eye eraser, mascara, pale lipstick—the works. No two mirrors have ever returned my same self to me. Some are kind and others severe. Sukie's mirror makes my face—in which my original beauty is buried, out of reach but not forgotten—seem soft and blurred. That's not bad, but a woman requires some image stability.

Last summer at the beach, after a few glasses of wine, Sukie and I had stationed ourselves before a mirror and, like little girls, created new faces by pulling back the skin near our eyes to test the effects of a future facelift. Ultimately we decided we looked like fifty-year-old Oriental women trying to look like young Occidentals, so we quit. But the very next day we went shopping for new frames for our reading glasses. We tried on an endless number, hunting for forms and shapes that would cover the lines radiating out like wings from our eyes. Eventually we each bought a new pair of frames that we didn't need and considered it a savings since it postponed possible surgery.

But now, finally, I am compelled to ask myself if I am making up in order to make up to Max. And if this is so, why I am doing it. I do not understand why I must still attempt to make such enormous changes at the last minute. Obviously, I am prepping myself to see what Max will see when he sees me. I have already tested the depth and range of my laugh lines by smiling at myself in the mirror and then watching the smile hang crepe around my eyes. Why, despite all my new-found independence, must I still seek to look good for a man toward whom I feel a considerable amount of disapproval? This man—for whom I am primping—wounded, perhaps mortally, my dead friend, yet I cannot stop wanting to look good to him.

It is at this moment I begin to hear yelling.

The voices carry over all the various room air conditioners, up the stairs, and into Sukie's bathroom in the rear of the house.

Elaine and Max are going at each other.

By the time I reach the kitchen they are positioned

diagonally across from each other as if in a boxing ring.
Elaine has her back to the stove and Max is leaning
against the door. Joanne is sitting, upset but silent, at
the table. Only Happy is in motion, tearing back and
forth between the two antagonists.

"Don't give me that long-suffering shit, Max," Elaine
warns. "Everyone knows what happened here and
what it did to Sukie."

"Oh, come off it, Elaine."

"You fragged her before you deserted," Elaine hisses.

"You're crazy, Elaine," Max groans. "You've gone off
the deep end. Just like Sukie did, for Christ's sake. After
all your talk about independence and autonomy and
equal time and all that shit, as soon as you arrange to get
left alone, you all freak out. What the hell's the matter
with you, anyway? You've turned into a crazy lady since
Nathaniel got remarried. What happened to all your
political commitments, Elaine?"

Their political enmity is ancient. Elaine always out-
flanked Max on the left. During the sixties, she was
constantly daring him to organize bolder antiwar actions and demanding more militancy from him and his
male comrades.

"Oh, gimme a break," Elaine moans, lifting her hands
in supplication. "You're a lightweight, Max. All you ever
did was chase little bimbos around. You're a phony."

"Oh Jesus, Elaine. We're here to . . . bury Sukie. She's
dead. She *died*. Can't you *ever* let up?"

"You're more than a little responsible for her dying,"
Elaine charges. "You'd been killing her for years. As
soon as you started making it, you dumped all the shitwork from your life on her so she had to run the house
and raise the kids and free-lance to earn some extra
money and she couldn't write fiction anymore. And you
didn't give a damn because she was just a woman. She
was just your wife. And then you took a powder when
you found a replacement and just left her to have a
breakdown all alone."

Max moves to the middle of the room and takes a deep breath before he speaks.

"Elaine, I did everything I could to help Sukie. But Sukie was a self-destructive woman with absolutely no self-awareness. I am not going to take the rap for either her life or her death. Do you understand me?"

"You fragged her from the rear," Elaine repeats wildly.

We have all experienced that feeling of flailing, objectless anger, of unfocused rage which won't let us articulate our most fundamental beliefs. But it is Elaine's style to plunge ahead, rather than retreat, even if words fail her.

"All those years she had no support system, no network, no nothing to help her survive. All during the sixties, it was every woman for herself and every woman against each other. Sukie spent so many years trying to patch the pieces of her life together, she never got the chance to accomplish what she really wanted to do."

"Shit. She just drank too much," Max rants irrationally.

"Sukie didn't start drinking too much until five years ago," I say with great authority, since it's the first time I've spoken.

"She always took those damn uppers. Sukie loved speeding. Face it. She was a speed freak and speed kills. That's what probably killed her. That's what probably caused the hemorrhage."

"You just got scared, Max," Elaine continues as if she's heard nothing Max has said. "You got scared because you'd crumped out of any real commitments. You were afraid because you couldn't provide enough excitement for her anymore, enough action. You were slowing down and you got scared you couldn't cut the mustard."

"You're so full of shit, Elaine. You make me sick." Then Max whirls around to face me. "I'm going over to find that stud of hers—who, by the way, is just one in a long line of studs of hers—so if you want to come, I'm leaving right now."

I look at Elaine for a moment, but then turn and follow Max out of the house and down the block to where he's parked a new Nissan Sentra. The heat is still hovering low over the city and there is a lot of traffic. Our ride to Georgetown takes a long time and I have several hot flashes on the way.

Hot flashes during a heat wave—back to back, one on one, white on white. It is a thermal redundancy. I am stoking up. Sukie's cotton blouse sticks to the leather seatback. The bottom of her skirt is glued to my thighs. I am thoroughly overheated. Although I don't remember much college chemistry, I think there is a flashpoint of evaporation. I believe my hot flashes are now approaching that temperature and that I am in danger of disappearing into a wet sweat. I can no longer tell when one flash ends and another begins.

We are temporarily gridlocked at 23rd and M streets, waiting to turn right into Georgetown, when Max finally speaks.

"Listen, I'm sorry about that scene back there. I know it sucked. But Elaine can be so goddamn overbearing and self-righteous. She gets herself all revved up and then she's all over the map. Personally, I don't know how Nat took it for so many years."

"She's a wonderful woman, Max. She's been a better . . ." I take a deep breath. "She stuck with Sukie when Sukie needed her the most. She was a better friend to Sukie than I was."

Max is staring straight ahead into the traffic. "Well, she's really got a hair up her ass about men and I can't stand that kind of talk. If that's the end result of the women's movement, it's a fucking shame."

"I don't need a lecture on *that,* Max."

Thoroughly sickened by the meanness Max displayed in the kitchen, I feel no need to appease him now by apologizing for Elaine. Instead, I wrap myself in silence.

Trapped in traffic, I realize my hot flashes often produce early-warning rushes of impatience, the same kind of irritability I feel when I'm trying to make a green light and the car in front of me dawdles taking a right-hand turn. A sharp-nailed, edgy anger scratches its way up my nervous system. My still-damp hair, rubbing against my shoulders, annoys me and angrily I push the wet ends away from my face. I cannot tolerate any intrusions or incursions upon my *self* during the spell of a hot flash.

"How are Loren and Lisa doing?" Max asks.

"They're good. They're both at Yale; they love it."

"Are they . . . coming to the funeral?"

"I'm not sure." My voice falters and my heart flutters. "We'll probably talk tomorrow so I can tell them when it is. Their classes start Tuesday morning and they're out on Long Island . . ."

I stop.

I will not allow myself to *expect* anything from my daughters any more than I allow myself to expect anything from any man. Nor will I allow anyone, other than Lisa and Loren, to expect anything from me. I've eliminated all expectations from my life. I haven't stopped living, I've only stopped expecting. I no longer want to be exposed to disappointment. I no longer want to be at risk. By eliminating expectations, I reduce those possible occasions for unhappiness to less than zero.

Still, Sukie's death has made me somewhat vulnerable. It has made me regress into wanting my daughters. It has unraveled the delicate sweater of indifference that I knitted for myself to wear and temporarily caused me to backslide into wanting some demonstration of love or loyalty from Loren and Lisa. I must admit, I would feel richly confirmed if my girls went through the major exertion of coming to Washington from Long Island on their way to New Haven in the course of a single day.

Now we are hunching along like an inchworm, looking for a parking space in Georgetown. Signs proclaim a new Saturday-night parking ban on Wisconsin Avenue, so lines of cars, like beetles, cruise through the side streets, circling the same blocks again and again. Finally Max leaves the residential area and drives down toward the river where there is a huge parking lot. Couples are emerging from the river flat to hurry up the long hill to the M Street strip of bars.

The sidewalks are congested and I can hear expectation beating its drum as we join the people parading up the hill. We are easily twenty years older than everyone else. These are young straights, gays, yuppies and college kids out for a night on the town. They are wired for fun, laughing and talking as they ooze across the sidewalk, forcing some of their group to limp along in the gutter.

3203 M Street is a doorway between two discos. It is, of course, locked. There is no bell, no mailbox, no security system, just a paint-smeared steel door. Max knocks for a long while and then resorts to kicking at the door with suppressed frustration. Finally he steps back and looks around. To the left of the entranceway is a disco called Peppermill. Max looks at me, shrugs, and then motions me to follow him inside.

The bar is a long, narrow space divided in two by a mirrored wall. On one side is a crowd of people milling around and on the other a few tables and a small dance floor fenced in by spectators. Max has seen enough movies to know what to do.

He approaches the bartender, orders us a couple of beers, and then parks his elbow on the bar like a nineteenth-century pioneer pausing on the western ledge of the United States so as not to plunge into the Pacific. When two barstools are vacated, he nods at me to take one. After a while, he too sits down and motions the bartender over.

Then he tells him he's looking for Jeff Conroy.

The gray-bearded bartender does not respond. Instead, he takes several swipes at a puddle of spilled beer. This man is clearly a former hippie and grossly offended by Max's self-conscious movieland performance.

I, of course, like this guy immediately and when he turns to look at me it's with an understanding based on our shared embarrassment over Max's macho manner. Our eye contact is a complicated hangover from the sixties, when we believed it possible to perceive people's characters visually. People who still practice that look trust each other. It's like the "high five" blacks use. It's part of our sixties code. Despite the gauze of age over my face, I know this man can see through it to who I am. Even if it's been a while, he knows I've been around the track a few times with the right team.

"Someone Jeff knows died," I say. "She was my friend."

He believes me.

"Jeff usually comes in here real late Saturday nights. This is pretty early for him. But if you want to hang around, I'll tell him you're here if he shows."

Max has missed most of this. The men of our generation resisted instinct and intuition. What Max knows is how to perform—walk into a bar, order, pay and exit. He has perfected his public style and handles all practicalities with liquid ease. He's learned how to seem superior to his actions, like a rich man who consents to abide by conventions only because he *chooses* to do so. Max remains above the fray while mining its resources. He doesn't contribute; he simply absorbs. So when it comes to one-on-one, Max often washes out because he doesn't let instinct inform his actions.

When we walk around to the other side of the mirrored wall, everything is in motion. Max captures a tiny table for us and we sit down. The air is vibrating with heavy rock music. The floor ripples from feet beating like drumsticks to the music. The dancers throb. They lead with their elbows. Their arms are pumping as if they are trying to fly. Their bodies speak style to each other long distance.

Nowadays dancers try harder. They have to be given credit. We used to let the music carry us. The kids here are churning up movement; they have to reach down deep to get it. Partners are not in sync, but they are still producing a lot of body heat, working hard to make their body motions emotional. They look highly stylized even though dancing is no longer a contact sport.

I glance at Max. He is not immune to this music. Rock is referential. We both know what it means. Memories of passion are as persuasive as any expectations of it. It is simply that we no longer feel compelled to play it out. We've done that; there aren't all that many riffs or variations.

The set ends. No one in the band has shaved in the last four days. They are all whiskered and whiskeyed up. They look weary and wicked, a look I like a lot. The guitarist has a special sweetness in his bleary eyes and I like the way he watches the women dancing. He likes girls; I like him.

"So what happened to you and Elizabeth?" I ask Max, hoping to catch him off guard.

He watches my mouth as I speak. The music has stopped, but the noise hasn't totally subsided. Couples are leaving the floor, walking past our table with the empty expressions of dancers no longer tapping the source. They seem embarrassed without the music, shy and awkward after the urgency is over. They resemble dazed moviegoers coming out of a theater feeling displaced and distant, denying the questioning eyes of those waiting in line to enter.

"She left Washington."

"When?"

What I want to know is if Sukie knew, if she found some solace from their split before she died.

"I don't know," Max shrugs. "Four, five weeks ago. What's the difference? She took a teaching job out at Berkeley."

He's been hurt. Bad.

"Is that why you took the kids to Europe?"

"Hey, gimme a break, would ya? We had this trip planned since last summer."

"Sorry."

Then we stare at each other through the smoky blue atmosphere. It is like looking into a mirror. We know each other too well. Our histories are parallel. Professionally we are on the same track. Personally we have suffered the same histories. Max, too, is a Depression Baby who lived through an explosion of suppressed sensuality, a premature marriage, extramarital flirtations, dangerous infidelities and a damaging divorce. He's been around the track a couple of times, too.

"You were together four, five years?"

"Yah. But she's young. She's just twenty-six. She wasn't sure about things, about what she wanted." He lights a cigarette to change the subject. "So how about you? What are your headlines? Happy to be single again?"

I nod.

"How's Leonard doing?"

"Haven't you talked to him?"

"Yah, once in a while."

"You never called me."

"Hey! You're Sukie's best friend. Why would I call you?"

"I thought *we* were friends too."

He gives me a powerful reprimanding look that insists we were always something more dangerous than friends. I'm flattered, so I let him have that point.

"Why'd you dump Leonard, Diana?"

I only pause for a moment. When I answer it's with something I've never said before.

"Because I couldn't bear lying *underneath* him anymore in bed."

"What the hell does that mean?"

Max looks both insulted and angry, but then he sights a waitress and signals her over to our table. When she arrives, I order another beer and Max asks for a double Scotch.

"I had too many equity struggles with Leonard to let him lie on top of me in bed at night anymore."

Max decides to turn it into a joke.

"There *are* other options, you know. Other positions. After a couple of decades it's probably time to try Number Two. You should have climbed on top. Nowadays all the girls want to be on top."

I ignore his humor since he's inadvertently offered me an insight.

"Leonard always had to top me. He had to best me and beat me. Whatever he did had to be more important than what I did. I traveled around the world with him on his business trips, but he would never *once* go on a field trip with me. And, of course, he'd never let me go alone. When the kids were little, he refused to take over the responsibilities so I could get back to Brazil. And every year after that he found some other reason why I couldn't go. Jesus, Max, I couldn't *proceed* with my life. I couldn't *progress*. But he *always* made me go with him to Europe for business or down to the islands for vacations. We must have gone to a million resorts."

Max shakes his head. "What the hell are you complaining about? You went first-class with Leonard, is that what you're saying? What's wrong with first class, for Christ's sake?"

The girl brings our drinks.

I just couldn't do it anymore.

I could no longer gaze across a wide beach boulevard, hemmed with haughty palm trees, at a handsome horizon above some turquoise ocean from a hotel terrace surrounded by frangipani, where we were served a sweet breakfast of mangoes or papaya while we watched some "lucky" native clean the hotel pool by slowly sweeping the surface of the aqua water with a rake as gently as a mother skimming the skin off a cup of hot cocoa for a finicky child. I could no longer drink glasses of fresh fruit juice or deep cups of fragrant native coffee beneath a green tree with chartreuse flowers and cerulean blue butterflies while some skeletal young boy hurried to set up chairs and chaises for the hotel guests before the sun began to heat up the day.

I could no longer swim in pools where rats had died during the night from drinking the chlorinated water and floated on the surface in the dawn's early light when I first opened the thickly lined drapes of our room to inspect the landscape and weather. I could no longer carry a loaded, but unused, camera over my shoulder to shoot scenes of harrowing inhumanity, or mail frivolous postcards from central post offices in enormous, under-developed capitals where handsome teenaged boys pushed broken wheelbarrows full of debris along the major boulevard from one place to another for no explicable reason. I could no longer go where it was unsafe to drink the water and where it cost too much—in human terms—to get high in the capital of a country whose primary export was dope.

What remained of my soul was no longer strong enough to support such enormous contradictions.

"Oh, I don't know, Max. Maybe our marriage ended from the slow burn. The slow burnout. Maybe it just died the same slow death any marriage does. Twenty years of misunderstandings. All I knew was that I didn't want to watch television with Leonard anymore. He defied my sense of myself. He denied me and I couldn't hack it."

"Did the sex go?"

"Yah. It was a case of mistaken identities. The guy I was fighting with every day turned out to be the same guy I was supposed to ball at night. That wasn't too terrific. It's hard to make it with someone who makes you crazy every minute you're *not* in bed making it. I mean, after enough time, a simple screw can get pretty complicated. Screwing just lets you have your fights in sign language."

"You're too clever by half, Diana. You always were," Max complains, finishing his Scotch.

"You know, there ought to be a word for twenty years of monogamous sex."

"Long term monogamy is as close as you can get to masturbation while still keeping up appearances," he laughs.

"Jeez. Two decades of sex with the same partner. Actually, there ought to be a medal for people who make it."

"Right. And an awards dinner at the White House so the Reagans could eat alone."

We both laugh, but then I feel heat flood the area below my neck that is always exposed by a V-necked blouse. Immediately, I am distracted by that launch pad, that Kennedy Space Center for hot flashes. Using my lower lip as a funnel, I blow my breath up onto my face as the heat mounts and look away to scan the room while my skin shrivels from the slow burning sensation.

Most of the tables around us are filled with groups of girlfriends rather than couples. The young women have good haircuts, blunt cuts that count—and cost—a lot. This summer they're wearing sleeveless cotton sweaters and straight, rather longish, skirts. They are far less self-conscious than we were at their age and also less wired. They clearly don't make a habit of sleeping with strangers.

Lisa told me that young men no longer dare ask women for their telephone numbers at discos or bars. Instead, the men write down their own names and numbers on pieces of paper and offer them to the women they find most appealing. I glance over at the

stag line —a lot of guys who look like former marines—
hanging out together near the dance floor. The ambience hasn't changed all that much since high school
mixers in the 1950s. There seems to have been some
regression. Some fifties fairytales seem to have come
back into style.

Hot flash . . .

In that bridge of time between 1955 and 1965 when
we lost our innonence, sex meant adventure to us. Back
then, there was little chance of our getting onto the fast
track under our own steam. Finished with college, but
unable to find any political, financial, artistic or professional mountains to scale, we began searching for men
whose lives contained a little adventure. In this search,
we traveled tirelessly—anywhere and everywhere. We
begged, borrowed, or stole money to make those trips
to Europe, again and again, first by boat and then by
plane. We wanted to be anywhere but here.

We sought love in Paris, romance in Rome, drugs in
Katmandu, God in the Orient and sex in the South
Pacific. If we weren't in the air, we were on the ground
sitting in a bar close to the tarmac. During those years,
we treated affairs and adulteries as little adventures
leading up to serious experiences. But then somehow,
at some point, we became confused and began to feel
that our affairs *were* the experiences we'd been seeking.
Click. That mistake might have been one of our costliest
ones.

Our manhunts, which began as hobbies, became habits. Our sexual safaris ended up as ends rather than
means. Our games were our Big Game. The men we
met and made it with became our missions, our cru-
sades, our epic battles, our new horizons, our works of
art, our last frontiers, our Moby Dicks. To us, each attractive new man became a mountain to be climbed
just because he was there. We saw interesting strangers
as unexplored and uncharted lands waiting to be
mapped and mined. In our urgent search for Graham

Greene adventures—where the bloated atmosphere buoys up both the action and the settings—we often ended up in seedy hotels with shady characters seeking sordid scenes. But back then, mood and place and tone and style were everything. We wanted to replay *Key Largo* and *Casablanca* again and again.

During that decade we had a lot of sexual self-confidence so we had a million all-night one-night stands. Since we had once dreamed of being torch singers in dark jazz clubs, hat-check girls in racy nightclubs, or showgirls in Las Vegas, we'd been practicing our lines for many years. We always knew exactly what to say at any given moment. All the guys got a big kick out of us because we gave such good dialogue. *Yah.*

For us, men were environmental intensifiers, enhancers and enlargers of experience. Men meant magnitude to us which might explain our addictions. We loved it when they reappeared after their showers wearing only aftershave lotion and a towel twisted around their waists, leaving bare the expressive prairies of their handsome midriffs. We liked their smells, their smiles, their contradictions. We liked the way they could grow both beards and roses, the way they could make both love and money, the way they could carry responsibility or a six-pack with the same sweet nonchalance. We loved the language and luggage they used, the grins and sweaters they wore and the enormous pleasure they got from playing a pickup game of basketball or balling all night long.

Even when the fifties started turning into the sixties, fun still meant meeting some handsome stranger when we joined a group of friends in a crowded, croissant-curved booth at the back of a smoky cocktail lounge into which we slid as if into the arms of a waiting lover. And, often enough, there would be a man there waiting to meet us, some flirtatious type who would casually wrap his arm along the back of the booth, surrounding and claiming us without a touch, and making the less interesting people smudge into background, become bit players present only to offset our performance in a play that was always about the possibility of passion.

Max starts signaling the waitress for another round of drinks.

"Sukie had a pretty rough time, Max. Did you know that?"

"Did I know it? I was the object of it. She made it pretty tough on everyone else, too. Look," he sighs, "what's the point of beating around the bush? You want to hear my side of the story, right? So I'll tell you. But we don't have to go through the whole rap. We both know all about the social and political inequities between the sexes in our country. I was married to Sukie for a long time so I learned a lot *from* her as well as *about* her."

The waitress arrives with our drinks and Max lights us two cigarettes in the old 1940s movie mode.

"So let's skip all the generalities and just see what was distinctive about Sukie's and my situation. I know Sukie did ninety percent of the work raising the kids and that handicapped her career. I know she should maybe have lived in New York instead of Washington. I know she wasn't paid half of what I would have made doing the same things and that there aren't enough women in Congress, etcetera, etcetera. I know the whole schmeer. But, dammit, that was just the tip of the iceberg. Her *craziness* was the icing on top of all the rest of that."

Max lifts his glass and touches mine.

"To Sukie," he says.

I lower my eyes as I taste my drink.

"The thing was that I had *had* it. She was just too self-destructive for me to live with anymore. I was tired. Do you know the divorce rate in our age group? The number of couples who split up after twenty-five years? It's an epidemic, for Christ's sake. I don't know. Maybe there's such a thing as marital menopause."

"Bullshit," I say.

The band is starting to regroup. They amble in from whatever dark alley they used for coking themselves up. Baby ripples of anticipation begin to spread through the room.

"Jesus," Max says in disgust, taking a last, serious gulp of his Scotch. "Let's get out of here. They're going to blast our heads off."

I inspect his face. He has purposefully been keeping the conversation general, away from any particulars about Sukie and himself. He had tried to talk about American women, not Sukie, and that was okay with me for openers. He was entitled to act gentlemanly and protective of a woman he once loved who had just died. But it was clearly also a way of keeping the heat off himself.

Now enough was enough.

"Okay," I say, with great intentionality. "Let's go someplace where we can really talk."

He finishes his second drink, leaves a bill on the table, and leads me outside.

CHAPTER 10

It is almost eleven o'clock when we reach the parking lot down near the river. Max drives out of Georgetown along K Street to reach Dupont Circle.

Dupont Circle is the watch face on the wristband of Connecticut Avenue.

In the sixties, it was our launch site for the war against the war—the place where we mobilized before proceeding toward designated battlefields on the Mall. It was here that Sukie and I always cautiously removed our earrings because women we knew had suffered torn ears when riot police rioted and caused panic among the demonstrators. It was here we used the fountain in the center of the Circle to dampen the large handkerchiefs we carried to protect our eyes from tear gas and kept wrapped in tinfoil inside our pockets along with any prescription medicine we might need in jail if we got arrested.

Of course Max would live near the Circle. The Circle is an easy statement about one's social and political values. That's what Dupont Circle tells the real residents of Washington who ignore the "official" city. By tradition, the Circle is a free, independent territory—a retreat and sanctuary for marginal people—in the center of the city. It is like an Indian reservation for foreign students who gathered there to play their native music

near the marble fountain which, as years passed, was
more and more frequently left dry.

The summers of the sixties enveloped everyone. Dupont Circle blossomed with flower children who grew
brown from sleeping in the sunlight. Drug-blissed hippies washed themselves in the forbidden white fountain
while long-haired boys and girls roamed the avenues
that moved around the Circle like hands on a clock.

In the summer, when the Circle was green, young
mothers, still anointed by their sweet new maternity,
pushed buggies or strollers full of self-important first
babies along the paths. I remember walking in the Circle with Sukie and our collection of three toddlers one
eerily quiet Sunday following an enormous 1967 peace
demonstration. That afternoon we both felt profoundly
dramatized by the political actions of the previous day,
which had polished our commitment to a high sheen.
That, plus the sweet sense of immortality produced by
baby fists gripping our forefingers, exhilarated us as we
walked through the Circle, and though I don't remember anything we said or did, I can recall the happy high
we shared that day.

Because Max has to park on a side street, we get to
walk back up Connecticut Avenue past the modest
office buildings housing various public-interest organi-
zations in dim offices above the street-level Oriental
antique shops. During the day, Pakistani and Ethiopian
vendors set up card tables on the wide Connecticut
Avenue sidewalks to sell cheap leather goods, used
clothing, or kitschy products from their homelands. At
noon there are cozy cultural interchanges as serene
secretaries, strolling by on their way to lunch at the
Golden Temple or Childe Harold's, pause to inspect the
wares, trying on earrings that they then study in huge
hunks of broken mirror held before their eyes by the
eager, dusty-faced vendors.

For a moment we pause in a pool of white light spilling out of Kramerbooks, which has a small café in the

rear that Sukie and I frequented during the seventies when I came to visit.

The thought of never having lunch with Sukie again whips the air from my lungs and I have to skip a few steps to catch up with Max.

The entranceway to Max's building is not unlike Jeff's—a narrow doorway set between a dance studio and a Karate center. Two flights up, Max unlocks the door to a handsome, white-walled, Brazilian leather and Scandinavian wood apartment. Crayon-green ferns lace the Parisian-style floor-to-ceiling windows overlooking Connecticut Avenue.

I am truly surprised by the apartment since few of the single men I know have the spirit to spend much time improving their nests. That's why the homes of single women are usually nicer than those of single men. But, of course, Elizabeth had been living with Max until recently, so he was not necessarily responsible for the warm welcoming hug of his studio apartment.

Max asks if I want something to drink. I choose wine before sitting down in an old-fashioned wicker chair facing the wall of windows. After a while he joins me, sitting down in a twin chair before beginning to talk.

"You know, after Sukie's mother died, it was around Christmastime in '79, Sukie just sort of . . . lost it. That summer Carol was a counselor at the camp David went to, so Sukie and I were alone for the first time in . . . maybe fifteen, sixteen years. And I want to tell you, all hell broke loose. Really. I never knew what to expect from one day to the next. Sometime in the middle of that June—I was teaching two summer courses to beef up our income—I came home one night and found Sukie gone. Just gone. The place was empty. I mean, it *really* felt empty. I went upstairs to our room, and there was this note tucked underneath her spray can of FDS. You know, that feminine deodorant spray? And you know what the note said? It said, 'The best way to get ahead is to give some.' I swear to you. That's all it said."

I smiled. I remembered when Sukie first penned that line.

"And I didn't even find it right away because she left it on top of some old Victorian bureau she was refinishing that wasn't really on my territorial track. I mean, I usually didn't go near that thing because the wood-stripper stuff made such a big mess. All I could do was lie down on the bed and read her damn little message over and over again, trying to figure out if it was a suicide note or what. But after a while I decided it was much too combative to be a suicide note and that it was just a continuation of the quarrel we'd been having for the past ten years. The only thing I couldn't figure out was if she had just left or if she had left *me*. You see the difference?"

I nod.

"I suppose that whenever I thought about her leaving, I guessed it probably would be like that—no warning, just an empty house one night with a note someplace where I wouldn't find it right away, and then that kind of smack in the face: 'The best way to get ahead is to give some.'

"It was just the same goddamn dramatic, destructive shit she always pulled on me. But I swear to you, I couldn't decode that note and I'm not playing dumb. What the fuck was she saying to me? That our whole lives together boiled down to a blow job? Is that what she meant? Really. Can you tell me, Diana?"

First I shrug, but then I warm to it.

"It's a pretty fair summation of how our lives feel to a lot of us, Max. When we look back at our various choices, we see how often we took easy outs, gave in, put out and shut up. A lot of what happened to us boils down to something like that."

"Like what?"

"Like being nice. Like keeping quiet. Like not making trouble. Like . . . giving head, you know? Giving in.

Going down. Going under. It's a metaphor, Max. Maybe men can't understand it. I think most women would know exactly what it means. It's about doing some things to make other things easier. Oh, I don't know, Max. I don't know. It probably just meant that Sukie was feeling bad. Sad."

"Okay. Sukie said it. You didn't. But I sure as hell didn't know what it meant that night and I just lay there trying to decide whether I should get up and make the bed or make some phone calls or make myself a drink. But then I decided that I couldn't decide, so all I did was lie there and think about Sukie. Because, really, she was basically . . . a paradox, Diana. She was both the thesis and the antithesis of everything she said or did. I mean, half the time she wanted to be the best woman writer in the country and the other half of the time she just wanted to sit around getting stoned and suntanned at some beach somewhere. She always talked one way and acted another. And there was always this huge discrepancy between her appearance and her reality. I mean, Sukie liked to dress like a whore, but in fact she acted like a nun in bed. I'm not kidding. Nothing about her was in sync. On the outside she liked to look wicked and wanton, but on the inside she was this prim, prissy little pricktease."

"Oh Max," I complain, laughing a little.

"And after her mother died, she *really* freaked out. She started collecting all these tiny paper things, these scraps of memorabilia that she made into miniature collages. I swear, Diana, she would sit around for hours gluing these scraps onto onionskin sheets of paper, which she folded twice, first lengthwise and then across the middle. She spent days arranging all these little papers—old ticket stubs and newspaper headlines and lottery tickets and cash-register receipts and pieces of her mother's birth certificate that she'd ripped up and little torn-off corners of bus transfers or tinsely gift-wrapping or other paper shit that reminded her of something. And then she'd paste all that stuff onto those onionskins. And the whole time she kept sniffing the model airplane glue she was using. She would just snip and glue and sniff, and then snip and glue and sniff some more. I tell you, she was making me crazy. And finally, when she had three full scrapbooks of these finished collages, one day she says she's going to Georgetown to see if she can find some gallery to give her a show, and off she goes and of course I never see those scrapbooks ever again, and when I ask her about them she doesn't answer. They're just gone. Forever.

"And I'm lying in this mess of a bedroom, in a bed that hasn't been changed in a month, feeling like a criminal because my wife has left me. *Me.* I'm feeling *responsible* and trying to remember if I did anything the past few days that might have ticked her off. I'm like some detective at the scene of a crime, trying to piece together a case against myself. But all I can remember is that she woke up sort of sad that morning, which was unusual because it was a Friday. Friday mornings Sukie was always full of false expectations about the weekend. There she was, in her mid-forties, still believing that every weekend was going to be 'fabulous.' Sukie was like some Broadway theater, lit up on weekends but always dark on Mondays. I mean, the end of a weekend had the same effect on her as the end of a love affair has on other women.

"Maybe I should have known something was wrong since she woke up acting weird on a Friday, but shit, I had to teach a class at nine-forty and I couldn't get it up to start in with 'What's wrong, honey? What's the matter? Something happen?' You know, all that shit husbands are supposed to produce at the drop of a tear. Anyway, she just got up and put on my dirty shirt I'd dropped on the floor and walked out of the bedroom without saying a word. Like I wasn't even there."

Sitting beside Max and hearing his deep voice delivering his persuasive perceptions, I realize I am in danger. His arm, resting beside mine on the wedge of the wicker chair, is turned to expose the blue highways of his veins running upriver, thin, sheer azure tributaries that ripple when he moves his fingers. I feel overwhelmed by his nearness.

"So when I went downstairs for coffee, I thought I'd try to buck her up a little and I asked if she'd like to play tennis that afternoon. But of course she says, 'No thank you, the water came back. My knee hurts.' Every time Sukie wanted to avoid any discussion about her emotional condition, she would claim she had water on the knee and that it hurt too much to talk." Max shakes his head hopelessly. "She was like a kid. I'd say, 'Sukie? Do you want to go to a movie?' 'No,' she'd answer. 'My knee hurts.' It was wild. Just wild. Before we got married I used to think I could handle women. Like I knew how to make salad without a recipe? But, nope. I was wrong. Not with Sukie.

"I started to think maybe she'd been doing some amphetamines again, because the last time we were in Mexico she'd scored like crazy. But when I asked her if she was, she swore she'd flushed all of them down the toilet. Uh-huh. Yyyyah. The way she was acting made me pretty sure she'd just crashed. But then all of a sudden she jumps up, goes out on the porch, and starts repotting some plants that didn't need repotting and making a big mess of dirt out there that I knew she'd never clean up. I guess maybe I said something before I left about her sweeping the porch after she was finished because that's the only thing I can figure that might have pissed her off. Anyway, she was gone when I got back."

"Where'd she go?" I ask casually, lighting a fresh cigarette and sipping some support from my wine.

"Who the hell knows? Four days later she comes back, but she isn't talking. Ten times I ask her where she's been, but she won't answer. Then all of a sudden she starts telling me that the Abramsons are getting divorced and when I ask her why, she says—and this is God's truth, Diana—she says they're getting divorced because John couldn't learn how to read faster. Apparently he took a speed-reading course that didn't help him much and Ceilly just couldn't stand how slow he read—how long it took him to finish a book—so she was divorcing him. Diana, I swear to you, Sukie believed every word she ever said at the moment she was saying it."

"She was burned out, Max," I say apologetically. "She tried to do too many things. She tried to be everything to everybody and ended up not being true to herself. They're . . . we're . . . writing lots of books about burnout nowadays."

He doesn't respond.

"The next morning she says she knows we shouldn't have gotten married because I cut my breakfast toast diagonally. She says people who cut their toast diagonally are traditionalists or something. Then she says she's never going to see her friend Myra ever again. *Really*. Myra was one of her best friends here in Washington and when I ask her why, she says Myra is too destructive, and when I ask her *how* she's destructive, she says Myra told her that people can still see the wrinkles underneath your eyes even when you're wearing sunglasses and that also it's wrong to believe you've only got *one* mouse in the house because how did you know you were seeing the same mouse *twice* rather than *two* different ones? And all this presumably proved that Myra was a destructive friend because she tried to destabilize Sukie's defenses. Or illusions. Or whatever the hell they were.

"Then, later on that day, we're in the kitchen and she tells me she wants to move to Chile because she thinks she might be of some use to the resistance down there. She says that there's this silent underground campaign being run in Santiago and she thinks she might be able to help them think up some new ideas. Apparently people have been writing *Libre* on the margins of their pesos—or whatever the money's called down there—and on the walls of buildings and on the backs of bus seats. Finally Pinochet had all the seats removed from the public transportation and all the defaced pesos recalled and the government announced that any factory women caught weaving resistance symbols into the fabrics they were making would be imprisoned on the spot.

"But when I didn't say anything, because I didn't know *what* to say, Sukie starts in yelling that I don't think she can do *anything,* that I don't even think she can learn Spanish or come up with any good new ideas about other kinds of silent protests for the people in Santiago. And then she starts crying and says that if she has *any* talent at all, it's exactly for thinking up new ideas for political dissenters to use against homicidal tyrants.

"And then, right while she's talking and crying about things like that, she starts making herself a three-layer club sandwich stuffed with lettuce and peanut butter and mayonnaise and jelly and some cold hamburger she found in the fridge. Listen, Diana. I know you all have hangups about your weight and your bodies and I even have some serious theories about the etiology of that whole syndrome, but I swear, Sukie's eating was *crazy. Crazy.* I've seen her fast for two solid weeks and then just sip watered-down orange juice from a wine goblet like she was Mahatma Gandhi or somebody for the next few days. But I've also seen her devour an entire sirloin steak, smeared with catsup on both sides, while holding it in her hands like a corn on the cob. And I've seen her eat *four* two-dollar boxes of popcorn during one movie and then nothing but cottage cheese for the next ten days. I mean, we're not talking *neurotic* here; we're looking at some major psychological problems."

"Oh, Max . . ." I protest, beginning to laugh.

But he continues.

"Of course she always felt ugly unless some guy was letching after her, putting the make on her in a big public way. Then she would feel better about herself. Then she'd feel good. And goddamm it, every time I got back from a trip I *knew* she'd been with some other man. I could *feel* it. Once she brought home this Arab she'd met on the shuttle coming back down from New York, this real chichi guy who clearly had the hots for her, and she says she's invited him for dinner because she wants the kids to know some *real* Arabs. But it wasn't jealousy that got to me, it was her damn self-destructiveness."

"You should have taken more vacations alone together," I say weakly.

"God, we did. A *lot* of times. I grabbed every opportunity to go to international meetings. And we always went to Mexico because she loved it there so much. But do you know why she loved Mexico? Because it has lots of drugs and lots of dysentery that she thought helped her lose weight. When we were in Mexico, Sukie would go around *trying* to catch dysentery. And if she wasn't trying to catch the runs, she was trying to catch the rays because she thought deep tans camouflaged her laugh lines. She was always *chasing* something. And when I said that the sun was like a drawstring that pulled all her wrinkles tighter, she said I was just as destructive as Myra and that with friends like us she didn't need any enemies.

"But listen to this, Diana. This you won't believe. In Cuernavaca, she bought a baby. I swear to you, that's the goddamn truth. Some old beggar woman offered her a baby on the street and she fucking went and bought it and brought it back to our hotel. And then she starts running around sending bellboys out to look for baby bottles and American formula and talking about

finding a Spanish-sounding Anglo name. She kept repeating that—that she wanted a Spanish-sounding
Anglo name—a hundred times while I tried to talk
some sense into her. And I want to tell you, I went
through hell trying to give that baby back to the authorities. First they claimed she'd kidnapped it and
then finally the American Embassy had to step in and
handle the whole thing. But those were the things she
never talked about to anyone else. I mean, I bet she
never told you about that baby, did she?"

I shake my head.

"See? She saved all her craziness for me."

"She sounds like she was . . . unhappy," I say. "Didn't
you try to get her to see a shrink?"

"A shrink? Are you kidding? Every time she saw a
shrink they'd give her tranquilizers and she'd bop them
down with a can of beer first thing in the morning and
then drink or do coke during the day so finally I had to
blow the whistle on that shit because I thought she'd
OD."

"Look, there are all kinds of different shrinks," I say.
"You know that."

But Max isn't listening.

"I never knew what she was going to do or say next.
Like whenever the subject of the Middle East came up,
she'd say the only really good thing about Israel was that
their coins were engraved in Hebrew, Arabic and
Braille. Diana, she'd say that in front of Israelis or my
parents, who are Orthodox, or in front of her own father
who would fucking freak out of his head. She was always
coming up with crazy political ideas that drove people
up the wall. I never knew what she was going to say
next."

I stand up and move closer to the windows. Across the
street there are neon lights spelling out ZACK'S BAR
AND GRILL. I watch the hot flashes of the bulbs slice the
darkness as I wait for him to continue.

"Then, of course, she could never sleep at night.

She'd do anything to keep me awake with her on a bad night. Except fuck, of course. *Anything* short of fucking. And she'd bite her fingernails down so low that half the time there was coagulated blood in the culverts of her cuticles. And she'd only stay in hotel rooms below the third floor because she once dreamed she died in a hotel fire. And after her mother died, she was unable—I mean *physiologically* unable—to finish anything. Anything at all. If she finally cleaned the kitchen, she'd leave at least one big pan soaking in the sink and it would stay there for days until it filled up with so many dirty dishes you couldn't fit a glass under the faucet to get a damn drink of water. And then, finally, she'd clean up again but leave *another* pan soaking.

"And for some reason she insisted on removing the straighteners from my shirts when they came back from the laundry before putting them in my drawer. I mean, I must have asked her a million times not to do that because that made them wrinkle, but I couldn't get her to stop. I mean, she was really getting eccentric. She would call information in Chicago because she thought all the operators there sounded like her cousin Phyllis whom she used to like a lot when she was little but couldn't locate anymore. Or she'd call the weather number in Ohio to see what kind of day it would be there for Carol. I swear Sukie knew maybe a hundred 800 numbers to call about things."

I return to my chair.

"Sometimes for weeks on end she'd go off on some tangent, you know? Right before she ran away, *Vogue* magazine came out with a big fashion spread showing Nancy Kissinger modeling fall suits and coats on top of the Great Wall of China and that really freaked Sukie out of her mind. She started carrying that damn magazine around with her every place we went, saying it symbolized America's insanity, and showing it to everyone at a dinner party we went to where there were a lot of State Department people. And then, after the dinner, she started in on all her theories about why certain women read *Vogue* from back to front—like a Hebrew book—instead of front to back.

"Or like when she lost her MasterCard. She refused to report it missing because she said no one else could actually use it since she'd exceeded her credit limit. Then, of course, when thousands of dollars worth of charges started coming in from Maryland and northern Virginia, all she could talk about was how surprised she was that someone was able to charge a new set of car tires at a gasoline station. 'I didn't know you could charge something like *that*,' she kept saying. She was much more impressed by the feat than by the fraud. But she was like that about a lot of things. Like she went crazy with excitement when she found out that the post office would accept personal checks for postage stamps. *Jesus.*"

Max shakes his head again.

"She just wore me out, Diana. And her cooking? That was as crazy as everything else. Sometimes there wouldn't be any food in the house for weeks on end and the kids would have to eat at McDonald's. But other times she'd cook up a storm, make five or six meals at the same time. I remember once she started making a moussaka while we were watching the eleven o'clock news. By midnight she'd done the whole eggplant bit and made a big mess and then she did the white sauce and then she got grease all over the walls while she was browning the meat and there were tons of frying pans and pots all over the kitchen. Pretty soon I could see she was getting more and more confused and finally she yelled at me to go to bed. But the next night when I got home, even though there was this huge moussaka sitting out in the kitchen, she was just lying on the sofa in the living room ignoring dinnertime and watching the news and acting the same as when she hadn't made anything at all to eat and was feeling defensive. I mean, I just could never figure her out."

"You lost sight of the forest for the trees, Max."

"But the worst thing of all was her writing. That was so painful, I still can't talk about it. She'd work on a short story for six, eight weeks and then tear it up. Or she'd work on some article for months and then decide that the research was leading her to a conclusion she didn't like, so she'd just dump the whole project. Or she'd start a new novel and work on it for eight, nine months and then just stick it in a drawer somewhere and never look at it again. It was crazy."

His words are only stirring up my love for Sukie.

"It was like . . . every time Sukie grilled a steak for dinner she'd invariably stick her arm too close to the broiler and get a horrendous burn. But see, all her injuries were self-inflicted punishments for what she considered her nonproductivity. And it wasn't like she didn't work hard. She did. She just never thought anything she wrote was good enough to publish. Like her second book. I just sent it off to her agent when Sukie was in Chicago and the damn thing got printed without any revisions. I tell you one thing, Diana, Sukie suffered over her writing as much as any genius ever did. I'm not saying she was a genius, but she suffered like one."

My grief for Sukie's pain is like a pillow pressed over my face, stifling my breathing and muffling any sound I might make.

"But what was really so weird about that summer was that I spent so much time with her. When the second session was over, we went all over town together, shopping in Georgetown and stuff like that. One afternoon I bought us matching shirts from some hippie vendor on Wisconsin Avenue and we hid in an alley behind the Riggs bank to put them on. And a couple of times we just sat around and got drunk at Clyde's in the afternoon and went out to a lot of good restaurants and saw a bunch of good movies and went to a concert at Wolf Trap, which we'd never done before, and did some fancy fucking in the afternoons because the kids were still at camp."

Max's monologue has moved me to a pitch of emotion more intense than any I've allowed myself to experience in recent years. I feel gratitude toward him for riding the roller coaster of Sukie's moods for so long, even though he understood so little about them. Still I want to remain wary because I don't want him to con me. I don't want to be seduced by any self-congratulatory description of his intense involvement with her.

"Of course, our sex is a whole other subject. I've made it with Sukie when she was stoned, drunk, speeding or high on coke. But this is the truth, she'd never been more turned on than she was that summer. I mean, I'd had twenty years of one-night stands with her because, sexually, she always acted like a stranger with me. But that summer it was different. It was like a second honeymoon or something.

"Sometimes I thought—or maybe *wished* is a better word—that she'd had a permanent lover all along. Someone who had been there from the very beginning of our marriage. Because I really wanted there to be a third party—some outside force—that was fucking us up. I wanted there to be some excuse for her weirdness. But if there was, I never found out. In fact, the craziest thing was that I could never guess what Sukie did when I wasn't there. Maybe she wrote or read or played with the kids. I just never knew. But finally I stopped wondering or worrying about what she did when we were apart and concentrated on trying to figure out what was happening when we were together.

"Still, she just kept on getting sadder and sadder that summer. And the sadder she got, the tighter the jeans she would wear. Finally she started wearing Carol's Levi's, which are size sevens and so small that they irritated the insides of her thighs and she finally got a skin infection. I mean, finding too-small clothes to wear so she could feel fat? Gimme a break.

"Actually, sometimes I think that one of her basic problems was that she read so goddamn much she started feeling like a fictional character. I mean, Sukie really got hung up on this woman, Marge, in *Dog Soldiers*. She read that book maybe eleven times. And pretty soon she started to talk like Marge and act like Marge and, excuse me, but she also started to fuck like Marge because I read that goddamn book in self-defense. And who was this Marge? A flake. A complete flake. A junkie. A dodo who pushed dope for her flake of a husband while balling his best buddy. I mean, Marge was a mess. And that's who Sukie modeled herself after in *my* bed."

Suddenly Max stands up and begins pacing around the room. I do not have to watch where he goes. I know where he is without looking. Because now I have a leash—woven from multicolored emotions—tied around my neck, tethering me to him. Now when Max moves, he takes up the slack and tightens the leash of feeling between us. I am yoked to him by the heat of his white-hot revelations.

"Diana, Sukie was *too much* for me. I just couldn't handle her anymore. I'm fifty now, but even five years ago I was too tired for that sort of shit anymore. I wanted an easier relationship. The kids were older and to tell you the truth, when I met Elizabeth, she seemed irresistible because she was so . . . easy, so . . . well, not transparent, but let's say predictable. I knew what was happening every minute. Or, more important, I knew what was going to happen the *next* minute. And when she fell in love with me, well, I just couldn't walk away from that. Do you understand?"

I didn't. But I was being buffeted about by enormous waves of contradictory feelings, feelings that Max had both reported and stirred up inside me. Here was a man swimming in an ocean of feelings just as I was splashing about in a sea of separateness.

After a while Max says, "I know how all of you feel

about what I did. And maybe to her friends, Sukie's behavior was charming. But twenty years of marriage under those conditions was all I could take. I know you're not supposed to speak ill of the dead, and God knows I loved her for a long, long time, but I just couldn't live with her anymore. Can't you understand that?"

Since I didn't know what to say, I didn't say anything.

"I don't know if she told you, but she started going through her menopause pretty early. Her mother did too; that stuff's hereditary. But after her mother died, Sukie started getting more and more irregular; she'd skip her period two or three months at a time. She was only forty-four when she first started getting hot flashes. Sometimes, and this is the only thing that makes me feel a little guilty, sometimes I think she got more erratic when her menopause started. And then I feel bad because if her craziness was chemical and not her fault, I should have . . . Sometimes I think some of her depression might have come from that. But of course she was always a bit off base before then, too."

"I get hot flashes all the time now," I say softly. "They're awful. No, not really awful. Just awfully upsetting."

"Yah . . . well . . ."

He walks to the window and stands, hands in his pants pockets, looking outside for a while. He is breathing heavily, apparently struggling for a full order of air.

"After she started skipping some of her periods, one night—we're up in our bedroom—she spills out a box of Tampaxes on the bed and starts ripping the wrappers off all of them saying that she's going to save them for rolling joints because they're the sheerest, strongest paper around. Oh, I don't know." Max shrugs his shoulders. "Anyway, now she's dead. I can't believe it. She was mad in a million ways, but she always loved life. You want to smoke a joint?"

"Okay."

Max always had good dope. The joints were already rolled and lined up like little soldiers inside a carved wooden box on the table beside his stereo. He spends some time looking for a compact disc and finally puts on the Verdi *Requiem*. We listen to the music and watch the neon sign from Zack's Bar and Grill across the street flicker on and off like a small-time light show while we smoke our joints.

For a long while, Max is silent. When he finally speaks again, his voice is muffled by hopelessness.

"Do you think it's going to be easy for me to live the rest of my life? I mean, after the turmoil of these days is over, I've got to go on living knowing that Sukie died so early, so freakishly, only a few years after we split. Or after I left. However you want me to say it."

Now Max begins to cry. He cries in a rather controlled way so that the sobs only seem to accompany his words.

"Do you think it's easy for me that Elizabeth moved out and left me just a few weeks before Sukie died? Or that the day after we get to Europe—the first time I was going to be alone with both my kids at the same time in five years—Sukie dies and we have to come back to this havoc here? Don't you think my life tastes like ashes in my mouth? What makes you think I'll ever recover from all this? Or if my kids will? They're going crazy because Sukie died alone when we were all away. And they hadn't even really recovered from the damn divorce yet. Do you think I like how things turned out? How things are going? What happened to our lives?"

Then he is swamped by his own cascading cries. His groans begin to crash down upon him like ocean waves, crushing him with their weight.

I feel his pain and anguish about all that has happened and I am submerged by a groundswell of feeling for him. A surging urge to comfort him, to wrest away his regrets, overwhelms me. I can feel an appeal forming within him and a response shaping itself, of its own

volition, within me. I wonder if Sukie would want me
to comfort Max.

After several minutes his cries start to subside.

"Don't you think men have feelings?" he asks. "I
mean, even if we don't talk about them all the time or
confide in our friends the way women do, don't you
think we feel pain?" Max is looking out the window.
"Don't you think I died a million deaths for not living
with David while he was still growing up, for not being
with him when he needed me? God," he groans. "Do
you really think I would have left if I could have stayed?
Doesn't twenty years in residence show good faith?
Even conceding the advantages men have over
women, does that mean we don't suffer over our family
disasters? Aren't we entitled to some peace and happiness as much as women are? Is it so wrong to want to
make our lives more decent instead of more difficult? Is
it so outrageous to want that? Is it wrong to want what
we feel we need?"

I am stoned. I am very stoned.

I see my past. I see my past like a message scrolling
itself across the dark blue canvas sky. At first my past
appears distinct and clear, like a fresh message left by
a skywriter, but gradually the letters grow larger and
more translucent. The puffy white words printed in the
sky inflate, dilate, and disappear, leaving only a white
smear across the blue. The past prints itself on the present, but fades into oblivion even as I read it.

This is not good.

"But you're fabulous," Max smiles.

Turning toward me, he extends his arms in an invitation to lift me out of the deep wicker chair.

"You're very special. And very, very beautiful. I can't
understand how we . . . missed each other."

I reach out to grasp his hands and he draws me to my
feet so that we are standing face to face.

"We're just something that never happened," I

shrug. "We're like a book we put on reserve and forgot to go back and read. You know, like the classics. Like Dante's *Inferno*. I'm saving that for when I have terminal cancer."

"I don't want to wait that long," Max says.

The flashing Zack's sign splashes light across our faces.

Now there is a very long silence. Somehow, during its duration, I begin to feel forgiven, although I am not certain by whom or for what.

"It doesn't necessarily have to be right now," Max continues, prompting a response I refuse to provide. "Although I do think we might be able to comfort each other."

That makes me smile again. My hands feel happily defined by the gentle pressure of Max's fingers.

He is watching me, waiting and wanting me to confirm him, to help make some sense out of his experience.

"Would you want to . . . stay here tonight?" he asks.

"No, I don't think so," I say. "If I wanted anything, I might want that. But I don't want much anymore, Max. I have no expectations anymore. I have no needs in regard to anyone else. I've simply stopped expecting things."

"What are you talking about?"

I shrug, and he laughs softly.

"You're stoned," he smiles. "I think you should stay here. I think we could . . . comfort each other."

"But see? You have some expectations about the end result of our being together—that you'll find some comfort, or that I will. And as soon as you want or expect something—comfort or love or passion or whatever—you've set yourself up to crash. I don't do that anymore."

"I swear I don't know what you're talking about."

"Never mind." I smile. "It's too soon to look for comfort. We're both too raw." Then I slip my hands out of his. "Should I call a taxi or can you take me home?"

"I'll drive you," he says wearily.

We walk back to his car in silence. The stiff, haughty streetlamps bleed light into the darkness. Dupont Circle is a black hole.

Max drives back to Sukie's house, but as soon as he double-parks to let me out, I remember I don't have a key and he has to let me in with the one he's kept on his keychain for more than five years.

CHAPTER 11

"Well. Where have *you* been?"

It's Elaine. She is sitting in the front room without any lights on. I close and lock the front door.

"You know. We went to look for Jeff," I say in a matter-of-fact voice that sounds totally false. "But we couldn't find him."

"Hmmmmm. So where were you if you didn't find him?" Elaine's voice is hot with hostility. "It's almost three."

I switch on the hall light which marginally illuminates the living room. The sofa has been made up into a bed and Elaine is wearing a nightgown, but she is sitting straight up, clearly wide awake. She has not been sleeping. She is holding an empty glass that makes me wonder if she's been waiting up for me.

"Well, we sat in a bar next door to Jeff's apartment," I answer. "The bartender there knows Jeff and said he usually comes in on Saturday nights, so we just waited."

Not wanting to mention Max's apartment, I have blundered into a provocative image—of an evening spent drinking in a bar—that sounds even worse. Now it sounds as if Max and I had gone out dancing on Sukie's grave. The hurt on Elaine's face makes me flush with shame. There is another long and wretched silence. I don't know how to prove my innocence without acknowledging her suspicions.

So, of course, a hot flash begins mobilizing for an attack. It moves rapidly and I can feel the flush start to fuse with the guilty blush already painting my face. For a moment I believe I might just boil over like some soup forgotten in a pot upon the stove. Miserable, I wait.

"So what'd Max have to say for himself?" Elaine finally asks. "How's he handling Elizabeth's split?"

"Badly."

I set my purse on the radiator beside Sukie's basket of mail, extract my pack of cigarettes, and walk wearily into the living room to sit in the armchair facing the sofa.

Friendship with Elaine since Nat left her has been difficult for all of us, but it's too late in life to give up a friend just because there's a patch of rough times. Sukie was really no easier, just more charming in her anguish and anxiety.

"Where's Joanne?" I ask.

"Sleeping. Mr. Smilow called. He'll be here tomorrow afternoon."

I light a cigarette. Elaine has been drinking. A lot. She is in a stubborn, intoxicated place. Her words are wrapped in cotton. Her eyes are glassy. Her lips have become lax. Everything about her has drooped. This is sad because Elaine was always our sturdy, headstrong old-fashioned headmistress, directing us in all our political endeavors. Now it is she who is in need of some leadership. If reading Sukie's journal has had any practical value, it must have been to alert us to the many varieties of female depression, which, like Joseph's coat, has infinite hues and colors. Perhaps Sukie's journal was preparing me to help Elaine.

"Why are you so angry?" I ask her in a voice full of curiosity rather than criticism.

"Why not? Why *shouldn't* I be angry is a better question."

"But what does it get you?" I keep my voice as gentle as I can.

"Nothing. Which is what I've got anyway. Don't give me any lectures, Diana. You're hardly in a position."

"What does that mean?"

"I'm sure you know."

"Look, I am not after Max, Elaine. And I would appreciate it if you'd quit giving me the evil eye and watching every move I make. Otherwise we'll never get through this weekend. Max just talked to me nonstop for three straight hours about what happened between him and Sukie. And I wanted to hear what he said."

"You and Max always had an eye for each other."

"Oh God."

"I'm not saying either of you did anything about it. But all those summers we spent together—everyone saw it. Nobody blamed either one of you. It was just one of those things. Like Paul Newman and Joanne Woodward on the same movie set. There'd have to be a click, no? Or even better—Dyan Cannon—that's who you look like, and someone like . . ."

"Did Sukie think that too?" I waver before asking the question, but I want to know the public position on this issue.

"She never said anything to me, but I assume she saw it. Everyone did."

"What was it you saw?"

"Feelings. Just feelings."

I shrug, confident of Sukie's confidence in me as she'd revealed it in her journal.

"I bet Sukie never said anything about anything like that."

Elaine looks thoughtful. "Actually, she did talk about it once. The summer we went to Bridgehampton. She mentioned something that had passed between you and Max on the beach. She said it was natural, or maybe she said inevitable, that you'd feel . . . something for each other. She said it was sort of like the rain. It wouldn't hurt anybody if you didn't stand around in it and get a chill. Or something like that. To tell you the truth, I think if you and Max were to get together now, Sukie would probably be glad. If it made your life any easier or happier, she wouldn't mind. She'd be more interested in your happiness than his. And she would have loved it if you'd unseated Elizabeth, if you know what I mean."

The shadows erase the lines from Elaine's face so once again I can see the perky, bright woman I met in 1963 at Sukie's house—the strong young woman with whom I later collaborated on draft-resistance actions.

"You want a drink?" Elaine asks.

"Sure."

She disappears toward the kitchen and when she returns hands me a large iced-tea-sized glass, full to the brim with vodka and tonic. I eye the drink warily, but of course start chipping away at it.

"To be honest, Diana," Elaine says as she returns to the couch, "I'm in a total panic because now that Sukie's gone I don't have a friend in the same boat with me. In the same fix I'm in. This kind of misery doesn't just *love* company, it can't survive without it. The fact that I'm fifty years old and could easily live another twenty-five years just like I'm living now is too much for me to handle."

"But why is it so hard for you, Elaine? So many people go through it and come out the other side. Why doesn't it let up or get any better for you?"

"I don't know. But everything Sukie wrote in her journal goes for me too. Only I can't even write it down. Everything she felt, I still feel. Of course, before today I couldn't understand why she started feeling better, how she pulled out so far ahead of me in the recovery department. But then this morning, when that guy, when Jeff, walked in, I realized she'd gotten herself a lover and that's why she started feeling better. That's why she lost the weight she'd gained and started her life over again. See, even though we talked to each other almost every day, I didn't understand why she started feeling better when I didn't. And that wasn't fair. Maybe it even slowed me down. Oh, I know you'll say she didn't want to hurt me by telling me some cute young guy had the hots for her, but it was worse for me not understanding how she could quit drinking—which I still can't do—and lose all her weight and start looking good again and start getting writing assignments again. And now I find out it was only because she was getting laid."

I gasp. "Oh, you don't really think it was just that, do you, Elaine?"

"Hey. I know what I know. If men don't matter to you, Diana, if you don't need a man in order to feel like a woman, that's great. But for the rest of us, we have to live with our own realities. And I am bitter, I'll admit it, even though I'm one of the lucky ones," she continues. "I got left with some money—blood money because Nat felt so guilty. Otherwise . . . see, I lived my twenties and thirties and most of my forties based on the premise of my marriage and family. And now, just because Nathaniel made a unilateral decision, I'm stuck in a dead end that could easily last another *twenty-five* years. I'm just left with a lot of leftover life to kill."

"Oh, Elaine, there's so much you can do."

"Like what, Diana? I tried so hard . . . to live a decent life, to try to make a difference, to do something of value, to help out. When I think of all those marches and sit-ins and demonstrations in Central Park, the Whitehall Induction Center. All those endless meetings, all those protests, *all that effort.* And what did it get us? What's different now? Everything's the same again; Reagan is just a pre-Watergate Nixon."

"We helped stop the war."

"I dunno. Maybe. We sure haven't had any impact domestically."

If we had ever gained any political power, we had two top priorities—nuclear disarmament and federal daycare. We would have converted our country from a war machine into a peace generator and reshuffled the social cards through a massive, world-class, national daycare program. However, for most of our adult lives we were either in the hands of the Republicans or in a state of war.

We are a generation of women who had everything, but found we couldn't enjoy it when others had too little or nothing at all; we wanted to find a political solution to this economic problem, but still haven't. We were the women who wanted to Make Love Not War and who wanted to restrict Arms to Hugging. This is probably because our generation can actually remember the hot flashes of the atom bombs that won us our victory over Japan but left us fearing future chilly scenes of a nuclear winter.

Elaine is not the only burnt-out case. At the present time, lots of us are suffering from severe political burnout. We are much more likely to send a contribution to some Sandinista support group rather than travel to Washington to demonstrate against apartheid or Reagan's Nicaraguan policy. Although we haven't stopped caring about the have-nots of this world and continue to buy and hang *arpilleras*—hand-embroidered scenes of oppression in Chile—we are no longer activists. If pressed, we will admit we prefer justice to freedom and that we are more interested in north-south problems than east-west ones.

"So I never developed a career for myself. Substitute teaching was just a chance to get away for a day once in a while. But all that time, Nathaniel was carving out his empire. I think our marriages started going down the tubes when our husbands got too successful."

That has always been Elaine's contention.

And maybe those were bad times for us when our men began sprinting ahead of us in life so that suddenly within our marriages there were winners and losers as well as husbands and wives. Maybe it was bad to feel as if the men had finally started their real lives while ours remained on indefinite hold. Confined by commitments, we felt excluded from the worldy adventures of our men, so some of us made other men our adventures. Then, guiltily, we became more watchful of our husbands and often made much ado about nothing. Jealousy is a tropical island where killer vines grow wild and strangle the giant trees to which they cling.

"I should have run for Congress. I don't know know how Bella and Shirley did it. They had kids and husbands, too. But I just couldn't juggle my time any better than I did. I felt too guilty about leaving the boys alone too much. It was only the volunteer stuff that didn't pay—or pay off—that didn't make me feel guilty. I know that's a crazy reason to settle for getting pamphlets printed and picket signs made, but it's the truth. So now I've got nothing to show for thirty years of volunteer political work."

Elaine is inhaling rather than sipping her drink.

"Elaine, I was reading some more of Sukie's journal and in one part she wrote about one night when she called you up crying about how empty her life was and how you talked real tough to her about getting back into shape and doing things for other people. You mentioned Nicaragua to her and helping Brenda out with the babies she adopted."

Elaine looks at me. "I remember that," she says sadly. "That was when Sukie was so bad off I looked like I was in relatively good shape. You know, all I think about lately are the wonderful summers we all had together. I think it was so wonderful, us being young mothers together with all our little babies. It was so fun. And so sexy. And nice."

"Yes," I say. Yes, yes, yes, yes.

"We looked like we were the mother's helpers that summer on Fire Island."

"Yes," I say. Yes, yes, yes, yes.

Summers were always the best times for us. Summers

were like recess—sudden freedom from our sense of solitary responsibility. Summers were the only times when our routines took on the quality of shared adventures, when we changed from being Robinson Crusoes into Swiss Families Robinson. Summers were our playtoys, the teddy bears of our years, when we could all be together and every meal was a picnic and every night a slumber party.

Being young marrieds together in the late fifties and early sixties was delicious because marital sex back then was equivalent to drinking right after prohibition had been repealed. Just the fact we could do it—if and when we wanted to—made it special. That's why there was always an overflow of afterglow at our group get-togethers. A blusher of sex colored the sweet young faces of our marriages and couples felt enormous sexual goodwill toward each other. People would come and go talking about *The Alexandria Quartet* and Durrell's two-backed monsters—those genitally linked, seemingly inseparable Siamese twins known as husband and wife.

"I think the sixties did us in," Elaine says reflectively. "All that wildness. We were married—but nobody felt married. Or else it was those open marriages that made being single seem so sexy. And now our marriages are gone and it turns out that being single sucks."

"Well, we've just got to pick up the pieces," I say energetically despite the enormous fatigue enveloping me. "Listen, I'm starving."

"I'll see if there's something to eat." Elaine stands up again—large, yet ghostly, in her nightgown. "But I know my major problem is that politically I'm burned out. You want a refill too?"

Reluctantly I hand her my glass.

Politics played an important part in our lives.

Domestically, few of us have been to any campaign victory parties above the local level. On the other hand, although we often arrived with different men, we went every four years to Democratic National Conventions so as to stay connected with the political mainstream. In Miami, in 1972, someone asked Sherril if she was a Marxist; she thought for a while and then said, "No, I'm a registered Democrat." We were always Democrats unless, of course, there was a reform ticket on the ballot. Some of us even saw ourselves as insurgents.

During the 1960s, when lots of people had no last names and gangs of white teenagers lived in Central Park during the summertime, we engaged in daily, hand-to-hand, jungle-style combat against the forces of evil. We worked with protest or poverty groups housed in ramshackle buildings above shops, wearing signs like ATLANTIC TRANSMISSIONS, on the wrong side of town. Lavish with our time and energies, we spent years working on doomed projects that always fizzled out but which the FBI believed dangerous to our national security. In later years, we often panicked when coming home from abroad because we feared finding our names listed in that big black looseleaf "lookout" passport-control notebook consulted by U.S. Customs officials.

The interminable seventies were sad times for us. Our friends became selfish and moved to the West Coast or to apple orchards in Vermont. Our children all wanted to go to Brown and our husbands looked unhappy. We still believed that war was unhealthy for children and other living things and though we tried desperately hard to Ban the Bomb, Stop the Draft, and End the War, we always clapped during performances of *Peter Pan* to show we believed in fairies—just in case.

And then, shockingly, even the seventies ended.

"I wish you could have heard everything Max told me," I say when Elaine reappears.

She is carrying fresh drinks but no food.

"Why?"

"Well, it was informative and . . . sort of moving in a way, how connected he'd really been to her. Max is a pretty intimate man."

Elaine starts to cry.

"Why did we junk our plans for this summer?" she asks me. "It was the first time we did that in seventeen years and it was wrong. We'd all have been together someplace this weekend and then maybe Sukie wouldn't have died." Elaine wipes away her tears with the back of her hand. "But I think none of us could bear how sad it was last summer, all of us alone, no men, none of the kids showing up, and feeling ashamed of how we looked on the beach. But the worst was the way we kept trying to act like we were having fun when we weren't. I think that's the real reason we canned our trip this year."

But now my head is spinning. The room is spinning. I am tired and drunk and almost comatose from hunger. The last thing I'd eaten was my miserly ration of pizza pie.

"I don't feel good, Elaine. I've got to lie down."

She slumps into a corner of the sofa, crying softly into the pillows.

I don't know how to help her.

Would the existence of a man in Elaine's life really save her? Is that all that matters? Is it only a man who can erase that kind of pain?

I stop and bend over to kiss the back of her head. She lifts her hand and I hold it for a moment.

"Go to sleep," I say. "It's almost four o'clock." I take the half-empty glass of vodka from her hand and leave it on the radiator before I run upstairs.

But as soon as I lie down, the riotous feelings Max stirred up in me return. Again I feel the rushes of tenderness, the unalloyed yearning, the terrifying physical desire. After holding back for so long, I had suddenly felt summoned again, as if I were being beckoned back from a point of no return.

What did Max want from me? His youth back? Another crack at marriage? A professional girlfriend in New York? Some sweet September sex? What did he

think we would be or do in bed together after so many
years of wondering, after a quarter-century of warily
watching each other. What kind of players would we be
after all that had gone down between us?

I lie in Sukie's bed while her room whirls around me.

Like beads on a necklace, bright broken pieces of the
past string themselves together into a chain of memories. The chain swings in front of my eyes like an infant
jungle gym hung across a crib. I hear bits and pieces of
brief conversations from ten or twenty years ago. What
I hear and see are scenes from a marriage. My marriage.

Once we were in Kingston where the rain provided
the sound effects. There was a steady dripping sound all
day long. It surrounded the small hotel where we were
living. It sounded as if a million faucets had broken at
the same time and begun splashing water onto the
ground. It sounded like when the gutter around a roof
needs flashing, so that water runs down in a steady
stream rather than draining. The dripping stopped only
when a solid downpour of heavy rain interrupted its
disconsolate tempo.

Leonard and I sat inside at the bar, helping ourselves
to beers from the unlocked cooler that was run on an
honor system. We were staring out through the lat-
ticework at the patio. The broad green leaves of a palm
tree arching over the terrace were funneling raindrops
down onto the tables from where they rolled, like marbles, onto the tiled floor below.

Leonard had made me come to Jamaica with him. He
said he had business there with men who would expect
him to bring his wife. He said it was vitally important,
that it meant a great deal of money to us. He also said
that though his business was with white Jamaicans, all
of them were deeply involved in helping to develop the
island for the betterment of the blacks. He said that
Michael Manley had failed to bring prosperity to
Jamaica but that the new president, Seaga, would improve the economy through foreign investments.

I made myself believe him. I made myself go down to Kingston.

Later, in our room above the bar, we got dressed to go out for dinner at the home of a government minister. I put on a white safari suit studded with redundant pockets, a pair of outrageously high linen sandals and huge golden hoop earrings.

Jazzy Petain picked us up at our hotel. He was a white Jamaican, bright, personable and friendly. He drove us far out of Kingston to an outlying village, where he pulled off the narrow country road and drove up a jungle trail before stopping at a wooden shack shaped like a kiosk in the center of a small clearing.

Jazzy's wife, Lina, looked like a Hemingway heroine—long hair the color of bleached muslin and pale skin licked by the sun. She welcomed us at the doorless entrance to their house and led us inside. The shack had few furnishings, all of which were authentically primitive. The windows had no screens. The floor sloped so that the rear of the house was only inches off the ground. The room was filled with the sounds of snakes slithering around in the bush, accompanied by the cymbals of larger jungle animals breaking through the thick underbrush that embraced the house.

Nevertheless, this rudimentary shack had a servant—a large black woman who had prepared a meal that she served to the four of us whites on an open deck off the underdeveloped kitchen area. The food was elegant, the setting exotic, the Petains unique. I was enchanted by Lina, whose British family had lived in Jamaica for generations. She explained that she was devoting her life to developing new agricultural products for the area. Her commitment to the island and its natives was awesome and I was enchanted with this handsome, resolute woman.

After dinner, Lina asked me if I'd like to take a walk around the farm with her. Flattered, I said of course. Then she led me outside and directly into the jungle.

I became terrified as she kept pressing farther and farther into the bush and I followed her in silent panic. My high-heeled sandals sank into the rich loam. I could hear invisible animals smashing all around us. Intimidated both by the jungle and by Lina's bravery, I forced myself to keep walking as she talked about teaching new agricultural methods to her neighbors and about the difficulty of raising experimental crops.

Finally we came to another scooped-out clearing which contained a shed made of flattened tin cans. A large black man was standing in the doorway.

Lina went up to the man and embraced him tenderly. He kissed her several times with insistent passion. After several minutes, Lina extricated herself from his arms and signaled me to follow her back into the jungle.

Obediently I walked behind her.

"I thought you might be wondering why we live so far from Kingston," she said. "That's my lover. I didn't want to be too far away from him. He's helping me farm my land. When you get back to the States, would you take the trouble to send me some almanacs that deal with raising corn in rainy climates?"

Although I said yes, I never got around to it. On the airplane home I tried to make some sense of Jamaica and that encounter in the jungle. Was Lina really trying to develop new crops to grow in the tropics or was that only a cover for her lover? Did she despise her husband's political equivocations or was she even more of a phony than he was? I felt bad. Sad. Had.

I said to Leonard: "I'm sick of the sorts of people you know. I'm going to find a seat in the smoking section."

Another time, after meeting a plane, we pulled out of Kennedy International Airport. In the backseat sat our friend, a white South African political activist who had just entered the country on a false Dutch passport. We were all feeling hyper after the pressure and tension of waiting for the flight and then waiting to see if Theo would get through passport control.

"Well," Theo said, taking some papers out of his inside jacket pocket. "At least I didn't have to use these Dutch work papers. That would have been much worse, more dangerous."

He began shredding the incriminating documents into small squares and then, opening the car window, threw them out so the wind would carry them away.

I was the first one to see the squad car with its twirling red light on the roof.

"Oh my God," I moaned.

Sitting beside Leonard in the front seat, I told him that the police were signaling us to stop.

The squad car parked close behind us. The cop who was driving got out and walked over to our car. Leonard rolled down his window.

"Okay," the cop said, holding out his hand.

Leonard produced his car registration and driver's license.

The cop carried them back to the squad car to call in the information.

"I need a lawyer," Theo said, breathlessly. "Who do you know in New York?"

"We'll find someone good," Leonard said. "I'll call someone as soon as they let us."

The cop returned. He leaned through the front window that was open and looked into the backseat.

"Something you wanted to get rid of pretty bad, back there?" he asked, looking at Theo.

Theo stared straight ahead, silent.

"You know the price of a ticket for littering?" the cop asked.

I turned around, stunned. Then I looked at the cop more closely.

"How much?" I asked, straining to make my voice audible.

"Fifty."

"Officer, we're on our way out to Long Island. Can we just pay you directly since we're not stopping in New

York and we won't be able to get to court to pay the fine?"

The cop looked at me critically. I reached into my purse, pulled out my wallet and extracted five ten-dollar bills.

The cop stretched out his hand.

"I don't have my receipt book here," he said.

"Oh, that's okay." Leonard smiled reassuringly.

The cop took the money and walked slowly back to his car.

Theo was shaking.

Leonard started the car and we drove straight home.

Leonard never participated in another political action after that one and soon my own involvement began to dwindle. I always felt that Leonard's behavior stifled my own, but now the past seems much more complicated than it used to be and I no longer understand things with the clarity and conviction I once felt.

Unable to sleep, I get up, select another hunk of Sukie's manuscript and then lie down again to I read it.

JUNE 1982

Here Are Some Things That Happened to My Friends:

Women I know, women in their forties, have begun having babies. Eve told me she was thinking about getting pregnant; she said it was hard to do after forty, but even if she ended up having a frog, she was still going to try.

Pat got pregnant at thirty-nine and went past her due date by several weeks. Quite desperate, she said to me, "If I don't have this baby soon, I'll be too old to have another."

Carolyn, who teaches sociology at NYU, became engaged to a colleague who had been divorced three times. When they went downtown to a jewelry store to pick out their matching wedding bands, he knew his ring size without being measured.

When Joanne's first lover finally, after three years of living together, asked her to marry him, they were sitting in a Parisian café. While waiting for her response, Ethan saw a beautiful young Frenchwoman walking past.

"Wow. Look at that sweet pussy," he said. "I could eat her for five days running."

Joanne didn't marry Ethan but she never got over him either. Apparently he whispered in bed a lot which was something she loved and didn't find again very often after they split up.

Myra once told me that her lover always remembered his former girlfriends by the car he was driving at the time of their relationship. He would say, "Okay. Let's see. In '77 I had my Corvette. I guess I must have been going with Lila."

I didn't mention that Myra always remembered foreign cities by the men she'd slept with there: Johannesburg was someone named Nels, Mexico City was Robert, and Katmandu was first Antonio and then Nicolas.

I think we live in very peculiar times.

Twice in recent years a woman who wanted to show me a picture of her lover handed me a newspaper clipping.

The last time that happened, I was talking to Beth, who had just returned from Ireland. Eventually her travelogue turned into a description of the Irishman with whom she'd been involved and she asked if I'd like to see his picture. Retrieving her travel-tired handbag, Beth extracted a deeply creased newspaper photograph. Lovingly she unfolded the frayed paper and smoothed it out to show me six tough-looking men, in heavy overcoats, carrying a coffin.

"That's him," she said tenderly, pointing toward the center of the picture.

My heart paused since I wasn't sure whether she was indicating the coffin or one of the pallbearers.

"His best friend died in prison from fasting."

"Oh," I said.

That was the second time. The other picture had been clipped from a Lebanese newspaper and showed my friend Laurie's lover—a member of the PLO—carrying the small casket of a child killed during an Israeli bombing of Beirut.

I think it is a very peculiar historical period if women carry newspaper photos of their lovers instead of snapshots.

Here Are Some Things I've Heard Lately:

I heard about a young woman who got married because she was five months pregnant and then miscarried on her wedding night. After delivering stillborn triplet girls, she left the States and went to live in an ashram in India.

I heard about a yuppie lawyer who was in group therapy for a year before realizing that another man in the group was having an affair with his wife. The other man liked and enjoyed the woman so much, the husband didn't recognize her from any of his descriptions.

I heard about a man who struggled for three and a half years to win custody of his young son and then died of a heart attack on the day his lawyer told him the court had found in his favor.

I heard of a man and woman—father of the bride and mother of the groom—who fell in love during the festivities preceding their children's wedding. After the ceremony, they threw rice at the young couple and then jumped in a car and took off for Hawaii. They call themselves "out-laws" and are still living in Kona.

My friends have all been terrific about sending me weird newspaper articles, great titles, and descriptions *of scenes they've seen or produced that they thought I might be able to use in a new book.*

Recently I became intrigued by the young California man, waiting for an L.A.-to-Oakland flight, who accidentally boarded a plane to Auckland, New Zealand. He was returned on the next flight and immediately hired a Hollywood agent to sell his story to the movies. . . .

I have only recently realized that every clever thing a person says or thinks is not *a two-word book title.*

Last month, trying to remedy all my medical problems while still covered by Max's health insurance, I discovered that I had traumatic arthritis in both my thumbs. This affliction was apparently caused by excessive typing at a desk of improper height. What an unromantic occupational hazard! Nevertheless, I find it difficult to hold a heavy Vogue *nowadays because my thumbs no longer exert effective opposable force. If I remember my high school biology correctly, an opposable thumb is one of the primary differences between apes and humans.*

Dorothy saw two policemen walking out of her apartment building when she returned home.

"What's wrong?" she asked, running up the stairs toward them. "What happened?"

"Nothing, lady," one of the officers groaned. "We live here. Cops got to live someplace too, you know."

Arlene went over to her lover's apartment, opened the door with the key he had given her, and saw him making love to his former wife on the living room sofa. Later that night, Arlene was sitting near her front window when a foreign student who lived in her building jumped off the roof. She saw his face as he fell past her floor.

Britt was helping her new husband fix up his study when she saw a letter to him from his first wife. The last sentence wasn't complete but it began, "I could have forgiven you if she'd only been my friend, but my sister . . ."

That was when Britt began to notice other things too. Marty's sexual preambles were coded for a different woman. He did things to Britt that his former wife, Ursula, had clearly enjoyed. Once Britt realized this, she stopped responding to her third husband's first wife's pleasure points.

Next she noticed that many of Marty's other habits were probably Ursula's preferences also. He folded the dishrag into a square before draping it over the kitchen faucet and turned paper napkins into tutored triangles with a practiced twist. Soon Britt began to identify with Ursula, and since Marty had betrayed her, Britt could no longer trust him. If it had only been Ursula's friend— but her sister! Marty and Britt broke up six months later.

Elaine. I think Elaine broke up her marriage because she had gained thirty pounds and was unable to lose the weight. She started a fight with her husband, orchestrated its escalation, and somehow established the idea that it was he who wanted to get rid of her. The idea hadn't occurred to Nathaniel before, but a few weeks after their fight, he moved out.

I think what Elaine was remembering was a previous separation when she had lost thirty-six pounds and turned from a fat woman into someone who could wear jeans and enjoy a different life-style. For several months she had lived in a communal house that provided her with endless companionship. She enjoyed this interlude so much that after she reconciled with Nathaniel, she found their affluent, opulent—but isolated—life oppressive.

Within a month of their second separation, Nathaniel met a beautiful young woman who worked at CBS and turned to her for consolation. In the next two years, Nathaniel married the young woman and fathered a new baby. After losing her husband, Elaine gained rather than lost weight. She became even fatter and was desperately lonely. Perhaps it would have been

*better if she had just gone on the Scarsdale Diet instead
of starting that first fight.*

*However, Elaine is a source of great comfort to all of
us now. Maybe it's because she's so noncompetitive. Or
maybe it's because her self-esteem is so low that anyone
in her presence has got to feel better. Perhaps it's
wrong to take advantage of that. But Elaine is our comfort station, our pit stop, our rest area off the high-speed
highway of life. She believes in basics—in cozy bedrooms with perfect reading lamps, in planned menus
and in reserve rolls of paper toweling and toilet tissue.
The last time I was in New York she told me that the
pickle in a Big Mac does not qualify as a green vegetable.*

I couldn't survive without Elaine.

*Once Jackie told me a story. Her bed was pushed
against a wall in her L-shaped bedroom, in her L-
shaped apartment, in her L-shaped building. On the
other side of her bedroom wall, Jackie could hear a
woman sobbing, hour after hour, in the middle of the
night, night after night. One morning, while waiting for
the elevator, Jackie saw the door of the adjacent apartment open and a middle-aged woman emerge and approach the elevator. She smiled sadly at Jackie but
Jackie was unable to speak or respond. Having overheard the woman's intimate pain, Jackie was stricken
with shyness. She was home several weeks later when
the woman OD'd on sleeping pills and the fire department took her corpse away.*

*When Carol was little she, of course, watched the tele-
vised funerals of the Kennedys and Dr. King. Later,
when a friend of ours died, she asked, "When's the
parade?"*

Here Are Some Things That Happened to Me Recently:
*An older man I know said, "Life isn't fair because
women have all the pussy." This was too weird for me,
especially since he seemed to be speaking seriously.*

Last summer I went to an Orioles game, in Baltimore, where I sat next to two young men wearing cutoffs with T-shirts that read: WE RENT BY THE PIECE: FURNITURE FOR LEASE. During the seventh inning, a good-looking girl walked past and waved to both of them.

"Hey, do you know Mary Ann?" one guy asked the other.

"Do I know Mary Ann?" the bearded man next to me echoed in italics. "Hell, I was once married to her for one night."

I knew what he meant. "We rent by the piece."

Three times in my life I've been in bed with different men who, stoned or drunk, said something they considered memorable and asked me to get up to find a paper on which to record their utterances.

I've slept with two men who went to enormous efforts to get me to bed with them and then turned out to be impotent. What did they want? Did they think I might cure them? I don't even know how the damn thing works. Did they want me to comfort or coax them into virility?

I've slept with two different men each of whom said he was considering divorce, but was also interested in another marriage. Both times I was able to stop myself from laughing. Recently I learned that in Brazil you can only get divorced two times. The third marriage is indissoluble. Final. Forever. Maybe that's a good idea.

I can't remember the last time I gave a completed manuscript to a man who didn't return it covered with chicken-scratchy editing marks.

I have met several men who wanted to give me their telephone numbers but, even after a long struggle, couldn't remember them. People who live alone seldom have cause to call home and consequently often forget their own numbers.

Once I met a very sweet divorced man who found his

Sundays so excruciatingly long that he walked nineteen blocks from his home to buy The New York Times *at a downtown newsstand, thereby killing some time, postponing the pleasure of reading the paper and emasculating his Sunday.*

Three years ago, when I was still me, I got an assignment to cover a meeting of Latin American bishops in Pueblo, Mexico. Afterwards I stopped off in Cozumel. There I got dreamy drinking Margaritas in the restaurant of the El Presidente Hotel after we lost electrical power so there was no elevator service or lights. Sitting there, half drunk, I watched an absurdly short mariachi trumpeter, whose pants were so tight he had to be lifted onto the stage, flirt with me. I thought, Is this what it's all about?

The next day, I dumped two pocketfuls of amphetamines into a garbage can at the airport when I saw security officers doing body frisks on the passengers ahead of me.

After Max left, I went to New York where a crazy lady at Penn Station who had been accosting a lot of people came up to me and asked, "What is your religion? What is your race? What is your creed? Who are you exactly?"

As soon as she finished her litany of questions, I burst into tears.

I still dilate upon my losses. The qualities of my pain are exquisitely distinct. Bittersweet or sour rushes of rage spiral through me. Geysers of grief erupt. I experience a rush of sobs for the past. To comfort myself, I pretend the truth hasn't happened yet.

I study my photograph albums, seeking to discover who I was when my children were babies. I am determined to retrieve a former version of myself from some earlier edition. This has become very important to me. A few days ago I decided I had simply forgotten the person I used to be. I believe people can erase their previous selves just as infants turn into babies and then into toddlers and then into real children in whom the newborn is eternally buried like a little Russian doll inside a larger version of herself.

I remember when all our friends had new babies and we used to take them with us to dinner parties and leave them centered on the host's master bed. Paul, who named his daughter after his dog, told me about a New Year's Eve party he went to in New York where rowdy, boisterous guests threw their coats over a baby sleeping on the bed. Later, right before midnight, the mother went in to check on the infant and began screaming as she pulled the heavy winter wraps off her baby, flinging them like parachutes into the air. The baby was dead.

My photo albums are almost too chaotic to serve as memory joggers. There is little order to them, certainly nothing chronological. The best-organized album holds baby pictures of Carol that I study carefully, trying to remember who I was when she was an infant. Am I still the same woman or has that girlish young mother totally disappeared? I am as surprised at seeing my young self as I was when I first saw photographs of only black faces in Kate's family album. Photos of black faces struck me as strange after a lifetime of albums filled only with whites.

Many famous people used to visit us; we went ice skating with them or on picnics or to parties, but I was too proud to ask for their autographs or take their pictures.

Max and I are still together in many photographs.

Who took those pictures? Where are those people now?

What I can't accept are the shared memories that were also divorced—devalued and depreciated by our separation.

What happens to memories that cease to be mutual and are no longer reinforced? Isn't the birth of a baby less dear when remembered alone? Isn't an averted airplane crash less real if only one person recalls it? Isn't a tragedy more painful, a fear more fearful, a dread more dreadful, when suffered alone? And what of the deaths of friends we suffered together, the illnesses of children, the intricate understandings of inexplicable forces from the past?

Certainly there were moments at restaurants when our family shimmered with closeness. There were car rides that didn't become irritable. There were mornings when mutual expectations fused into familial joy. I am very sorry I didn't keep a journal back then, when the kids were babies. As a writer that would have been as natural to me as a photographer taking pictures of a new infant. Now I remember so little. Just a few things. I do remember when David said to me, "I'm sorry you and I couldn't be little at the same time together. I would have brought you home from school." He wasn't yet six when he said that. But he was right. We would have been great pals. In fact, we are.

In our family, more was always better. Less was never enough.

I can no longer recall the extreme anguish I suffered in the first few days after Max left. I do know that for the first week I wore sunglasses around the house, even at night, so my children wouldn't see how much I'd been crying. I believe God fixes things so that even enormous losses, like labor pains, are forgotten. If women could clearly recall giving birth, they might very well embrace celibacy and cease to reproduce. If I were able to relive my sense of loss when Max left, I would probably cease to love anyone ever again.

So God lets losses fade.

What I can still remember clearly is my anxiety. I remember it as if it were an old house in which I used to live. I can remember all its nooks and crannies. I lived within that edifice of anxiety for so long that it

*became a permanent kinetic memory that won't quit.
I would do anything to avoid having anything like that
anxiety ever again.*

NOVEMBER 1982

*Early this morning—it is Friday—I decide to spend the
day outside my house. I get dressed in black corduroy
jeans with a black turtleneck pullover sweater that
David says makes me look like I have a whiplash. In a
sense I do. Briskly I walk down Connecticut Avenue to
the Bread Oven, a French patisserie on 19th Street. I
come here hoping to encounter some old friend—or
perhaps to meet a stranger. I will, at least, taste the
sweet residue of thick French coffee in my mouth as I
squander my morning.*

*The restaurant is full of sunlight that shimmies across
the long baguette ovens lining one wall. The din of
dishes and dim voices reminds me not of Paris, but of
novels by Jean Rhys, who painted such lovely scenes in
pale pastels. I have always cared fiercely about Rhys'
heroines, who try not to look shabby while eating their
single meal of the day in some Parisian café. Her stories
provide lyrics for our songs of loss.*

*The light inside the restaurant feels fictitious to me,
filtered through literary prisms; it offers clues to someone else's memories, not my own. This makes the past
seem once-removed. I am now in such a state of es-
trangement that I am even separated from my own
senses, unable to manufacture any authentic feelings.
This place makes everything seem distilled and since
my emotions lack any immediacy or authenticity I feel
sensually dumb.*

*Seated there alone, among clusters of tables crowded
with morning couples on their way to work, I feel lost.
I want to stand up and cry out. Can it be that one's
loneliness is the result of one's own character? Is it possi-*

ble that one is unloved because one is unlovable? Can a person be considered lovable whether or not she is loved? This is an interesting question; it throws some light upon the despair of loneliness.

I know no one in the restaurant. I try to imagine some of my friends walking through the doorway. I try to think of them as I used to, as an ever-present, permanent army of occupation. But now my friends have become discrete individuals with whom I have complicated and confusing relationships. They are no longer just there; now everything has to be negotiated.

Pride cometh before the fall.

Falling.

It's not death that's feared, but the falling first.

How far in sensations is any window from the ground? Do people struggle to stop the fall and fight fright even as they're falling?

Perhaps everything was prophesied in the Bible and I just forgot to do my research. Perhaps I neglected to use the one reference book that would have illuminated my life for me—or at least have identified my problems before Max left.

The days are so long. A quarter of an hour can feel like fifty laps in an Olympic-sized pool. And the nights. How long is a night? The length of a window shade. The difficulty of traversing time hasn't diminished much. Time seems even slower now as I sit alone at a table in the Bread Oven.

Lately the ground below my bedroom window has begun to summon me, to serenade me with seductive siren songs. I know for a fact that bloodstains do not come out of sidewalk pavement. The stains spread and darken, then finally just stay there. Once I met an American girl in Florence whose father had jumped out of their second-story window and permanently stained the paving outside her house. I can't handle the thought of David having to walk around a splotch that used to be me, his mother.

I recently read a newspaper article about lab rats made to feel increasingly more helpless. Next they began developing cancer at a phenomenally faster rate than the control group. Helplessness hurts a lot, no doubt about it. It is exactly at the moment when you are unable to pick up a man that you pick up the flu.

Visits to the post office and grocery store have become reassuring rituals for me. In my mind I have begun to inflate paltry appointments into important engagements, casual invitations into required events. Terror tightens my sense of obligation. I can no longer remember the sweet taste of casual encounters. I can barely recall when my life was clotted with people and engorged with experiences.

This restaurant is more French than some restaurants I've been to in Paris which proves a culture is as much an idea as it is a place. I had a French friend once. Her name was Jackie. She died of a heart attack in her elevator when she was forty-three one afternoon when I was supposed to visit her but didn't. I will always wonder where she was going.

Max stopped taking my phone calls long ago. He didn't want to hear any of it anymore. I still want to recall the good things of our past to him—our riveting relationship, our obsessive quarrels, the incredible intensity of our lives. Coldly he asks what is causing my obsession. I inquire what caused his stubborn insistence on staying with me for more than twenty years. His affair, which he tries to inflate into some monumental love, seems to lack the magnitude of our past. But perhaps passion became too much for him after a while. To me, life without passion is nothing more than a broken promise. Now that the negative irritations have disappeared, all I can remember about Max is the unconditional love he gave me, the rich security he provided.

Is loneliness more extreme in some situations than in others? Is a quiet room more lonely than a large restaurant, an empty car more difficult than a crowded bus?

For a while, I joined a psychotherapy group. After a short time I began to feel an enormous contempt for the other members of my group because their pain did not seem comparable to mine. Only the outrageous anguish of a woman whose twelve-year-old daughter was dying of brain cancer reached me. Then I wondered how I could complain of loneliness in her presence. What was loneliness next to death? On the other hand, wasn't loneliness a living death? Wouldn't I exchange the slow passage of time when my soul was strangling from loneliness for the peace of death? Either way, I couldn't say much in that group, so I just quit.

My journal. I try to keep enough notes to set the scene and the mood, record the characters, and choose some clue as to the meaning of what happened. Anyway, besides my notebook, there are still plenty of scribbled notes all around the house. They are on the backs of envelopes, the margins of newspapers, the covers of matchbooks and crumpled paper napkins that I carried home from bars or restaurants. Now whenever a thought travels through my mind, I write it down on a piece of paper for later insertion in my notebook. I call these scraps of papers my Freudian slips.

One day, shortly after Max left, I had this conversation:

"But what do you do when you're alone?" I asked the fifty-year-old woman who had never been married. I felt absolutely consumed by curiosity.

"I just do what I do," she answered rather sharply, tired of our talk, weary of my monomaniacal anxiety about surviving alone.

"But what do you mean?" I persisted.

"I mean—people do what they do."

We were sitting in Renée's kitchen at the table drinking coffee. Renée has already left for work. The lady and I had both spent the night there—for different reasons.

"But like what, for instance?" I pressed her suggestively.

"You read," she answered sharply. *"You clean your room. You pop corn. You watch television. You lie in bed."*

She was only a friend of a friend; I didn't really like her.

A short time later I went home.

Although I have been an intellectual all my life, I never thought to look for any books concerning my situation. Helen ran off a bibliography for me on "divorce" and "separation" at the Library of Congress, but it never occurred to me to read any of those books. I just stuck that long list of titles in my desk drawer and forgot about it.

I can no longer remember how many times I have sat alone in some strange beach house hearing acorns, or maybe magnolia leaves, falling on the corrugated porch roof outside a bedroom window while I wondered if I was going mad. Twice since Max left, I have gone out to the ocean where, lying on the warm sand beneath the sweet summer sky, I felt as if I were beginning to heal, as if my heart were growing warm again, losing the chill of its loss. I would watch the children and babies playing with their pails near the water and I would begin to feel gentle once again, available to life.

But when I returned to the city, my pain would crystallize once more, making my heart as hard as melted sugar boiled until it burned.

Of all the summer houses I ever rented, I loved the little Rehoboth Beach cottage best. There I always tried hard to wake up early so I could hurry across the highway to the bakery and buy thickly frosted doughnuts for my family—as a morning promise to be sweet to them all day. But though I struggled hard to maintain my equilibrium during those summer holidays, I had little control over the twin self that developed inside me during the long hot hours when the heat of the sun inflated my yeasty moods.

A sudden rainstorm could create havoc in my soul.

*Undefined yearnings and longings would rise and de-
velop into unfocused rage. Sharp winds would make me
intolerably restless. The sight of certain couples on the
beach, young mothers with toddlers, or a provocative
collection of windblown teenagers could set me off. But
I am not near the sea now and it is no longer summertime.*

*I am home alone. The mailman just slid my mail
through the door. There are eleven letters. I have to
forward nine of them: Carol's to New York, where she
is visiting a friend, and Max's to his office. David never
gets any mail; adolescents seldom do. I wonder if I
should go to the post office and get some change-of-
address cards. I wonder if I should notify the authorities
about what has happened to me. Why is there no
women's bureau here as in France? We could use one.*

*Eventually I realize why this day is so difficult for me.
It is the second anniversary of my aloneness and I am
reexperiencing the pain that accompanied the end of
my marriage. Even the memory of that pain destabilizes my equilibrium. A sudden loss of identity such as I
suffered makes the world tilt and the self seem smeared
across time.*

*I have learned that anniversaries are much more im-
portant than I previously believed. Jan has a friend who
survived the Allegheny Airlines crash in Connecticut
and, every year a few days before the anniversary of the
crash, the woman feels a burning sensation in her feet
just as she did when she walked out onto the hot metal
wing of the plane to escape.*

*On this anniversary of mine, I feel once again the loss
of definition from which I suffered so severely just two
years ago.*

*I would gladly die right now if I could see my mother
just one more time. I want to tell her that Max left us.
I need her to know this piece of information.*

CHAPTER 12

"*D*iana, Diana, wake up."

Joanne is crouched beside the bed, her face close to mine.

"What's wrong?" I ask. For a moment my mind is murky, but seconds later reality rushes in and I remember Sukie has died.

"Shh. I don't want to wake Elaine," Joanne whispers, "but I want you to come someplace with me."

"What time is it?"

"It's only eight, but I really need you."

I sit up. I have only slept a few hours and I feel headachy and hung over. My night with Max is segregated in a part of my mind I can skirt and avoid, but Sukie is still gone from this world and I will never feel safe again.

"Where do you have to go?" I ask, swinging my legs off the bed.

Joanne is wearing a long T-shirt under which I can see the outlines of a bikini. With a rubber band, she has pulled her hair back so tightly from her face that it appears darker than usual and makes her look even more glamorous.

"I've got to get some exercise," Joanne says. "Really. Like sometimes you need a drink or a cigarette? Sometimes I have to . . . move. I was inside here all day yesterday without any fresh air."

I look at her groggily but in my heart I relent. Although I have never felt much urge to exercise, I have come to concede its authenticity as a human need.

"I found Sukie's membership card to the Hilton," Joanne whispers. "And I found a bathing suit in Carol's room that looks like it will fit you. Please," she pleads, standing up. "Please?"

"Okay."

I take the tank suit she's holding and go into the bathroom to try it on. It's tight, but I manage to get into it. Quickly I cover the suit with one of Sukie's sundresses and then hurry downstairs. Joanne is waiting for me in the front hall, twirling Sukie's keychain around her forefinger. Happy is sitting beside her, thumping her tail against the rug with erroneous excitement. We both look guiltily at the dog, but let ourselves outside without walking her.

The air is a little cooler and lighter than yesterday, but that is probably only because it is early. There is no sign of a breeze or any actual change in the atmosphere. Indeed, this false freshness begins to evaporate as soon as we start walking toward the Washington Hilton, which is set back on a hill off Connecticut Avenue. After a few blocks we feel the heat swallow us again.

That is when I notice Joanne has developed a serious expression on her face and I realize I am going to catch some shit from her about last night. Obviously she knew how late I had stayed out and she is clearly going to stick it to me for socializing with Max. I can't really blame her for being suspicious. Whatever Max's faults, he is still one of the few men we know who knows how to be intimate, which makes him fundamentally seductive.

But instead, when she finally speaks, Joanne asks, "What did you think of Miranda?"

"Oh, I'm not sure," I answer, relieved not to have to explain about Max. "Sometimes she sounded pretty sincere, but other times she sounded a little too facile for my taste. Oh, I don't know. Sukie never knew what to think about her either. Sometimes these new women just go with the flow and let whatever happens happen. Guilt or innocence isn't quite relevant. By the time they get to be thirty, they're hard nuts to crack. You never know what's going on in their heads. I guess it's because they're so embattled from having to support themselves on lousy salaries and from dealing with men who won't make even a minimal commitment."

"But I did get the feeling Miranda really liked Sukie."

"Sure. But that doesn't mean she might not have done a lot of damage. You know, it's not like it used to be when we could tell in a minute if some woman we'd just met *understood*—when there was a pre-verbal, chemical connection. These new women are different. They always have to ask what it is you *expect* them to understand, and if they have to ask, then they don't. They don't even consider themselves feminists."

"I think feminism left them holding the bag," Joanne says forgivingly. But then suddenly her voice cools off. "So what's the story about last night?"

"Oh. Well we couldn't find Jeff so we just sat and talked. Max had a lot to get off his chest."

"I'll bet. What'd he have to say?"

I begin to repeat Max's monologue and Joanne listens without any comment. Since she walks more purposefully than I do, I have to insert little half-steps to keep up with her, but my summary lasts until we reach the hotel driveway. I can tell she is as mesmerized as I was, and when we turn off the avenue she reaches out to take my hand.

"Thanks for coming with me, Di. I had to get some non-air-conditioned air or I was going to have a breathing attack." She pauses a moment and then says, "I suppose there's two sides to every story. Just because we loved everything about Sukie doesn't mean she wasn't difficult for him to live with."

So we walk into the Hilton holding hands—to hell with the Ethiopian and Eritrean cabbies hanging around outside the main entrance harnessing their ancestral hatred into rowdy roughhousing and rude comments. We totally ignore all the short squat American businessmen clustered around the lobby who look at our locked hands with ugly anti-Lesbian leers. We couldn't care less what anyone thinks about us anymore.

Sukie had often joked that whenever she wanted to feel like she was in a foreign country, she simply walked over to the Washington Hilton and had a drink outside on the terrace beside the pool. She said the same Americans appeared there as at any other Hilton around the world, and she could pick up exactly the same types as were available in Abu Dhabi or Amsterdam—minus a few Red Adair jocks whose careers kept them careening around the world outside the United States.

It was from visiting Sukie over the years that Joanne and I had learned the drill for Hilton summer "members," city residents who paid to use the tennis courts and swimming pool. Confidently, we walk through the lobby and out the terrace doors, past the café area sprouting striped umbrellas, and up to the gate where an attendant checks membership cards and distributes towels. Finally we reach the long aqua pool petaled, like a daisy, with yellow lounge chairs.

Joanne selects two chaises near the diving area and then wanders off toward the side reserved for swimming laps. I pull off Sukie's sundress, adjust the tank suit, and walk toward the diving board. The ceramic tiles, baking in neat margins around the pool, burn my feet, so I dive hurriedly into the water, swim two laps, and then climb up the ladder and retreat back to my chaise. From there I watch the early-morning hotel guests stationing themselves around the pool before I close my eyes.

I want to think about something. Max and I both did the same thing. We both ended our marriages. But I feel he was wrong and I was right. Essentially I asked Leonard for a divorce so I could be alone for the first time in my life. Max wanted his freedom so he could be with some else. Those are two very different things even though untangling the thick skeins of any marriage is painful, regardless of the reasons.

Actually Leonard had been a lovely husband to me, at least in the beginning, when he was young and idealistic and more interested in politics than money. But when the Movement began to shrivel, he panicked and cast about frantically for something new to care about. It turned out to be money. He still does a lot of *pro bono* civil rights work, but he's really interested in money.

Perhaps Leonard never believed that I had no romantic attachments or entanglements when I asked him for my freedom. Maybe he didn't believe I was truly content with the natural silence of my solitude which I saw as the only natural resource for good, if not great, work. Perhaps Leonard never believed what I said about enjoying the sensuousness of a solitary life undisturbed by the needs of another.

Perhaps his hurt is still too great to let him accept the fact that my work is now flourishing, that my time with our daughters is more nourishing, that reading and studying comfort me, and that the simplest excursion with a friend satisfies my now minimal social needs. Perhaps he'll never understand how the emotion and commotion I abandoned had already fertilized the soil in which I now plant the seeds of my own interests so as to yield the last and—hopefully—greatest harvest of my life.

And if, sometimes, a Sunday morning seems too unnaturally silent, I can always go out to meet any number of wonderful friends for coffee and compassion before returning home again. And if sometimes I awaken alone during the night, I can always listen to music, watch late movies on television or write in my Hot Flashes notebook where I am planting images and pruning ideas about my generation. Or if, in the most uncomfortable of all situations, I need the comfort of a man, I can always call my not-so-significant-other—knowing he tends his aloneness less well than I—and that he will appear promptly at my door. The rest of my life is in good order.

My friends and I don't travel much anymore but when we do we stay in first-class hotels with our second husbands or much-younger lovers and leave most of our lingerie behind for the maid when we check out. Actually, we are most comfortable now in the assorted beach houses some of us acquired during the past decade of divorce settlements. We view these summer properties as communal resources where, in case of emergency, we can always send one of our teenagers to recover from some severe complication occasioned by growing up. We can also use these mountain or beach houses when we need solitude more than sisterly sympathy or when, on those choice occasions when inspiration strikes, we want to write something of value. Of course we are discreet about not intruding when these recreational retreats are being used by their owners for family reunions, rendezvous or reconciliations.

Our beautiful friend Liz, who ran for Congress in Wisconsin, sent her two boys off to summer camp and then went up to the Vineyard to stay with Ellie. One morning they went to the beach and were sitting back away from the water when Liz saw her biological husband sweep out of the parking lot and sprawl, with his new wife and her three small children, across the sand down to the shore. Since Steve didn't have his glasses on, Liz knew he couldn't see her so she was able to observe everything in a relaxed, leisurely way.

Late in the afternoon, Steve had his new wife and new family pose for some snapshots. As he began taking the pictures, Liz said, "Do you know that we're going to be in the background of all his shots? His eyes are too bad to see us, but I know the range of that camera. You and I are going to be in every one of those pictures. He's going to freak out when he opens them up in the drugstore. I wish I could be there. He won't believe it. He'll think it's just my vindictive spirit."

Whenever possible, we still try to coordinate some summer weekends so our children can be together for a few lazy, happy days. "Come to me," says Anne, who summers up north in Maine where she owns a home and can find neighboring ones for overflow friends to rent or sublet. "Come to me," says Ellie who has a pondside cottage up in the Vineyard; "Come to me," says Janet, who has a farm in Vermont; "Come to me," says Mary from her condo down in Kitty Hawk, North Carolina. "Come be with some black folks," cries Eleanor, who inherited her parents' cottage in one of the first and only all-black resort towns on the Chesapeake Bay; "I swear there's no jellyfish until August." And when we do go there, it is like no other place in America.

But no longer will we have to travel to a patch of peninsula called Delmarva which Sukie, for some mysterious reason beyond geographic convenience, loved but which none of the rest of us could endure. Next to Ocean City, Maryland, Rehoboth, Delaware, is the tackiest town on the Atlantic seaboard. On that Boardwalk there are more underdeveloped, weird, out-of-it misfits than in any other resort town in the country. They come here because the place doesn't make them feel odd or out-of-it. Here, freaks prevail—genuine sideshow freaks plus circus families, adolescent girls with deformed feet, identical twins dressed exactly alike in homemade clothing, palsied old derelicts talking to themselves, bag ladies in their summer costumes, Baptist ministers singing and preaching aloud as they walk the streets, motorcycle freaks, ugly young lovers who kiss and pet in public, people propelling themselves in automated wheelchairs from which they play endless carnie games, and blondes wearing terrycloth shorts without any underpants.

Now there is no Sukie to nag us into trying Delmarva just one more time.

Now there is no Sukie.

When the chill of a shadow falls upon me, I open my eyes.

Joanne has interposed her body between me and the sun. She is glistening with water and looks svelte and taut bending over me, although from this angle I can see that her waist has begun to soften slightly. She has removed the rubber band from her hair so it will dry, and the long tangled strands fall forward over her shoulders like a careless scarf. I look away. I love Joanne's beauty and I don't want her body to melt as mine has begun to do.

But when she finally settles down on her chaise, I hear her breathing rapidly, and when I look at her face I see that she is crying.

"Hey," I say softly.

"It hurts so much," she sobs inconsolably. "And there were things I'd been saving to tell her."

I wait while Joanne wipes her eyes with the corner of the hotel towel.

"I feel so shitty that I didn't know what she was going through."

Now Sukie's anguish has become her deathbed where we must keep our vigil. Because her death preceded our discovery of the illness that probably killed her, we feel compelled to grieve for Sukie's pain as well as for our loss of her. It's like back in the sixties when hippies used their women's afterbirths as the base for a celebratory stew that they ate at postpartum parties.

"I suppose everyone knows by now," Joanne says softly, "but I think we should call someone from her old CR group. At least to say we're here and staying at the

house. Or something." Soberly she observes the heavy
sky. "And I suppose we should try to call Lindy. She'll
want to come down for the funeral. She loved Sukie."

"Did you know Lindy had a bad breakdown?"

"Yah. Sukie told me. Have you seen her?"

"No. She wasn't allowed to have any visitors at first
and then I went out to Long Island. But last week I saw
Bob out there and we had a cup of coffee together. He
feels real bad about Lindy's being in the hospital, but
he's got no intention of going back to her. Did Sukie tell
you the reason he left?"

"No, what?" Joanne asks.

"He was doing his yoga when Lindy walked into the
living room and said he should lift his legs up higher for
the lotus position. And that was it. He just stood up,
went into the bedroom, packed his clothes and moved
out."

"After five years?"

"Yup. And when Lindy asked him if he didn't think
he was overreacting, he told her she couldn't even fucking *do* the lotus position, so where the hell did she get
off telling him his legs weren't high enough?"

Joanne flashes her awesome smile, but after a few
seconds it flickers like a fluorescent light fading out.
Then she shakes her head and sits up to light a cigarette,
priming herself to speak.

"You know, I missed the mating season," she says
mournfully. "That's all. It's simple. I just missed the
mating season. But not having a man is not my number-
one problem right now. What I can't accept is that I
don't have any children. I can't accept that. I'm absolutely bloated with undelivered love. That's what I
wanted to tell Sukie. I wanted to say that to her. I've
had it with men, Diana. And I've had it with est and all
the personal-growth encounter jazz and all the feminist
c-r stuff and all the exercise classes and all the group sex.
I've done it all. I'm just not a groupie anymore. I lived
through the whole sexual revolution and the women's

movement and now I'm stuck in the postfeminist famine. I've run plenty of personals and I don't ever want to do that again. I don't ever want to try explaining myself to some asshole who can't understand anyway. I've *had* it, Diana. I'm just burned out. Jesus . . .

"When I think of all the men I slept with—it *freaks me out.* I mean, I've been with *so* many men. I've gone with a guy who kept a separate Rolodex for women from Dallas and one who kept a spritzer under his bed in case some woman he picked up had her period and smeared his fancy Porthault sheets. And for one entire year I went with a guy who used to say, 'I've got to be alone right now. Right this minute. It's not personal. Please just leave.' I have screwed standing up in the bathroom of a 747. I've screwed standing up in the stationery closet of a senator's office."

"Who was that?" I'm compelled to ask.

But she doesn't answer. We are known for protecting married men with legitimate excuses for adultery and elected officials with good ADA voting records.

"I think I've done more one-night stands than any big-name group in the country. And now I'm done."

She has finished toweling her hair and lies back to look directly up at the sky. After a few moments she closes her eyes.

We didn't start sleeping around until after our hideous high school years had ended and we finally escaped to college. Although we had been discusing free love since ninth grade, we had been unable to give ours away because there were neither takers nor opportunities. But as soon as we got to our respective colleges, we threw away our rubberized Playtex girdles-with-garters and became moody existentialists who wore no underwear at all. Then we took down the chintz curtains we had brought from home and began to use our dormitory windows as late-night rendevouz routes.

Now officially recognized refugees from conformity, obsessed with the absurdities of modern life, we unloaded our virginities on the first available organ recipient we could find and began "sleeping around" as if it was going out of style instead of just coming in. We rationalized our outrageous promiscuity in Marxist terms, viewing it as a means of redistributing the wealth. The works of Sigmund Freud became our sexual manuals. Having grown up during the Cold War, we were well schooled in maintaining long-term hostilities so our sexual liaisons were as urgent and neurotic as Russian/American relations. Each of our affairs was epic. We spent our nights going out, making out, breaking up and making up.

Nowadays I hear Loren and Lisa talk about "fooling around," by which I think they mean screwing. We never "fooled around." We were deadly serious about sex. We geared up for it. We dressed for it. Screwing for us was a fashion statement as well as a political posture and for a while we used up more Tampax absorbing morning-after sperm drainage than our own menstrual blood. We loved our love-hate relationships and discussed them in dreary detail. We came to love the color purple. We loved purple prose, purple lipstick and purple nights.

At Radcliffe I roomed with Doris from Dayton, who carried *The Stranger* around with her and hummed songs from *The Threepenny Opera* to show she was an intellectual. Our dorm was a time bomb loaded with books, bennies and boys. Every day, as soon as we woke up, we began yearning for the unavailable and craving the unattainable. We condemned Korea, criticized conformity, cursed McCarthy, got diaphragms from the Student Health Service and spent a lot of time trying to identify the tip of a cervix which the doctor had said felt like the cartilage at the tip of a nose. We dated, dieted and discussed Sartre endlessly.

Those were the days when we refused to declare a major until the very last minute and read everything on the recommended—as well as the required—reading lists. We read relentlessly, argued passionately and screwed incessantly. After making up all the Incompletes we'd collected, we graduated from college and went to New York where we collected unemployment comp while trying to test our talents. Since we'd never learned the numbers at the top of our typewriters—blissfully believing the letters were enough for writing poetry—we were unsuccessful as stenographers or typists. What we were good at was suffering-with-style and doing-without.

We wore turtleneck sweaters with no makeup and no bras. We picked up men on trains and in coffee houses, airports and depots, in the streets and on the sidewalks of New York City. We hung out in the Village and made the art scene at Max's Kansas City. By the time we finished college we had learned how to drink bourbon, rye, wine, Scotch, beer, vodka and even cappuccino when stuck in coffee houses during long poetry readings. We drank to excess in bars, bathrooms, boats and bedrooms. We were intensely intense about everything. We went to plays and museums and old movies, and if a date paid for a meal, we paid him for paying. We played and prayed we wouldn't get knocked up. We loved being bohemians and we couldn't get enough of anything—especially sin.

Sin still existed back then.

During that bridge of time between the mid-fifties and mid-sixties, college bohemians became on-the-road beatniks and the Beatles exploded, smashing middle-class hypocrisies. We immediately bought navy-surplus pullover sweaters and walked along Macdougal Street in our new custom-made leather sandles eating Italian sausage sandwiches and Italian ices on our way to see some arty Italian movie full of malaise.

It wasn't until the disorienting discovery of *truly* casual—rather than *intensely* casual—sex in the 1960s that we really got into some serious trouble. It was Hippie-style free-love that eventually turned out to be the

most costly of all. It was sixties free-for-all-love that left
us with so many *outstanding* debts.

"And when I think of the abortions I had . . ." Joanne's
chin beings to quiver. "For all I know, I probably can't
even get pregnant anymore."

Tears well up in her eyes. I can see her swallow forci-
bly in an effort to gain control over her voice.

"Jesus. The way Elaine snapped my head off for men-
tioning *The Big Chill* almost makes me afraid to say
this, Diana. But really, I've been thinking about getting
knocked up by somebody and just not telling him. Some
stranger who seems like a decent human being. I mean
pretty soon, with this AIDS thing going around. . . . I
mean, I'm almost forty-four and if I don't try soon, and
I mean *really* soon, it will just be too late for me."

"Oh, Joanne." I laugh gently and cautiously, knowing
she experiences all her enthusiasms as authentic and
serious.

"I just want to pick out a man and forget to put my
diaphragm—do you say *in* or *on?*"

"I don't say either anymore."

"Actually, three women I know pretty well in New
York did it. They picked out some guy—some friend—
to knock them up and now they have babies. Real, live,
darling little babies. And the men don't know shit. They
probably couldn't care less anyway. Look, the seventies
sucked. There wasn't a chance in the world to meet a
man back then and make things work out. Everything
was too tense. The war between the sexes really got out
of control there for a while. We were facing some *major*
disorders back then.

"But now I'm down to the wire, Diana. Really. And
I feel frantic. I want a baby. I want to raise a child. And
if I'm going to do it, I have to do it now. I mean, I did
think it was a little weird when Glenn Close provided
her own husband for her girlfriend. That did seem like
a little bit much. But with a stranger or with someone
like Jeff, who Sukie cared about and who loved her

. . . Anyone who loved Sukie that much couldn't be a bad human being, could he? And he'd never know. He wouldn't even bump into us at the Children's Zoo in Central Park, since he lives here in Washington. I really would never see him again.

"And I don't want to get shot up with a turkey baster full of sperm from some pricey sperm bank. Every time I'd look at the kid, I'd think of a turkey. And I don't want a baby from Bolivia. I can't even remember my Spanish. I want my own baby. Now. Before it's too late forever. Because I've got an apartment and enough money and all this love to give. What am I supposed to do with all my love? Eat it?

"I tell you, I'm scared to death I'm going to go into menopause any minute now. I go crazy waiting for my period every month. I wait for it like back in college when I was scared I'd get knocked up. So twenty years later I'm still running into the bathroom every ten minutes to do the old toilet-paper oil-dip routine, you know. Remember? Swiping the sides to see if anything's happening? Looking for some show-and-tell."

She begins to cry. Hard. Very hard for a very long time. She's off on a jag. She's crying for herself and for a baby and for the past and for Sukie. She doesn't even try to stem the tears or the harsh noises she's making.

I wait.

"What did I do wrong, Diana?"

"You didn't do anything *wrong*, Joanne," I say gently. "Your life just got out of sync. Go ahead and get pregnant if you want to. There's nothing wrong with it. Let Phil Donahue worry. So he'll have a show called 'What About the Biological Father?' So what? Nobody worried about the 'biological father' back when unwed mothers existed. Then it was always *her* fault and *her* problem and *her* baby. So if you want to do it, just go do it. Do some dope and do Jeff. What the hell?"

Although decades have passed, essentially, we have not changed very much over the years.

Except for Sandy and Nadia (both brilliant but un-recognized research scientists who helped Sandy's husband win a Nobel Prize and who aren't afraid of dropping a vital syllable when they use the word *organism* in polite society), most of us remain science-and-technology virgins. Although we have learned how to operate PCs, like our mothers we still cannot load a camera, remember the number of cups in a quart, use the metric system, open someone else's car trunk or reverse angles in order to get a table back through a doorway after getting it through frontwards.

We still do not wash our lettuce unless someone is watching, bake anything from scratch (although we say we do), or stick our heads inside the toilet to scrub away the high-water marks. Occasionally, we have been known to emerge from a restaurant rest room with a piece of toilet paper stuck to the heel of one shoe and, on a bad day, to abandon a stuffed shopping cart at the checkout counter of a crowded supermarket for no apparent reason to the total bafflement of the management. Many of us persist in cutting our own hair with manicure scissors, burying our feet in the sand so as to hide crooked toes, kissing with our lips closed to cloister bad breath and thinking—whenever we are drunk—that we are about to be able to speak, or at least understand, Spanish.

We still order magazine subscriptions under false names, listen to odd radio stations in hopes of catching interviews with old friends, and join the BOMC every few years to receive cheap introductory books before canceling our memberships. We continue to carry breath fresheners in our purses in case we bump into an old lover, and will never stop curling and/or straightening our hair, waxing our legs and bikini areas, or maneuvering the bathroom scale around to find an advantageous floor slope that will produce a tilt that allows us to detect a weight loss.

We are still terrible spellers. Phonetically crippled by 1940s "sight reading" methods, we never learned how to sound out words or distinguish between long and short vowels. We still can't tell the TV networks apart or dare to make non-changeable airline reservations seven days in advance. We continue to be self-conscious dancers, impatient gardeners, fast typists, good drivers, erratic cooks and lazy—but inventive—lovers. We remain firmly convinced that grapefruit juice can destroy already digested calories and that wearing a tampon all day before a heavy date will tighten up tired, slightly stretched-out, sexual passages.

Suddenly I am invaded by an enormous but imprecise feeling of peril that makes my heart start pumping iron. I slide off the chaise and onto my feet in a swift swirl of motion, hoping to preempt any opposition.

"Don't you think we should be getting back, Joanne? Elaine doesn't even know where we are—and Mr. Smilow will be coming in this afternoon."

Joanne immediately senses my feeling of urgency and prepares to leave without any protest at all.

CHAPTER 13

So it is still before ten when we unlock Sukie's front door and walk back toward the kitchen where the telephone is ringing. Elaine, who is sitting in her customary chair at the table, answers it as I push open the door.

"Yes?" she intones. Barefoot and wrapped in her caftan, she listens, nods, and says yes several more times before replacing the receiver.

"Who's that?" Joanne demands, following me through the doorway.

"Norman Naylor. That shrink Sukie used to date."

"No shit," Joanne groans. "What'd he want?"

"He wanted to know if someone would be here so he could come over and pick up something he'd left."

"Like what? The family silver?" Joanne sneers. "Oh boy. I'm really going to keep my eye on him. I'm not going to leave him alone for a minute."

Elaine shrugs, stands up and walks to the refrigerator. Opening the door, she studies the interior as if reading a table of contents. After a few minutes she returns to the table carrying a restaurant-size enamel baking pan covered with tinfoil.

"Where were you?" she asks.

"We went to take a swim at the Hilton."

"I know this is a lasagna," she says, removing the tinfoil as if unveiling a portrait. "I saw it Friday when we got here. I can't believe Sukie made a lasagna."

We all look into the pan. It is three-quarters full. There is a thick frosting of half-melted mozzarella cheese and several chunks of undissolved canned tomatoes clinging to the ghostly white noodles. Elaine fetches a fork, sits down and starts eating the cold lasagna directly out of the pan. Her fork cuts a swath through the noodles, moving methodically from left to right and then back from right to left like a typewriter carriage.

It is now midmorning of Day Three as I sit watching Elaine transport heaping loads of pasta up to her face. I wonder whether she likes eating the lasagna because Sukie made it or whether she is just hungry. I wonder if Sukie made it for some special dinner the night before she died. Perhaps Jeff would know something about this lasagna if we ever see him again and can ask. Certainly it's unusual to find a pan of pasta in Sukie's refrigerator. She was the one who always reminded us that Gloria kept only grapefruits and club soda in her fridge, and since Gloria has remained scrupulously slim, she serves as our anti-fat touchstone or talisman.

Joanne gets up and walks over to the silverware drawer. She extracts a fork, pauses, looks at me and then down again at the utensils.

"You want one?"

I nod.

Back at the table, she sits down, hands me my fork and plunges her own into the pan of lasagna. I do the same.

We are about to expand our suffering with a siege of suicidal overeating.

Here is a list of what we consume during the next forty minutes:

⅓ jar sweet pickles
½ quart Oreo-flavored ice cream
½ jar artichoke hearts marinated in heavy oil
2 stale jelly donuts

½ jar stuffed green olives
1 package pressed ham
1 stone-hard whole-wheat pita bread
3 hard-boiled eggs, so aged that the yokes taste metallic
¼ package Entenmann's cherry cheesecake
⅓ jar capers
1 teenager-sized bag of Utz Bar-B-Que potato chips
¼ half-frozen Entenmann's Bavarian cream coffeecake
3 Amstel Light beers

While eating, we retell several of our favorite eating epics.

"Remember when Sukie went out to the beach for a weekend with that lawyer she liked from Boston and starved herself so bad that by Sunday afternoon when they stood up to shake the sand off their blanket, she fainted? And then the medic on the ambulance told the lawyer she was suffering from self-induced dehydration?"

We laugh and keep on eating.

"Remember when Joellen did the same kind of number? She didn't eat anything solid from Friday night until Sunday morning—only a little white wine—so when that guy she still goes with took her to a restaurant Sunday morning and went into the men's room, Joellen stuck her fingers inside a jar of jelly on the counter and got them jammed in so tight that what's-his-name had to drive her to Southampton so the jar could be broken by a doctor in case the glass severed any of her arteries?"

Joanne giggles at Elaine's story. I hadn't heard that one before either and the thought of chic, sleek Joellen Darling getting herself in such a fix makes me laugh so hard some sweet pickle juice tickles my throat and makes me choke.

Elaine decides to elaborate further:

"Later on she told me that the whole time she was in the emergency room, all she could think about was a scene from some hard-times Depression movie she'd seen, where a starving drifter went into a diner, drank a whole bottle of ketchup and then escaped before anyone could catch him."

Oh, how many times have we gobbled laxatives in frenzied guilt over our orgiastic eating or swallowed toothpaste in an unlit motel bathroom because we had starved ourselves into delirium? Joanne once told me she ate half a tube of Dentagard in the bathroom of a new lover's apartment because she felt faint from hunger but too shy to ask for any food. And even then, when reduced to eating toothpaste, she remained nervous enough to carefully observe the direction in which the man had squeezed his tube, so as not to cause him any aggravation the next morning that might turn him against her.

For the first time, Joanne pauses in her nonstop eating. "You know, there's a new over-the-counter high-fiber pill that kills your appetite if you take it thirty minutes before a meal."

"How would we know?" Elaine inquires, raising another forkful of lasagna up to her mouth. "I mean how would we know we were about to have a meal?"

We are impulse eaters, the culinary equivalent of kleptomaniacs. Often we discuss the binger found unconscious in her New York apartment surrounded by empty deli containers of coleslaw, pasta, three-bean and potato salad, who had passed out from overeating and was rushed to a hospital to have her stomach pumped. Later she told a psychiatrist that she was unable to stop herself from hitting every delicatessen on the way home from work and buying a pint of each item on sale.

Joanne is now gliding between the cupboard, the refrigerator and the counter, busily smearing butter and garlic flakes over some English muffins she's discovered in a recycled Medaglia d'Oro coffee can. Sukie believed muffins stayed fresher refrigerated and that the design of a coffee can—perfectly shaped to contain a stack of muffins—proved her theory.

Joanne is preparing to toast the muffins when suddenly the doorbell rings. Although we are momentarily startled, a second later we calmly rise and methodically but swiftly begin to clear away any signs of food consumption. Quickly Joanne sweeps the garlicky muffin crumbs off the counter into the cup of her hand while starting to stuff emptied containers into the garbage can. Elaine whisks the empty lasagna pan into the sink where she directs hot water from the rubber vegetable spray (that only devoted homemakers such as Elaine and our mothers used) into the burnt, crusty corners, while I dance between table and sink, whipping a wet sponge over one surface after another.

Within minutes, the scene of our culinary crimes is spotless and Elaine rushes off to answer the second, louder and longer ring of the bell.

When she reappears, Dr. Norman Naylor is following her, making wide irritated sweeps with his arms to push Happy away. The dog is trying to get the doctor's attention by leaping up and lunging at his thigh before snowplowing, with uncut nails, down his trouser leg.

Dr. Norman Naylor is short, stocky and close to fifty. He has beautifully bonded teeth, a contact-lens gleam in his dark, darting eyes and an undulating hairline. What remains of his thin lusterless hair is reluctantly parted into something resembling an EKG wave, since he draws longer hairs from either side over his central bald spot. Even on this sweltering Labor Day weekend, he is wearing a suit and tie.

"Hello, I'm Dr. Naylor. Norman Naylor," he says in a nasal voice that betrays serious allergies as well as a possible deviated septum. "I was a good friend of Sukie's."

"Yes," I say sarcastically. "Sukie told us all about you."

Immune to sarcasm, Norman Naylor tosses me a quick, insincere smile before sneaking a covetous look at Joanne—the prototypical shiksa star of major Jewish wet dreams. Joanne, although still wearing the long T-shirt over her bikini, looks, as always, as if she's on her way to a cocktail party. Glamour oozes from her pores like sweat from lesser women.

"This is truly a tragedy," Norman continues, stationing himself in the center of the kitchen. "A great tragedy. Sukie was a fine woman. She'd been going through a rough period, no doubt about that, but then most women her age getting divorced usually do. That's why I have an ironclad rule not to date any woman who hasn't been *divorced*—and I don't mean just separated—for more than two years. Before then, they're simply too upset. In fact, Sukie was the only exception I ever made to that rule, and that proved to be a bad mistake. But it's really tragic she died just when she was beginning to come around."

Now it's a shocked silence that bounces around the room. Joanne is staring at Norman with incredulity. I see a flush of anger stain Elaine's face and I feel my own heart start to pound at the door of my chest.

Hot flash . . .

Dr. Norman Naylor has been sent to us to diminish any discord in our ranks by providing an external threat that will automatically reunite us. Actually it feels quite wonderful to be gathered in Sukie's kitchen hating Norman Naylor in unison. We know, from Sukie, that Norman is a divorce vulture who makes a career out of exploiting newly single-again women. Indeed, Norman is obviously suffering an internal struggle over whether to go for Joanne, the chancy super-shiksa, or Elaine, the clearly available Jewish Geisha who would obviously be grateful for any opportunity to be of service. A risk-averse person, Norman is in a wretched state of conflict reminiscent of comic-book Archie, who was always torn between blond Betty and brunette Veronica.

By now, all the women of our generation are fed up with all the Normans who have passed through our lives. A classic Norman is immediately identifiable because he has a totally unwarranted, swaggering attitude similar to the kind sported by MVP athletes.

"I bet everyone teases you about Norman Mailer, with your names rhyming the way they do," Elaine ventures with a visible absence of malice. Clearly she recognizes a suitable suitor for herself, even though a classic Norman is biologically incapable of spontaneously warming up to an Elaine.

"Oh, sure. All the time. But I'm used to it," Norman says, smearing his words with mucus manufactured by his overactive sinuses. "Actually, even though he's a *little* better writer than I am, we're not totally dissimilar types."

He says this lightly, tone-deaf to who we are and how women like us feel about men like Norman Mailer. Joanne lowers her sunglasses. She had pushed them high on her head to restrain her chlorine-wild hair, but now puts them back in place to hide an expression of enormous contempt in her eyes.

"So, tell me who all of you are," Norman says with a saccharine smile.

Wearily we offer him our names.

"Listen, if you're sitting *shiva* here, I'd like to join you so I can get to know all of you better and hear what each of you does and how each of you knew Sukie."

"This isn't a singles club," Joanne says sourly.

Norman smiles. "Of course not. But there's no reason we can't try to comfort each other at this time of bereavement, is there?"

Elaine, who had started the dishwasher, returns to reopen the door and insert some more dirty silverware she'd overlooked.

Norman releases a howl. "Hey. You can't . . . edit that thing while it's going. All the water'll come out."

Elaine looks up at him as she closes the dishwasher door without releasing a drop of water.

Norman has now exposed himself as a *nudge*.

"Well, just let me take care of one little piece of business before we start to talk," he says. Then he turns and looks directly at me. "I know it's hot out there, but would you mind stepping into the hallway with me for one minute?"

Although startled that Norman has chosen me as his confidante, I follow him out of the kitchen. Away from the air conditioner, the air is so stagnant and heavy that it is difficult to breathe. The house feels like a car with its fan running when someone accidentally turns on the heater instead of the A.C.

"Listen," he says. "This is a little embarrassing, but there's something I left here I need to retrieve."

"What is it?"

"Actually," he says, "I'm not sure where it is, but it might be up in Sukie's bedroom."

"Well, why don't you tell me *what* it is, so I can go find it?"

He looks at me with increased discomfort and, opening his pouty lips, tries to speak without any success.

Ahhhhh, I think.

Hot flash . . .

A sweet revenge is moving within reach.

I step a little closer to Norman.

"Actually, Diane . . ."

"It's Diana," I say gently but firmly, hoping to further disconcert him. "Dian*a*."

"Well, Dian*a*, it's a videocassette." Norman lets the last word spurt forth like a belch for which he isn't responsible.

"But how long has it been here?" I ask with innocent incredulity. "I thought you'd stopped seeing Sukie months ago."

"Well, yes, I did. I mean, we did. Of course, I was sorry that it had to happen, but she was getting serious and I thought it best to slow things down."

Internally, I cringe at his *chutzpah*. Sukie was only able to tolerate his company for limited periods of time at times of intense loneliness and then only as comic relief.

"Anyway, I forgot my film here before we parted company."

Click.

He takes a deep breath. "I guess it's probably up in Sukie's room. So why don't I just go up and look?" he asks with a touch of impatience.

Instantly, I move ahead of him to lead the way upstairs.

As soon as we enter Sukie's bedroom I glance behind the TV where several cassettes, which I'd noticed while remaking the bed, are stacked on the broad sill of the bay window. As Norman begins prowling along Sukie's desk, jarring her books, lifting her papers and carelessly shifting her file folders, I reach for the videocassettes, grab one marked *Linda Lace*, and quickly insert it into the VCR.

At the sound of the mechanical clatter, Norman whirls around. But in the time it takes him to cross the room, I hit the control buttons that activate the video and watch the title and pseudonymous credits leap onto the screen.

"That's it," Norman cries, reaching out to turn off the TV.

But now I insert myself between him and the controls, planting my body in front of the screen as the peculiar percussive music—located somewhere between a Lindy and a twist—that plays in most pornographic films begins to pulsate. Immediately I am transported back to my nightlife with Leonard, the big civil libertarian and defender of First Amendment rights, who was a porn junkie.

The film begins with a good-looking couple awakening in their conjugal bed. The Handsome Hubby reaches over to turn off the clock-radio and then, stark naked, heads to the bathroom while his wife curls up and goes back to sleep. Once in the shower, the Hand-

some Hubby begins soaping himself and starts to fanta-
size into cinematic existence a woman who prayerfully
kneels down before him under the shower to start playing with his pale pink prick.

"Good Lord, I've never seen *anything* like this," I lie.

"You mean you've *never* seen an X-rated film before?" Norman asks with excited disbelief.

In truth, there was one porn movie that Leonard
enjoyed and played so often I came to feel I was also
married to the leading couple.

"Really," I answer.

This one's for Sukie, I think. Yes sir, this one's for
Sukie.

Now Norman is standing near the foot of the bed,
paler and more anxious-looking than before. "Listen,"
he whispers. "This is not the right time to play a movie
like this. This is a real pornographic film. Maybe you
and I can go back to my place later and watch it, since
you've never seen one before."

"Wait just a minute," I insist.

This one's for Sukie, I repeat to myself, as I watch
Handsome Hubby soap his chest while the Fantasy
Lady sucks his organ, playfully gliding her tongue up
and down the slightly distended, rolled hem of his
penis. Next she starts licking the whole thing as if it
were a popsicle, and then, afterwards, as if it were a
melting ice cream cone.

"Listen . . ." Norman says, searching for but unable
to remember my name. "I'm going to turn this off."

He moves toward the television once more, but I
reach for Sukie's remote control and, the minute he
turns off the set, I turn it on again.

"Good Lord, Norman," I say in what I hope sounds
like an anguished cry. "I've got to see this. I've *got* to."

And once again Norman relents.

Finally, like a sleepy reptile, Handsome Hubby's
penis starts coming awake, stretching, yawning, and
sleepily shaking its head while opening its cyclopean

eye. When the organ reaches its full, impressive growth, the Fantasy Lady tries, like a sword-eating swami, to swallow it. The camera zooms in and follows the intrusion of the mushroom-like head of the cock down the Fantasy Lady's throat.

Norman is profoundly embarrassed.

"Oh God," he groans, looking at me venomously. "Why are you doing this at a time like this?"

He reaches out again to hit the stop button, but I instantly restart the film.

"How do I know this is your movie, Norman?" I ask, as the slim blond wife arrives in her hubby's fantasy to station herself behind him. There she begins licking his wet buttocks and low-slung scrotum, which dangles between his legs like a poorly packed, unevenly distributed shoulderbag purse. Eventually she swivels around to join the brunette on her hubby's front.

"Well, I can tell you what's going to happen," Norman says confidently.

"Well you could *guess* that, Norman. Anyway, that just proves you've watched it, not that you *own* it. This might belong to Sukie's"—I have to pause before uttering the word—"estate. I mean, these cost a lot of money, don't they?"

But now Norman is watching the screen, suddenly transfixed, and his voice evaporates from the heat of his own suppressed emotions. By now the slim blond wife, who has turned out to be a psychiatrist, is at her office. On the other side of her desk sits a visibly uncomfortable, awkward young male patient whose problem is his inability to achieve orgasm. Our lady shrink instructs him to unzip his fly and allow his lazy organ to hang out.

"Now do this," she says, showing him how to roll up the sleeve of his penis. "Now do this," she says, showing him how to slide it back down again. Diligently the young man works the glove of his penis back and forth until his organ grows to monstrous length. Then the doctor gets horny and, lifting her skirt, shoves the crotch of her panties aside so she can stroke her labia. The mutual masturbation continues for a long time, but Norman, gentleman that he is, waits with professional courtesy until both his colleague and her patient come before turning back toward me.

"I know you're doing this for some ulterior motive," he snarls. "I think you're trying to embarrass me."

"Norman," I chide. "why would I want to do that? I simply wanted to see an adult movie for once in my life."

Now, with a certainty he hasn't displayed before, Norman presses the rewind button and stations himself between me and the set.

"I just don't understand what you're trying to accomplish," he says sourly, "but I can certainly understand why you and Sukie were *such good friends.*"

Then, with great deliberation, he ejects the video and, holding it firmly in front of him, marches resolutely out of Sukie's bedroom for the last—if not the first—time.

We have known numerous Normans in our times. Indeed, some of us even married Normans. After the 1984 TV debate between the Vice-President and Geraldine Ferraro, Jane and Barbara wrote an article for *The Wall Street Journal* in which they said George Bush had reminded every female American viewer of her first husband.

Wrong.

George Bush might have reminded Jane and Barbara, who are both Christians, of their first husbands, who were both Gentiles, but the ethnics among us, myself included by marriage, were originally married to men more like Norman Mailer than George Bush. Many insecure Depression Babies married Nice Jewish Boys who turned out to be disappointingly one inch too short all over.

But we are onto men now. Actually, we have been onto men for quite a while. We always knew what they

expected when they empaneled an all-woman jury.
They were wrong. We always knew what they expected
when they said, "Hey, wouldn't a cup of coffee taste
great right about now?" They were wrong. Barbara H.
said power was an aphrodisiac. She was wrong. That
wasn't power. That was expensive after-shave she was
smelling. The whole L.A. Airport smells like that.

We have done lots of things for lots of men. We have
scored for men, lied for men, cheated for men, passed
bad checks for men and moved pre-Columbian art for
men. We have looked up to men and gone down for
them. We have worked with, under and out for men;
we have worked some men over. We have put men up
and put them down; we have put up with them and
been put out by them. Constantly, throughout our life-
times, we've carried on about men—about carrying on
with them and about carrying on without them. Although Florence claims a woman needs a man like a fish
needs a bicycle, lots of us identified with the Little Mer-
maid who died in her effort to dance for her prince. She,
of course, landed on her tail just as we usually did.

While our sisters married CPA's or orthodontists, we
married the medical students who, during the sixties,
became shrinks who wore lovebeads or a single shark
tooth on a leather thong around their necks and eventually ran off with female patients much more neurotic
than we. If we married law students, they could never
pass either kind of bar and if they did, often became
alcoholic public defenders or public-interest advocates.
The poets we loved wouldn't marry anyone and most of
the Ph.D.s in psychology whom we dated ended up in
Haight-Ashbury on one side of the couch or the other.

Those few of us who were virgins on our wedding
nights, had no basis for making any sexual comparisons.
What does a cherry know about the pits? As virgins, we
were too ignorant and insecure to trust our own instincts, especially since our husbands insisted they were
great lovers—conveniently confusing their pussy-lust

for talent. Those of us who were not actually virgins, but who withheld our sexual favors from men who wanted virginal brides, realized—only too late—that our first lovers were the best. However, we stayed married and eventually, over the years, discovered that our first lovers were the only guys who never showed up at class reunions.

Although Sukie had told me about Norman Naylor with great wit and much laughter, I knew he had hurt her feelings when he said she was too moody and too much trouble to see any longer. When she had replied that she had never wanted to be anything but friends, he said he didn't have the time or the temperament to be "just friends" with *any* woman. Sukie had also said that Norman was enormously cheap and was always afraid she'd want buttered, for a dollar more, rather than plain popcorn at a movie. She said that he insisted on autopsying movies to death, scrutinizing the product of every noseblow into his grungy gray handkerchief as if trying to locate the live virus responsible for the common cold, and drove like someone we would hate driving behind.

None of us any longer bothers to try impressing men like Norman. It was Sukie who said that if you leave the *t* out of *outrage,* you have "ourage" men. No longer do we twist ourselves out of shape for ourage men. Nowadays, when we rendezvous with either old or new ourage lovers, we no longer bother to apologize for—or even identify—the various scars on our bodies, let alone our souls. We assume that most ourage men have had enough experience to be able to distinguish between appendix, hysterectomy, cesarean and fibroid surgery scars designed and cut with care for wear with bikinis. They also have personal familiarity with stretch marks, although they sport theirs in different locales than ours.

Since we grew up believing that physical fitness meant brushing our teeth twice a day and eating something from each of the Four Basic Food Groups we are not in great shape.

However, though fat, flab, veins and wrinkles now mar our bodies, we believe these are offset by our sexpertise, which can be defined as maintaining a good sense of humor while assuming weird positions. Along with our muscles, our expectations have relaxed. We no longer freak out when men call us by the wrong name, and we never expect multiple sexual encounters from the same man in the course of a single evening.

Several years ago, we made a policy decision not to listen anymore when ourage men use adjoining bathrooms, since the sound of their urine has changed considerably over the years and their streams have become much slower starting, less steady and markedly weaker than ever before. Indeed, the infrastructure of our male peers has begun to resemble that of our aging family homes where corroded pipes are taken for granted.

Needless to say, their hair (both kinds) is as gray as ours. Maxine, who until she was forty-three thought all pubic hair was black, finally escaped from the sexual shtetl in which she had been segregated and discovered that Wasps have totally different color schemes. Also she learned that she wasn't the only person in the world guilty of leaving a stray gray question mark stuck to the side of a bathtub after a long soak. Nevertheless, because of the paucity of special agents in our skewed (some say screwed) sexual economy, Maxine came to believe we must forget the old American adage about a chicken in every pot and share the few male resources available. In other words, some of us have taken up with other women's husbands.

The feminist party line on sleeping with someone else's husband is fuzzy. Basically, we could never decide whether we were committing adultery if our lovers were married but we were not. We were always unclear as to whether both parties had to be married to commit adultery, or whether an innocent single woman could be found guilty by association.

The adultery question continues to plague us. As we all know, for the past four years Joanne has been having an affair with a married man who visits her from six-thirty to seven-thirty every morning while supposedly jogging in Central Park. We consider this harmless since it keeps Joanne happy and her lover away from marriage-hungry younger women who can only hear their biological clocks ticking. Joanne maintains that she is helping her lover's wife maintain the status quo and that she should be commended for her altruism. Needless to say, we have been unable to settle this issue to everyone's satisfaction. On this question there are two camps—and one is full of camp followers.

Although it used to be that we could forget our troubles by sitting in a bar until an appropriate stranger (someone with whom we could talk and feign or feel love for a finite period of time) finally appeared, we admit that that is no longer feasible. Nowadays it takes far too long to meet a man imaginative enough to see our appeal through the veil of our years. As Gracie's George said recently, "It now takes all night to do what I used to do all night."

We have finally acknowledged that we can no longer hang around an ocean marina, looking slim, tan, and mysterious, until some Special Agent docks his yacht, comes ashore in faded T-shirt and cutoffs, and engages us in a conversation so crackling with sexual static that he impulsively invites us to sail off to Micronesia that very afternoon aboard his boat with his all-male, deeply tanned crew for the next six weeks.

Although we did not necessarily like *all* men *all* the time, we loved being with some man most of the time; we loved being with men for the same reasons we loved going to movies. Both offered us quick trips out of our own heads. Men could modify our moods, unleash our ids, enlarge our egos, and suppress our heavy-duty, overdeveloped consciences. Men and movies offered delicious excursions out of ourselves; like enabling legislation, they helped us get from one place to another.

After lifelong addictions to passion, for which we would gladly sacrifice sanity and security in pursuit of some momentary thrill, it is difficult to forget that search for the quiver that quickens life. So we continue to hunt for the Perfect Lover, who will provide us with an escape route from inferior realities, through the old tried-and-true, trial-and-error method, despite our decreased patience and diminished faith.

When I start downstairs, I see Elaine and Norman standing together at the front door. Elaine, now wearing a fresh cotton dress, is holding a large box and she looks up at me with a surprised but easy smile. The sour expression that so often stains her face has evaporated and she looks lighter and brighter than she has in years.

I quicken my descent, avoiding Norman's eyes.

"Where are you going?"

"We're going to the funeral home," Elaine says, flashing some of her old conviction and competence. "I put together an outfit for Sukie—a blouse and the paisley suit." She pauses. "I'd been planning to take a taxi over there this afternoon, but now Norman's offered to take me."

Her smile is like an old friend I haven't seen for a long time.

I turn, shamefaced, toward Norman. But he shows no sign of a grudge. Either he missed the point of my performance upstairs or he is actually rather good-natured. There's even an outside possibility that he has some professional perspective that remains operative despite his personal foibles.

"How nice of you, Norman," I say, genuinely moved. "How . . . very nice."

He nods at me but then turns to touch Elaine's arm and propel her forward.

"Then we're going to the police precinct to tell them

about Sukie's car," Elaine continues hurriedly. "I found her insurance policy with the serial number and everything. And after that we'll go over to the *Post* and drop off the funeral announcement Joanne wrote."

"Gosh, Elaine," I smile, truly impressed by her renewal.

Then, I lean against the smooth silky banister as I watch them walk outside talking animatedly to each other.

CHAPTER 14

When the doorbell rings late that afternoon, we know that it's Mr. Smilow. I look at the faces around me, realize I am the unanimous choice of a welcoming committee, and reluctantly go out to open the door.

He is wearing a wide-ribbed blue seersucker suit with a white shirt upon which, right above his heart, he's pressed his panama hat as if acknowledging the national anthem before the start of a sporting event. As a fight promoter and gambler, Manny Smilow mixed it up with many of Chicago's diverse elements, and his semi-legit life, as described by Sukie, had tinted his basically decent character with a tinge of corruption.

Since Manny Smilow has taken a Northwest Airlines Chicago-Vegas gambling junket once a month for the past twenty-five years, he has a vague Vegas tan, the variety acquired by walking between casinos during the daytime. His stubbornly black, naturally wavy hair succeeds in covering his skull, and a raunchy racetrack squint elongates his eyes. It is obvious this man has scanned the heavens many times to see if some game was going to be rained out.

Beside him stands a woman whose face, and particularly the set of bags beneath her eyes, identifies her as his sister. She was once very good looking, and a scent of sensuality still clings to her, suggesting she had relied heavily upon her handsomeness to get through life. Now her body looks like the "before" shape that shadows a newly reduced figure in a diet-pill ad.

Her hair is totally disciplined and "done." Educated waves hug her head, and palette-platinum locks mingle with naturally light strands for a highly stylized "frosted" look. She is wearing a dark cotton sleeveless sheath with a matching, long-sleeved jacket draped over her shoulders—a perfect hot-flash fashion.

Shifting her handbag so as to extend her right hand to shake mine, she says, "I'm Rosetta, Sukie's Auntie Rosetta. This is one of the greatest shocks of our lives. We lost Clara, Sukie's mother, only five years ago. A problem with the heart; she went quickly. But I'm afraid this is too much for my brother. It's been a terrific shock. Manny's just holding on. No parent should bury a child, regardless of age. It's not in the natural order of things. This is out of order."

Mournfully, I agree with her by bobbing my head.

Rosetta is now inside the foyer, beckoning her brother to follow.

"Hello, Mr. Smilow," I say, extending my hand again. "I'm so sorry."

"Darling, I recognize you," he says, "but I've forgotten the name. The shock . . ."

"I'm Sukie's friend Diana Sargeant—I mean Satz. I mean I was Satz when we met once here in Washington, but that was a long time ago. I live in New York. I was . . . the one who called you."

"Of course," he agrees, inspecting me from top to toe. "And I know you're Sukie's friend because you're a real looker. All Sukie's girlfriends are good lookers. Ten years younger than your age, you look. That's why I never understood why you all didn't find more happiness. That's what I'll never understand. Should've been better men around to take better care of all you fine women."

He is inside now, blinking in the diminished light. Finally he begins walking toward the kitchen with Rosetta and me in his wake.

"We've got lots to talk about," he says, pushing open the swinging door.

Inside, they are waiting for us—Elaine, Joanne and Norman—seated sedately around the table.

"Okay." Manny Smilow nods as he registers all the faces. "Okay, so I knew my sugar plum had enough good friends she wouldn't be left alone now. She was always good to her friends. Plenty of money I gave her to lend her girlfriends when I had it. When times were good. A couple times I paid one girl's tuition at Chicago University because my Sukie asked me to."

"Please sit here," Norman says to Rosetta, leaping out of his chair in a way that acknowledges the past history and present prerogatives of a well-preserved Jewish princess.

Joanne disappears and returns with two more chairs from the dining room so we can all sit around the table.

Mr. Smilow takes off his suit jacket and drapes it over the back of his chair before sitting down. His eyes are a pre-cataract blue, so that even though he isn't crying, he appears tearful. His mouth is bent into what seems to be a permanently broken smile, as if he had been interrupted long ago by a stroke that flash-froze his features into an eternally crestfallen expression. However, there is another angle from which he looks more cheerful—more like the kind of guy who would buy a round of drinks for anyone congenial enough to sit at the bar instead of a table.

"Well," he sighs. "At least Sukie's mama didn't live to see this. That's good."

Suddenly Happy springs to attention and comes skittering across the kitchen floor, sniffing for the owner of the raspy voice she's recognized. At the same moment, Mr. Smilow remembers the dog and reaches down for her, locking his hands around her head to steady it as he looks into her eyes.

"It's the dog," he says, in a voice stricken at having forgotten and now flooding with remembrances. "I forgot her dog." Then, for the first time, he allows a few sentimental tears to surface. "At first it doesn't seem fair a person dies and a pet goes on living. But after a while it's sort of nice, like a link. . . ."

At that point, everyone suddenly begins to move about.

"Coffee, Mr. Smilow?" Elaine offers. "Tea, Rosetta? May we call you Rosetta?"

"Schnapps?" Norman asks.

A brief ballet of beverage service begins, as if we are on a plane that has suddenly reached its cruising altitude.

Mr. Smilow accepts a gin and tonic, removes the slice of lime Joanne has dropped in the glass, mumbles something about "garbage," and then leans back in his chair.

"So at least she won't have to bury me. That's good. She buried her mama and that was enough. The city owes me my burial."

"Manny, what are you saying?" Rosetta complains, pressing one hand to her head and the other over the plump round breast hiding her heart. "You're making me crazy."

"And I never sent Sukie her mama's mink coat like I promised. My sugar plum didn't want it. She said Washington didn't get so cold."

His sister watches his face as he speaks.

"So now, Rosetta, you'll take it. It's that ranch mink. It's a good one. Full-length, half-belt in the back. Got it as a replacement for the midnight one that got stolen from Clara's dentist's office. Was a thief who just walked through the Medical Arts Building taking fur coats out of waiting rooms. Insurance company paid in a minute. Knew all about that *gonif.* Then I upgraded a little. Got her a little better coat. And who else should have it?

Carol? She wouldn't be caught dead in a fur that came off an animal. And now there's no other family left. Also there's a few white-gold cocktail rings." His voice falters. "First the divorce and then she dies."

Finally Mr. Smilow breaks down, folds his arms on top of the table, tucks his head into their dark cave and starts to cry.

Actually, he doesn't cry. He shakes.

We watch him.

I try to think of him as a young man, the fight promoter who took his little daughter to the gyms where his fighters worked out, and to the Standard Club where he played cards in the afternoon. Sukie told me that when he won big, he would return home to their South Side apartment with extravagant gifts for her. One winter, when she was five, he brought her a matching white rabbit coat, hat and leggings to wear to a Golden Gloves welterweight championship fight.

Another night, during a bad blizzard, he came home with snowflakes clinging to his bushy eyebrows and the furry collar of his heavy storm coat, and called Sukie into the hallway. Saying his hands were cold, he asked her to fish his keys out of the deep dark secret of his coat pocket, and when she did, a Chihuahua puppy curled up inside peeked out and Sukie screamed as she delivered it into the light.

Clearly, Manny Smilow had been a decent, loving father because Sukie always liked and often defended men by factoring their frailties into her explanations of what seemed, to the rest of us, impossibly unforgivable behavior.

"The children?" Mr. Smilow finally mumbles.

"They're in New York with Max's parents," Elaine answers. "They'll get here tomorrow."

"Soon enough." He nods thoughtfully, grieving for the death of his daughter's family as well as for his daughter. "She'd be ashamed to leave them. A mother never wants to abandon her children, even if they're almost grown."

Then he gets up and goes to stand by the back door to look out through the barred window at a small piece of striped blue sky. "It's selfish, but I wish she'd gotten sick first before she died. Then I could've come here to take care of her for a while and we'd have gotten a chance to talk."

He snaps his fingers so that Happy comes running over to jump up and dribble down the side of Mr. Smilow's leg again and again. Finally her excitement peaks and she rolls over on the floor, inviting Mr. Smilow to scratch her stomach.

Slowly, Manny Smilow bends down to oblige the dog. "This is a calamity," he says, thoughtfully extending the span of his hand to increase the territory he's scratching. "This is a true calamity."

Then he returns to sit in his chair again.

"And the *schlemazel?* Max?"

"He just got back to Washington," I say.

He registers my words with a nod. "Max," he says, shaking his head. "Max."

The name becomes a song of despair on Mr. Smilow's tongue.

"Max never helped her. All he did was listen to his stereo while she took care of the kids. When they all had to go out as a family together, he got himself ready and then sat down to wait for Sukie to fix herself and the children while he played *The Firedance* on his hi-fi with a bass boost.

"He was a real *luftmensch,* Max, you know? Above it all. So she had to pick up after him. For twenty years she picks up after him and then he picks up and leaves her. Can you believe that? *He* leaves *her?* Him? Who never made a decent living with his big social group theories and his big ethnic gangs book? But that's what she wanted. She didn't want to know from the rackets or from the business world. The middle class? It made her want to vomit. She was an idealist. She wanted equality in the world. So." He shrugs. "Look at the equality we got. It's *schrecklich.*"

Manny Smilow crosses his legs, locks his hands around one knee, and begins to rock back and forth.

"And temperamental? Sukie was a prima donna from day one. Never satisfied with the ordinary, always wanting something more. Oh, her mama could tell you. Sukie had a rage to live. From the minute she was born, she wanted to do everything, go every place, know everybody. No. She wanted to *be* everybody. First she wanted to be Sister Kenny and cure polio. Then she wanted to be Eleanor Roosevelt and help the Jews. Next she wanted to be Natalie Wood in *Miracle on 34th Street* and then Elizabeth Taylor in *National Velvet.* She even wanted to be Roddy McDowall in *Lassie Come Home.* Lots of times she wanted to be a boy. Maybe that would've been better for her. Who knows?"

He nods his head solemnly in rhythm with his rocking.

"Everything she wanted to do and learn. But at school? Nothing, absolutely nothing. She even got suspended from kindergarten. From kindergarten! She wouldn't stand up for 'The Star-Spangled Banner.' Why not? Even Sukeleh didn't know why not. And her sewing class? That she fails. Into junior high school. On probation. The genius, on probation. And algebra? Forget it. Civics? I had to go meet the principal because Sukie sassed the teacher. A Miss Yates. Oy, a real battleaxe. She told the class all labor leaders were crooks, so Sukie called her a name and got tossed out of school again. *Again.*"

We are all quiet, soothed by hearing Sukie's history in her father's intimate immigrant voice.

"Reading. That's all she wanted. A book a day she read. Right through the card catalogue at our own public library. And the librarians? Very nice ladies—they liked her. Miss Rood. She let Sukie take out more than the five-books-a-day limit when she was only eleven. It's Miss Rood decided to let Sukie into Adult Books. So there, right away, my sugar plum finds *A Tree Grows in Brooklyn.* Eleven times she read it. She cries and cries because the little Francie in that book doesn't know from menstruation and thinks it's her heart that's broken and bleeding. Instead of the other. Next Sukie reads *The Egg and I,* then *Cheaper by the Dozen.* Those are okay. But then, God help us, it's *Forever Amber* and nothing's ever the same again."

Elaine smiles with enormous gratitude. "I think it's *wonderful* that you *knew*—I mean, that you can *remember*—what Sukie read, Mr. Smilow."

"What? I shouldn't know what my own child, my only child, was reading? As soon as she finished a book, then I read it next. Then her mother. So we could see what got into her head. We were a reading family. Together. And also we had to so we would know what was coming next. Because after *Forever Amber,* nothing was ever the same for my family ever again

"The minute she got to high school, she got completely boy-crazy. Right away she wants to wear makeup, a color purple lipstick, 'Orchids to You' is its name, I still remember. And straight skirts. Tight, that tuck around the bottom. But her mama says no, no way, lipstick at fourteen. No way, straight skirts that tuck under, because now our Sukie already wants to go to parties where they play post office. She wants to go steady and wear some boy's *schmatta* club jacket that's too big for her. Oh no. So we sit on her for a while; we don't let her go noplace.

"Then next what does she want? To go to college. To go to Chicago University. To enter early, right? Early entrance they call it. At fifteen. She couldn't wait. So what then? Then she wants to 'place out' of everything. At that *grosse* university, you pass an examination from a certain course, you get the credit and don't have to take the course. Now she wants to place out of all the classes she wanted to go to college to take. She wants to be done with college before she starts.

"And who does she find there at the big Chicago University? Philip Roth she finds, the big dirty-mouth, the turncoat against the Jews. Him she falls for. Never does he talk to her, but she keeps washing clothes all the time so she can see him at the laundromat. She even wears high heels to do her laundry. And every night she has to eat at the Tropical Hut so she can see Mr. Big Mouth who sits in there because he's after some shiksa waitress. Now my Sukie goes there to watch him watch his shiksa. Sick. Sick. This I needed? This her sainted mother needed? Like a hole in the head."

I laugh.

Mr. Smilow looks a reprimand at me.

"Crazy she was about life and about living. New York. Next she wants to go live in New York and be a writer. A Grace Metalious she wants to be, fat like a pig in blue jeans. Or else to San Francisco to find the beatniks. Jack Kerouac she wants to find. To the City Lights Bookstore she's running, to find them all. Allen Ginsberg? That's a Jew? A homosexual Jew? *Vey ist mir.* Her mama and me, we had to hold on tight to her. But one day she disappears and next we know she's a stewardess for Delta Airlines. She tells them she's twenty-one years old and a German Lutheran, no less. Where did she get that from? Nineteen she was, from a good Jewish home.

"So right away she's the valedictorian of the stewardess class and her prize is she gets to choose her base. Then back she comes to Chicago because now she wants to take her masters. Her masters? Three days a week she's a flyer and two days a week she's a scholar. And that's how she found Max. Back at the university. He sees what he thinks is a shiksa in her flying uniform with the wings on her blouse, on the breast pocket, no less, and right away he gets hot pants. So then Sukie's happy. Oh, he's *so* smart, she tells us. Uh-huh. So smart that boychik was. A *nahrisherkind.* A big sociologist. A

student of mankind. A *bulvan* he was, a *shlubb*. A
dreamer, a wild dreamer.

"Together they were going to save the world. They
were going to work for racial equality. For nuclear
disarmament. For whales. For seals. For environment
protection. For civil rights. For *blacks.* Say 'blacks,'
Sukie tells me. No more should I say 'Negroes.' Instead
now I'm supposed to say 'blacks.' But I couldn't say it.
You've *got* to say it, Sukie yells at me. You've *got* to.
Finally I could say it and then that makes Max happy,
so she's happy. They're happy together because now I
can say 'blacks,' *nu?*"

Mr. Smilow begins to cry.

We wait.

Rosetta stands up and pats her brother on his head,
which only makes him cry harder. There is heavy silence until he regains his composure. Gradually he revives, sips his drink, and returns to his epic.

"So at last he finishes his degree. His doctor's. Not a
real doctor's, a Ph.D. *PH* is for 'Phony.' So they move
to Washington because at last he gets a job. But in Washington—my Sukeleh worked hard, with a job full-time
and two kids, and staying up half the night to write her
stories, working all day, and running back and forth.
Always she's schlepping the kids to marches and
demonstrations and sit-downs and stand-ups or making
fund-raisers for Schnick. And always people are staying
at their home for marches. Why? Why such a hectic life?
But she was a *shtarke,* schlepping groceries and liquor
cartons and making parties for Max's friends. She was a
regular life force."

He makes a valiant struggle not to cry again.

"And then right when she could start to take things
a little easier, the kids are almost grown, she's sold a few
books, then Max leaves. Just like that."

Mr. Smilow snaps his fingers.

Immediately, Happy rushes back to resume their relationship.

"I'm not saying she was an angel. She tested Max. She tested Max for a long time with her moods, her discontent, her disappointments. That's not easy for a man, either. I'm not saying it is. But he didn't act like a *mensch.* Right after her mama dies, he takes a powder.

"But look how much I'm talking about myself. I should ask about you. How much each of you will miss Sukie. Because I don't know any of you except I know that you all must have cared for her because she loved her friends. Always on the telephone she said, Daddy, This One just wrote a fabulous book and This One just finished medical school, Daddy, and she has three-year-old *twins,* and this one just did this and this one just did that. She loved you all. She was proud of her girlfriends." He pauses for a moment to look at Norman with puzzled curiosity, but then decides not to inquire about his connection to Sukie. "Always she was running to someone who just had a baby or, God forbid, a female operation. A heart of gold she had. But was she ever happy? Who knows? A part of her died when her mama died. And her own children? Aach, who knows?"

His voice evaporates and he seems to drift away.

"Mr. Smilow," Elaine says, "we'd like to talk about the kind of service . . ."

"Not now, sweetheart." Mr. Smilow shakes his head.

"Just give him a minute to recover," Rosetta suggests. "Also back at the hotel I have a box with my baking pans I brought on the plane. My other brother had the best bagel factory in Chicago. Of course, it was my recipe he used. But tomorrow, first thing in the morning, I'll get here early and start baking. Everything we need for the reception. For how many? Maybe a hundred? Two hundred?"

"The reception?" Elaine echoes in a shocked voice.

"Of course." Rosetta nods vehemently. "We need to have a reception. Directly following the burial. Everyone should come back here and I don't want there to be any store-bought sweets. . . ."

"But the worst," Mr. Smilow moans as he suddenly starts speaking again, "the worst were our fights about politics. She had no respect for authority. My own grandfather was cut in half by the Cossacks because he got stuck in the trapdoor of a hayloft, and then I have a daughter who's too good for America. America, she says, is too materialistic, too middle-class; capitalism corrupts, she says. She has no respect for the American government, for the American way of life. No gratitude that they gave me a home so she could be born here.

"And for Israel? Forget it. A long, hard struggle the Jews had before they could finally come to rest in Israel, and does she care? No. The *Arabs* she worries about. . . ."

The doorbell rings.

"This is starting to sound like a sitcom," Joanne whispers to me as she gets up.

Several minutes later, when she returns with Max, it is clear she has warned him about Mr. Smilow. Max sidles through the swinging door looking totally subdued and bereaved. He approaches Mr. Smilow silently, grief and guilt making him walk gingerly.

Mr. Smilow does not stand up.

Max stops. Then, slowly and purposefully, he extends his hand.

Mr. Smilow suddenly busies himself with his drink.

"Hello, Max," Rosetta says, without stirring from her chair.

A hot flash flushes my face. I feel beads of sweat form like a headband along my hairline.

Max is nodding.

He is nodding at everyone and everything. By nodding, he is conceding the circumstances. He is accepting Mr. Smilow's scorn. He is accepting the ironies and cultural contradictions of this situation. He is accepting his own defection and deficiencies. Finally he moves away from the table area and leans against the sink, out of Manny Smilow's view. Max owes him that much, not to contaminate his field of vision and just to stand in disgraced attendance while accepting the blame for his blasphemous behavior.

"So," Mr. Smilow says, as if Max had never appeared, "Sukie told me she was writing a new book. . . ."

"She was," Joanne responds eagerly, returning to her chair. "She didn't tell us about it, but a friend of hers who's been editing it says it's quite good."

"Did she finish?" her father asks.

Reluctantly, Joanne shakes her head.

"I'd like to see it anyway," Mr. Smilow says, smiling.

"Manny," Max says, stepping forward to seize the opportunity to be of some service to his former father-in-law, "I heard about the book from the kids, so I asked about it as soon as I got back. I was pretty upset to hear"—he pauses and adopts a falsely forgiving tone— "that some young man friend of Sukie's has the manuscript. So last night I went looking for the guy, since he doesn't even have a telephone."

"What?" Manny Smilow shouts, jumping out of his chair. "You? You went to pick up my Sukie's book? *You?* How dare you?"

"Not for *me,* Manny," Max says nervously, stepping back and bumping into Happy, so that he has to jump sideways to avoid stepping on her. "For the children. For their sake. Whether it's finished enough to be published or not, they're the heirs. . . ."

"You are not to lay a finger on Sukie's book," Manny Smilow says, moving threateningly into the center of the kitchen. "No way. Not one finger. Not even for one minute."

As Mr. Smilow moves deliberately and theatrically toward Max, Happy begins rushing around in a circle, yapping at her own tail rather than confronting her conflicting loyalties.

"I wouldn't trust you with the garbage," Mr. Smilow snarls. "And I'm glad you deserted my Sukeleh. Glad. Glad you divorced her like some Muslim saying it three times. I'm glad. And do you know why?" he thunders, leaning forward on the tips of his shoes so he is inclined into Max's face. "Because of the settlement. Yes, the divorce settlement. Because the settlement says half the house belonged to Sukie and the other half to my grandchildren and you're out, mister." Now he begins to waggle a finger in Max's face. "You're stone cold out of the picture. You won't see a penny of the proceeds from this house. Directly it goes to the children, with me as the only executor."

Max is not exactly cowering. Rather, he is contracting into himself, physically withdrawing, reducing the provocation of his body from Mr. Smilow's sight.

"I thought," Max begins rather bravely, "I thought maybe I should move back in here so that when the kids come home from school for summer vacations . . ."

"No way, Jose." A sheer spray of sputum floats out of Mr. Smilow's mouth. "Over my dead body, you'll move in here." He is panting as he speaks. "*We* will sell this house. *We* will realize the profits from this place. And from whom did you get the down payment in the first place, mister? Huh? Tell me that. Tell me where you got ten thousand dollars in ice-cold cash? Huh?"

"Well, they'll just have to stay in my apartment," Max warns. "And it'll be crowded because it's only a one-bedroom, Pa—I mean, Manny. A very small one-bedroom."

"Then maybe your girlfriend will have to take a room somewhere else. Did you ever think of that?"

Now Mr. Smilow whips around, whirling on the heels of his shoes. But he glides too fast, swivels too hard, and completes the circle so that he is back facing Max once again.

"I only wish Sukeleh could see what a good property settlement we arranged for her. It's a better deal than a will. And one more thing, mister," Manny Smilow bellows into Max's face. "That book of hers comes to me." He begins to poke himself in his chest with a blunt forefinger. "Directly to *me*. Me. Do not pass Go. Directly to me. And then I will see how to handle that book, not you. Me. The father of the bride."

At that, he begins to howl with great gasping sounds. By the time Rosetta reaches him, he is rocking on his feet. I can see his knees begin to buckle, but his sister grips him around the waist and, draping his arm around her neck, leads him out of the kitchen into the dining room.

Slowly, Max turns around and pastes his forehead against one of the cupboard doors.

The rest of us sit in silence, listening only to the tinny hum of the tired little window air conditioner.

At this moment I can feel Sukie's presence more keenly than at any other time since my arrival. Her spirit seems to be tiptoeing around the kitchen, debating how to bring some accord into her family so she can be buried in peace.

I feel tears touching my cheeks and I lower my face so that no one will be able to read my eyes.

"Listen," Joanne says in a choked voice. "I'm going to go find Jeff. I'm going to tell Mr. Smilow that I'll take responsibility for getting that manuscript into his hands."

Max whips around. "Jesus, Joanne. How can you give that old man a manuscript no one's seen? Who knows what's in there? Who knows what she wrote? She was pretty unbalanced there for a while. He might not be up to reading what she wrote. Why should he suffer any more? Why should he be subjected to Sukie's craziness?"

"It won't be him who will suffer," Elaine predicts ominously.

Joanne walks out into the dining room without responding.

Seconds later, Rosetta returns to the kitchen. "I'm going to take my brother back to the hotel," she says. "He hasn't slept and I think he should have a nap.

You've all been very nice." She retrieves Mr. Smilow's
hat and jacket, as well as her own belongings. "He says
I should say goodbye and he'll be calling up over here
later when"—she casts a long look at Max—"everything's quieter."

Then she leaves through the swinging door.

Several minutes pass in silence. Joanne returns.

"I'm going to *drive* them back to the hotel," Max says
suddenly.

"You think they'll take a ride from you?" I ask.

"I'll make them," Max responds. Then he kicks open
the door and disappears.

"God. That was pretty upsetting," Elaine says flatly,
after we observe a few moments of silence.

"Really," Joanne agrees.

The scene between Mr. Smilow and Max had caused
a general rise in my body temperature which is now
triggering a run of hot flashes. Sustained agitation seems
to activate and aggravate my condition.

"How did Sukie get along with her dad?" Norman
asks in his professional psychiatric voice.

"I never heard her complain," Elaine responds
quickly. "And I roomed with her at Chicago. I think she
sort of liked bouncing off him, if you know what I mean.
He was her straight man. Whatever he liked, she didn't.
Except living on the edge. She learned that from him.
That's where he lived—with all his gambling and making book and promoting boxing matches and stuff. He
was a real high roller and he spoiled Sukie like crazy.
She had seventeen cashmere sweater sets when she
moved into the dorm. I remember watching her un-
pack them. They were all those 1950s Day-Glo colors.
But I know one thing. She always suspected her dad of
having a long-term 'thang' with his secretary who was
always hugging and kissing Sukie when she went to visit
her dad's office. Sukie said she used to get sick from the
secretary's perfume. I know it made her feel bad for her
mother. She was crazy for her mother."

Now Joanne, who seldom speaks about herself and even less frequently about her family, begins talking. Standing near the back door, she is looking out through the window into the past, just as Mr. Smilow had done.

"My dad really faded after the war ended," Joanne says mournfully. "He had a bad leg so he didn't get drafted; instead he got this really great job in a war plant outside Boston, and he made more money than he ever did before. Or ever did again. My mom worked in a plant too, so we really had loads of money. But as soon as the war was over, my dad lost that job and never found another decent one the rest of his life."

Joanne sighs as if—forty years later—her original pain was still perfectly preserved.

"We had seven kids to support. And I can remember when everyone in the family was sitting around the kitchen table crying because Roosevelt died. I was so scared. I didn't understand what was happening. I thought the Germans were coming. And every Sunday morning my mother made all of us go to mass with her to pray for a victory in Europe." Joanne turns back toward us and laughs. "But I think when Japan surrendered she was a little bit sorry."

When we were little girls, someone named FDR died and we saw people crying whom we had never seen cry before. I lived in Marshall, Minnesota, then and I remember my mother throwing herself across her bed and lying there all crooked and making funny noises. When her parents got home they sat next to each other on the sofa and cried. It seemed that after the Great Depression and the Second World War, they all needed a Big Daddy as much as I did. But my father was in Europe and I never believed he would come home. That's why it scared me to see everyone else that scared.

Some of us lived in the country on family farms or in small towns with only one movie theater which, like shopping in Moscow, eliminated any decision-making. When my father came home after the war we moved to Minneapolis, where he taught at the university, and then I became a city girl. It wasn't until I went to Radcliffe, though, that a window opened up in my life. To get there I took the train from Minneapolis to Boston and wore a pair of white gloves the whole way. My mother also gave me a fresh pair in an envelope, which I was supposed to put on right as the train reached Boston. I did that.

And that was the last time I did what my mother told me to do. Once I got to Radcliffe, I met and hung out with students who had been red-diaper babies, gone to the Little Red Schoolhouse, run for student government at their high schools, and eventually gone on to take Ph.D.'s in history at the University of Wisconsin. Having grown up in the Midwest, I was very different from the Eastern girls. I had stayed home practicing togetherness right up until I took that train to Boston.

Sweetpea.

That's what my daddy used to call me when he came home from the war.

What did you do in the war, Daddy?

He would throw me up high in the air, but I knew his big hands would catch me—would save me from a shrieking plunge into the abyss. Always. Forever. He would stop my free fall through life. He would never drop me. He would never let me down.

Once, when we lived near the campus in St. Paul, some professor friends of his came over to visit. I was playing across the street in my green, green park and when he came to fetch me, he sat down on a bench to comb my curls before taking me home to show me off to his friends. He held me between his knees and gripped my hair by the roots so I wouldn't feel him untangle the ends. He pulled my hair much harder than my mother did.

When we were little girls, we wanted to be little boys.

There. It's said. It's not so strange. Who wouldn't rather be a Have than a Have-Not?

When we were little girls, we wanted to be wanted.

Little daddy's-girls-with-curls needed attention, affection and approval at all times. Little daddy's girls listened to pop songs and played only zero-sum games. *It's all or nothing at all.. . .*

When we were little girls we wanted to grow up to be mothers.

Some enchanted evening, you will see a stranger, you will see a stranger across a crowded room, and then you will know. . . .

It wasn't wee-wees we wanted as much as the promise, potential and power our brothers and the other little boys on our block possessed. So we swallowed our stinky codliver oil and turned into tomboys—first on trikes and then on bikes. We spent our childhoods proving and improving ourselves. Once when I was going to play marbles in the park with the little boy triplets from across the street, I rubbed some dirt on my face first. That was my dark dirty little secret.

Together we all played war. We surrounded houses, invaded backyards, attacked alleys, conquered parks and climbed crab apple trees to raise our flag à la Iwo Jima. Together we all played doctor; I, of course, only planned to become a nurse. Together we all played marbles, baseball and kick-the-can. When we got tired we would stop and listen to hot news flashes about the war over the radio.

Suddenly I realize Norman is looking at me with quizzical eyes that suggest I have something to hide. For some reason I suddenly feel compelled to volunteer some story:

"Once when Leonard and I were here in Washington, it was in the early sixties, Max and Sukie took us out drinking with a novelist they knew named Billy Lee and his wife, who was very beautiful. Her name was

Nadia. Actually, the Lees had been separated for quite a while, but Nadia had flown in from California 'to stake her claim,' as Billy said, because he had just sold one of his books to the movies.

"So we all went out to a beer garden called Harrigan's, down in Southwest by the river, to celebrate. It was a really hot, humid night in August and we sat outside in the garden behind the bar where we could hear the boats on the river and the cars speeding past on Maine Avenue and we just kept drinking more and more beer and getting drunker and drunker and talking and laughing and having a great old time.

"And then all of a sudden Nadia kicked off her shoes and climbed up on top of our table. It was all slick and slippery from spilt foam, but she began twirling around and around. She was crying these big beer tears and twirling so that her skirt, it was a dirndl, flared up straight out around her thighs. She had these beautiful long legs that were all tan and this wonderful shiny brown hair that went swinging out like a velvet ribbon around her head when she twirled. And the whole time she was half-singing and half-crying, 'I want a Big Daddy. Oh, I want a Big Daddy. That's what I want. Oh, so bad. Just a Big, Big Daddy.' "

"Most women want a Big Daddy," Norman appends pedantically. "It's a universal phenomenon."

None of us bothers to respond to him. None of us looks at him.

We are all staring off into space, seeing some larger truth.

CHAPTER 15

"Well, I certainly don't want to go running around town looking for Jeff," Elaine states flatly, when Max reappears.

"No one said you had to," Joanne snaps back. "Diana and I can do it."

"And me," Max adds. "In case he gives you any trouble."

"He's not going to give us any trouble," Joanne says sharply. "But you can come if you want to."

"I'll just hang around here, if you don't mind," Norman says to Elaine with studied nonchalance.

Elaine doesn't reply, but she looks pleased.

Joanne and I go upstairs to change clothes. Once again I rifle through Sukie's closet and this time pick a soft white cotton dress with small rosebuds on it. If Sukie could buy something with flowers on it, she always did. I put the dress on and feel it hug me as gently as a friend.

When I meet Joanne in the hallway, she looks at me with a mildly critical expression, and suddenly I wonder if my borrowing Sukie's clothes troubles her. She is wearing a loose white cotton shirt and her skintight jeans, the crotch seam of which disappears into the seam of her crotch. I cast a glance toward her groin and then neither of us mentions each other's outfit.

Max leads Joanne and me up the block to where he's

parked his car and very purposefully I climb into the back seat so Joanne won't feel I expected to pair off with Max in the front. There's little traffic today and we're even able to park on the same block where Jeff lives. The door of the Peppermill is open and inside I can see a restless, late-Sunday-afternoon crowd huddled around the bar.

Max is still pounding aggressively on the steel door of 3203 when it suddenly swings open to reveal Jeff standing at the bottom of a narrow staircase. He is wearing a fresh white shirt with the same jeans and boots he wore yesterday. Although clearly startled to see us, he doesn't seem alarmed.

He stares at Max for only a moment before extending his hand.

"Hey, you're Max. I'm Jeff Conroy. This is rough."

Max shrugs his agreement.

"Jeff, Sukie's dad's in town and he wants to see Sukie's manuscript," Joanne says a bit precipitously. "I came to get it for him."

Jeff looks at Joanne and me, and then returns his gaze to Max again. Obviously troubled by the possibility that it may be Max rather than Sukie's father who wants the manuscript, Jeff hesitates. It is clear he intends to protect Sukie's book from any danger, especially that of a worried former husband. His only loyalty is to Sukie.

"Hey," he says softly. "Come on up. Let's have a glass of wine. Funny you came by right now. I just got back from the funeral home. I went to see Sukie."

The three of us freeze.

Both Max and Elaine had gone to the funeral home and not viewed Sukie. Neither Joanne nor I had even considered it. So now it is Jeff, the Vietnam vet, who calmly announces he's seen Sukie. Perhaps he'd seen enough dead bodies in Vietnam to be able to view death with impunity. Perhaps he felt closer to Sukie's corpse than any of the rest of us because he had been the lover of her body. Whatever. His loyalty diminishes us.

Silently we file up the dirty, uncarpeted staircase
with Jeff in the lead and Max at the rear.

Jeff's apartment looks like a set for a movie about a
war-weary, war-ruined Vietnam vet in search of his
MIA self. It's a studio apartment with two undressed
front windows offering a view of M Street, a row of
kitchen appliances, a very large aquarium, and an open
door to the toilet against the rear wall. And that's it. The
room is furnished with a variety of battered tables, sofas
and chairs. There are books everywhere—stacked and
piled, opened and closed, shelved and floored. Tall piles
of newspapers erupt like islands on the woven-hemp
South Seas rug.

The room is deadly hot. The air is motionless. There
is no sign of an air conditioner. Indeed, the heat is so
oppressive that it seems to isolate us from the city outside.

Jeff walks over to a table displaying an assortment of
bottles and asks each of us our preference. By now Max
and Joanne have selected chairs in which to sit, so I
slump into a beat-up sofa and wait for Jeff to bring me
a tumbler full of wine.

"How's her dad doing?" he asks me.

"Just fair."

"And what about David and Carol?" he asks Max.

Max flushes. I know he views Jeff's question as imper-
tinent and I can see him struggling to control his tem-
per before he comes up with a nonresponsive, logistical
answer.

"They're probably in New York with my parents by
now. Carol's boyfriend will be driving them down here
tomorrow. We couldn't fly home together because
there weren't any flights with three seats available."

I can see he despises the defensiveness that's crept
into his voice. He knows Sukie must have delivered
extensive and damaging evidence against him, so now
he must shadow-box with what he imagines Jeff knows
or thinks about him. But Jeff senses Max's discomfort

and retreats since, on the issue of the kids, he has no grievance. It is only in terms of Sukie that he feels himself more legitimate than the husband who left her.

Meanwhile, Joanne has risen again to reconnoiter the room, inventorying the fish in the aquarium, Jeff's various military souvenirs and the large Peace posters that are handsomely framed and nicely installed on his walls.

"How long were you in Vietnam, Jeff?" she asks.

"Two and a half years," he answers in a terminal tone. "From '69 to '71."

"And you went to school after you got out?"

"Yah." Jeff turns around to indicate a strong distaste for talking about himself. Having provided everyone a drink, he now sits down beside me on the couch.

"Listen," he begins. "I'm not sure Sukie's manuscript is the sort of thing her dad should read. I mean, rightfully I suppose it should go to him, but it's sort of raw, if you know what I mean."

"You don't have to worry about that," Max says.

This is precisely the least reassuring thing he could have said. Now Jeff is totally on guard. Seated beside him, I can feel a heavy resistance begin asserting itself within him.

"See, I promised Mr. Smilow I would get the manuscript back from you." Joanne speaks calmly and matter-of-factly. "He's just worried because he doesn't want it to get . . . knocked around. It's no big deal."

Silence.

Everyone has staked out a different territory to defend.

"Hey. I told you yesterday what it was about," Jeff says reproachfully to Joanne and me.

"I know," Joanne nods. "But that's really no big deal."

I can feel the heat of Jeff's eyes on her.

"Okay." Max straightens up in his chair. "I figure this novel is about me, right? I'm sure Sukie did a real job on me, but that doesn't matter. The book's got to go to her dad. And since he doesn't lose any love over me either, it's not about to hurt his feelings."

I know Max is telling the truth, but Jeff doesn't. Jeff and Max can never trust each other because their serial relationships with Sukie make them natural antagonists. The men of our generation have trouble coping with contiguous sex and feel that subsequent lovers diminish them. While we believed it proper, or at least preferable, to space lovers, we were sophisticated enough to know that sometimes confusion peaked and produced an out-of-town beau—reducing us to such sanitary considerations as douching more than once in the course of a single day.

While Joanne and I see Max as the heavyweight man in Sukie's life, Max views Jeff as having the edge over him because he was Sukie's last lover. Men and women keep very different sexual score cards.

"Hey," Jeff says. "Let's cut the crap. You want to hear how this book begins?"

He stands up, walks to his desk, opens a folder and pulls out a handful of papers. Then he returns to sit down on the sofa again.

"Okay. Get ready. '*Death Sentences.* Chapter one,'" Jeff says.

" 'Samantha (Sam) Cronik lay on the frequently reupholstered sofa in her floral-papered living room and flipped TV channels with her remote control. The TV was a hot item she had recently purchased through her youngest son from a fence on 18th Street. On the coffee table beside Sam was a gallon jug of vodka, a half-full bottle of Diet Coke, a large ashtray containing two still-viable roaches, a box of Morton's Kosher Salt, which she used when mixing vodka with grapefruit juice to make Salty Dogs—her favorite alcoholic beverage—a two-week-old issue of the *Nation* and a container of Flagyl capsules. The medication was for her defiant case of trichomonas (medically defined as a form of vaginitis, but considered by Sam's best friend, Glenda, a venereal

disease since it required immediate notification of all
one's partners to report their exposure to a doctor who
would then initiate the standard twelve-day Flagyl
treatment during which time no alcohol could be consumed). Sam once heard that out in California a person's refusal of a drink at a cocktail party was
tantamount to announcing that the abstainer was on
Flagyl and thus a contagious trich carrier to be assidu-
ously avoided.

" 'Next to the Flagyl was a large container of Yoplait
low-fat cherry yogurt into which Sam periodically
dipped a teaspoon upon the advice of her family practi-
tioner/gynecologist, who prescribed yogurt to fight off
the yeast infections frequently produced by Flagyl,
which destabilized the chemical environment of the
vagina. The yogurt could be taken orally or introduced
directly into the guilty orifice. (When Sam asked Dr.
Mulberry what flavor yogurt to use, the doctor had answered, "Whatever turns you on," and Sam had felt
forced to exchange sophisticated smiles with her family
practitioner.)

" 'Sam put down the pocket calculator on which she
had been adjusting her budget in accordance with some
recently released data showing that a husband's ex-
pendable income increased seventy-two percent in the
year following a divorce while the wife and children's
income decreased forty-three percent. Stretching toward the coffee table, she turned on her also newly
acquired (through the same source as the TV) ghetto
blaster, which was tuned to OK100 where Sam's favorite deejay was playing some golden oldies that fit in
perfectly with the dismaying heavy fog being dispensed
on this ashen, isolated January afternoon. Alternating
with the golden oldies were some newsy bluesies to
which Sam attended carefully so as to memorize
enough lyrics to enable her to mumble along with the
music in case it began playing when she found herself

in some uncomfortable sexual situation during which she was unable to think of anything to say.

" 'Only four days ago, beneath her glass cocktail table, Sam had discovered the corpse of her white French poodle, Haggie, who had died of old age—or, more specifically, cancer, according to the vet to whom she had carried the corpse in a large green garbage bag, uncertain about the legal requirements for its disposal. The death of the family dog had affected Sam adversely since it occurred *after* the death of her family, which meant she was the only one still home and available to deal with the final details.

" 'This last betrayal paralleled the original one, when her three sons had promised to take complete care of a puppy if they could have one. Of course what had happened was that Sam ended up working as a support staff —for over fifteen years—purchasing and delivering crates of canned dog food, shampooing, grooming and styling Haggie's hair—more frequently than her own—and clipping its nails when she herself needed a manicure.

" 'Now shoved into the newly available space beneath the coffee table were all the books Sam had been reading: Shana Alexander's *Very Much a Lady, The Jean Harris Story,* Diana Trilling's version of the same trial; the paperback *Scarsdale Diet* (to give Sam a clearer picture of Dr. Herman Tarnower), *Widow* by Lynn Caine, a Penguin edition of *Medea,* a copy of *Moving Violations,* which Sam had published six years ago in 1979, *I'm Dancing as Fast as I Can,* by Barbara Gordon, *Crazy Time,* by Abigail Trafford, and a five-section college theme notebook in which Sam was keeping her divorce diary.

" 'In the first section of the notebook, Sam was recording all the symptoms of her deterioration which she planned to use in her next, nonfiction, work—*Sex and the Single Grandmother.* The second section contained many of the herpes and cunt jokes that Sam collected because she felt they carried a lot of social significance in terms of contemporary attitudes toward women.

" '*What's the difference between love and herpes?*

" '*Herpes lasts forever.*

" '*What is a woman?*

" '*A life-support system for a cunt.*

" '*Why is it good that women have cunts?*

" '*Because otherwise no one would ever talk to them.*

" '*Why do women have two holes?*

" '*So you can pick them up and carry them like a six-pack.*

" '*What do you get when you mix a computer with a JAP?*

" '*A system that won't go down.*

" '*What does a good JAP make for dinner?*

" '*Reservations.*

" '*Have you heard about the new Jewish porn movie* Debbie Does Nothing?

" '*Why does a JAP make love with her eyes closed?*

" '*Because she can't stand to see anyone else having a good time.*

" '*How do you know when a JAP has an orgasm?*

" '*She says, "Sorry Mom. I'm going to have to call you back later."*

" 'The third section contained an outline of a new novel that Sam intended to write while she proceeded with her plot to kill her estranged husband, Seymour Cronik. The book, which she planned to have published in conjunction with her trial, was entitled *Death Sentences: The Assassination of an American Jewish Prince.*

" 'Following the outline was a page of other titles that she planned someday to use: *Tight Ends, Split Ends, Enemy Lines, Raw Material, Dirty Linen, Intimate Relations, Root Canal, Double Extraction, Third Parties, Cross Purposes* and *Second Opinion.* Often after writing down a good title, Sam no longer felt any compulsion to write the book to go along with it, but this time her rage at Seymour and her monetary needs made the writing of *Death Sentences* nonnegotiable. Luckily her financial neediness coincided perfectly with the unclogging of her creative passages. For the past two years, Sam had suffered from a writer's block that she believed was really a strike by her talent for better working conditions. But now that her marriage was over and her life had become preposterously simplified, *Death Sentences* was actually being written in daylight—so her block and/or strike had ended.

" 'With a sigh, Sam closed her notebook.

" 'It was Playoff Sunday. The Redskins, whom Sam had come to know and love during the NFL strike that had coincided with the long winter of her own discontent, were in Dallas to face the Cowboys, a team that had not given unanimous support to the Player's Union. Jess Ransom, the Skins' tight end, had become Sam's favorite football player both because of his body and his up-front role as union rep during the strike. Indeed, Sam had become a fanny fan of his, so that she was very eager to see Ransom play and display his designer buttocks tucked into tight pants that grabbed his buns and gloved his genitals.

" 'Still, she resented having to watch the game alone.

" 'Even though she genuinely enjoyed pro football and was committed to the Redskins because of Jess Ransom, Sam resented the fact that she had raised three perfectly fine sons, none of whom was any longer in residence or available to watch the game with her when she craved company and companionship.

" 'The problem was that Sam was in such an intensely insecure period of her life that she felt her present solitude reflected her character, her social status, her sexual circumstances, her professional plateau, her advancing age, her fading appearance and her financial straits. Insecurity had become Sam's major personality trait.

" 'Just last Wednesday, when she walked past the fresh fish counter at the Safeway, she had shriveled with shame, momentarily certain that the fishy odor in the area stemmed from her own carefully deodorized crotch. Later, only after hand-testing herself while driving home, she realized that her spasm of self-consciousness was simply a sign of her heightened insecurity.

" 'Indeed, at the insistence of her family practitioner / psychiatrist, Dr. Mulberry, Sam had registered for her first adult education extension course: Self-Assertiveness I, at Georgetown University. The first assignment required each class member to assert herself in some way and then write four paragraphs describing her feelings before, during, and after the chosen assertion. These paragraphs were to be read aloud to the entire group—consisting of five other women besides Sam—at the next class meeting.

" 'Sam had used the assignment as an opportunity to teach Haggie, who was still with her then although already desperately thin, how to slip between the bars of the new gate Sam had installed on her back door after her seventh robbery. By teaching Haggie how to squeeze between the bars, Sam could avoid unlocking and relocking the gate every time Haggie had to do her business. It had taken close to two hours, and a half-box of Treats, to teach her old dog this new trick. Although Sam had felt guilty about taking advantage of Haggie's boniness to fulfill her assignment, she was shocked when the teacher refused to accept her recitation on the grounds that asserting oneself with a pet didn't meet the intent of the lesson. So Sam had been doing a makeup assignment when Haggie slipped away through pearlier gates.

" 'However, compounding Sam's confusion was the fact that only three students had registered for the second semester, Self-Assertiveness II, and the university had canceled the course. Now, several times a day by telephone, Sam was trying to assert herself sufficiently to get her prepaid tuition refunded by the bursar's office. Needless to say, her ineffectiveness in this endeavor only underlined her suspicions that she should receive refunds for both her first *and* second semesters' tuition, since her first genuine effort to assert herself sufficiently to get her tuition back wasn't working.

" 'Sam reached over for her pack of cigarettes which was buried amid the debris on the coffee table. The tabletop was strewn with random objects which she liked to keep within reach now that she was spending an inordinate amount of time on the living room sofa. Lately, the majority of both her sleeping and nonsleeping hours were passed on the sofa since she could no longer find any reason to go to any other areas of her awesomely empty house to eat or sleep, when all essential functions could be accomplished right in one place.

" 'The major problem with Sam's new life-style was that the coffee table was quite crowded. Ashtrays overflowed, tepees of open paperback books formed Indian villages, empty coffee cups and vodka glasses squeezed for surface space while fruit peelings, sandwich crusts and empty cigarette wrappers wilted along the periphery. Two toothbrushes (one firm for teeth, one soft for gum massaging), a scratchy nylon hairbrush, a strong skin astringent and some Sassoon spray deodorant for men (because Sam believed her perspiration to be of male, rather than female, ferocity) cluttered the tabletop.

" 'Reaching beneath the sofa to extract the soft mohair blanket her mother had knitted for them years ago, Sam wrapped the cover around herself.

" 'She had been cold all winter.

" 'Although a longtime participant in the Year-Round Budget Plan of the Griffith Oil Consumer Company of Cheverly, Maryland, for $141 a month, Sam couldn't warm up. She was still cold although she was wearing a pair of Mike's woolen soccer socks on top of a pair of run-ruined nylon pantyhose beneath a pair of 28W by 30L Levi's (unsnapped and unzipped for comfort), a black turtleneck T-shirt and a large Bulgarian machine-made sweater, purchased for a five-dollar bill from the Pakistani street vendor outside the Riggs National Bank Universal Branch on Connecticut Avenue (out of which Sam intended to take her $194.53 checking account balance because of the bank's rumored investments in South Africa).

" 'Actually, she believed she was cold—both inside and out—because she had just made a truly chilling decision.

" 'Within a week, Sam Cronik was going to murder her estranged husband, Seymour Cronik, who, after twenty hectic years of marriage, had decided to run off with his red-haired, pug-nosed, slightly pigeon-toed secretary.

" 'Sam was angry. Very angry. Having previously relied exclusively (and heavily) upon drugs and alcohol to deal with her rage, Sam had now decided that homicide was the only suitable solution—the only act serious enough to express the magnitude of her magnificent rage. Murder was definitely dramatic and dramatically definitive. It appealed to her on a number of levels and was the only sort of action appropriate to her current condition.

" 'Also, it was clear that Sam needed an organizing principle—some means of tying up the various loose ends of her life. Without some grounding action, her mind would continue to leapfrog from one fright to the next. Recently, all she could do was obsess about getting old, fat or sick. She spent hours wondering what she would lose first—her mind, her money, her parents or her hair.

" 'Sam needed an organizing principle just as she needed certain office organizers, separators for the cards in her recipe box, individual makeup containers for her purse, small plastic boxes for her tool chest. She yearned for heart-shaped containers in which to keep paper clips or aspirins—anything that would put a little order back into her life. She even wanted to do something permanent with the cigar box full of her children's baby teeth, sweet white pearls that she meant to preserve for posterity.

" 'This was why her impulse to kill Seymour seemed perfect. It would catapult her simultaneously released novel onto the best-seller lists while ridding the world of a man who had never once refilled an ice-cube tray, a salt shaker, a guest's drink or his own prescriptions. She would rid the world of a man who couldn't pump gas in a self-service station or control his own at home. She would do away with a man who had difficulty locating a clitoris in the dark, lighting a match so the sulfur would absorb the stench he left in the bathroom, or speaking in a normal tone of voice to a good-looking blonde. She would do away with a man who couldn't drive in a single lane on a high-speed highway, adjust to daylight saving time or keep his pajama fly closed when he was vertical and ambulatory . . .' "

Suddenly Jeff's voice breaks.

At first I think he is laughing, but then he lowers the hunk of manuscript down to his denim thighs, raises his empty hands to cover his face, and starts to cry with coarse groans.

Joanne flinches, rises as if to go forward to comfort him, but then sinks back down again.

Max, clearly unnerved by Sukie's book, sits motionless near Joanne, sullen and injured by the comic treatment of himself that he's just heard read by his former wife's young and handsome lover.

And though my heart is aching for Jeff, whose grief is a palpable presence in the room, I feel myself lighten— as if before a birth. Because now some of the heaviness surrounding Sukie's death is diminished by the fact that she had begun to alchemize her tragedy into comedy before she died, had attempted to transform rage into art. Like Lois and Allison and Nora and numerous other women writers we know, Sukie had begun to spin her grief into gold.

Jeff's sobs continue for a long while; no one speaks.

Sukie has done it again. She has left her survivors wallowing in chaos, unable to deal with her death because she continues to reinsert herself into our lives. We are now interacting with her work as if it were a living entity.

I sigh heavily. Joanne looks at me and shifts her shoulders in a slight shrug to indicate there's nothing to be done about the current situation. Finally, Jeff stabilizes himself, stands up, inspects a messy heap of tapes near his tape deck and inserts one. Immediately Tina Turner's raucous voice begins shouting "What's Love Got to Do with It?" and the music provides a cover under which each of us retreats.

"How 'bout a joint?" Jeff asks helpfully. "I can't handle wine; it really brings me down."

Max nods. "Sounds good to me."

So Jeff busies himself with a little red cigarette-rolling machine, and we all watch, like children, as he slowly crumbles and folds some marijuana into the paper and fondly licks it closed. He hands Joanne and Max their joints and then passes me one before sitting down on a nearby chair.

"It's not fair," Jeff finally says, sucking in all the relief the dope can provide. "Maybe a guy who's thirty-five shouldn't feel like an orphan, but I do. My folks are dead, my best buddy got killed two days before we were supposed to leave Vietnam, and now Sukie dies for no fucking good reason."

"Look. Let's try to relax a little," Joanne suggests. "Let's try to think about something else for a while."

I start puffing away on my joint.

CHAPTER 16

So we sit there, an ad hoc committee of Sukie's survivors: her former husband, her last lover, and two of her best friends, all getting high together the night before her funeral. The four of us form a sexual pentagon—two men, two women and a ghost—linked together by invisible pencil lines that connect the dots of our lives.

Gradually the dope unknots my tension so that it unravels and slips away, falling like a ribbon to the floor.

After another long, fuzzy while, there is a shifting and softening so that the hard geometric frame connecting us turns into a soft-spun gossamer pentagonal spiderweb. No. A Sukieweb. Our pentagon becomes a sweet, connective Sukieweb.

Max is sitting quietly on the sofa, but I know his mind is rioting. His head lolls back over the rim of the sofa to rest against the wall while he stares up at the cracked and water-stained ceiling. He, too, is caught in the Sukieweb. He cannot defend himself against her portrayal of him. There is no way to respond to her book because the author has died. The indictment she brought down means Max will have to prove his innocence. He is shaken and angry.

Like twin Nancy Drews, Joanne and I are staying on top of The Case of the Missing Manuscript. The atmosphere in the room is full of white-hot electricity. Cartoon lightning bolts are being hurtled all around us.

Much is happening. We're making a heavy-rock music recording without any lyrics. Lots of sound and fury. No language.

"The last thing this world needs is another *kvetch* novel about Jewish husbands," Max finally says. "I think we've OD'd on those. And given the circumstances, we don't really know what Sukie would want done with the book. So I think we should just turn it over to some neutral third party until we sort everything out."

"That's not the way it's going to be," says Jeff.

He is sitting in an old, misshapen armchair, clearly his favorite roost for drinking morning tea or coffee and reading the newspapers. He looks handsome, slouched and comfortable in his own digs, more relaxed than when he had sat in Sukie's kitchen. There is a stillness that encircles Jeff like a spotlight, setting him apart, making him seem special.

Beside his chair is a tall, tired avocado plant, listing like a palm tree during a hurricane. A cluster of four brownish leaves droops sadly over the chair, serving as a weathered beach umbrella. Jeff takes a final drag off the roach he's holding and tamps it out in an ashtray. Then, reaching up, he pats the dying avocado leaves as if petting a dog.

"This avocado loves me," he sighs philosophically.

Joanne smiles so that warm lights rush into her eyes.

She is curled up at the end of the sofa, the spill of her hair running down over her thin shoulders. Her bleached muslin shirt drapes over her faded sea-blue glove-tight jeans that trace the length of her body, tapering down her long legs.

I can see she is positioning herself for love. She is flowing forward toward Jeff, like a glass of spilled water. I can almost feel her senses becoming indistinct and indiscriminate as she softens toward the object of her affection. Her neediness, like a steady rain, is preparing the ground for seduction.

Occasionally Max looks over at Joanne with accusative and warning eyes, because he, of course, doesn't know that her objectives this time are serious rather than frivolous—meaningful rather than meaningless. Only Jeff remains oblivious to Joanne's eager availability because he is still thinking of Sukie.

"This book was important to her, not just because of its intrinsic value, but because it marked her recovery, understand? It was a sign of her recovery. People own their own survival stories as well as their own horror stories, you know?"

In the bookcase behind Jeff's chair, empty spaces have destabilized his library. His books are listing like the tall stalk of his avocado plant. Missing books have caused the dislocation of the remaining ones, leaving them to tilt, precariously off-balance, a physical manifestation of removal and loss.

Now Max is studying Jeff with stoned concentration in a high-schoolish, but somehow endearing, attempt to size up his opposition. Max is struggling to control the final image of Sukie's life. If Jeff establishes preemptive control over her book, he also achieves a proprietary position toward her life. His closeness to Sukie, right before her death, can make their relationship definitive and thus diminish the importance of her marriage to Max. This is the phantom Max feels he must fight.

We are now in a time of life when our cumulative history is as active an agent as the present in determining our behavior. The past has become our savings account and, of course, has a much larger balance than our paltry NOW accounts. Max doesn't want to be robbed of his savings, but Jeff is quietly chipping away at Max's preferred version of the past.

"There's a good joke I know about a situation like this one," Max says suddenly. "You think you're up for it? No one's going to get insulted?"

We shake our heads.

"Okay." He sits forward on the sofa and dons a boyish,

but earnest, expression he must have created years ago when he told his first dirty joke.

"A man's wife dies. For years she'd been having an affair with her husband's best friend who, of course, turns up at the funeral. The lover is hysterical with grief and collapses sobbing beside the wife's grave following her burial. Then the husband walks over to his friend, puts his hand on his shoulder, and says: 'Don't cry; don't worry. I'll get married again.' "

We all look at Max with astonishment.

It's Jeff who laughs first.

"Jesus," he groans, chuckling and shaking his head to indicate his incredulity at both the joke and Max's perception of the present situation. But then he stands up.

"I know it's just a joke, Max, but it seems you've got everything turned upside down and inside out. I didn't take your wife away. You dumped her. I just picked up the pieces and helped her get through some of the last rough patches before she died. See—I think you treated her like shit."

"Hey." Max stands up, compelled to defend his honor in front of Joanne and me. He cannot allow such an accusation to stand unchallenged. "You don't know shit about anything."

"Sukie told me everything."

"Sukie told you her side of the story."

"You left her, didn't you, Max? And you never once looked back, did you?"

"Fuck you." Max grabs the front of Jeff's shirt. He's shorter than Jeff, but solid on his feet,

"I had plenty against you even before I saw you," Jeff says, stiff-arming Max. "So don't fuck around here. This is my cave. Now back off."

But when Max moves away, it is only to create enough space to swing at Jeff.

Clearly Jeff wasn't expecting an actual strike, so when Max connects he falls back against his desk, sending papers and books spilling down onto the floor. Then, outraged by such a violation, Jeff comes at Max with full speed and fury.

"You're an ego nut, Max. You can't even see anything that's right in your face."

Joanne and I are both standing up.

This is a movie. This is television. This is not real.

Now the men are clenched together, dancing around the center of the room, edging back to get space and then embracing each other again, hugging in hatred.

"You asshole," Jeff says. "Don't you know enough not to fuck with a grunt? What do you think we learned over there?"

And then he pulls back and releases the cudgel of his arm. Max turns so that Jeff's fist only sideswipes his face and grazes his head, but then he stumbles backwards and falls against the aquarium. The heavy glass case totters for a second atop its wrought-iron base and then crashes onto the bare floor of the kitchen and explodes. The glass shatters, in what seems like slow motion, sending shards, water and silver piranha flying upward—like birds in a silver arc—before they crash back down to the floor.

Jeff howls as if he's been knifed.

Rushing forward, he falls to his knees, grasping for a fish. Then, holding it in both hands, he gets it to the kitchen sink and turns on the water. But there is no drain stopper and the fish starts throwing itself against the sides of the sink.

Now Jeff panics.

The other three fish are flopping on the floor as he rushes into the bathroom. I can hear him stopping up the tub and running water into it. Now one of the fish is thrusting itself up and off the floor, flopping against a cabinet so that the door thumps like a heartbeat again and again. The third piranha is already spent and waiting to die.

"Help me," Jeff yells. "Get them in here into the

bathtub." He is standing half inside and half outside his bathroom. "Get that one. Sacco. Vanzetti."

Obediently I move forward but I am unable to touch, let alone lift, either of the slim silver fish flopping upon the floor in a struggle to live.

Joanne, too, remains frozen in the center of the room.

"I'm wiped out," Jeff howls. His body is heaving and his face is wet.

It is Max, shamefaced and frightened, who finally clasps the last two fish and carries them to the tub.

"It's too small," Jeff groans, but he stays inside the bathroom for a long while, apparently putting some kind of cover over part of the tub.

Silently, Joanne and I begin to pick up the books and papers that have fallen off Jeff's desk. Max finds an empty grocery bag and slowly begins picking up the biggest shards of glass. He has withdrawn into himself, ashamed of what has happened and the vulnerability it has exposed. His distress acknowledges his understanding of Jeff's anguish.

I wonder if Jeff, like Joanne, has only a limited number of objects to love and if the fish were on his endangered love list.

"Look, I'm sorry as hell," Max says when Jeff finally reappears. "I'll pick up a new aquarium for you tomorrow if you tell me where to go and what size you need." He pauses and then shrugs as he remembers the funeral. "I guess it'll have to be first thing Tuesday morning."

"Let's get out of here," Jeff snaps. "What time is it?"

"Nine o'clock," I say, squinting at the expensive watch I could finally afford to buy, but can no longer read without glasses.

"Let's go get a drink."

Joanne watches without objection as Jeff puts Sukie's manuscript back on his desk.

Immediately, Max moves forward, gesturing toward the pile of pages. "What about that?" he asks.

"Let's have a drink first," Jeff says firmly, gesturing us to precede him through the door.

"But we've got to settle this tonight," Max insists.

"We will," Jeff promises.

Outside, the heat has lessened.

"Wow, it's crowded," Joanne says, looking at the suburban kids in urban drag strolling along M Street.

"Actually, it's kind of deserted for Georgetown," Jeff disagrees, eyeing the passing crowd like a cautious driver entering freeway traffic from an interchange. "Most folks aren't back from their vacations yet. Georgetown doesn't really get crowded till next week. Hang a left," he says, starting to steer us upstream against the crowd.

Night is drifting down upon Georgetown, igniting soft lights and sweet illusions. We walk past narrow boutiques, fast-food outlets and hanging-fern French bistros. All the doorways are indented like new paragraphs in the justified line of red brick storefronts. Glassed in by bay windows, people are eating expensive meals inches away from passersby on the sidewalk.

Max has his hand cupped around my elbow. Still mildly stoned, we feel little impulse to speak. Jeff and Joanne walk ahead of us, moving closer together as they talk. Tall and narrow from the rear, they seem to belong together—slim, blond, casual Americans who can cruise crowded streets in any city around the country with consummate confidence.

The humidity hovers above us like an open parachute. The faces of the people who approach and do-si-do around us are glistening with sweat. Although my mouth is dry, my dress and hairline are damp. I am very tired of being hot. The heat of the city and my grief over Sukie have been stirred together like sand and water into a brick of summer discomfort.

Suddenly I experience a hot flashback that returns me to a winter morning, several years ago, when I was bent over the sizzling steam radiator in my apartment trying to recover a keyring that had dropped behind it. Dry fingers of heat reached out to claw my face, making my features flinch and my skin curdle. A hot flash, backed up by my sizzling hot flashback, plus the Washington heat brings me to the cusp of hallucination. My body temperature soars and even though it is almost dark, I think I see waves of hot air quivering above the sidewalk as we walk along the strip. I step over them as if they are puddles.

We are inspecting saloons, entering and standing in the doorways while we measure the sex appeal and weigh the potential embrace of each particular place. We receive long looks from people who wonder who we are and what we're doing. But we don't care. We are just "out drinking."

We go out drinking as though it hasn't gone out of style the way it has. We go out drinking like back in the fifties when we set out with that sole goal, that single purpose, in mind. Back then, we sometimes called it bar-hopping, because that's what it was. We'd hit a place, have a drink, have a second, and stay only if we got a boost off the atmosphere. Otherwise we'd hop over to the next bar with a decent name above its door and try again. We did it for hours. It was an old-fashioned, 1950s way of bonding.

And bonding we are.

Joanne is flashing herself at Jeff, showing her stuff, and Jeff has finally begun to notice. Although thoroughly distraught and distracted at first, he becomes more centered as he downs more drinks. Ordering two drinks for each one of ours, and drinking twice as fast as we do, Jeff is both drowning his pain and surfing on the tidal waves of the alcohol he's consuming.

By the time we hit the fifth bar, we are, of course, drunk.

Walking beside Max, entering saloons and sitting beside him, talking as a team with him to Joanne and Jeff, brushing against him accidentally, watching him jockey

Jeff into confrontational discussions, feeling him operating at full capacity every minute, I realize that he is exactly the kind of trouble we used to crave years ago. Men like Max confirmed us—assured us that we were really players in the game. Now, moving around Georgetown with him, I can feel what Sukie wanted from Max—the possible conquest of a male supremacist. A home run with the bases loaded.

I am on my fourth vodka and tonic. Still slightly stoned when I started drinking, I am now far out in orbit and suddenly—in a hot flash—I see this scene from Sukie's celestial perspective. It does not look good. Sukie would not be happy to see her biological husband, her handsome young lover and two of her best friends tanking up together in a raunchy tavern, each couple getting a contact high off the other, and all four players only one bounce away from bawdiness.

—What's happening, Diana? You're not even going to wait until you bury me?—Sukie's spirit inquires inside the inner sanctum of my mind.

—Sukie. This is so complicated. It has to do with you. We're all in a lot of pain.

—So was I, Diana. You're not planning to sleep with Max are you?

—He wasn't always your enemy, Sukie. You had some good times with him. We all did. Great times. Remember all our summers out at the beach when the kids were growing up?

Suddenly I wonder if I'm talking out loud.

"Why don't we take a ride somewhere to cool off?" Jeff suggests, dispatching Sukie's ghost from our party.

We are sitting in a dark wooden booth in a bar above a disco.

"Maybe down to Haines Point. Or wait. Have you seen the Vietnam Memorial yet?" he asks Joanne.

She shakes her head.

"Well, let's go over there. You should see it."

We go outside onto M Street again and then up to

33rd where we turn right. Here the first-floor windows of haughty Federal row houses flash long drapes like taunting tongues stuck out at trespassing tourists. Jeff's battered Checker cab, parked directly in front of an enormous mansion, is a hulking insult to the insularity of the neighborhood. As soon as we're inside the taxi, I feel Max's presence expand and start to crowd me in the spacious back seat. I move further away but I can still feel his willfulness like a tent around me.

Then I embark upon a roll of hot flashes. They start coming closer and closer together, while growing longer and hotter, until they produce a sudden, white-hot insight: Sukie's cerebral hemorrhage was the ultimate hot flash, a streaking sensation of roiling, boiling blood which raced up to her brain while her life flashed fast forward before her eyes. Perhaps death is the final hot flash. Perhaps death is life's menopause.

I stare out the car window as Jeff drives along the Potomac River before swinging off onto the surprising broadness of Constitution Avenue. There he parks his cab and we all slide out on the curb side because the street has become a river of splashing headlights. Walking away from the white water of lights into the tree-studded darkness of the Mall, we can see no sign of the Vietnam Memorial. From where we are, the memorial—like the dead it honors—is hidden below us in the earth.

"If you don't mind, I'd like to go stand by my buddy," Jeff says, walking purposefully ahead of us. "I mean his name."

Silently we follow him past a high podium where the Book of the Dead, protected by a plastic shield, is open to its alphabetical list of Americans who died in Vietnam. An elderly couple is methodically consulting the Book as if it were the Yellow Pages. The short, shapeless, gray-haired woman is wearing a catalogue-style cotton outfit—a blouse tucked into the elasticized waist of matching slacks. She is from the Midwest—dressed by Monkey Ward with makeup from Maybelline. Although she is clutching a collection of tote bags, a camera and road maps, the paraphernalia of tourism does not detract from her dignity. She and her tall, thin, farm-tanned husband have clearly traveled to Washington as the parents of a dead soldier.

The government, pressured by a small group of veterans, had finally raised this memorial to acknowledge their loss. Something about the couple suggests that they have taken a great deal of friendly fire during their time—even before their country took their son.

Clearly agitated, Jeff leads us past the weekend tourists milling around near the bronze statue of three Vietnam vets that traditionalists insisted be placed near the unconventional black granite memorial wall. He is moving steadily deeper into the earth as the slope of land sharpens and the wall bearing the names of the dead grows higher beside us. We descend into a darkness illuminated only by low-set spotlights. Suddenly I feel as if I am inside a tunnel, a tunnel like the war, a tunnel like the past leading up to this particular present. The L-shaped memorial directs attention out toward the Washington Monument on one end and the Lincoln Memorial at the other. The wall points at the places where peace marchers met to protest the war.

"This is it," Jeff says, suddenly stopping near the right angle where the wall turns eastward.

He moves forward to scan the long list of names engraved in the granite, seeking the friend he'd lost first in Vietnam and now in the crowded inventory of dead soldiers.

"This is the biggest fucking tombstone in the world," Jeff says, squinting as he tries to read the names stacked like corpses one atop the other. "Fifty-eight thousand dead souls. It always takes me a while to find him."

Finally, Jeff reaches out to touch the name of his friend with flat fingertips. We wait. After a few seconds he steps back and rejoins us. "But the real weirdness is that—now my time in Vietnam is starting to look good compared to what came after."

That is silencing. How could Vietnam seem preferable to anything else? But in one sense I can understand: it is not the war that vets miss, but the camaraderie of fighting together. By now, both participants and protesters find their experiences sweetened by the kiss of time. Resisters and soldiers alike crave the crowded past like aging junkies. The decade between 1965 and 1975 bottled the best years of our lives—as we slipped from our thirties into our forties—making everything that followed feel like epilogue.

And who would not feel nostalgia for a past when people felt linked and loved, when our togetherness was like a lovely summer day full of sweetness? The war years were busy years when we were taking care of babies, testing the current, challenging the old order, ricocheting inside the security of our marriages—rebelling and relapsing as regularly as ocean waves—within our relationships. We never limped until our spirits were broken.

I turn and look at the black wall which some people call the healing memorial. Camus wanted to be able to love his country and justice too. Same with me. We all feel that our generation didn't get a chance to make any positive political contributions because we were totally occupied with just trying to stop the madness.

Some of us went abroad to do good. Back in the fifties, two of our Barbaras drove one of Franco's prisoners out of Spain under a blanket in the backseat of a rented car. Margaret lived in Mexico, Cuba, and Nicaragua for twenty-three years before coming home to discover that the INS didn't want to grant her citizenship again and wouldn't even give her a green card. Elizabeth is still writing about Cambodia, Elsie is in the South African underground and Carla is working with the Sendero Luminoso.

For years, Perdita received grateful telephone calls from Algerian men whose names she didn't recognize. They would provide detailed accounts of experiences they'd shared with her when she was nursing wounded guerrillas in the mountains near Algiers. But last Christmas, Perdita suddenly realized that these men who telephoned her had simply forgotten their "war names"—their revolutionary aliases—the only ones by which she knew them. She only remembered who they used to be and they only knew who they were now. She said she'd sent this message on a Christmas card to Sukie for her modern metaphor file.

Jeff's blond hair is gleaming in the soft spotlights and his face is illuminated both from within and without. Other tourists are making wide detours around us, courteously not walking between Jeff and his patch of wall. The rest of us stand in bereaved silence as we stare at the names of the dead. A line from Faulkner flits through my mind. The past isn't dead, he said, it isn't even past.

We start walking again. But as we approach the end of the wall, where the names of the last Americans to die in Vietnam are engraved, we see the couple who had been consulting the Book of the Dead. By now they have found the name they were seeking and are taping a small American flag, a red plastic rose and a folded paper—clearly a letter—beside the name. Standing in the shadows, we watch them affix their message.

Suddenly, Jeff makes a deep, guttural noise that rises like a groan from the dead. Then he turns and begins running into the darkness.

"Hey," Max calls, starting after him.

Joanne and I follow. It is too dark to see the ground we cover as we move farther away from the Memorial. Dimly I make out the shape of the two men near a distant tree and as we approach we hear Jeff being violently sick. He is doubled over, leaning against the trunk. His body is lurching in rhythm with the spasmodic retchings that have begun to convulse him and he seems near collapse.

Max is holding him.

Max is keeping Jeff on his feet, supporting his weight, while Jeff, totally out of control, is vomiting both on the ground and on Max, retching from the dope and the liquor and the struggle with his fish and Sukie's death and the memorial and the parents leaving a letter to their dead son and the war and the people who went and the ones who stayed home and for himself and his life. And the longtime husband of the woman he had loved holds his head as tenderly as a father supporting a child over a toilet basin, one hand pressed to Jeff's forehead to comfort, as much as cradle, him while he is being sick.

I feel somehow as if we are watching a scene we shouldn't see, so I take Joanne's hand and walk her back toward Constitution Avenue, where we find Jeff's cab and lean against its hood while we wait for the men.

Eventually they materialize out of the darkness.

Max is walking in front of Jeff. He is bare-chested but carrying nothing so I assume he threw away his shirt. He looks handsome wearing only jeans and walking through the fast flashes of lights flung at him from speeding cars. After a while I see the hot flash of his cigarette lighter in the darkness as they approach us.

Jeff seems almost shriveled as he hugs the shadows while unlocking the car doors. When we get inside the taxi we can all smell the odor of vomit still clinging to both men. Jeff pulls out of the parking place and makes a U-turn in the middle of Constitution Avenue.

"Want to hear something crazy?" he says tersely. "When you came over to my place before, I had a Bruce Springsteen tape on and I was listening to his lines about throwing up after he strafed his old high school from a B-52. I think that's maybe what made me barf."

No one speaks until we're back in Georgetown. Jeff double-parks near Max's car.

"What about the manuscript?" Max asks.

"I'm going to take care of that," Joanne says softly, but firmly, from the front seat. "Jeff and I are going out to get coffee somewhere and talk about it a little more. I'll get home under my own steam later. Don't worry about the manuscript, Max. I'll take care of everything."

I begin getting out of the cab, but Max is still seated, watching Joanne anxiously.

"It's okay," I tell him. "She'll take care of it."

Reluctantly, Max gets out of the cab and transfers us back into his own car. Then he drives me to Sukie's house in total, uninterrupted silence.

He doesn't even say good night.

I don't mind. In what is fast becoming a habit, as soon as I'm ensconced in Sukie's room, I strip off my clothes, randomly select another portion of her journal, prop up the pillows and get into bed to begin reading again.

CHAPTER 17

SEPTEMBER 1984

I have a new doctor. Her name is Dr. Annie Austen. I met her on the bus. Her office is near the zoo and she was sitting behind me when I started to cry. She thinks she can help me. She is going to let me run a tab. When I asked her why, she just smiled. I have to go to her office first thing every morning to plan out my day. I must attend one or two AA meetings, play tennis for at least an hour in the morning or afternoon, put in four hours of writing (articles only, fiction's too scary at the moment, although she thinks I should start a funny novel about a woman like me who looks for the perfect act of revenge against her unfaithful husband), and have dinner with some friend who might like or need my company.

"Don't you have any homework, David?"
   "No."
   "Nothing?"
   "Just a little Spanish."
   "You want to play some Ping-Pong?"

This is the AA Serenity Prayer: "God grant me the serenity to accept the things I cannot change, the cour-

*age to change the things I can, and the wisdom to know
the difference."*

No matter how hard I try, I can not memorize the AA
Serenity Prayer. I copied it down in the pink floral
notebook that I carry in my purse all day and keep
beside my bed at night, but I still can't learn it. I can
remember some of the AA slogans, although I am also
unable to recall the twelve steps, or the twelve tradi-
tions, that bind the group together. I know they say, "A
day at a time," "Turning it over," and "Letting God."

At one AA meeting, a woman spoke with flat matter-
of-factness: "When I'm alone at night," she said, "my
favorite hotlines are AA and something called FACT,
which is a family counseling group."

Ah. A slight shiver slides through me. So other people
have favorite hotlines for when they feel suicidal. That's
how they survive those black hours when the city is
asleep and there is nowhere to go and no one to telephone for help to get through the night.

I wonder if there is an 800 number for God.

Sometimes I go to AA meetings just to feel the fellow-
ship of decent strangers struggling to survive. Occasionally I drop into the basement of a church on Rhode
Island Avenue for their noon brown-bag lunch meeting.
It is warming to hear other addictive personalities
speaking about their pain and their plans and their loyalty to this program. Sometimes I take a drink before I
go, but either way I always sob softly when the members clasp hands at the end and say the Lord's Prayer.
That is still a very beautiful and moving poem to me.
Afterwards I like to have coffee with some of the eager,
friendly people.

Once I met a handsome man at an AA meeting—well,
not met him exactly, but noticed him noticing me. Before, when I saw such a man, I simply assumed we
would smile and chat and then go out for a drink to
some dark bar. Now I was stymied. He, however, came
over to me while I was emptying my ashtray.

*"Do you like Häagen-Dazs ice cream?" he asked.
I guess where there's a will there's a way.*

Sometimes when my children write me letters, they forget to put a comma between the word *"love"* and their signatures. Perhaps they don't forget. Perhaps they're saying, *"Love me!!"* But I do. I have always loved both of them according to their needs.

Possible titles for a spoof: Dirty Linen, Second Helpings, Bad Connections, Split Ends.

Margaret from up the block called and wants to fix me up with some shrink friend of hers who saw me down at the tennis courts. His name? Norman Naylor. I didn't believe it.

Just last month I started having a few dinner dates. Wanting to look svelte, I would fast all day so my stomach would be completely flat beneath my black velour dress. Luckily, anticipation always dims my appetite and late in the afternoon I walk around the house hugging memories of lovely dinners I've eaten in elegant restaurants, warmed by a velvet ambience and serenaded by a soft chorus of stylish voices.

I remember back to the mid-fifties when I was flying for Delta and dating a lot, going out for expensive dinners that were sexual preludes played to the tune of sumptuous foods that left languorous tastes upon the tongue like a lingering melody while we sipped a last glass of wine and anticipated passion. Back then, of course, the last course was always intercourse—part of the dinner. I can also remember sipping slow cocktails afterwards in dark corners of hotel bars, while I knitted a new mood around us, crocheting postcoital intimacy into a shawl for our shoulders.

But the realities of my so-called dates with so-called suitable men now are completely different. Restaurant

*dinners are totally without romance. People eat in dark
ethnic dens that serve Ethiopian peanut-butter sauces
in which to dip raw, damp-tasting bread. Everything
seems austere again. Meals are no longer extravagant
gestures, silent but passionate promises; now they are
exercises in avoiding excesses. My dinner companions
pay practical attention to the economics and logistical
details of eating, rather than elaborating upon any
meanings. These evenings are profoundly disappointing to me, although I try not to expect too much.*

*Actually, I only accept these invitations because Dr.
Annie Austen wants me to. I can't really make myself
care much anymore. Now I just wear some old silk
blouse tucked into my faded, quite-tight jeans. I top it
off with my fur jacket, which I no longer dare wear over
a dress anymore. My tired fur jacket and worn-out cowboy boots serve me as a memo about changing times
and my new life-style.*

How sad it is. How shabby.

*Lately I have begun to yearn for the smell of garlic and
onion on my hands once more. I want to brown bits of
beef in olive oil, turning them over like dice, again and
again, before stewing them slowly in red wine alongside
plump yellow carrots and new potatoes whose thin
spring jackets seem too skimpy to keep them warm. I
can remember all the times I resented going to one
grocery for a superior steak and to another for the most
verdant vegetables. I remember past impatience standing in line to buy pastries at Avignon Frères, liking the
thought of a French conclusion to dinner, but disliking
the inconveniences of marketing. I remember the first
time I ever pressed the butcher's call button at the
supermarket to ask for a special cut of meat. That made
me feel so matronly I never did it again.*

*Now she's put me on Antabuse. This is getting serious.
This is a whole different trip altogether.*

MAY 20, 1984

*I've met a man. He picked me up. Not in the old way,
but in a taxi. Ha ha. He was the cabbie and he liked how
I smelled because I had vanilla smeared all over me on
account of the Antabuse. He said I smelled like his favorite kind of cookie, that I smelled good enough to eat.
Ha ha.*

*His name is Jeff Conroy and he's thirty-five, hand-
some and enormously sweet. He took me out for lunch
at Clyde's and then asked me over to his place. He said
he lived right across the street. He did. I did. We did.*

*But not that fast. First we had omelets in Clyde's
mirror room where the light is a real presence, like
some rowdy drunk who sits down at your table to make
trouble. The sunshine comes pouring through the sky-
light and then splashes up against the mirrors that toss
it back and forth across the room like white water.*

*It was too bright in there for me. I could actually feel
the imperfections, the impurities, in my complexion,
growing larger as we sat there. I thought people could
see it happen, like you think you can hear corn growing.
But Jeff didn't seem to notice anything. He kept smiling
at me like I was lovely, like I was maybe Anouk Aimée
in* A Man and a Woman.

*"So. You're in AA," he said. "What got you into so
much trouble?"*

*I told him. I gave him the Garvin's Laugh-Inn sce-
nario.*

*He laughed and told me about two women he'd gone
with who'd made scenes like that with him. Beautiful
women, ugly scenes, he said. But he couldn't understand why women never learn that husbands don't have
the heart for big scenes. Lovers have to handle them,
but they're too heavy for husbands. He said men get
married just to avoid having scenes like that in public.*

*"Were you sleeping around right before it hap-
pened?" he asked me.*

I was stunned.

"Around where? I mean when? When do you mean?"

So he dropped it.

"What do you plan to do now?"

"Nothing," I said. "I've got a new shrink. A woman. She's great. She doesn't jerk me around. She's more like a teacher. She's teaching me a lot."

"I bet you're teaching her a few things, too."

Then that sweet smile. Wonderfully white squarish teeth that look super strong, like he could chew glass or something.

"So what's your story?" I asked him.

He said he'd been in Vietnam, gone back to graduate school, wanted to get married and have five kids. He wanted to name them Ricki, Rory, Robin, Randy and Arthur. The first four names could cover either boys or girls. Even crazier, he meant it.

That hurt my feelings. For the first time I felt a bit barren and bitter. Out of it.

Lunch didn't take long because he didn't order anything to drink either. I think he was trying to be helpful. So afterwards we walked across the street to his studio, which is a second-floor walkup right on M Street in the center of the universe.

"This is it," he said watching my face when he unlocked the door at the top of the stairs.

"It's nice."

Actually it was plain and sort of poor-looking. It looked like the home of a guy who'd been living alone a long, long time. I can recognize that look now. Almost four years later, I should be able to do at least that much.

There was a large aquarium near the kitchen, so I walked over and watched some fish swimming around. One of them looked at me and kind of wagged his tail, so I smiled back.

"Where you at now?" Jeff asked next.

I shrugged. "I don't know. I guess I'm still sort of grieving for my marriage or something."

"Don't you work?"

"I'm a free-lance writer. I write fluff for women's magazines."

"And what's your position on smoking dope?"

"Well, it's not kosher at AA, but my doctor doesn't mind if it helps me not to drink. I was . . . drinking a lot."

"So how about we have a joint and listen to some music?"

"Don't you have to work? Drive your cab?"

"Not if I don't want to. That's why I do it."

He has a real slow smile that sort of develops like a photo print, getting lighter as it comes into focus. His eyes are as smoky as the air around us.

He likes me.

"You got any kids?"

"Two. Seventeen and twenty."

"Well, at least you're lucky there."

Suddenly it felt as if we were old colleagues in a lousy world.

I hadn't been with a man for more than three years.

I asked him some questions about Vietnam, but instead he told me this story:

Once he and his younger brother, Arthur, were walking home from grade school in Missoula, Montana. Some bigger boys were out to get Arthur and five of them jumped out of nowhere. They pummeled Arthur until his face and head were bleeding. By the time they ran off, Arthur was in pretty bad shape—crying and wheezing from asthma. Jeff took him home, calling their father while they were still walking up the front stairs. Their dad ran out and listened to Jeff's story about what had happened.

"From now on," their father said, looking at Jeff, "if one of you gets beat up, you'd both better come home crying."

"So I took good care of Arthur after that," Jeff says

seriously. *"Even though he got most of the sweet pussy when we were in high school, I didn't really care. I loved that kid. Then I went to Vietnam and my Dad died and Arthur became a junkie and moved out to San Francisco. He OD'd while I was in Saigon. So I didn't do what my dad asked me to do, after all."*

Jeff walks over to his bookcase and removes a shoe box filled with rolling papers and pipes and a big cellophane bag full of grass. Then he sits down on the sofa beside me and rolls three big joints in a little red rolling machine.

"I used to have a hard drug problem," he says easily. *"I was in a program for three and a half years. Now I only smoke a joint once in a while."*

Then he puts on a tape and heats some water for tea.

We got stoned real slow. For a while I felt an uncomfortable craving for a drink—for the controlled action of alcohol—but then it passed. Vaguely I wondered if this man would make love as nice as he made tea. About half an hour later we went to bed. We had been sitting on it anyhow.

Whoever said you can't recover your virginity hadn't gone through menopause yet. You hang around long enough, history repeats itself.

His foreplay was fabulous and, after my long famine, perfectly sufficient. But finally he shifted and lifted himself on top of me. I pressed my hands against his chest in an insincere gesture of shyness. I was not afraid as much as nervous. The warm object pressing between my legs seemed enormous, its blunt head butting me like a billy goat. But I remained closed and tight and dry. It had been a very long time since I melted for a man.

Patiently he continued prodding me.

For the first time in my life—since the very first time of my life—I was unable to receive a man.

He stops and returns to caressing me, but this seems false to both of us and clearly beside the point. I feel almost innocent again. Fleetingly I remember some blah-blah about postmenopausal vaginal atrophy I'd read in a ladies' magazine.

This was a problem? This was a consolation prize.

Jeff too seems appreciative of the delicious drama of his forced entry, his armed—ha ha—assault. Though not savage, he's persistent about pressing onward and upward like the good soldier he must have been.

Ah. The ache of such arch rejection, the drama of such halting penetration! The unrequited constancy of it all! Decades of sex are deleted with quick strokes. Passion impedes our breathing. I become intoxicated by the sweet pain of his persistence and my own ambivalent resistance. I am unable to surrender to the monstrous machine seeking entry into my secret. I can do nothing to make myself welcome him. I cannot admit him and thus everything is severely dramatized and intensified. This is no scene from a newish-Jewish novel; we are definitely in a Regency romance now.

And what else could be the value of virginity if not the joy of deferred gratification? Deferred gratification is clearly another sweet experience wasted on youth. My deflowering makes Jeff and me delirious. Even our dialogue is delicious.

"That must hurt."

"Not too bad."

"Seems it would."

"Well, a little."

He resumes his labors.

"You . . . doing okay?"

"Ummmm."

"Oh, sorry. Am I hurting you?"

"Uh-huh. Now you are."

"This is too much."

"I know."

"IS THIS GOOD OR WHAT?" he shouts.

I have to laugh.

We begin falling in love from making love. By definition some things are sweetly circular. Other than a

*baby, what else can lovemaking produce but love?
Where does breadmaking lead?*

"Oh! Wait a minute!"

"Sorry. Sorry about that."

"It's okay."

"This feels like high school."

"That I wouldn't know."

"You're really out of shape. I mean practice."

"I know."

Rest time. Then a sweet, softening internal massage.

"I think you're loosening up."

"Really. *I* think *you're* getting my Change Cherry."

*We laugh so hard we have to wait a while, lying side
by side on his pullout sofabed, holding hands. I look
around the studio again. From here, I can see a small
patch of live sky and his ailing avocado plant. It seems
like a sufficient amount of nature for me. After a while
I hear him stifle a moan of discomfort.*

"I know you're sore, but we could . . . try something
different," *he offers.*

"Why would we change?"

"You're right. You're absolutely right. We're definitely on a roll here. We'll just take it real slow.'

*Ah. Then some progress. There is a partial entry but
no maneuverability. A shiver of expectancy rattles me,
but Round Two ends in a draw again before another
recess.*

"You're going to be sore as hell," *he predicts.*

"I am already."

"That's what I thought. How about . . . some more
tea?"

He stands up. I am shocked he is detachable.

"I'll never eat another piece of pecan pie or rice
pudding ever again without remembering this. That
vanilla . . ."

*He shakes his handsome head with appreciation. He
is standing nude, clearly still on-call, beside the bed. He
is a little winded. His smoky eyes study me intently.*

Then he flashes a white, white smile. He has a wonder-ful bedside manner.

"I wonder if you could use it for suntan lotion, too?"

"I don't know. Why not? It is a little sticky, though."

"What did you drink?"

"What do you mean?"

Now he is back in bed, tea forgotten. "What was your drink of choice, as they say?"

"Oh, vodka. Vodka with grapefruit juice."

"Uhuh. Salty Dogs. I've played a few sets with those too in my day. Down in the islands."

Down in the islands.

He's nuzzling me, licking vanilla off my neck.

"Did you see Atlantic City?"

"Yes."

"Remember Susan Sarandon rubbing lemons all over herself to get rid of the shellfish smell?"

"Uh-huh."

He's still licking me, a proud cat grooming his kitten, learning as he goes along.

"We're going to have to get you moving a little," he says gently after further examination. "You're not really in too bad shape. We'll just get some of those Salty Dogs out of your system. We'll go jogging on the towpath."

"Ummm."

He misses my lips and kisses my chin, smiling, friendly.

And then, quite unexpectedly, my body remembers the music.

I turn to look into his already dear face.

Of course, I do not have to speak.

He knows.

And this embrace is as slow and as lovely and as per-fect as any in my long career and he knows that too and we are very close for a long time after it has ended. Lying in bed, listening to his tapes and talking and drinking tea, we touch each other to remember and wait for the future to happen again.

It is already getting dark when his voice changes and he grips my arm too tight.

"I really want to . . . reach you, Sukie," he says, turning my face toward him. "I want to find out who you really are. I don't have the foggiest . . ."

He begins again. He is panting. He is straining upward and inward to find me.

He does.

But then he starts to lose it.

He loses it.

After a sweet while I do too.

Later, tenderly and lovingly, he touches the laugh lines around my eyes and the smile brackets around my mouth. Then he gathers me up into a giant hug that warms me like a great overcoat.

We screw again. And again. And again. We cannot stop. We screw until midnight. Then he puts me in a taxi, his—ha ha!—and takes me home.

The next afternoon I go back as I'd promised, and he opens the door, real excited:

"You like chicken? I barbecued us some wings. A whole big slew of them. About thirty."

"Sure," I say.

*So we ate a lot of chicken wings, got high again, got back in the pullout bed that he'd left pulled out and started ***** like bunnies.*

Sweet sex.

That first afternoon in Jeff's apartment, I felt as if he were pumping life-restoring glucose intravenously into my system. The fact that he used the vaginal canal route was almost irrelevant.

Sex as consolation goes a long way.

Other Sexchanges:

He likes fiction a lot. We talk about who's writing what. Since we don't know any of the same people, we talk about characters we like or don't like in books. I tell him

I really loved Ray Hicks in Dog Soldiers, *so he says, "Oh, yeah?" and gives me this big white grin and then forces me down on his bed to do something to me that Ray Hicks did to Marge.*

Hmmmmm.

He wants to know about my books. He pesters me and pesters me, so after a couple of weeks I bring him a copy of each.

He responds differently from anyone else who ever read anything of mine. He takes them seriously. He assumes I am serious, that I am consciously working within a tradition, trying to do certain specific things.

What hurts me most is that he wants a baby. Oh God. No more babies. I hadn't really thought about that before. Before now, who cared? Who cared about life and love? I only loved loss and losing. Now I remember the sexiness of pregnancy—the body as a testimonial to the dark, secret stirrings of nightly love.

Once I caught Max looking at me when I was pregnant with Carol. We were out somewhere and suddenly he looked at me like a high school boy seeing a hickey peeking out from the neckline of his girlfriend's sweater and then looking around to see who else had noticed. I think Max was shocked that he'd left such a public mark upon my body.

The last time I visited Mama, I accidentally got off the elevator on the maternity floor and saw a young couple—no, a boy and a girl—holding on to each other. They had clearly become parents and he looked as shy as she did, standing there by the elevator, burning with pride and shyness because now the world knew what they had done. He was only a boy—like Max had been when we had Carol.

Jeff is so sweet. He coaches me sexually. He is like one of those flamboyant, hands-on, TV-star pro basketball coaches. He's always urging me to go for it, to dance all the way downcourt to score. His voice hums in my ear.

"Was that a nice one for you?"

"Hmmm."

"Can't you say yes? Say yes so I'll know."

"Yes."

"It was a biggie, wasn't it? Would you trade ten little guys for one biggie? Oh-oh. You getting shy again?"

Hardly. This is shy?

We move with economy. We don't need or like too much motion. We like staying locked together for as long as we can bear it. (How can you tell if a JAP has an orgasm? She moves.) Stoned, we savor the small, shivery sensations. Small is beautiful.

"This is going to be a very big one," *he announces to me in advance.* "Now just stay still, be quiet for a minute. Ssshhh. You are really going to love this one."

Waves of breathing.

"Oh, good for you, sweetie."

He is always happy to make me happy.

I am happy.

He can hold back for hours. In fact, he holds back far too long and too often. I don't know how or why he does that. Sometimes I wonder if there's something physically or psychologically wrong with him.

Ha ha.

In the beginning I was too shy to ask. Finally I found the nerve to say, "This is all about me. It shouldn't be all about me. What about you?"

"Don't worry about that. I like what we're doing. Tomorrow's soon enough for me."

"Tomorrow? Are you kidding?"

"Hey. Don't be a Jewish mother about that too, okay?"

"But—"

"You don't get to control the action around here. This is my pad." *Flash of white.* "I can come and go as I please. Now hush," *he whispers.* "Just let me love you a little. Come on. How's this right here? Nice, huh? Is that nice for you?"

"The sixties were never lonely," he says one night, breaking my heart. "There were so many things to do."

A friend he knew in Vietnam is coming to Washington. Jeff is pretty excited. I ask about the man and Jeff says his name is Roger and he's bringing "the lady he lays with." I'd never heard anyone say that. I couldn't get it out of my head. It spoke of ultimate choices.

We've had some bad times. Some real bad ones already. Once I got to his place at the agreed time and he wasn't home. All I could do was stand there kicking his door, angry as hell. He didn't call for a couple of days, either. When he finally did, he said, "There's no excuse for what I did, but there was a reason." He would say nothing more, so I kept pondering the tense tautology of his words for days and days afterward.

Once he called me at midnight.

"Did you know that Andrea's coming?" he began.

I had been asleep. "What's an Andrea?" I asked, thinking of a hurricane.

In fact, it was his girlfriend from New York. She stayed with him a week. I thought I might die. During that week I felt like the soft white filling of an Oreo pressed between my grief over Max and my yearning for Jeff. I was simply the center of a pain cookie, the frosting between a layer of agony on top and another on the bottom. Actually, though, the diversification of pain, like a financial portfolio, was somewhat liberating. It showed me that my original grief over Max was not absolute—only relative. It was also a good lesson about sexual jealousy. No longer in a position to claim any exclusivity, I was glad just to be included in Jeff's stable.

When Andrea finally went back to New York, Jeff invited me over. I pouted around his apartment for a long time, looking for signs of her, signs of their togetherness.

Finally I asked. "So how was Andrea?"

*"She has very weak gums," he answered seriously.
"Very weak gums. They bleed. She has bleating glums."*

*That was all. That was it. That was all he would ever
say.*

*But he did make very, very sweet love to me that
night and he kept smoothing back my hair whenever it
got damp from sweat and stuck to my forehead. He
kept smoothing my hair all night long.*

*Once we were over at my house. I was trying to
shorten a pair of jeans for David. I couldn't find a thim-
ble and I was going crazy trying to push the damn
needle through that heavy denim and getting nowhere.
Finally I threw the jeans across the room.*

*"Damn it," I said. "I can't do anything with my
hands."*

*"That's not true," he said immediately, with his deli-
cious smile. "You do nice things to me with your hands
all the time. You just don't know it."*

*He loves his fish. They are really his pets, like a dog
or a cat. Their names are Sacco, Vanzetti, Pol Pot and
Kissinger. Every week he buys them fresh shrimp to eat
from Cannon's Fish Market. He says taking care of
those fish reminds him of positive values. He says taking
care of his piranhas, his ficus and his tape collection
keeps him off heavy drugs.*

*On the day the time changed from daylight saving to
standard—or whatever—I took down his kitchen clock
and moved the hands back one hour while he was sleeping. On the way home I felt rich, as if I had given him
a gift of an extra hour of rest.*

*The next time I was there I smoked a big joint by
myself because he didn't want to. He was sort of in a bad
mood and he poured himself some vodka, which he
doesn't do often in front of me, and then sat there sipping it. So I said, "It's lonesome getting high without
you."*

And he told me that he loved me.

That was the very first time.

*One night when I was already encased in the blankets
of his pull-out bed, he reached up to the top shelf of his
closet and pulled down a sweater. After pausing to
think for a minute, he threw it onto a rattan chair in the
corner. Then he began pulling down all his sweaters,
one after another, beige and gray, navy, brown. They
flew past the bed and fell like leaves on the woven straw
chair. I watched the colored sweaters winging above
me and remembered Jay Gatsby showing Daisy his silk
shirts.*

*"I'm going to wash every one of those suckers in
Woolite," he growled.*

I loved him so much I thought I would die.

Last night we were lying in the same bed miles apart.

*Nothing had happened, but everything was wrong.
On one level there was mutual irritation for no particular reason and below that were layers and layers of
hostility. I felt despair like a cancer in my soul because
I was unable to readjust the balance between us. I also
felt grievously disadvantaged. Jeff's behavior had
thrown me entirely out of joint. I felt old and ugly,
unable to operate on even the most minimal level with
him. I felt unequal. Less than Andrea.*

*We lay in the sofa bed and watched Paul Newman in
WUSA.*

Jeff didn't speak. He wouldn't speak.

I applied myself to watching television.

The silence increased.

I watched the television more furiously.

*After some fifteen minutes, I looked over at him and
asked how he felt.*

"Fine," he answered.

*When the next commercial came on, I felt more des-
perate and asked, "What's happening?"*

"Nothing," he said, not very nicely.

He kept dozing off, snoring softly, comfortably.

I rolled on my side and looked at the wall clock.

It was 11:35. I was still watching the clock when it turned into a quarter of twelve. Suddenly I was inspired. I did not have to stay there in Jeff's apartment when things were not going right, when nothing felt right. I could simply get up, get dressed and get out.

That discovery surprised me. I reached over to reclaim my clothes from the floor. My jeans were stiff from the cold. My boots felt hard. He had woken up again and began to watch the TV. I stood naked in the blue light and pulled on my shirt.

"Where are you going?"

"Home."

Escape was both plausible and preferable.

"We should maybe see Reds *tomorrow," he said sleepily.*

"Sure," I answered and then I left.

Inside the car was safety. Even the dark streets—with their real threats—seemed manageable as opposed to the psychological imbalance in Jeff's apartment. I parked my car and ran home up the block, staying away from the bushes and shrubs of neighboring houses.

I love to watch him get dressed.

He keeps his socks and underwear in the side table near his sofa bed. There are several packages of unopened boxer shorts in the drawer which he always has to remove and hold while digging for a pair of socks that match. There are also several pairs of new socks still stuck together by their labels. These, too, he always holds aloft. For some reason it touches me enormously that he remembered to buy himself new underwear that he doesn't really need all that badly yet. I like that very much.

Everything in his medicine chest has its own proper place. If a cough-drop box is tall and thin, it's parked vertically rather than horizontally. His few kitchen cupboards are also well organized. His narrow little broom closet is outfitted so that it also serves as a tool chest. Every space in that single room is utilized, organized and compartmentalized.

What does this mean?

That's easy.

I am crazy for this guy. Nuts about him.

With his love, I begin to recover. Slowly he revives me.

Now both Dr. Annie Austen and Jeff are nagging me to write a novel. They keep asking me leading questions. They seem to be in collusion, except they've never met.

Anyway, I have this idea and I've already started working on it.

CHAPTER 18

*E*lena, now reduced to a tropical storm, hits Washington early Monday morning. We are already in the kitchen drinking coffee when the storm sounds begin.

I had come downstairs at 6:00 A.M., in search of some time for reflection, only to find both Joanne and Elaine already seated at the kitchen table. Joanne, still dressed in last night's outfit, has clearly not been to sleep yet and the whisker-rub burnishing her beauty this morning amounts to an announcement that she's spent the night with Jeff making love and—perhaps—a baby.

"You want leaded or unleaded?" she asks, rising to show me a pot of rewarmed coffee as opposed to some fresh that is still dripping through its filter.

"I'll wait," I say, avoiding her eyes.

Having just read Sukie's account of Jeff's lovemaking, I feel shy, but Joanne is too blissed out to notice my awkwardness.

When the rain starts, Joanne opens the back door and the three of us step out onto the porch—Elaine and I in our nightgowns. Holding our coffee cups like hymnals in both hands, we watch hot flashes of lightning streak across the steel-gray sky. Rusty thunder growls in response and long raindrops, warm as tears, blow against our faces.

"Who will stop the rain?" Joanne whispers. "How can we bury Sukie in the rain?"

Elaine looks at her sullenly.

Ten minutes later the storm stops as casually as it started, leaving the heat unimpaired and the humidity still heaving, undiminished, around us.

Only then does Happy leave the shelter of the back porch to traipse down the stairs and daintily cross the wet grass to use the garden. We leave her there when we go inside.

Sukie's Aunt Rosetta arrives alone at seven-thirty. She is wearing a housedress and carrying a totebag full of cake and cookie pans, small sacks of flour, heat-disfigured sticks of margarine, a rolling pin and other baking paraphernalia. After making herself a cup of tea, she claims a large area of counter space and begins rolling out dough like a highway construction crew paving a blacktop.

Elaine and Joanne go upstairs to dress for the funeral, but I remain glued to my chair, watching Rosetta's deft motions like a little girl jealously trying to absorb some skill through osmosis. In truth, I am totally focused on the fact that neither Loren nor Lisa has telephoned yet to inquire about our situation here or about the funeral arrangements. I am shocked for Sukie's sake, if not for mine, because they had always cared deeply for her. Though I try to ignore them, stirrings of anger and betrayal have begun to invade the lowlands of my soul.

So it is really out of total self-absorption that I say the most outrageous thing to Rosetta. The words slip from my lips like smoke from a cigarette.

"It's hard being a mother, isn't it?"

And though I immediately dig my teeth into my bottom lip, my silly rhetoric has already flown off to hit its target.

"Well, of course, I wouldn't know." Rosetta's mouth scissors out the words. "I am not a mother. I was never married. I only know from Sukie's mama, who was much more than my sister-in-law. She was my friend, my best friend. I know from her that raising a daughter was frightening. There was a lot to worry about . . . and fear." Rosetta increases the elbow action to her rolling pin. "Sukie's mama could not have survived this unnatural disaster. She was always afraid of disaster."

Rosetta lifts her head for a moment to look through the window above the sink. The import of what she has just said, and the way she now appears profiled against the window, gazing into the past, ignite a burning flush that starts locket-low on my neck and rushes upward to scald my face. Helpless, I surrender to the heat and the flashback it brings. . . .

None of us wanted to do any of the things our mothers did—nor anything the way they did it—during the postwar years.

Oh no. We would never keep coasters conveniently located for guests to set beneath their highball glasses to protect the surface of a distressed cherrywood free-form cocktail table on which sat a silver Ronson cigarette lighter, a leatherbound photograph album (that twirled like a Rolodex, displaying our baby pictures) and a fruitwood Lazy Susan (religiously oiled after each use, just like our wooden salad bowls) which offered a variety of fifties-ish dips starring the brand-new onion-soup-mix-and-sour-cream variety.

Oh no. We would never own a kidney-shaped, organza-skirted, mirror-topped dressing table carefully cluttered with a casual assortment of fat-bottomed atomizers and fancy, albeit often empty, perfume bottles reproduced in reverse on the mirrored surface. We would never sit upon a seat upholstered in the same fabric as the dressing table—whose skirts parted like those of a cancan dancer to offer legroom or an indoor parking space for the stool—as our mothers did when putting on their makeup. Oh no. We do not collect or treasure such trivial, distracting possessions or make such a production of drawing on our public faces.

Nor do we collect the coins our husbands empty from

their pockets and heap or scatter on bureau tops late at night from which they retrieve only quarters or better the next morning before going to work, leaving us the pennies, nickels, and dimes to be stashed away in some large jar like our mothers used to save up for some special or secret purchase. No. We do not mend our men's socks, reinforcing sheer spots on the heels or toes by planting a red strawberry pincushion beneath the vulnerable places to plump them up for preventive patching. Nor do we stop runs in our nylons—rinsed nightly with Lux in lukewarm water and hung on a towel over the shower-curtain pole to dry—with dainty dabs of colorless nail polish.

Yet in many ways we are still our mothers' daughters. We still suspect that pigeons carry polio, that it's healthier to blow-dry our hands in a public toilet than to use the roll of toweling that might rewind and recycle itself, and that it is dangerous to play a radio in the bathroom. We believe it is important to call ourselves from a hotel lobby shortly after checking in to verify that the operators have us correctly located in the right room, and that it is prudent to peek back inside a mailbox to make sure our letters have actually dropped down and disappeared so they can't be retrieved by a random thief happening to pass by and look inside.

Like our mothers, we believe Clinique is the proper cosmetic for us, that it is essential to own one piece of "important jewelry," that it is best to wipe front-to-back rather than back-to-front, that it is nice to wash off the hand soap in the guest bathroom when company is coming and that it is appropriate for a woman to fall on the floor to cover a de-elasticized half-slip, runaway sanitary pad, dead mouse cat-delivered into the house, or a pile of dog doo-doo on the carpet. Although we will deny it if men say so, our mode of thinking remains discontinuous—the exact opposite of a legal brief.

Suddenly the back door is flung open and Kate Constant, the once-famous black folksinger who inexplicably lost her voice, bursts into the kitchen looking extravagantly beautiful and dangerously upset. She is wearing a multicolored Indian dress, enormous earrings and an Afro that frames her head like a halo. Close to forty, she looks like a teenage girl.

"How can this be happening?" she demands in the deep, throaty tones that have replaced her once-soprano voice. "I mean, what in the name of God is *happening?*"

I watch this glamorous creature, whom I've never met and only know through Sukie and the media, lean up against the refrigerator and start to cry. She lets the tears skip down her sculptured cheeks unimpeded as she stares at me.

"Who're you? One of her gang from New York?"

The image of Sukie describing us as her "gang from New York" makes me begin to cry. At first my sobs are quiet, soft and manageable, but then they pick up momentum and I begin to keen and grieve aloud perhaps for the first time. Over the sound of my own cries, I hear Kate Constant inquiring about a glass of wine and Rosetta introducing herself as she pours her one.

"Did you *know,*" Kate Constant demands, detonating each word like an explosive, "that Sukie was the first person I met in Washington who even *thought* to invite me over? I mean, she just stuck a note in my mailbox asking me to come here for dinner. She was the only one who wasn't *afraid* of me because I'd lost my voice. So I lost my voice. So what? She'd lost her husband. We were both hurting, right?"

Keeping her dark cheek pressed against the white enamel of the refrigerator, she fidgets with some imitation-fruit magnets stuck to the surface. Her explosive eyes continue to spit angry tears.

"I met most of my friends right here," she says emphatically. "Right here in this kitchen. Including the guy I'm living with now. I mean, we're looking at some major influences here, some major changes Sukie made

in my life. And then I turn my back for a minute, for
two days, I had *dinner* here Thursday night, and she
dies."

Then, with silent but dramatic style, Kate Constant
recrosses the kitchen, reopens the screen door, and
runs outside to lean against the porch railing, rocking
and wailing with grief.

I sit paralyzed in my chair, holding my cold coffee
cup, watching Rosetta spread raspberry jam on a floury
stretch of dough, and listening to Kate's moans float
back into the kitchen.

Oh, how many times have we looked into the face of
a friend as if into a mirror to see who we were? How
often did we look into a friend's eyes to discover the
truth? How often did an experience feel paltry—a decision impossible—until we shared it with our favorite
confidante? How many times have we felt the rich rush
of pleasure as a friend raced forward to meet us—open
and unarmed to offer sanctuary within her embrace,
with never any need for explanation?

Female Depression Babies are addicted to friendship—our one act of faith throughout feckless times
when again and again we made that great leap forward
toward another woman. Despite cynicism and sarcasm,
disillusionment and despair, we seldom disparage those
dear sweet friendships we won with our own love for
another. For us, the best relief from life was the presence of a friend who seldom asked us for more than we
could give. From what depths of our agnostic souls did
we extract the strength to offer and receive such gifts?
And what else did we learn from all the novels we've
read—all the stories crafted by sisters who told cruel
tales about the way we live now—but of salvation
through friendship—the extension and acceptance of it
which never ceases to stun and . . . fulfill us.

When Carol walks in, I disbelieve my eyes. Suddenly
she is just standing there in the kitchen, a twenty-two-

year-old, taller, slimmer Sukie, dressed in tired jeans, a denim shirt and dirty espadrilles.

Throwing an apologetic glance at me, she heeds protocol and first hurries forward to embrace her great-aunt. They cling to each other in awesome silence for several minutes. Then, overcome with emotion, Rosetta turns and runs out of the kitchen, apparently to regain her composure and not break down.

So Carol is left standing in the center of the room, Rosetta's floury fingerprints on the back of her shirt. Her widely spaced, Sukie-brown eyes are full of loss and anger. Her silky dark hair is mussed and forgotten. Clearly she had time, first in Portugal and later on the long trip home, to experience her initial rush of emotions. Now she seems primarily focused on surviving the reentry into her home where her mother's absence is centered.

"Poor Diana," she murmurs, turning toward me.

I open my arms to her and she drifts into my embrace in a neat, controlled way. Never encumbered by Sukie's kind of frenetic energy, Carol always hummed along on a quiet battery that had steady starting and staying power.

"Poor you," I say, rocking her in my arms.

Although she rests her head upon my shoulder for a moment, she disengages quickly.

"I can't pretend I'm not mad, Diana. I mean, I'm not going to put on any big act or anything. You know how my mother and I got along."

"Oh, Carol, honey. You have to forget all that now."

"No. I don't *have* to do anything. Not anymore. Never again." Carol steps back to face me from a formal distance. Her face is flushed with heat and anger. "My mother's death was an act of revenge. She didn't want David and me to go to Europe with Dad, so she literally died to get us back here."

"Oh God, Carol," I moan. "Don't talk like that. Not

now. Don't do this to yourself. Just try to lighten up a little bit."

Carol shrugs, walks to the sink, and fills herself a glass of water.

"I know she wasn't really strong enough to arrange the timing of her own death, but she did a pretty good job of it."

"I can't believe you're going to act like this. Right now—right before her funeral," I grieve.

The back door swings open and Kate Constant comes inside. One glance at my face causes her to spin around. Then she runs toward Carol.

"Oh, baby," she groans. "Baby."

Carol lets Kate hold her briefly.

"Where's David?" Kate asks nervously, when Carol backs away from her.

"He and Neil are at my Dad's. They wanted to shower and clean up before they came over. We left New York at four this morning, and the air conditioning in Neil's car wasn't working."

"Baa-ad," says Kate, reaching out to wipe a smear of flour off Carol's cheek. "But you'll have plenty of time to shower and everything here. You want some coffee or anything?"

Carol doesn't answer. Instead she walks to the back door and looks out at the garden.

"My mom just freaked out when we told her we were going to Europe with Dad," she continues dimly. "She kept making up excuses about David needing more time to get ready for college and complaining that she was getting left with all the shitwork like shipping his trunk and stuff. But it was all just a cover story because she was jealous. That's all. And in the end, she won. She might as well have jumped off a bridge."

"Hey," Kate exclaims, shocked by Carol's anger.

"You've got to stop this now, Carol," I say evenly. "Let's bury her first and then we can talk about your anger."

Carol shrugs before she kicks open the screen door. "Happy," she calls. "Happy."

The dog comes wheeling into the kitchen, skittering across the linoleum just as the front-door bell rings. Kate hurries into the hall and returns with Miranda, who is wearing a tight black jersey dress that cups her breasts and buttocks. Unhesitantly, Miranda hurries toward Carol, but Carol kneels down to fondle Happy and evade the embrace.

"Give me a break, Miranda," Carol moans, looking up with a wild expression in her eyes. "Don't come sucking around here now, after everything you've done. You probably helped kill my mother, so don't put on one of your performances about what a great friend you are, okay? I've had enough of you."

Miranda recoils and staggers back against the counter. "I know you don't mean that," she says breathlessly. "You know I never meant to hurt anybody. I loved every one of you."

"With a friend like you, we didn't need any enemies." Carol delivers the line calmly.

Now Elaine and Joanne walk into the kitchen. Already dressed in their dark fall cottons, they rush toward Carol, who rises to receive their embraces and politely thanks them for coming to Washington. But a few seconds later, unable to restrain herself, Carol turns on Miranda again.

"Really," she insists. "I don't see any reason why you should be here or why you should come to my mother's funeral. I think it would be a travesty."

Silently, Kate, Elaine, Joanne and I form a supportive semicircle around Carol.

"I mean it," Carol repeats coldly. "I don't want you here."

Miranda looks at our clock of faces and then slowly turns to walk out of the kitchen. No one moves or speaks until we hear the front door close behind her.

"My mother was hardly an angel," Carol says fiercely, "but that bitch wasn't good enough to wipe her shoes."

I see Elaine wince and then revert to form by beginning to make a fresh pot of coffee.

"But everybody knows my mother had pretty bad judgment about everything. Especially people."

"That's a rather rude thing to say in front of her friends," Elaine remarks.

"Oh, I'm sorry," Carol apologizes as she reaches out to take Sukie's purse from its place on the table. Scavenging through its contents, she extracts a package of Merits and lights one, which she then proceeds to smoke awkwardly, without inhaling.

"My mother let that viper into our family. In fact, she actually *invited* Miranda into our lives."

No one speaks.

I am silenced by bafflement. I cannot understand how the little daughters we adored—the little girls we dressed in forest-green velveteen party dresses with square, lacy collars, black patent-leather Mary Janes, with straps they couldn't buckle, and white tights we had to tug on over the rosy apples of their buttocks— grew into censorious, unforgiving young women who often treat us as their primary adversaries. All too often, I, too, have been stung by the same kind of scorn from Loren and Lisa.

"She was soooo possessive," Carol continues. "She just couldn't stand the idea of David and me traveling around Europe with Dad. It was driving her crazy."

When Rosetta, freshly composed and made up, reappears to put her *kamishbrot* in the preheated oven, Carol calms down for several moments in deference to her. But then she explodes again.

"I mean, I think she died from her own jealousy. I think she got a cerebral hemorrhage because she couldn't stop David and me from going."

Although Rosetta has her back to us, I can see her shrivel beneath the impact of Carol's words.

"If autopsies could show emotional causes for death, I bet that's exactly what it would show."

"Stop it," Elaine shrieks. "You don't talk about the dead like that. This is your own mother you're talking about and she's not even buried yet."

Joanne, who consistently tried to maintain independent relationships with her friends' children, now walks over to stand beside Carol in an effort to show some understanding of her anger. But Carol ignores her, an act of extreme hostility.

Almost all our children honored our friendships over the years since they were always respectful of genuine articles. Often, as time passed, they even held us responsible for each other's objectionable words or actions. At other times, they turned to us to help reconcile seemingly irreconcilable differences with their mothers. We were, in some way, all part of a great motherland.

"Now, you all stop this," Kate Constant interrupts in tones that are terrifyingly deep and authoritative. "This kind of family fighting hurt Sukie. No wonder she couldn't ever get the time to take herself or her work seriously. Sukie was a fabulous woman, Carol, and you're not going to talk about her like that while I'm around here. Shit. Wait till you see who turns up at her funeral. She was important. *Important.* And she loved you *so* much it was bor-ing, bor-ing how much she talked about you. You kids"—the *you* is a stinging racial slap—"don't appreciate *nothing.*"

Carol, a member of a generation that is totally colorblind, ignores Kate's blackmail.

"Believe me," Carol insists, speaking directly to Kate, "it was easier to be my mother's friend, and see her only once in a while, than to live with her like we had to. I mean, living with her was a real trip."

Now the door swings open again and David, Max, and a tall blond young man clamor into the kitchen.

David is wearing jeans, sweatshirt and blue running

shoes. He has inherited Max's best features—the deep-set denim eyes, the dark hair, and the boyishly open expression that makes him look much younger than eighteen.

Glancing at each of us in hot confusion, David first rushes to fling his arms around Rosetta and wail, "Where's Grandpa?"

"He'll be here in a few minutes, honey." Rosetta clamps David against herself in an effort to absorb some of his pain. "Before ten, he said. In just a few minutes."

For a moment, David rests against her sturdy frame. Then he frees himself to rush across the kitchen and tumble into my arms.

What tears me up is that I can feel him trying to acknowledge my loss while struggling with his own.

"Diana, she died. She's just . . . dead," he announces, gripping me with quivering arms. "The day after we left for Europe. All by herself. With nobody else around."

It is clear that David has turned his grief inward upon himself. All I can do is hold him carefully, like a baby bird fallen from a nest, and hope my hug communicates a promise of myself to him in reparation for the loss of his mother. I know he still needs maternal support and I want to help him—to talk him through his first year of college, to welcome him to my apartment over holidays, to be there for him. But at this moment, all I can do is hold him tight.

Sukie always thought David's generation was the first of really "new" men in America—men who genuinely *liked* and found women *interesting*. Certainly David understood the dear dependencies of his mother and her friends and accepted our network as a serious and legitimate one.

"Why right now?" he demands, pulling back so he can see my face. "I needed her. I still . . . wanted her."

David, like Carol, feels that the timing of Sukie's

death is her ultimate betrayal and he is challenging me to defend her defection.

"She never took care of herself," he continues fiercely. "She smoked and drank and ate greasy food. She didn't care if she left us alone."

"Oh, David, that's not true. She would never have wanted to leave you. And you're not alone."

He is my height. Our eyes lock.

"I don't think it hurt her too bad, do you, Diana? I think she died too fast to feel any pain or anything."

"I do too, Davey," I moan. "Don't think about that."

"Come, David," Rosetta says briskly and firmly. "Let's walk out and go meet Grandpa, huh?"

Eager to submit to her mothering, David pauses only long enough to put a leash on Happy before following Rosetta out of the house. Then Max, aware of the residual tension in the kitchen, tries to distract everyone by introducing Carol's boyfriend.

Neil Scott is a tall, pale young man who peers out at us from behind horn-rimmed glasses. He clearly senses something has gone wrong since he and Carol parted less than an hour ago and he moves quickly to stand beside her.

Max is looking anxiously at all of us. His dark hair is rumpled and his eyes, framed by the pleats of previous smiles, look strained. He is sweating. His shirt is glued to the flat plane of his chest, showing the shadow of dark hair beneath the damp cotton. His khaki pants are creased angrily around the crotch. His fatigue and distress create a sense of looseness and license about him.

I have to look away.

"What's going on?" he asks. "What's happening?"

No one responds.

"Don't tell me there was a fight already," he says threateningly, looking at Carol.

Neil Scott puts his arm around Carol's shoulder and pulls her closer. I glance at Carol to see if she'll absorb some comfort, but anger is still scribbled across her face. She is silent now only because the one person in front of whom she won't complain about Sukie is her father.

Though some of our daughters sided with their fathers during our breakups—teaching us that daughters and divorce don't mix—and often bad-mouthed us to their friends as well as to ours, few (to our knowledge) betrayed us in front of their fathers or their fathers' new wives. Although Martha's daughter Jessica agreed to "stand up" for her father's new wife (his former secretary) as maid of honor at their wedding, and went to Saks where she charged a $559 dress to Martha's charge account without asking permission, she refused her father's invitation to join them on a honeymoon trip to China, so as not to leave Martha alone at Christmas.

When I bumped into Carla's biological husband, Conrad, on Madison Avenue, he told me he still felt terrible about leaving Carla—after twenty-eight years of marriage, right when she was stricken with multiple sclerosis—and that he *always* thinks about her in the evening while watching the sunset in Pago Pago, where he currently lives with his new bride. Stunned by his words, I had the presence of mind to tell him not to worry about Carla since their daughter, Emily, is a selfless angel in terms of caring for her, and that we all pitch in to do Carla's grocery shopping and other errands.

So while divorce offers a perfect opportunity for daughters to express any innate distaste for their mothers, essentially they don't betray us in any ways that really matter.

Pouring myself another cup of coffee, I think of all the times Sukie and I exchanged helpless looks, silently conceding the daughters of strong women often feel compelled to resist or even reject us in order to achieve their own autonomy. I remember how often we suffered estrangements from the daughters we adored because they despised the very strength that generated our passionate maternal love. And though we couldn't have loved them more, we were often unable to lessen our key disagreements or modify their disapproval of us.

Some of our daughters have been quite difficult.

When Sarah's daughter Cindy came home from college for Thanksgiving vacation and decided to make it with her high school boyfriend for old times' sake, she simply went into Sarah's bathroom and borrowed her diaphragm. When Sarah discovered it missing, Cindy simply apologized for neglecting to return it. There then ensued an argument during which Cindy accused her mother of being unwilling to "share" because she was jealous of Cindy's more active sex life. When Sarah explained that her diaphragm was a 75 and probably too large for Cindy, Cindy said that her mother had a "humongous" body-image problem. Several days later in a restaurant, Cindy said that if it was true what Sarah had always said about "being what you eat," Cindy, by all rights, should turn into a spermatozoan.

When Arlene's daughter had a miscarriage, she brought home "the product of conception" in a jar and left it on Arlene's bedroom windowsill.

When Phyllis's daughter Liz was a senior in high school, she discovered her boyfriend in bed with her best girlfriend and simply walked outside and set her boyfriend's father's Mercedes on fire. Liz was on probation for two years, and Phyllis had to get a waitress job to pay the damages. She wore her full-length sable to work at the Pizza Hut near their $400,000 suburban house because it was the only coat she owned and she didn't have the money to buy a cheap one. Her cash-flow problem was monstrous, but she laughed when her electricity was cut off because she thought she looked younger in candlelight and she'd begun seeing the Pizza Hut manager at home on weekends.

It is difficult for us to admit that our children—the linear descendants of Hippies and Yippies—are now the Yuppies of the 1980s. Apparently the confusion and chaos of our broken families frightened them into a kind of conformity we spent our lives avoiding. They like their brand-name clothes with the labels on the outside so as to expedite their identification of each other and remain very selective about the messages on their T-shirts, carefully avoiding any metaphysical overtones. But despite their quirks, our children have decent instincts and we believe that eventually their designer jeans will recede and their genetic ones triumph.

Our daughters' lives, though enormously different from ours, are also difficult because in many ways the feminist revolution further convoluted male-female relationships. None of our daughters will date men they consider chauvinists (defined as any male who must be reminded to do his share of the chores), and they genuinely despise scoundrels (those very men their mothers most coveted). Our daughters only like considerate young men incapable of making any commitment—which is sad, because many of these attractive young women would probably postpone their careers if Mr. Right came along and consented to marriage and the production of bumper-to-bumper, post-Boom babies with them.

The differences between our generation and our daughters' are extreme. While we carry "notes from underground," secret feminist *samizdat,* and Swiss Army knives in our Gucci handbags, our daughters have to purchase and carry slippery packs of condoms and sickly rubber medical gloves in their purses. Also, because of the way we raised them, they find it difficult to "be nice" to men just because they are men—which is good, but which of course causes problems. So our daughters have problems, and some of our friends have really horrendous problems with their daughters. No matter how bad Sukie and I occasionally felt, we always knew we were fortunate with the girls we'd raised.

"Come on," Max says, loud and angry. "I want to know what the hell's going on here now."

"Oh, knock it off, Max," Elaine answers, raising her voice. "You don't get any input on this one. This is for *women only.*"

"Oh Lord," Kate Constant moans to Elaine. "You really do have an *at-ti-tude.* A serious *attitude.* You've got a real problem. You all do, as a matter of fact. Sukie did too. You *expect* so much from your men. You're all so spoiled. I mean *spoiled.* If your old man doesn't want to wash the kitchen floor or listen to you read what you wrote that day, you *freak out.* I'm not saying your men do the right thing at the right time at the right place. But the fact is you *expect* them to. *And that's crazy!*

"Because you ladies don't know what it's like when there ain't a man around. Not a man within miles. Not a one. Not a daddy or an uncle or a grandpa or a boyfriend. And a husband? Are you kidding? Hey. I grew up in a world without men. Shit. I was afraid of men until I was fifteen. I thought they talked too loud. Their voices scared me and I didn't know for sure if they were really talking English, because I never heard much English *spoken by a man* before I was four. I didn't recognize it as the same language. So when I tell you ladies you expect a lot, you'd better believe it. Now let's just knock off all this shit and get serious."

Mau-maued, I stand shamefaced while Kate, the black woman, defends Max, the white man. Seconds later a hot flash rips through me. The white women of our generation are compelled to listen to the black women because they often speak truths of which we've lost sight. In the arena of human emotions, they frequently remind us of lessons we've learned but, unfortunately, forgotten.

It's then that I notice Max motioning to me and Joanne. After a few puzzled moments, we understand enough to follow him outside onto the back porch.

"Well, did you get it last night?" Max asks Joanne, after closing the door behind us.

Caught off guard by his phraseology, Joanne begins to blush profusely and remains silent. Max immediately grasps the reason for her misunderstanding of his question. Her silence is an admission of its accidental accuracy and he erupts with rage.

"Ohhh. I don't fucking believe it," he groans. "This is too much. Aren't you getting tired of quickies yet, Joanne? Haven't you had enough of them? Isn't it time you grew up, for Christ's sake?" Especially the night before Sukie's funeral? With *her* boyfriend?"

Then Max whips around and thunders down the backstairs into the garden. His hands jammed angrily into his pockets, he walks around looking at the late bloomers and early fall flowers that Sukie so erratically but successfully raised. Max clearly feels that both Joanne and I compromised and betrayed him. Obviously he dreads facing Manny Smilow without some resolution regarding the manuscript.

I am left alone facing Joanne on the Victorian latticed wooden porch.

I watch her face begin to crumble from this last great insult. The shrine of her hopeful lovemaking has been sacked with an attack of obscenity that she both does and does not deserve. She begins to cry. I can think of nothing to say to comfort her, so I just hold her in my arms while she sobs, and rock back and forth a bit to quiet her.

After a while, I lead Joanne to a narrow bench set against the latticed wall of the porch and leave her there so I can return to the kitchen where everyone has regrouped to stand around in unalloyed grief and unresolved conflict.

CHAPTER 19

*E*ventually Max and Joanne reappear, separately, from the back porch, but the general uneasiness is intensified when Jeff Conroy suddenly comes stomping down the hallway to enter the kitchen. Although he has changed his jeans for clean chinos, he still looks slightly disreputable, which helps to deflect any general realization that he has again let himself into the house with his own key. It is so preposterous a thought that no one thinks it. Under one arm he is carrying a recycled box clearly containing Sukie's manuscript.

After a painfully long look at Joanne, he turns and swallows David in a warm, gentle bear hug. When this aching embrace ends he walks over to Carol.

"Hi," he says gently.

I can see Carol's body vibrating with internalized sobs when Jeff embraces her.

"Hey," Jeff says, cupping her head with his hand. "It's going to be okay."

His concentration on Carol cancels out the presence of Max, Elaine, Joanne, Mr. Smilow, David, Rosetta, Kate Constant and me. When he releases her, Carol moves back toward Neil and Jeff stands alone in the center of the kitchen, holding the manuscript in his outstretched hands.

"You all probably know this is Sukie's book," he says quickly, nodding at the box in front of him. "I've been editing it," he explains, turning toward Mr. Smilow and Rosetta. "I'm Jeff Conroy. I know you must be Sukie's family." He moves forward to shake their hands.

Mr. Smilow squinches up his eyes as he studies the casual-looking stranger who seems so at home in his daughter's house.

Mr. Smilow is not happy.

"Because everyone came in at a different page in this event, nobody knows the whole story." Jeff continues. "The only important thing is that I reread Sukie's book again this morning, and it's *really* terrific. Also, it's much closer to being finished than I thought."

"Just what I thought." Mr. Smilow nods. "Exactly. My suspicions were correct."

He flashes an I-knew-it-all-along grimace around the kitchen.

"But you've got to hear me out," Jeff insists. "This is not an easy situation. There's been a lot going on around this manuscript that you kids, and probably you too, Kate, don't know about. First off, all your mom's friends have been trying to get their hands on it." He flashes a fast I'm-just-teasing smile at Carol and David. "Then your dad came looking for it—over at my place—and then your grandfather"—Jeff pauses to nod politely toward Mr. Smilow—"sent a pretty tough rep over last night to nail it down for himself."

Jeff looks at Joanne for another longish moment.

I am unable to determine whether I am experiencing a flash or a flush, a rush or a blush, but I am *very warm.*

"Now wait a minute, sir," says Mr. Smilow. "Don't mess with us today. Our family is suffering a terrible tragedy. I am the father of the author. I am the one in this family who can recognize if something has a value. And I want my *tochter*'s book manuscript. If it has any value, it is part of the estate."

Jeff's ignores Mr. Smilow.

"To tell you the truth," he continues, "I didn't know what to do. In some ways I thought I was the one who best knew what Sukie meant this book to be and do and say. But I stayed up real late last night trying to figure out the right moves and just this morning I realized what Sukie would've wanted."

"If you think you know what Sukie would have wanted, you're fooling yourself," Max interrupts. "Sukie never knew what she wanted, so how could you?"

"What Sukie wanted, you took away from her," Mr. Smilow howls at Max. "A little bit of security. A little bit of peace and quiet at the end of her life."

"We don't have to accept your decision anyway, you know," Rosetta says prissily.

My heart is hammering.

Jeff takes a few lateral steps and puts the box in Carol's hands. Then he waits until a slim smile of surprise slides across her face.

"Now wait a minute here," says Mr. Smilow. "How should a young girl like Carol know what to do about a book of fiction? How should she know?"

"Okay. Let me tell you why I think Carol should have it," Jeff says simply, turning toward the Smilows. "The reason is that I suddenly remembered, just after dawn this morning, right before the storm broke, something Sukie said to me about a week ago. She said, and I'm repeating her words to the best of my memory, 'You know, I wouldn't be at all surprised if Carol starts writing soon. She always wrote real well and I think the only thing that keeps her from starting is the fact I'm a writer. But now I'm getting a feeling that things are about to change and that she's ready.' "

I look at Mr. Smilow. With voodoo impertinence, I *will* him to accept this decision, to understand the psychology of the moment, the human importance of what Jeff has said and its possible redemptive power in reconciling Carol to Sukie.

"She really said that?" Carol asks Jeff with confrontational directness. "She said all of that?"

He nods.

"Actually, I can go along with this decision," Max says in a generous tone of voice, edging closer to Carol. "I really can."

"What you can do is your business," says Mr. Smilow. "Give me the box, Carol."

The room becomes quiet.

David is watching his sister with pale concentration.

"Grandpa, I'm going to be in charge of Mom's book," Carol says.

That's all. But it is with a kind of authority few women, and even fewer *young* women, could take with the patriarchal head of their family. Carol watches her grandfather absorb the meaning of her comment. Then, and only then, does she turn toward Neil and break into rough uneven sobs.

I hear Neil expel a soft whistle of relief as he watches Carol finally crack. Clearly, he had been apprehensive about her inhibited response to Sukie's death, so it is with unrestrained joy that he embraces her.

"Just cry, Carol," Neil says again and again. "Go on, cry."

"I didn't even know . . ." Carol is fighting hiccups that quarrel with her words, ". . . I didn't even know she thought I *was* a good writer."

"Hey," Jeff cajoles her. "Sukie always thought you were a *great* writer."

Glowing now with gratitude at her mother's posthumous confidence, Carol rests against Neil's chest.

"How is it?" she asks Jeff in an attempt at a business-like voice.

"You'll have to read it and see what you think," Jeff answers seriously. "You do whatever you think is right. That's an order. Okay, come on now. You and David walk me to the door."

"Aren't you coming to the funeral?" Carol whispers over a spray of new sobs.

"No. I'm going to take a pass on that," Jeff says.

Then he nods to everyone in the kitchen, links one arm around David and the other around Carol, and leads them out into the hallway.

A moment later Joanne slips away to follow them.

The rest of us shuffle about until Rosetta orders everyone to sit down at the table so she can serve the first loaves of *kamishbrot* that she's taken from the oven. Their sweet aroma stains the air, mixing with the smell of fresh coffee. I follow Rosetta's instructions and take my usual place. Mr. Smilow sits in the chair beside mine, subdued and thoughtful.

"I'm sorry," he says to me. "Yesterday I couldn't think clear." Wearily he bites into an oval-shaped slice of *kamishbrot.* "But now I want to hear the plans. Who's the rabbi for our Sukie? Someone who knows how to do it right, how to do it up brown?"

"Mr. Smilow," Elaine begins matter-of-factly, "we finally found a Reform rabbi who agreed to conduct a service in a nondenominational chapel. That wasn't easy. But we decided to follow him up with something a little unusual, which is allowing anyone who wants to speak about Sukie to come forward and do so. That's the way the Friends do it."

"What friends?" Mr. Smilow trumpets. "What's all this?"

"I meant the Quakers, Mr. Smilow. But actually, in this case, I do mean Sukie's friends."

"What are you talking?"

"It's a new . . . custom, Manny," Max intervenes. "The manager at the funeral home said lots of Jews are doing it nowadays. It sounded nice to me."

Mr. Smilow ignores him.

The discussion about Sukie's friends carrying her coffin is more dramatic, although actually much shorter.

"I never heard of such a thing," Rosetta gasps. "It's heresy, God forbid."

Mr. Smilow is too dumbfounded to speak.

Max remains politically silent.

Elaine again becomes the whip on this one. "We expect that a lot of Sukie's Washington friends will come by the house here this morning before the funeral, so we're sure to find one or two more women who will do it with us."

"This is insanity," Mr. Smilow moans.

"I don't like the open-forum idea either," Kate says, frowning.

Her facial expressions are so dynamic that Mr. Smilow is half hypnotized by her skittish eyelids, her rambunctious eyebrows and the Popsicle-pink tongue that peeks out occasionally to lick her heavy lips. He watches her surreptitiously, uncertain whether or not it is legal to study a black woman's face so intently.

"No. It's got to be better organized than that," Kate insists, setting down her coffee mug emphatically on the table. "We can't just have anyolebuddy getting up there and starting to ramble. We've got to decide who we want to say what and when we want them to say it. I mean, this is *important.*"

"Well, maybe Diana could talk about our generation," Elaine suggests. "Along the lines of the piece she had in the *Times.*"

"Hey! Don't get me wrong," Kate says in her usual energetic style to me. "That was a good article. But it was a real downer and I don't want to get written off so soon—the way you wrote off 'your' generation. I mean, maybe the ladies *you're* talking about went down with the plane, but *I* certainly didn't. I wasn't on that passenger manifest. So don't write me off yet. I'm just getting started."

"How old are you, Kate? Thirty-seven? Thirty-eight?" I ask.

"I'm forty-three." Kate whips off a triumphant smile. "I was born in 1942, but I'm still one of your Depression Babies. A couple years either side of the 1930s don't matter. Believe me. Nothing's so neat. In fact, I think you should include all the War Babies in your DEBs generation, because we had almost exactly the same set of experiences.

"See, Sukie and I talked about your article for a long, long time. Really. But I just couldn't buy all your conclusions. And I don't think Sukie did either, even though she might not have mentioned that to you. See, both of us thought that if you fight long enough, you don't know how to stop fighting. You get hooked on surviving— seeing how to get out of the next fix, what the next catastrophe will be. Who'll come out of the woodwork to help you, like Sukie helped me last year. You survive this long, it's hard to quit trying.

"Kate," I say, "I don't want you to quit trying."

"Anyway, there's too damn much left to do. And we'll do it. We'll do it with husbands or without them. With boyfriends or without them. We'll do it with jobs or without jobs, with money or without money. We'll do it after all the kids we've grown dependent on leave us home alone again. We've done it before and we'll keep doing it. All we ever needed was a little help from our friends and that's what friends are for, right?"

"Just what is it we're going to do?" Elaine asks with a touch of desperation. "What is it we've saved ourselves to do now?"

"Well, first off, one of the first things I suggest *you* do is make peace with the enemy, if you know what I mean. I think that'd do you a world of good."

"Uh-huh." Flat, noncommittal. "And what else?"

"Hey. I don't know. Whatever needs doing. We'll do sit-ups and volunteer tutoring and different political actions and our hair and some dope once in a while and our nails and our jobs and careers and our families and our men. We'll just do what we always do. But maybe we'll do it better. Maybe that's what we'll do. We'll do good and we'll do it better. We're going to do some good works. Godworks. We're going to think about other folks a little bit more. Help out a little more.

"Who knows? Maybe we'll run for Congress or join

the Peace Corps or invite a man over for dinner or take
care of our kids' kids or write a book about the forties
or the fifties or the sixties—our herstories. They've got
to get written. Hey, don't look so hopeless. Don't try to
scare *my* horses. I lost my voice, okay? And my voice
was my career and my identity and my union card and
my meal ticket and my sex appeal and my line of credit.
My voice was my *everything*. Maybe losing a leg is
worse, but *I* didn't think so.

"We're just feeling our oats now. We're just learning
how to run a campaign and get elected to office, how to
run a business and make some bread, how to write and
sell our work. And just look at everything women our
age are doing all around the country. So we're going to
do this funeral right for Sukie, too. Here's the deal, see?
We're going to write a eulogy that will really honor her.
We're going to write a herstory of what's going on these
days. This generation isn't wiped out. Hell. We're just
getting freed up now to start the rest of our lives. So let's
all go sit down at Sukie's desk and bang out this eulogy
right now."

And moments later, Sukie's other friends begin arriv-
ing. They appear individually or in pairs, some with
men at their sides, a few with teenaged children. They
greet whoever admits them and then walk immediately
back into the kitchen. There they introduce themselves
to Rosetta and Manny, take a cup of coffee and a piece
of cake from the continental-style buffet on the table,
and then move out into the living room, where they talk
among themselves in frightened whispers. Most of
them are dressed in dark cottons and are wearing end-
of-the-summer scuffed sandals and sunglasses which
they leave on while inside the house.

The first wave of arrivals are Sukie's Cleveland Park
neighbors—white Ward Three liberals, as she described
them. They are well-intentioned, well-educated women
married to more-than-moderately successful men, and
the mothers of high-achieving children. Sukie fre-

quently felt threatened by her neighbors' stability, but they adored Sukie for her chaotic passions and forgave most, if not all, her sins.

Each of the women who arrives has a totally different way of dealing with her sorrow, but most of them cry at some time or other during the endlessly long wait for the funeral to begin. One thing they have in common is a physical restlessness, and they all keep moving around the house, touching Sukie's possessions with heartbreaking gentleness and loving familiarity. They seem to achieve a certain dialogue with her through the statement of a small wooden table, an old-fashioned lamp, or the needlepoint footstool that used to belong to her mother. The majority keep returning to the kitchen again and again.

Oh, how many times have we used the excuse of "helping a hostess" to slip out of a public space back into the kitchen, to be reabsorbed into our basic clan where we feel most comfortable, where we don't have to look beautiful, where we can communicate without words, deliver complaints without disclaimers and make accusations without explanations. Together we can laugh at the character of an individual man, without having to present a bill of particulars, or at the nature of all men, whose traits are now as familiar as an old joke that no longer requires a punchline. Women, like longtime married couples, seldom have to complete a sentence or thought. Our tribe is rich in resources and resonances.

Kate Constant has quite naturally assumed seniority among the Washington women by virtue of her personal charisma, minority status, and enormous love for Sukie. Eventually she moves into the study to work on the eulogy with input from different women who drift in and out. Elaine takes me aside to say that Kate and Mary Murphy have already volunteered to join our coffin brigade, and each of them is recruiting other pall-bearers.

A while later I see Marlene Bennett, whom I met at Sukie's during various visits because she went to many peace demonstrations with us. Silently she wraps her arms around me in a hug of shared, shocked loss.

"This is not fair," she moans.

She is a thin, trim woman in her mid-forties, whose grief, though different from mine, is as intense.

"Aileen and Sandy Ratner and I are going to . . . carry the casket with you," Marlene says.

All morning long, the front doorbell rings and after a while Neil takes charge of admitting and welcoming the guests. Old friends Sukie thought she'd alienated arrive early; to them Sukie was still without question part of their intimate circle. Around noon, a warm blond woman arrives to spend a long time talking mostly to Carol, and later I learn from Aileen that the woman was Annie Austen, Sukie's savior/doctor.

Norman Naylor arrives. Max and I happen to be standing near the front door, so I introduce them. For a brief moment, Norman seems enormously interested in Max, but, when he sees Elaine flashing some high cleavage in her low-cut cotton sundress, he turns away to make his moves on her. Against all odds, Norman seems to have decided that a connection with Elaine has some value, if only to assure himself of a bed-and-breakfast stop in New York.

At first, Elaine seems flustered by Norman's high profile approach, but then she calms herself. I see the involuntary flutter of her hand, rising like a phoenix to plump out the side of her hair with hopeful fingers, and the innocence of her pleasure brings tears to my eyes.

"I've got my car here," I hear Norman say. "So you can ride over with me."

Now I see Elaine flush and nod, flattered despite herself.

Max is still standing nearby, watching me watching them, which irritates me enormously.

"I'm going upstairs to get ready," I say.

He looks into my face, but he is actually posing the question of himself to me. He is challenging me as young children challenge parents—presenting themselves and demanding that their presence precipitate a response. Indeed, Max is flashing his *self* at me.

"Well?" I ask, meaning what does he want from me. He shrugs.

I am completely impatient. I am feeling the kind of impatience that precedes a hot flash. Any moment now I will feel the heat start to scramble up my neck toward my face.

"Well," I shrug again, in a more conclusive way. Then I turn my back on him and run up the stairs.

From my suitcase in Sukie's room, I retrieve the slim black linen sheath I had for some reason—premonition?—taken out to the Hamptons and, even more surprisingly, remembered to throw in the car Friday when I rushed back to LaGuardia. In the bathroom I turn on the hot water and hang my dress over the shower-curtain rod to steam it out. Stripped to pants and bra, I station myself at the mirror, which has begun to steam up, and wash my face before reapplying my makeup for the second time in two hours.

Why I must curl my eyelashes to go to my best friend's funeral, I do not know. However, I cannot analyze such idiocies at the moment and I just do it—standing there with a knock-off of a medieval torture machine clamped dangerously close to my eyeball while I rhythmically tighten the handles to produce enough pressure to bend the lashes. Presumably this adolescent compulsion is too deeply ingrained to excise and probably serves to reduce some of my ancient *angst* so that I can continue to function.

Then I watch my tanned face start to disappear as the steam curls toward the center of the mirror. Suddenly I feel frightened and terribly old. My almost colorless eyes look panicky. The curves etched around my lips look like parenthetical brackets that punctuate my smiles and set them off from the serious statement of my features. As the mirror erodes, I see myself fading away and I remember Sukie's journal passage about feeling unloved while she sat in The Bread Oven.

When my face is finally lost in the fog of steam, I experience a sense of total bereavement. I am lessened and endangered by Sukie's death. Often our identities are fixed by our friends' feelings about us, and Sukie's vision of me was vitally important to my own self-image. She saw me as strong and self-confident, and I both needed and used that reassurance. I always trusted Sukie's view of me and her admiration was important to my own sense of identity.

I clear a patch of mirror, using my hand as a windshield wiper, but it immediately fogs over again. A little panicky, I open the door a crack to let some of the steam escape, and then turn around to check the condition of my dress. It is precisely at that moment that Max materializes in the doorway.

I blush, flush, and resist the urge to cover my body with the dress I'm holding. Instead, rather boldly, I walk back toward the mirror and station myself at the sink while I pull on the dress as if Max were not watching me.

Then I reach behind my neck to fasten the zipper. Of course, some of my hair has already become tangled in it. Lowering my elbows, my arms still locked behind my head, I watch Max watching me in his dead wife's mirror—somehow summoning her image up with mine—and I feel a hot flash of recognition. Looking back at him through the glass, I remember my husband watching me in the same sweetly studious way. The last vestiges of steam soften our features and suddenly all the images converge so that the past superimposes itself upon the present and there is a sense of unity published, some continuity of the past within the flux of the present. Then the steam is gone, clearing the looking glass.

I smile through myself back to Max.

"You left the door open," he apologizes.

I nod, still tugging at the hair immobilizing my zipper. I am trying to segregate some strands so I can break them off like threads. But then, silent and serious, Max takes over my job, so I no longer see his face in the mirror as he bends over to examine the problem.

"The limos are coming here at two-thirty to take us over."

I nod again.

"There are two. I told Rosetta that she and Manny should take one and ask whoever else they want to ride with them. But I'd like you to ride with the kids and me in the other, okay?"

"Okay."

"I'm going to take David back to my place now. I think I have a suit he can wear this afternoon."

I nod.

Through the glass I see Max raise his face for a moment. His eyes are fond and smiling, but still absorbed by the zipper problem. Finally he lifts the full weight of my hair off my neck and, holding it back with one hand, lowers his face to work on the individual strands more closely.

My hands, gripping the edge of the sink, begin to shake.

The feel of his face against my neck is producing waves of weakness in me. Through the looking glass I see only the top of his head streaked with silver flashes. I cannot see his face.

"Did you know you're a liar, Diana?"

His words slap me so unexpectedly that my face flinches in the mirror.

"What?"

"You're lying when you talk about having no more expectations—which really means no more needs or wants or desires. You're just lying to yourself to avoid any possibility of pain. Because no one can turn off those feelings. That's some kind of autohypnosis you're talking about. Like lowering your own blood pressure or speeding up your own digestive enzymes. You can't do that. No one can."

I smile nicely back at him, not arrogantly, but with the certainty I've savored for more than three years.

And that's when he releases my hair, letting it fall loose upon my back again. Putting his hands on my shoulders, he turns me around, curling his forefinger to knuckle my chin up higher.

"What you're saying is that you would *like* to stop having all these feelings that open you up to disappointment or hurt or fear. But you can't. If people really could do that, we'd all be home free. We wouldn't let ourselves need or want anything from anyone else, because the danger there is obvious. That way we'd be safe from every painful emotion in the book. In fact, we could throw the book away. But no one can just turn them off. You're kidding yourself, Diana. And I'm not going to go along with the gag. We've got to talk about things. About the past and the present and the future. And you can't be lying to yourself while we do it, because then we'll both lose out. We'll both be two-time losers."

"Don't be silly, Max," I say looking straight into his eyes. "I'm not a kid. I know what I'm feeling. I've thought about all this. A lot. I know what I know. I know who I used to be and I know who I am now."

"Look, Diana. I know who you were, too. I was there, you know? And you're not this person you're impersonating. Someone frozen. Paralyzed. You're so afraid to make a wrong move now, you can't move at all. You're not even running scared. You're stationary. But I don't believe you're burned out. I think you're just scared. I want to say one thing. You don't have to me afraid of me. I'm not going to hurt you."

Then he puts his arms around me. He holds me very tight and close to him.

He is holding me too tight. He is holding me for dear life. He is pressing my resistance, like grapes into wine, so that I feel myself relenting.

We remain like that for a long while. Finally he draws back.

"You okay?"

"Yah," I nod, almost believing it.

Then he turns and walks away.

CHAPTER 20

*I*n the plain, unadorned chapel, the Amrams sit on one side of the main aisle while the Smilows sit on the other as if at a wedding. David is between Max and Max's parents, who look like civilized New Yorkers trying to cope with the funeral of a former daughter-in-law. Carol and Neil sit beside Rosetta and Manny Smilow.

Sukie's friends try to blur the hard edges of this division by filling in empty seats on either side. I find myself in the front row of the Smilow section, unable to turn around to see the people filing in and filling the seats that stretch back from the stage to the ominously wide double-door exit. I can hear only the shuffle of flat shoes on the uncarpeted parquet surface of the aisle and the heavy silence of awesome grief.

The one time I wedge myself against Elaine so that I can turn around, I see hundreds of women. Hokey and embarrassing as it feels, the truth is they really are of all different ages and races and colors and sizes and styles. Weirder yet, they all look alike. They all look like they've just lost their best friend. And they all look like the kind of women who could hear the song Sukie sang, with its crazy, bittersweet lyrics about the way we live now. The women coming to bury Sukie must have felt she was prototypical and responded to her as a symbol for all women who struggled to survive in the same psychological subsistence society. They must have seen Sukie as allegorical, symbolic, mythic *and* real.

There are fewer men in the chapel. Those men who are not simply accompanying a female companion seem especially intelligent and sensitive—the kind of men women like us like most. Gradually there begins to develop a certain comfortable closeness among those present, almost as if we are already back from the burial and sitting around Sukie's kitchen, indulgently eating Rosetta's freshly baked sweets.

Having turned forward again, I misunderstand Elaine's nudge. When I do look up, she nods to indicate something in the rear of the chapel, and when I turn around again I see my two beautiful daughters standing in the aisle just inside the double doorway.

They look a mess. They look as if they have just driven eight or nine hours on Labor Day weekend from the tip of Long Island to Washington, D.C. They look as if they have turned themselves inside out and the world upside down in order to get here. I should have known.

Assuming I would worry if I knew they were driving, they simply took off without telephoning to tell me first. It seems I have become so self-protective I have lost my perspective. Of course, Loren and Lisa wouldn't miss Sukie's funeral even if their classes did start in New Haven tomorrow morning, because Sukie was their favorite of all my friends and they were crushed by the news of her dying. Also, I mustn't fool myself. My daughters would kill to get here to be with me at this terrible moment in my life. I should have known.

I should not have anticipated rejection before it occurred. Or perhaps I was actually *soliciting* rejection. Perhaps I am doing the same thing with Max—courting the worst in him.

Loren and Lisa are pressing inside the hall, each holding one of their matching blue suitcases. Somehow they had actually found quite suitable dresses and decent shoes to wear to Sukie's funeral and the fact that they are totally disheveled does not reflect badly upon them or me. They did the right thing and look messy only because of their travel.

Then, staring at those two, tall, slim, towheaded beauties who are my daughters, I begin to cry.

A minute later, Max rises from his front-row seat and hurries up the aisle, somehow embracing both of them simultaneously. Very shyly they each give him perfunctory, European-style kisses on both cheeks, remaining as reserved as politeness allows, for they too are women and understand the disasters of the Amram divorce. I see them asking Max about Carol and David, and that's when they catch sight of me and together wave sad little waves in my direction. Loren blows me a kiss, a hang-over habit from childhood.

I am so proud of them—of their grace and their beauty—and I know they have come here for me as much as for Sukie. Then, because I am weeping uncontrollably, I have to lower my face and I don't see where they sit. A little later Max returns to his seat on the aisle again. He was dear to go and greet my daughters, knowing they had traveled so far to come here, acknowledging the awkwardness of their reunion after more than five years and all that had transpired. Max obviously noticed their reticence with him, but he still related to them as the little girls he had watched grow up. The three of them also share a history and Max had to welcome them as young women he knew well and for whom he had feelings.

But I am not ready when Max suddenly turns his faded-denim-blue gaze upon me. Silently, but very clearly and specifically, he is asking me something. He is asking me to take a chance. His eyes are saying, What the hell, let's proceed with the possibility of who-knows-what from this point forward, from this place where we've come to bury a loved one—whether loved intermittently or with constancy, whether loved poorly or loved well, but loved in this world where love is hard to come by. Because now we are sharing one of the most painful moments of our lives and we must prepare ourselves for afterwards, ready ourselves for a future.

A rush of tenderness toward Max momentarily destabilizes me. I remember the riotous feelings he stirred in me that night in his apartment and uneasiness invades and occupies my mind. Now I must honestly ask myself whether I really have stopped wanting, stopped expecting, stopped needing anything from anyone else. Perhaps I've only trained myself to simulate indifference, to practice calculated withdrawal prior to rejection, to avoid people and abort events prior to any possible disappointments. Perhaps I am not being wise but cowardly.

But I am not yet ready to commit.

Shortly after three o'clock, a young man wearing a yarmulka rises to approach the lectern set beside the elevated platform on which Sukie's closed casket rests. The young, New Wave rabbi leads us in Hebrew and English through those few essential prayers for the dead required by Reform Judaism before offering some carefully chosen words of condolence to Sukie's father, aunt and children.

Then he leans against the lectern and speaks modestly to everyone gathered in the chapel.

"It is in the nature of organized religions to have their priests and rabbis deliver the eulogies for the dead. However, nowadays, religious leaders most often do not know the deceased personally and can only try to intuit, through hasty descriptions provided by the bereaved— sometimes only minutes before the service commences—the nature and character of the departed. Thus it falls to strangers to speak eloquently, at the most significant of moments, about a valuable human being whom we never knew. This is difficult—if not impossible.

"Unfortunately, in modern times, religion no longer plays a central role in many people's lives. Nowadays, especially in this country, people build their own communities or join networks that help them survive. Mothers of young children, senior citizens, students, divorced individuals, workers in different industries, various victims, political activists, singles, handicapped persons, artists, athletes, alcoholics—all types of people now build intimate communities to meet their most fundamental needs and to assist each other in achieving chosen goals. Where once people looked to religion, they now look to their own networks.

"Because Suzanna Smilow Amram lived the last years of her life with her children in a community of cherished women friends, it is members of her community who will now say farewell to her. Sukie's son David, her daughter Carol, and her friend, Diana Sargeant, will deliver her eulogy in my stead.

"We are also going to witness another . . ." he pauses uncertainly for a moment, smiles nervously and then continues, "departure from tradition. Eight of Sukie's female friends will carry her casket out to the hearse which will bear her to the cemetery. I suppose the fundamental reason why women have not, to my knowledge, ever carried a coffin before is because historically women have always been viewed primarily as the bearers of *life*. This is true. But because death is also a part of life, and because women are belatedly expanding and extending their life functions and activities, they themselves should have the final say as to whether or not they choose to carry their dead to a final resting place.

"If I have erred in my judgment in allowing this break with tradition, I alone accept the responsibility for my decision. Will the spokeswoman for Sukie's friends please come forward at this time?"

Suddenly I am behind the lectern. I do not remember walking up on the stage. I look down at all the faces, take a deep breath, and clutch the pages Kate Constant has given me. But even as I start reading aloud, I find

myself editing and adding as I proceed, much in the
same manner as when I give a lecture from prepared
notes which I use primarily as memory-joggers. Each
sentence I read triggers a rush of my own memories.

"Sukie was one of us: Sukie was all of us.

"She was a bundle of contradictions in total sync with
the contradictory times through which she lived.

"She was many things to many different people in
many different situations. This perhaps is the genius of
American women. And she was very much an American—an instinctively political person who struggled
with—and against—her government to achieve those
basic decencies and freedoms she believed inherent
to—and implicit—in democracy. But Sukie was also a
woman of the world—in both senses of that phrase. She
knew her way around and saw herself as a citizen of the
world. She often cried about the many painful contradictions existing on this planet of ours.

"Once she told me a story: She said the first time
she'd tried to explain the Biafran famine to her children, when they were young, they thought she'd said
'salmon' when she had said 'famine' and they thought
she'd said 'trout' when she had said 'drought.' And those
childish errors had made her weep because the innocence of affluent children was as authentic to them as
pain is to the have-nots of our world. She also wept after
a huge Mexican earthquake because it was reported
that the impoverished Indians who suffered the most
destruction believed they had inadvertently done some
terrible wrong to cause God to hate and punish them
with such vengeance. That broke her heart. The world's
children belong to all of us.

"Sukie was a student of American literature in which
she sought information and reassurance about the nature and character of our people through the art and
skill of our writers. She was also a writer who could bat
out journalistic pieces in a night or suffer for centuries
over a single sentence of fiction. That was because she

believed a higher truth affixed itself to fiction than to fact. She loved some of the things she wrote and disowned others—as if they were good and bad children.

"For a long while Sukie was a wife. She loved it when her family was whole and when it broke apart she grieved for its death as if it were a real person. As Sukie would say: There are plenty of resource materials to read up on this subject if you want to pursue the nature of her experience. You can check out *The Pumpkin Eater, A Woman's Place, Smart Women, Love and Friendship* and innumerable other studies of broken families, broken hearts and the consequences of both. There are also many movies dealing with this subject that Sukie would suggest you'd see if you haven't already: *Alice Doesn't Live Here Anymore, An Unmarried Woman, Shoot the Moon, Hannah and Her Sisters*—all well-done studies of this contemporary condition.

"Sukie was also a mother. She would have died for her children but didn't necessarily want to spend every afternoon in the park with them. For further information see: *Up the Sandbox. Diary of a Mad Housewife, Loose Ends, A Mother and Two Daughters* and so on. Sukie adored both her son and her daughter. She once told me her children were like precious jewels set into the bracelet of her marriage.

"Sukie bought a lot of her clothes in thrift shops and later donated them back again. In that sense, she only borrowed her wardrobe for the various roles she had to play. She lived on the fast track but feared high-speed highways; she believed the heaviest traffic was in the outside lane which made life there very perilous. She cared about kids and justice, disarmament and art. She was a liberal, a humanist, a feminist and a friend. She cried about prejudice and poverty, injustice and indignities.

"Sukie was part of a generation that has been called many things: Depression Babies, the Silent Generation, bohemians, hot properties, beatniks, hippies, peace-niks, women's libbers, gray divorcees, late bloomers and crazy ladies. They can call us what they will. We are twentieth-century survivors. Every morning we rein-vent ourselves according to that day's demands. We have to go with the flow because we don't know how to dam and control it. Perhaps there is no way.

"Sukie read and Sukie wrote. She worked, she pro-tested, she married, she mothered. She gave, she took, she tried, she failed, she loved, she lost, she despaired, she triumphed and then she died.

"She was a woman.

"We are going to miss Sukie in a big way, but some-how we will have to continue on without her. We al-ways thought that when we got old, our gang would live together in some huge communal house out in the country where we would each have a private room where we could work and write and receive visits from our aging lovers and growing-up grandchildren. Down-stairs would be a common room, no, *two*—smoking and nonsmoking—where we would share meals and memo-ries. Maybe we'll all still do that, but it won't be much fun without Sukie there. She was the best and the brightest that we had.

"She was our friend.

"We were such good friends. Really."

I leave two little damp handmarks behind on the lectern when I return to my seat.

Then Carol takes my place and wraps her hands around the microphone.

"I have lost my mother and I feel . . . lost. She was everything, my mother. She was a million different emotions and feelings all rolled up into one. She was wild sometimes and frustrated and ambitious and aim-less and interested and bored. She was everything.

"This didn't make her easy to live with. We certainly had our fights and quarrels. I don't even want to pre-tend that our relationship was smooth and without conflict. But no matter what went on, she never stopped loving us and never stopped giving us—herself. I loved her so much. We were good friends, too.

"My mom was a very modern woman. She lived and loved and lost a lot and I'm sure whatever she left us, she'd think it wasn't enough. But all of her losses happened because her life was full of living and loving. I know everything she left unaccomplished, the books she never wrote and the failures that plagued her. I know all the things she didn't get to do, that she postponed, and how sometimes she'd go to get her hair straightened instead of working on an article that was due or go charge a dress at Bloomingdale's when she didn't have a dollar in the bank and should have been writing a book.

"But I also know all the different people she helped in different ways, and all the dreams she dreamed for David and me, and how much she laughed about the world, which she thought had gone crazy, and all the political things she cared about. She thought the Maryknoll sisters were the bravest nuns ever and she really admired them. For us, maybe her greatest gift is that I'm not afraid of being a woman and my brother David is not afraid *of* women.

"That's important for people.

"But maybe the best thing about my mom was the great books she wrote. She was funny, and her books sound just like she did. This fall I'll be getting her new book ready for publication. It's called *Death Sentences* and it's much better than any eulogy I can give her. . . ."

Carol trails off. She is struggling to control herself. Finally she shakes her head and begins walking off the stage toward Neil, who has come halfway up the stairs to meet her.

David, too, is shaking as he passes Carol on his way to the lectern. The suit he is wearing is too large for him. It fits as poorly as his new role, his new manhood, which hangs, like the too-large jacket, from his still-ambivalent frame. His tentative maturity is clearly threatened by this crisis. Carefully he keeps his head turned so that he will not see his mother's coffin. When he first attempts to speak, he makes no audible sound, but after clearing his throat several times, he finally begins to talk.

"Today I can only say a few things, because I don't really believe this is happening. I can't believe my . . . mom died. She was really a great mother. We always had a lot of fun. I had a lot more fun with my mother than most of my friends did with their moms. I remember once when we went to see a certain movie. We'd waited all week to see it on Sunday, but when we got there, the projectionists were on strike and my mom . . . she just couldn't cross their picket line. I knew she was upset for me, but she just couldn't do it. So she started to say things like there was really a much better movie back at one of the Circle Theatres, one that was a lot better than the one we went to see, and that this other movie had gotten these great reviews and that even though she didn't say so before, she'd really wanted to see the other one right along. And she kept on talking like that and acting so excited the whole time we were walking back to the Circle until, honest to God, I really wanted to see that other movie instead.

"So that's one way she always used to make my life real fun—acting all excited like that about everything all the time. But I could always see right through her.

"And when we first . . . started living alone together, my mom went to Sears and bought a Ping-Pong set and strung the net right across the middle of our dining room table. And then she said we were going to have a year-long worldwide Ping-Pong championship tournament that would go on every night after supper. And we did, and it was really great therapy for her. Anyway, there was no chance of inviting anyone over for dinner anymore, which I really liked a lot because I don't like having company. And finally I beat her two hundred eighty-nine games to two hundred twenty-four.

"We were sort of poor, though. She never made much money from being a writer. Once she tried to make some guy in a Mercedes pay her a quarter for the time left over on her parking meter and when he said no, she said then she'd just stay in the space until her time was up and the guy started laughing real hard and gave her a five-dollar bill so we went out to McDonald's for dinner. A lot of times she dressed sort of weird, but she said people would just think she was too rich to care.

"And once we were at Woodies buying me some school clothes and the salesclerk looked at Mom's charge plate and said she should get a new one because it was getting old and wearing out even though it still worked and my Mom laughed and said 'Perfect. Just like me.' And another time, when two of our neighbors said that our house needed painting, we didn't have any money left that month at all, so Mom just went out and charged four gallons of housepaint and we painted just the front of the house ourselves with a little strip going around the sides so nobody'd know it didn't go all the way around the back.

"She always cared about me, and even when . . . she had some problems, she still tried to pretend she was paying attention, even if she couldn't, right at that minute. And after . . . she got separated, she really learned all about pro football and watched the Redskins with me all the time.

"The other thing I want to say is that she had some really good girlfriends and I'm really glad . . ." he chokes up, stops, waits, goes on—"that they want to carry my mom's coffin, because really she'd like that a lot and I don't think me or even my dad or any of my friends who are here today could do it, because even though we might be stronger, we're all too shaky. But I know my mom's girlfriends can do it, because"—he chokes again—"they're pretty strong for women." He looks down at us, surveys the row in which we're sitting. "What I mean is that they *are* pretty strong women."

Then he staggers off the stage and back to his seat beside Max, who has covered his face with his hands.

Now the four funeral directors, somber men in grave gray suits, surround Sukie's casket and motion us out of our seats. In a ragged line, Joanne, Elaine, Kate, Mary, Marlene, Aileen, Sandy Ratner and I walk up the stairs to the stage where the men are waiting. In a lightning-swift maneuver, two of the men rearrange us, probably according to height, and place us in proper position so that there are four of us on either side of Sukie's casket.

I feel weak. My legs are trembling and there is a tingling sensation in my arms.

Down below, I see row after row of anxious faces. I see Sukie's friends, watching and waiting, wanting and willing us to do this right, to do justice to Sukie and to avoid any disaster. An enormous expectancy radiates up to us from the women down below. Each of us, of course, wants to carry out her self-assigned obligation. Moreover, we want to do it well. We want to carry Sukie to her grave with all the dignity she deserved, the dignity that often evaded her during her lifetime. We want to bury her with all the glory she never captured on her own. We want to carry her high with pride, but gently with love. We want to show that even though she harbored greater expectations of herself than she achieved, she did—and was—enough for us just the way she was. She was the most user-friendly friend we ever had.

Silently the four men close in on the coffin and then there is a startling scraping and scratching of metal as they first dislodge and then lift the coffin off its bier before lowering it down again so that it is even with our shoulders. I see one of the men nodding at me, so I reach out to clasp one of the ornate carved handles jutting out from the side of Sukie's casket, assuming everyone else is doing the same.

And then suddenly, unexpectedly, the men move

away, withdraw their support, and there is a shaking, rattling, plunging moment when all the weight falls upon us, so that the burden of Sukie's coffin does, indeed, rest solely upon our shoulders.

And that is when I feel the weight—yes, the dead weight—of our dear friend (she's not heavy, she's our sister), and realize that somehow we have to bear this horrendous burden. (But who else should carry Sukie? If not us, who? If not now, when?) So I take a deep breath and try to transmit strength to my arms from some other, unknown center within myself, cursing the sedentary life I indulgently lead, the lack of fitness and form I allow myself.

And it is at that moment that Sukie moves, shifts recklessly and restlessly within her coffin, as if seeking some escape, and then our slippery hands slide sidewards, crazily seeking a more secure grip while we fight to stabilize and re-steady the coffin on our shoulders.

Now we are silently trying to soothe Sukie, to quiet that always restless body and soul, so she will lie still. We want to calm her spirit one last time so that we get a grip on her (on ourselves) and assert control over the coffin. All I can hear is the suctioning of fleshy palms skidding across the surface of the coffin.

Above the gentle curve of its cover, across from me on the other side, I see Elaine and Joanne and Marlene and Aileen. Their faces are damp, beaded with drops of sweat and tears.

But we cannot move; the weight of the casket is too much for us.

Again Sukie shifts, and each of us presses up flat against the side of the coffin, seeking stability, trying to anchor the weight. But Sukie is tipping and tilting toward me, so I know I am not holding up my end of the bargain, not carrying her weight well, not holding up my end of the deal. (Can it be that Sukie's weight, as she always claimed, is not well distributed?)

Hush, I whisper silently to Sukie, trying to calm her

soul. Lie still, dear friend. We have you. We've held you up before and we can do it again. We can hold you up now, just like you held us up so many times. Rest, Sukie. Hush. Go with it. It's your turn now to lie down in darkness.

"Oh God," I hear Joanne gasp.

I am grappling with the handle, hanging on with both hands, feeling the coffin slide against my body.

Behind me, Mary is struggling.

"It's too heavy," Elaine moans. "It's too heavy."

"Hail Mary, full of grace," Mary Murphy prays.

But above all else, this is frightening. Someone we loved, someone like ourselves, is inside this box, this heavy crate. Sukie is now an inanimate object, a sliding weight, a *heavy* weight, a pun playing itself out like all the puns played in plays.

So we falter, each of us chained in our own cell of uncertainty, manacled as always by a sense of inadequacy, insufficiency and inexperience.

Down below, there is a rustling as people stiffen in their seats. Now they are afraid we might allow our insecurities to prevail so that we will indeed fail and let down our friend.

But then, mysteriously, there is another reversal and somehow we recover control, restore order so that, after a few seconds, we are greater than the weight we carry and we now can raise high that coffin, finding our strength from below and beneath it. And then we are able to steady it, steady its contents, quiet our sweet friend, absorb encouragement from the women waiting below, willing us the strength to carry this burden.

And then I see Elaine and Joanne and Marlene and Aileen take their first short, trembling step, pausing like the tightrope-walkers-without-nets so often used as metaphors in feminist fiction, to reclaim their balance and then slowly repeat the motion with another baby step forward.

Suddenly, surprisingly, we are all moving, all walking

toward the edge of the platform, down those two treacherous stairs, straining to keep the coffin flat, straight, level as a buggy with a baby inside, which each of us so often found the strength to lift and carry up some dark flight of stairs while our purse thumped like a heart against the side of our thigh.

And then we are down, down, down and moving up the wide, wide aisle, holding tight with our damp hands to the slick surface of those handles, but doing it, doing it, doing it, carrying our friend, at great cost, to her too-early grave, to her final, or perhaps first, place of real rest where we shall all—in the end—lay down our burdens to assume our dreams of sleep.

We pass the rows and rows of faces, the hurt, frightened, injured faces of the friends Sukie left behind, frightened by her dying, her thoughtless leaving of half-grown, still-needy children. And then I see my daughters, clinging to the seatbacks in front of them, half swooning, half swaying, their eyes fixed upon me, pleading and praying, aiding and abetting me.

I cannot tell if my ears are ringing or whether I actually hear a faint ripple of applause for us and for Sukie as we move down the aisle. Are we finally being applauded for our effort, for our strength? Are Sukie's friends applauding her for the life she led? For the death she died? Or are my ears ringing, my brain buzzing, my body roaring for relief?

Then suddenly we pass through those double doors that open mysteriously before us, so that we are outside in the midday heat, in that hot flash of sunlight that temporarily blinds us so we instinctively stop where we are at the top of the stairs to look down across a wide ribbon of green grass to the rhinestone-studded sidewalk and that long black hearse about which we sang songs as children . . . the worms crawl in, the worms crawl out, your stomach turns to sauerkraut. . . .

It is hot, hot, hot. I can no longer distinguish between internal and external heat. And, anyway, what is the difference? Is a hot flash any different than the sting of the sun? Does it matter whether heat is engendered from within or without? Can't a white-hot flash shed as much light and illumination as a steady glow of lower intensity? And aren't hot flashes, perhaps, really spiritual awakenings—or reawakenings—metaphysical messages masquerading as menopause?

The same four men, still stiff and starched, are now below us, waiting beside the hearse. They talk quietly among themselves as they watch us push through the hot, heaving heat of this September afternoon with the sky sagging from the weight of its own heavy humidity, dropping its dazzling jewels, its bright pendants of light down upon us.

I feel a trembling, a deep, fundamental trembling inside myself as we begin moving again, still holding high the coffin as we descend those last harsh stairs.

Our faces are wet. Our hair, shrunk from the humidity, is flattened like yarmulkas against our skulls. Our dresses, our proper, prissy dark fall cottons, are wet and wrinkled. And yes, yes. There is a human odor arising from our bodies, from our own carefully deodorized parts. Like Nadine, I can suddenly smell *myself*, a sin of such magnitude that a drunken dizziness rises up to engulf me. A hot flash of shame rushes from my heart to my head.

So we carry Sukie's castle, casket, over the curb, into the street.

Once again there is the scraping and scratching of metal as the back doors of the hearse open, harsh sounds like the clang of prison doors in jail flicks—the fateful clang of eternal captivity.

The men are closing in upon us, stealing the air I need to breathe, creating a climate that causes another hot flash to race through me.

Then the men are helping us lift the coffin into the back of the hearse, hurrying us.

And now we know the funeral directors are taking

Sukie away, sliding her casket into the rear of the hearse onto rollers like the ramps in repair garages, so that instinctively we all steady it from underneath its silky belly, guiding it into the tracks, keeping it on track, staying on track. . . .

Suddenly, I do not want to let go. I do not want to release my last hold on my friend. I reach out to feel her coffin again. My shoulder aches for its weight once more. . . .

But now I am so weak, so faint, so shaken because she is gone . . . going, going, gone. . . .

I see one of the men walk toward me to take my arm.

I surrender to another burning hot flash that threatens to consume me with its fire. Perhaps I shall sacrifice myself upon the pyre of my own person.

And then I look up and see Max. He is moving toward me like a mirage, shimmering, quivering, an oasis in a hot, empty desert.

He has his hands upon me. He is giving me a transfusion of strength.

His hands are cool and he is moving me, walking me back toward a patch of green green grass . . . green as I would have thee green. . . . And then I see Loren and Lisa and David and Carol in a blur of color and motion coming toward me, coming to get me, coming to contain me, creating a sudden sweet circle that I can reach out to touch and I am touching all of them at the same time and all of us are sobbing and I feel like I've come home.

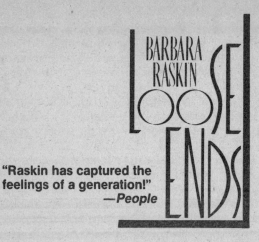

BARBARA RASKIN
LOOSE ENDS

"Raskin has captured the
feelings of a generation!"
—*People*

**By the author of the million-copy *New York Times*
Bestseller *Hot Flashes***
BARBARA RASKIN

LOOSE ENDS
_____ 91348-6 $4.95 U.S.   _____ 91349-4 $5.95 Can.

Publishers Book and Audio Mailing Service
P.O. Box 120159, Staten Island, NY 10312-0004

Please send me the book(s) I have checked above. I am enclosing $_____
(please add $1.25 for the first book, and $.25 for each additional book to
cover postage and handling. Send check or money order only—no CODs) or
charge my VISA, MASTERCARD or AMERICAN EXPRESS card.

Card number _____

Expiration date _____ Signature_____

Name _____

Address _____

City _____ State/Zip _____

Please allow six weeks for delivery. Prices subject to change without notice.
Payment in U.S. funds only. New York residents add applicable sales tax.

LE 1/89